Lazy Blood

– ROSS GREENWOOD –

An environmentally friendly book printed and bound in England by
www.printondemand-worldwide.com

LAZY BLOOD
Copyright © Ross Greenwood 2018

'In order to understand, I destroyed myself.'

Fernando Pessoa

PART ONE – THE END

1

25ᵗʰ August 2014

Prison. Again. This time though, people have died. His mind flickered back to his previous stay all those years ago and he remembered smiling at the banal promises of the great unwashed as they assured each other this would definitely be their last time inside. Did they believe it? Was it just more jail bullshit? Or was it the need to talk and to hope? Well he had known back then it would be his first and only spell inside and he had scornfully smiled at those deluded souls, confident that he wasn't like them. Yet here he was. No short sharp shock for a driving offence that had typically been Darren's fault. Now he could spend the rest of his life here.

He shook his head gently; even now he was still blaming Darren. Well he wouldn't be doing that anymore. The thought of his friend started to unlock the door on the compartment in his brain where he had put last week's nightmares. Not now he thought. He could feel the horror building there, bulging and pulsing, demanding to be heard and let out. It was like the police investigating a crime, gently knocking and peeking through curtains before quietly leaving. They would be back though and more insistent, until the door was broken down and all hell was let loose.

The prison van lurched as the obese driver got out, bringing him back to the present. He could see him through the tinted window searching in his pockets. The huge sweat patches on his shirt seemed to grow bigger as he hunched his back to light another roll up. An hour they had been parked outside the prison. This would be his third cigarette. He might as well have had it in the van as he seemed intent on blowing the smoke back into the cab. It could have been his intention to wind them up. He must have known nearly all of the prison population smoked and after the trauma of today's events the new residents would all be begging for one. More likely though it was just a lack of thought, or interest, but Will was confident it would soon provoke the idiot in the cage in front of him into another round of ranting.

He let himself debate for a moment which part of his anatomy he would donate right now for a shiny unopened pack of Benson and Hedges Gold, but Will doubted he would have been able to smoke it anyway as he was so dehydrated. As luck would have it the van was parked at such an angle that the powerful evening sun was beating directly on his side. They called them sweat boxes and the sensation was that of a takeaway rotisserie, gently cooking those within. The last drops of glistening moisture collecting on the glass sides. He could almost hear God's voice in the distance saying 'Your punishment starts here'.

Not only was he parched, but bloated too. He could remember very vividly an old man on the wing saying 'Do not get nicked on a Saturday, it's nasty. That's two days until the courts open, so you are in the cop shop until then. That's two days of microwaved all day breakfast, three times a day. No showers, no books, no sleep, no fun'. Sage advice as it turns out. Since Saturday he must have had five meals, admittedly not all breakfasts, but reheated aeroplane food basically and he had the bloating feeling that went with it. He felt like if he could get a fart out it would last a good minute, leaving him kneeling on the floor exhausted but temporarily happy.

No such luck. He also had the cramps such fare induced and was bursting for a wee. Two hours he suspected he had been stuck on the van as obviously they had taken his watch, as well as his shoe laces, to add to his disorientated state.

The other two occupants were already inside when he got on, possibly from another court. That meant their bladders too must be under considerable pressure. He had only heard the guy on his left speak once about an hour ago. He had a mature voice, even elderly sounding. Most likely he sounded different this morning. Suddenly from nowhere he had cried out.

'Please sir, I really need to use the bathroom' he had said. Almost like Oliver Twist, polite and educated. He suspected it would be a long time before the poor guy would be using a toilet that could even remotely be described as a bathroom. No-one bothered to reply.

As the driver got on and the van lurched the same way, some liquid rippled into Will's compartment and he knew someone's resolve had broken. Don't think about it, he thought. You clearly wouldn't need to be Galileo to locate the source but it was the weakening effect it was having on his own self-control that was more concerning. He stared at it as it trickled around his lace-less shoes and into some slits in the floor and idly wondered if the van was designed that way, or that the drainage system was a lucky fluke. It wasn't going to make the van smell any worse however, as that would have been impossible.

He knew he was responsible for his part of the aroma, maybe more than his fair share. His shirt was attached to his back like a layer of cling film and his jeans felt like they weighed three times more than when he had put them on. They sat below his hips all heavy with sweat, his belt long gone. The worst was his underwear. He could have rung the sweat out of his socks and he dreaded to think on the state of his boxers. It felt like he wasn't sure where the drone of the idling diesel engine finished and the hum of his own body began.

He was perched forward on the small seat with his head resting on the panel in front. Another trickle of sweat ran off his head and down the side of his greasy face, leisurely bouncing off his stubble as it slalomed down to his chin and then hung there like a diver on the high board. As it dropped, he felt a pressure on his chest. A rising panic coursed through his body, his brain fluttered with thoughts of completely losing it. Deep breaths, Darren always said. Control your breathing and you control your fear. A deep breath of the fetid enclosed air was far from appealing but he didn't want to be one of those carried off the van, a sobbing, snivelling, weeping mess. It always got back to the wings, so he sucked it up. Steady breaths, desperately trying to think of anything but his situation. He blinked the stinging moisture out of his eyes and tried to think of happier times. He remembered a sunset, the moment the sun went down and the temperature dropped and tried to sear the moment onto his fragile mind.

2

The van jumped forward as the driver suddenly engaged the gears and Will banged his forehead on the front partition forcing him into the present again. The barrier rose in front of them as they rolled toward the entrance. He wasn't sure if the prisoner in front had been asleep and this had woken him, or if he had been waiting for this moment to resume his baiting. As the huge prison entrance door slid open and welcomed them into its dark mouth the kid let out a cheer, stamping and drumming his feet, shouting through the crack in his door.

'Yee haa paedo. Welcome to hell. Bruv you're gonna need a new ass after they've finished with you in here. No escape in those cells. You'll be like a kid fiddling rat, stuck in a trap. If I see you man, I'm gonna cut you up.'

Jesus, he winced, YOs. Bloody Youth Offenders. All bluster and posturing. No doubt chest stuck forward as he bellowed in his best street accent. Surely he hadn't been so irritating and stupid when he was young. He grimaced as it came to him that it was more than twenty years since he had turned eighteen and he was pretty sure he was in deeper shit than most in here. So who was the fool?

These kids nowadays all seemed to have ADHD and verbal diarrhoea. Surely with all that pent-up energy being locked in a cell was the last place you would want to be? No wonder they went nuts when they were let out on association.

The banging caused the guard to shout through to the back.

'Jake, can it now you idiot, or I'll issue you with a warning.'

'Like I give a shit, screw,' the lad retorted. 'You make me laugh with your fucking bits of paper. You don't know who you're dealing with here. Go get your friends, put your riot suits on, I'm gonna fuck you up.'

Will pushed up on his seat to give his arse a break from the unforgiving hardness and gave himself a smile. It should be very concerning when you are on first name terms with the prison transport staff. He had heard a similar threat from a prisoner on his last stay but it had come from a forty year old black man who could do the frog song with his chest muscles. The man had been bear sized, well over six feet tall and holding a pool cue and ball. It had carried a lot more weight. Prison was surely a great place for role models and learned behaviour. He suspected the officers would know exactly what they were dealing with here and his young friend would be sobbing for the mum he never knew before the night was out.

The screws weren't your enemy here anyway, time was. Time was a strange commodity. Here you couldn't give it away, yet to a dying man it was the rollover lottery; an unattainable dream he would never acquire.

He remembered reading the 'Power of Now', a book on living in the moment, whilst reclining on a tropical beach in Indonesia. Even then, when he focused, he had struggled to really see and hear the waves gently lapping at his feet, bathwater warm and startlingly transparent. He could not focus on the heat of the sun bronzing his body, or feel the crumble of the baked sand as he scrunched his fingers into it. Even in paradise his mind was whirring about whether there were going to be any girls tonight, or dreading the next ten hour bus ride on the local death-trap, or what he was going to do for a job when he got back to the UK when his CV had more holes in it than a piece of rotten wood.

Yet here, in a place where time meant thinking and he would rather forget, he knew it all.

The bored scuff marks on the panel in front of him, the gentle whistle of his shallow breaths. The exact feel of his hands on his eyes as he held his face. The smudged imprint of his forehead where he had rested it on the window and worst of all the awareness of what he had done and what was ahead of him. All this was his, with no effort at all.

They came to an open door as they trundled through some high metal prison gates topped with vicious looking barbed wire where a big man stood blocking the view inside and the van pulled up. The driver went inside for a few minutes then returned and climbed into the back. His weight on the other side of the vehicle caused the remaining piss to wash away like the tide. Through the gaps he saw him help the man on the left out. He shuffled like a geriatric, stiff from being in the same position for a long time.

Will immediately thought of Darren's joke of dodgy looking old men in Thailand, 'If it looks like a paedo and walks like a paedo-'. The man's face was flaccid white, etched with fear, although no doubt this would be unfounded. He would be put on a foul smelling sex offender's wing, or vulnerable person's wing as they called it so as not to upset the foul smelling sex offenders, with a load of other dirty old men. No-one would ask what anyone else was in for, everyone would be innocent and the sick bastards would swap pictures of each other's kids and take turns with the underwear section of the children's section in the clothes catalogue. The unused showers a final testament to their warped mind-set.

He knew though it was fear of the unknown that unhinged most. This man's experience of jail would probably be gleaned almost entirely from the Shawshank Redemption and the Daily Mail and he would be shitting himself. He was looking at many months of remand time himself and he too was tingling with the knowledge that it was going to take a superhuman effort not to fold under these conditions. Innocent until proven guilty but incarcerated nonetheless. The not knowing when he was going to be put under the critical gaze of some bitter old judge, who no doubt would be savouring the thought of his rambling verdict making the national news. Months of poor sleep leading to a zombie-like existence. He had seen strong men broken by these long haunted nights.

He had said nothing during the police interview. Rarely muttering the words 'No comment', and feeling like an idiot as if he had watched too many US cop shows. By their questioning it seemed they had little idea what had happened. Huge pools of blood and spent bullets everywhere, but no dead bodies.

He was jerked from his recent past by the lad in front asking him what he was in for.

He thought for a minute, then replied. 'A mistake, when I was young.' Wanting to change the subject quickly he commented on the stench in the van. 'Hums in here, I can't believe the old guy pissed himself.'

'That wasn't him. I did it,' the youth said laughing. 'I asked the fat bastard if I could go and he ignored me. So I pissed on the floor. Ignorant prick can spend the end of his shift mopping it up. I didn't even need to go that much.'

As Will shook his head thinking at least the youth hadn't needed a shit, his own door opened.

'OK Mr Reynolds, out you come, nice and easy.'

He too struggled out, his back stiff, shoes slipping on the wet floor. He went through the reception door remembering the way from before and blinked at the glaring lights. There were officers everywhere. He recognised a few who must have been here from all those years ago. Prison had aged them as surely as it did the inmates. They had tired eyes and blank faces which no amount of fresh horror would surprise or shock. There were younger ones too, round eyed and nervous looking, more than likely not much older than Jake on the bus.

The Senior Officer at the desk gave him a hard stare. His red badge announced him as John Cave. He had a substantial beard shadow on a heavy jaw. He looked familiar to Will but he suspected he would remember someone so aggressive looking. He had huge arms and a barrel chest and the red faced demeanour and look of someone who had spent a wasted day and got sunburnt doing it.

'William Reynolds,' he stated. 'Put your finger on the scanner'.

The computer gave a confirming beep and the man looked at the screen and then directly at him with a cold smile on his face. 'Welcome back.'

Trying to add some levity into the situation, he looked around and nodded to the bank of officers behind him.

'Bit of overkill isn't it, for dragging a naughty boy off the bus?'

'It's not for him,' Cave replied. 'It's for you. It's not often we get murderers here.'

Will felt a cold sheen of sweat appear on his body and almost felt his legs go. His head buzzed as though he had stood too close to the edge of the platform as a tube train screeched through. The court earlier had been a blur and his solicitor worse than useless. Refusing to think about anything had clearly not prepared him for this. Saturday's madness would no doubt have been all over the papers and on the TV. He pulled his eyes away from the man's magnetic gaze and stared at the floor.

Unsure how to react, he just grumbled, 'OK.' In the background the radio began playing 'Nothing compares to you' by Sinead O'Connor and another wave of emotion threatened to engulf him. Unbelievable he thought, that song again and as he desperately tried to prevent the collapsing dam of memories from engulfing him, he felt a tap on the shoulder.

'Mr Reynolds, here please, you know the drill.'

He turned around and looked at the officer behind him, who gave him the hint of a commiserating smile. It was an older man, mid-thirties, with a paunch hanging over his belt and a hairstyle that was failing to hide his glistening pate. He had been here before, Prison Officer Duke he recalled. One of the more reasonable professional officers who had realised it was fine not to treat the inmates like they were all the scum of the earth.

He motioned for him to sit on the BOSS chair. A hard, black, plastic, full bottomed seat device you could imagine sitting in to play a video game at the arcade. The piece of equipment whirred and gave a ding, so he got up assuming that it had confirmed that he hadn't got a phone wedged up his arse. Chance would be a fine thing. He was wound so tight that if he had tried to insert a blade of grass in there it would have caused him to go screeching off around the ceiling like a rapidly deflating balloon.

'Follow me Mr Reynolds.'

He scuffed along behind him down a long white corridor, the only method he could use to stop his footwear coming off. He slid through a suspicious pool of liquid on the floor as he did so and past the ubiquitous wet floor signs. They passed multiple holding cells, all of which were empty. It was painfully white and bright compared to the gloomy interior of the prison van and eerily quiet. He felt like a bride coming out of church as he walked between the officers lining both sides, but they had relaxed now, realising he wasn't a frothing lunatic, just a tired, balding, middle aged man.

They reached the searching area which consisted of two changing cubicles with sides as high as an average man's shoulders. A younger officer came in to join Duke as Will went in to the nearest one and turned around and faced them. His missus had told him when you went in to hospital to give birth you left your dignity at the door, with all and sundry looking at your privates. Prison was much the same.

They at least had the good grace to look uncomfortable, like it had to be done but they weren't enjoying it either. Not all did that, perverts and power freaks were commonplace here. Of course it was a cooler windowless room and he felt dirty, smelly and embarrassed. He involuntarily shivered and he felt his mind imagining a blasting, boiling-hot shower sluicing through the film of grease and filth that was glazing his entire body.

'Any chance of a shower please Mr. Duke?' he pleaded.

'Sorry mate, it's late and we have been flat out. The prison's chocker, that's why you had to wait so long. We had ten lifers on their way to HMP Long Lartin unexpectedly arrive just before you. All murderers doing big stretches with so much stuff it was like they were moving house. I've never seen the SO so angry, and that's saying something.'

In a way they were moving house, he thought, the only house they would ever live in again. Even though he knew that prison rules stated every man was permitted a shower on arrival, he also knew now was not the time to ask. Prison was about getting as much as you can, when you can, and being smart enough to know the balance.

'How was the old guy?' Will asked, unsure as to why he cared.

'He collapsed and pissed himself after he came in,' Duke grunted. 'You just walked through the aftermath. He went straight to healthcare.'

Duke handed him his underwear back after searching it, his nose wrinkling at the smell.

'Look Guv, as you can see I reek. I know it's too much for a shower but if I can just have some clean underwear, I'll wash in the cell.'

Duke looked him in the eye about to say no, but for whatever reason nodded. When they got to the property desk he turned to the orderly and barked instructions to him.

'Eighteen, get this man a full kit, clothes too, whatever's left and fast, I want to get home.'

Small things Will thought, but he felt an insane amount of gratitude for something he was no doubt entitled to. The orderly returned and handed him a big opaque bag, tied at the top with HMP Paston Hill on it and gave him a conspiratorial smile. He should get a single cell considering what he was in for and all he wanted to do was get back to it and get these foul clothes off.

The orderly had been there last time too. He was a small overfriendly guy with a pasty complexion who looked a bit like Elvis with about three chromosomes missing. He also knew why they called him 'Eighteen'. He had thought it was a joke like the one about the guy's IQ in Aliens. It had piqued his interest though and he had looked it up when he got out. Turns out he was one of the UK's most dangerous sexual predators and eighteen years was his sentence for grooming and interfering with his neighbour's children.

Not a PC nickname but pretty witty. A very sick man he may be but reception orderlies had power, so he winked back and took the bag. Ironic that half the cons would have weighed him in had they known his depraved history, but as they arrived back late from court having missed dinner and he gave them a baked potato and cheese they thanked him profusely instead.

'Sorry Mr Reynolds.' The younger officer had come over to them. 'The SO said we haven't got time to process you and you will have to come back tomorrow morning. You need to go straight to the wing.'

'Do I get a phone call, or reception pack?' Will asked.

From behind the property desk someone grudgingly said 'Here' and he signed for his tobacco pack. He could have had phone credit; in fact he was entitled to a free call right now. He thought about mentioning it, but who would he ring? He didn't know anyone's mobile number off by heart and his phone was no doubt being held for evidence which only left his dad's landline. He could imagine how that call would go; 'You were given every chance, and this is how you repay us. Lazy blood is what you've got. I said go and grab life, instead you float about like a leaf, letting any old gust blow you where it wants.

Well you got your just deserts'. He could do without that chat.

He wondered how his relationship had soured like that as they left him alone on a bench, head tilted back, counting the ceiling panels. He remembered sitting opposite his dad at the breakfast table just before he started senior school, him all smiles, his eyes keen and interested, asking him what he wanted to be when he grew up. He should have just said 'Prison, twice please' as it would have saved a lot of disappointments. It couldn't have turned out any worse. Back then he had been waiting for someone to tell him what to do, to guide him, but no-one had and now thirty years on he concluded nothing much had changed.

Looking back towards the reception entrance, Will allowed himself a small smile. So much for Jake's grand entrance. He stumbled in like a shabbily dressed stick insect. Curtain haired and tall, but painfully thin. Head drooped, floppy limbed and eyes fixated on his footwear. He looked like a marionette whose strings had been cut. He could hear him mumbling his acquiesces and Jake was soon standing next to him, signing for his things.

Jake looked at him and shrugged, as if to say, 'You know how it is'.

The big senior officer walked past and bade them follow him through a succession of double doors, locking them behind. They arrived at the house blocks and Will saw the big clock in the central hub said nine p.m. as Cave took them onto a wing with a big A1 sign above the gates. Thankfully it was after bang up and it was empty and pretty quiet. He took them to cell twenty-two and gestured them in with a provocative point of his fingers.

'Here's your kennel,' he snarled.

Jake's question came out in a feeble high pitched squeak.

'Which one of us?'

'Both of you fuckwits, now move'

Will couldn't stop himself replying. 'Surely you don't put murderers in with YO's?'

'He's twenty-two Einstein,' Cave replied, leaning in so his face was only a few inches from his. His breath was foul, as though hunks of rotting meat were hanging off his teeth. 'And you will go wherever the fuck I tell you to go, just so I know where you are.'

Like children they trailed in. The sparse cell smelt atrocious, like a decaying swamp. Ill-fitting curtains blocked out some of the fading light and a lonely black sock floating in the toilet was the only sign of its previous inhabitant. Two narrow bunk beds were screwed to the left hand wall and on these were laid the dirtiest pair of mattresses Will had ever seen, and he had seen some. Only the bottom one had a pillow, although this looked like a dying haemophiliac had spent the last year blowing his nose on it. Before he could ask for bed linen the door slammed shut behind them.

Jake stood in front of him looking more than a little stunned. Like he had put his hand in his pocket expecting to pull out an apple but had removed a hand grenade.

Will sighed. 'You can have the top bunk Jake.' He watched as Jake pulled himself up as though the floor was on fire. He put his bag on the bed and heard a light crinkle so he looked inside. Eighteen had put two bags of crisps in, Walkers too and two yellow looking apples. Thinking that was a little unusual he shrugged and passed an apple and a bag of crisps up to Jake and then said, 'Here, you can have the pillow too.'

Ross Greenwood

Will eased himself back onto his bunk and unsuccessfully tried to get comfortable. The mattress was wafer-thin in the centre where a hundred other unlucky souls had compressed it over the years. He shuffled onto his side and facing the wall thought that now was as good a time as any to remember what he had done. He closed his eyes and pulled the weight of his memories over himself with as much enthusiasm as a tramp with a heavy wet blanket.

3

26ᵗʰ August 2014

He completely awoke just after dawn but he hadn't slept. The whole night was a haze of sweating semi-conscious thoughts. You would have thought in prison you would have all the time in the world to sleep, but few did. It was baking in the cells, an oppressive close heat which had you dreaming of breezy clifftops. He recalled last time, sweating in just his boxers, day dreaming of wind farms and hailstorms.

It was the noise that kept you awake though and last night had been no different. The shouts of the bad, conducting their business after bang up and the shrieks of the mad and the sad as they tried to come to terms with their predicament stretched into the night long after the idiots had given up competing on who had the loudest stereo.

He knew he had partaken in the cacophony, jolting upright, a shout still on his lips and banging his head again on the base of Jake's bed. Despite his nonchalance Jake too groaned and grumbled in his sleep.

The constant roll counts with bright torches shone through observation panels and the jingle of heavy keys and slow clump of heavier footsteps harried you through the night. When exhaustion tipped you into the abyss just before dawn you were pulled out soon after by the slamming doors and the loud jingle of locks being opened as they roused and then argued with that day's reluctant courts. To say Will felt less than prepared for what today might bring was a serious understatement.

Jake leapt down from the bunk like a Barbary ape as the rhythmic unlocking of the fifty-six cells reached their door. A poor night's sleep had seemingly restored his energy levels and confidence.

'Come on man, I'm starving,' he beamed. 'You snooze, you lose. I know these weasels.'

Will nodded. That was very true. Even though breakfast was only a 200 ml carton of long life milk, a few tea bags, two sugar sachets and a bowl of cereal, it was another commodity. The wing workers would work with unusual and efficient haste knowing that the busy officers would only hold them so long and anything left was theirs. That carton of milk or the sugar could mean an extra smoke at the end of the day, or a couple of squirts of aftershave before your woman's visit.

Will tried to relax as he stood in the line behind Jake. He had a protector last time he was here, but he was long gone and he felt exposed and vulnerable. He could smell the man behind him. His rank morning breath curled over his shoulder like a mugger's embrace. It seemed like he had eighty sets of eyes on him, but as he glanced around he never caught anyone staring at him and tried his best to put it down to paranoia. The servery inmates nodded at him but seemed only interested in getting back to bed and the officers didn't give him a second glance. He inhaled his breakfast in his room and soon found himself hastening to the showers, knowing it would be busy but desperate to be clean.

The shower room was basic indeed. A bare square tiled room, four metres by three, with four showers slightly too close together so it was infuriatingly easy to touch the man next to you as you raced through your ablutions. All the heads were taken but as he arrived two guys on the end spaces turned around and looked directly at him. They were big, well-muscled stereotypically Slavic looking types, with shaven heads and square features.

Prison showers are not a place for the timid and Will was tempted to do some over the top Mr Bean type charade where he pretended he had forgotten his soap and back out. The stench of his own body made him stand his ground and he braced for some conflict but they both just nodded at him and walked past, towels wrapped around their waists, one of them whistling like they had just come out of some highbrow sauna.

He showered quickly, his mind now going into overdrive and was grateful to get back into the relative safety of his cell. Jake returned later bursting with gossip.

'Hey man, they all know what you are in for,' he whispered, as though it was a good thing. 'If you need anything just ask, everyone knows me here, I'll look after you.' Will suspected Jake would struggle to look after a hamster but nodded anyway.

Before he could say anymore the door was pushed opened and an evil-looking mature man came in. He had a greasy shock of yellowy grey hair, slicked back and pulled into a small ponytail. If he had any teeth they had retreated out of sight for safety. He had a head like Skeletor and a complexion that suggested he had never been in the vicinity of a fruit or vegetable. He pointed at Jake and growled in a thick Irish accent.

'Fucking out, now!' Jake's loyalty clearly didn't stretch very far and he raced out the door like a greyhound leaving his trap. His place was taken by a wide fellow with a face that looked like he had been losing at boxing all his young life. The eyes that stared out of this visage though were aged, flinty and wired. Will felt his legs and arms go instantly weak and numb and he involuntarily backed up to the window. The big bloke soon had him by the throat, his back being moulded onto the bars of the window. He didn't try to struggle; God knows he wasn't a fighter. Instead of receiving a blow, the smaller man came to his side, pressed his face against his ear and began to talk in a low threatening voice. His breath was hot and sour, a combination of cigarettes and absent dental hygiene.

'I know what you did and I'm not fucking happy about it. Darren was a fucking mate. Now this is a taster, to let you know this is my fucking wing. I want anything of yours, you give it to me. Quickly. Or Jo-boy here, takes a lot more.'

With that he stepped back. Will's mind quickly cleared and he had time to breathe deeply as everything all of a sudden seemed to be running in slow motion. No answers came so he just tensed his stomach as the inevitable punch arrived. He still let out a whoosh of air and sprayed his milky rice crispies over Jo-boy's chest and then slumped to the floor.

Incredulous at this impromptu shower, no doubt the first for a while, Jo-boy lifted him off the floor by pulling both of his ears up. His face was a mask of hate and he used the lifting movement to arch his back. As the head-butt came, Will did the only thing he could do to save his face and looked at the floor. The bang of heads echoed around the room and his legs gave way and he slid back down. All of a sudden a loud voiced bellowed into the cell.

'What's going on here?'

'We accidentally bumped heads Guv,' Jo-boy laughed.

'Leave,' the officer replied. As the two travellers left, the man looked down at Will. He was in his late-twenties and had the usual apathetic attitude to violence most prison officers seem to develop. 'You OK?' he asked. Will nodded, still stunned by the blow. He could almost hear the man's brain whirring over whether he could be bothered with the necessary paperwork that reporting the incident would generate. Idleness or indifference won the day. He nodded his head and spoke as he put his key in the lock.

'No induction for you this morning, you got a legal first thing, so be ready for mass movement.' With that he stepped out and Jake came in, the officer locking the door behind him.

'Great,' sighed Will. A legal would mean a visit in the prison from probation, the police or a solicitor. None of which were particularly welcome. Mass movement was the time for work, when the wing gates were opened and five hundred or so of nature's finest were shepherded towards work like a herd of unruly, angry bulls. There was a complete lack of control and it was easy pickings for those out for revenge.

'Sorry man, I didn't know what to do. I shit myself,' Jake simpered. 'They say Jo-boy killed someone in Pentonville. I told a screw when no-one was looking something was going on in our cell. I wasn't sure if you could handle it or not.'

As Jake helped him onto the bed, Will figured this would be a painful stay. The bleakness of his situation caused his breath to catch in his throat. If things didn't change he would be having some long nights here, waiting for the doors to open. You can't run away here, or move home. Not unless you wanted to squeal and then he would be joining old matey from the bus ride here on the nonce wing. Jesus he thought, imagine twenty-five years of mainstream prisoners trying to spit through the wing gates at you.

* * *

He waited until the last minute to leave his cell when the prisoners were let out to go to work and walked to the visits hall where they did the legal appointments virtually on his own. The slippery stoat of a fellow who had been appointed at the court was nowhere to be seen when he went into his booth. Instead there was some sharp suited elderly city type with an attractive but efficient-looking woman. She had a note pad and thick trendy glasses. Neither of them stood as he entered. Neither of them offered their hand.

'My name is Grant,' the man declared. Will assumed it was Mr Grant, as his tone dismissed any notion of informality.

'Sit down Mr Reynolds. I only really have one question for you. Have you talked?'

He did have only one question but he asked it about ten different ways. When he seemed happy that Will hadn't talked, he spoke in a tone that suggested he was used to being listened to.

'Your legal representation has been paid for by a helpful third party. They have hired the best. I have not come here for particulars, just to explain the general defence. You three were set upon by heavily armed persons who were unknown to you. You were out for a drive with old school friends and know precisely zero. You 'hit the deck' as they say, saw nothing, only looking up when everyone was gone. We will be laying this at Darren's door. He won't be answering any questions. With his personal history it will be perfectly believable. They may even drop the case. No-one likes to see war heroes dragged through the mud unnecessarily. You say nothing, to anyone, at any time, unless directed by me. I'm sure you understand the consequences of not adhering to these rules, in both the short and long term.'

★ ★ ★

As he left the legal visit booth later that morning he was almost too stunned to make his way back to his cell. He filtered in with some new arrivals on their way to the wings. They hauled heavy bags with slumped shoulders, each with their own cross to bear. The only person who could have arranged and paid for all this for Will was Radic. Well he had certainly lightened his cross. The last phrase Grant had said kept recurring in his mind though and he wondered what he had meant by it.

'Your time on remand may be lengthy, but steps have been taken to make your stay as comfortable as possible', he had said with a wry grin. That half smile being the only display of emotion from his side of the table throughout the entire meeting. As he arrived back at the wing he could feel his headache subsiding, although he pushed down the rush that this glance of a different future had given him. He wasn't sure if his head ached through his situation or the fact he was continuously banging it on things here. He frivolously wondered if Radic could get him a crash helmet sent in.

The wing was mostly empty as the officer let him back into his cell. Jake was bouncing around the cell singing along badly to 'Counting Stars' by One Republic, which was blaring out of the radio channel on their ancient TV, looking pleased as punch.

'It's only sandwiches for lunch Will, you relax, and I'll get them for you. The screws been in too, you're moving to a single cell later and I'm going in with an old mate from Glen Parva. Sorted Bruv.'

He stretched out on his bunk and allowed himself a fond thought of his daughter, and Elaine. He was so close to losing everything, could he hope for an escape. As Aiden often said, he had it all and didn't appreciate it. He understood that now. What he would give now just to sit on his sofa and watch Baby TV with Jessica. Darren had always said that everything came up trumps for him though and he sent a small prayer up to the no doubt overworked prison deities. Strange how he thought he was directionless and scraping through life with a succession of near misses.

When they unlocked for lunch, true to his word, Jake shot off with Will's plastic plate and returned fifteen minutes later with a look of awed respect on his face.

'Man, I knew you were the nuts. You won't believe what happened,' he shouted. Then he paused and said quietly, 'Actually, you probably do.'

'Tell me,' he responded as a mixture of dread and hope got his blood racing around his body.

'Jo-boy's on his way to the hospital. He fell on a fucking screwdriver in the workshop. Full of Russians that place and no one's saying nothing,' Jake gleefully replied.

At that moment there was a knock at the door. Jake opened it to find the skeletal inmate from earlier. He respectfully stayed at the door and in a subdued, quiet and raspy voice asked, 'Do you young fellas mind if I come in, looks like tings got off on the wrong foot, so to speak. You need anything at all, then you tell old Terry and he'll do right by you.'

Young, Will considered. He supposed Terry was probably the same age as he was, but he was an advert for the 'Just say No' campaign. He could have been anywhere from forty to sixty. On top of that he had experienced the old prison adage there is always a bigger fish. His pasty visage which had earlier looked like the underbelly of a shark had been replaced by one with a livid set of colourful bruises. His right eye was swollen and near shut and his left ear was a furious purple with streaks of fresh blood on it. Will could not resist standing next to him and whispering closely into his normal sized ear.

'That was a poor welcome you gave me, Terry.'

Terry visibly flinched. You could almost see the fear emanating off him like radio waves from a cartoon antenna. He decided against any more close chat as the man smelt as though cleanliness and he were like chalk and cheese. Will knew not to push it though. Things changed daily in jail. All of a sudden someone got taken out, the balance of power edged the other way and your world altered. There would never be a shortage of men scrambling to the top in places like this. Men prepared to use whatever levels of threats or violence they deemed were necessary to achieve their goal. So he gave him a pass.

'Look at me and remember this please Terry. I'm going to be here for quite some time and I really don't want any aggro. So let's not mention this morning's activities again and we will move on.' With a raised eyebrow he laughed and said, 'If you could find your way to getting us a couple of pillows, that would be greatly appreciated.'

Terry looked like a man who had been told by the cancer doctor to book a holiday and to make sure it was in the next few months, only to be corrected a few minutes later and informed it was just a nasty case of piles. He threw down two boxes of Amber Leaf and two Mars Bars

on the bottom bed and with saucer eyed relief backed out
of the cell, shouting as he went.

'No worries Mr. Reynolds, consider it done.'

It appeared Radic's reach was both long and mighty.
Jake looked longingly at the goodies, as though a naked
model had wandered into his cell, sat at his bed and
winked at him. Clearly pleased as punch to be thought he
was included in the power struggle, but momentarily
unsure of his position.

'Just take it Jake,' Will smiled and then laughed.
Catching himself, he wondered ruefully if Jake would end
up paying for his involvement in this series of events. The
boy shot out of the room again, Mars Bar stuffed down
his trousers.

'Sweet, I saw them cleaning your new cell. I'll give
you a hand packing later.' He beamed as he left.

Will laughed out loud at that too, as he suspected he
would be able to carry a pack of tobacco and a bag of
sweaty clothes on his own.

As Will debated having a shit in their cell toilet, which
wasn't really prison etiquette if the communal one next to
the showers was free, someone slid a newspaper under his
door. It was two days old but it was another little
luxurious piece of normality sorely appreciated by those
with time to burn.

He decided to do his business in the cell, payback for
Jake pissing in the van he thought. He would need to
make room for tonight's culinary banquet. The prison
menu generally consisted of deep fried carbs with a carb
topping, served on a bed of carbs and generally made you
shit for England. This evening's extravaganza would be no
different. Jamie Oliver would not have been pleased with
the overcooked lasagne, lukewarm greasy chips and
nuclear hot, bullet baked beans but Will was looking

forward to some real food even though it was no doubt served to instil a mood of general lethargy on the prison populace.

An officer came to his open door and knocked on it. He smiled at him and gave him a key, 'Penthouse suite fifty-five, the wing workers are just mopping it now.'

$$\star\ \star\ \star$$

He waited until not long before bang up to leave his cell and move to his new one. Jake had grimaced at the smell when he came back but didn't mention it, instead happy to noisily carry his meagre possessions up to the next landing for him whilst waving to people like he was some kind of local celebrity. As they entered the cell Will let out a long breath of relief. Maybe he could do this now. He had a decent TV, a pleasant fresh aroma and some functional curtains. That was the holy trilogy for any prison. Jake clapped him on the shoulder with a big grin and smiled.

'Too easy eh, laters,' he said as he left.

Will flopped on the bed, temporarily pleased with the smell of clean linen. He reached into his pocket and pulled the letter out that he had been given earlier. It was Elaine's handwriting. Great girl he thought. She must have hand-delivered it to the prison so he would get it today, although he did wonder how she would have known to do all this. His telephone numbers should be on his pin by midweek so he needed to face things now as she would be expecting a call.

It appeared he had another protector. It was funny how things turned out. Almost as though if you expect salvation it never comes, but once your hope has gone it arrives from an unlikely source. The wing noise reached a climax as he heard the officers shout out.

'Two minutes, get your water.'

He heard 'Behind your doors' and people running, then again the steady rhythmic click of those same fifty-six doors being locked and bolted for roll count. He closed his eyes and let his mind wander. Let's start from the beginning he thought. That fateful first day, thirty years ago…

PART TWO –
THE BEGINNING

Ross Greenwood

4

2nd September 1985

H is mother wiped the inside of the windscreen with some used tissues from her pocket to clear the condensation. Visibility was poor, with the heavy thunderstorm rocking the red Ford Sierra estate and Will really wished she had worn her glasses.

He knew she was also struggling because it was her number two son's, as she liked to refer to him, first day at big school. She gave him a quick glance and smiled, causing the car to swerve slightly. 'You look so grown up in your new uniform and smart haircut. I'm glad I spent so long getting that fringe straight, you look very handsome.'

Will pulled the vanity mirror down and checked out his thick brown hair. It was the same colour as the spray of freckles across his face. She was always telling him what a good-looking boy he was.

She always told them she loved both her children equally, but Will knew she had had a soft spot for him. There was also no doubting the other boy was odd. The one and only pastime that Nathan seemed to get any pleasure from was trying to undermine Will's confidence and enthusiasm. He found great pleasure in Will's mistakes and endlessly probed his worries.

'Mum,' Will shouted, pointing at the windscreen. She seemed to have been in a trance but suddenly remembered what she was doing. She looked forward and noticed the rapidly approaching van, red lights burning through the mist like two angry eyes. Braking hard, the Sierra skewed slightly but caught its grip and stopped about a centimetre behind the van.

'Bloody Hell,' Will said. He knew he should have cycled, even in the rain. His mother's driving was on a par with 'The Mouse' ride at the pleasure beach. A noisy, jolting, juddering experience, culminating in you lurching from the car, shocked, pleased and more than a little surprised that you were still in one piece. He looked in the rear window for the arrival of the inevitable shunt, but the wiper cleared to see a relieved and shocked face gawping out about half a metre away from their car. Will forced himself to exhale and tried to unclench his toes which felt like they had curled up like how a crow would perch on a branch. His new shoes had already felt like he had somehow wedged his feet into a couple of bowling balls.

On top of this he was nervous as hell. His hands felt all numb and clumsy and it didn't seem to matter how much he had drunk, his tongue was still clacking around his arid mouth like a dusty castanet. His brother Nathan had informed him repeatedly throughout the summer holidays, in a polite manner, that the prefects molested and sodomized the new kids when they used the toilets. He needed to go now.

He wasn't exactly sure what this really meant but he had looked up molested in his Griffin dictionary, unable to find sodomized and immediately regretted it. Although he suspected they would not be so keen if his mum's driving deteriorated any further and he pooed himself.

His brother was in the back, his mum having let Will go in the front as it was his first day. Nathan was a dick, he thought as he looked at him over his shoulder. As he caught Will looking at him he formed a ring with his index finger and thumb and was poking his other index finger through it.

'Oi Nathan, do you hear, stop that,' his mother commanded. She slammed the car into first gear, the van having long gone and through slit eyes she pushed the wipers up to maximum and to a cacophony of irate horns, gingerly pulled away. The radio began to play Queen's new song 'I want to break free'. Will suspected it would be many years before he was able to do so.

When they arrived Nathan grudgingly took him to the area where the first termers were to meet. Will was shocked by the unexpected gesture, not knowing of his dad's drastic threats to Nathan's pocket money if he didn't. Will trudged along behind him, hands clammy and face wet from his mum's parting kiss.

The school seemed huge, full of strange buildings and teeming with life. Will had not wanted to come to The Prince's School. His father and grandfather had, but all his friends were going to the school near his house. If he wanted to live through the experience he was going to have to cycle two miles to school every day past many of his friends. To make matters worse football apparently was a swear word here.

His brother left him with a parting dead leg, telling him to meet at the gate later and Will, feeling very alone, surveyed the scene. The new students were all waiting in a big playground near some large double doors. The majority cowering in close proximity, huddled together for safety like a crèche of baby penguins, as hordes of giant children prowled past. Will felt like a gate crasher at a party, waiting for someone to tell him he didn't belong and had to leave. It was to be a feeling he would often have here and may have accounted for his general lethargy throughout his school life.

There seemed to be about a hundred kids waiting, all in varying states of attire that were a shade too big for them. His own thick purple blazer came down to his knuckles and was making him sweat despite the fresh morning air and his nervy disposition.

Will picked out the half adults as they cruised past, prefects' gowns fluttering in the breeze, looking effortlessly cool as they chewed gum, arms slung casually over girls' shoulders. He also kept an eye out for Carl, the only other boy he knew from his junior school who was coming here too.

Carl was a tragic figure, a genius of giant intelligence but a geek of epic proportions. He had stereotypical thick glasses and greasy hair but the one feature which really made him stand out was his amazing ability to cultivate a staggering array of sickening whiteheads on his neck in next to no time. No doubt Will mused, he would be hoping his nickname of Carlbuncle would not follow him here.

Sure enough he was standing on his own on the far side with a ring of space around him. His parents must have been intent on ensuring he had a poor first day at school as his blazer would probably still not fit him when he left for university, yet his trousers were already half-mast. Will turned to melt back into the throng before he was spotted, but bumped into what felt like an immovable object.

He turned around to look at a big barrel chest and almost hated to look up, expecting to see some kind of an ogre. Instead he stared into a big, red, round, sleepy face with a sloppy grin on it. His hair had been cut as though the barber had used a perfect bowl to create a blonde helmet to crown his huge head. Will had to stand back to take him all in. Will could have slept under his huge jacket, already tight at the shoulder and it was evident his trousers would wave the white flag shortly under the ferocious assault of a pair of thighs that would have not looked out of place on Arnold Schwarzenegger.

'Hullo,' he said in a mellow soft Scottish accent. 'I'm Aiden, is it your first day too?'

Will nodded, put at instant ease by his gentle voice and nature. At that point, the doors opened and a tall, slightly stooped robed man in his sixties looked out at them over his glasses as though he had discovered a new species which was unpleasant to the eye.

'I am Mr. Thatcher,' he announced in a strong voice that commanded attention. 'Head of the lower school. You may call me sir! Welcome to The Prince's School, whose good name will always go with you. As you enter the building behind me there are four classrooms.'

'First group,' he roared, 'Will proceed now!' and a hundred ears strained, praying they didn't miss their name as he began a procession of surnames, pronounced in a gravelly voice as though just saying them made him feel ill.

As though it was a sign from above, Will and Aiden were directed to the same classroom and therefore naturally sat next to each other. Apart from the fact the table moved every time Aiden moved his trunk like legs, he was pleased not to be on his own. He was about to smile when he felt some hot breath on his cheek and a high pitched voice squeaked in his ear, 'Greetings Burt.'

Typical he thought, but as Carl sat opposite him he seemed so pleased to have found a familiar face that Will couldn't help but grin at him. He would have a word about Carl's nickname for him later. Aiden smiled at Carl with the same dreamy expression he had given Will. He suspected Elvis would have received the same response if he had hip-shaken his way over.

Just as it looked like theirs would be the only table of the seven foursomes with one person missing and the teacher was hushing the class to settle down, Will noticed the door open and a late arrival turned up. Will watched the lad who stood at the door with his shoulders back as though he meant to be late and wanted everyone to see him.

The teacher directed him to the remaining empty seat. As he got closer it was evident he already had what looked like the beginning of a black eye, which Will thought was some serious good going as it wasn't even nine o'clock yet.

He sat next to Carl and gave him a smile that barely troubled his cheeks, never mind his eyes. He gave Aiden a look-over like you would seeing a remarkably big donkey at a sanctuary and then Will felt like he was being assessed for a grisly experiment as his gaze was turned on him. The eyes were keen and sharp yet at the same time seemingly devoid of emotion, like a crow eyeing up some recent squashed hedgehog, but constantly assessing for dangers.

The young, bright eyed and enthusiastic teacher interrupted the examination and all turned towards her as she started the register. Will began to feel on edge again as she began to talk of a first week of tests to ascertain which groups they would be in, so their minds could be 'stretched appropriately'. She rattled on.

'This will be your home room for the next year and these your seats unless told otherwise.' She too exclaimed how lucky they all were to be attending the best school in the area and then announced that they could spend the next five minutes introducing themselves to the others on their table.

As the four lads all looked in on each other, the new arrival rapped his knuckles on the table.

'I'm Darren. I like football and martial arts.' He had short black hair, in a side parting, pushed up into a Tin Tin type quiff at the front.

'Nice to meet you friends,' he stated.

He then got up and went around the table and shook Will's hand, looking him directly in the eye. A strangely adult thing for an eleven year old to do, Will thought. He seemed so confident and his grip was hard and cool, making Will involuntarily wipe his comparatively warm and sweaty soft hand on his trousers. His other hand moved to his fringe, all of a sudden conscious of his own style's lack of cool. Will just stated, 'Football and sweets.'

Darren shook Carl's hand who proclaimed to like 'Chess and war' which received an appreciative nod of respect. However he still flicked his hand in the air above his head with a grimace after, as though he had failed to find a penny in the pot of thick honey he was looking in, which Will suspected was a joke about Carl's oily nature.

After squeezing Aiden's hand and pretending it had been crushed to pieces by his hydraulic grip, he looked at him with raised eyebrows.

'Well?'

'My name is Aiden.' Aiden then looked up to think, as though he had been asked for his take on the theory of relativity. In his soft brogue he then simply replied.

'Food. And bigger trousers.' They all roared with laughter.

5

A dizzying blur of rules, timetables and responsibilities soon sobered them up and the bell went for what they assumed was a break. The teacher declared they would be sitting a spelling and numeracy test after and woe betide anyone who was caught cheating.

The four boys went out of the class together and back to the courtyard. There seemed to be a huge game of football going on, played with a tennis ball. There must have been about twenty-a-side, all bigger, older boys, raucously racing up and down, bellowing and barging.

They stood on the edge, all four in a line. Will looked at the others as they watched the game. Carl did so with a look of horror, Aiden with a bit more focus than he had shown all day and Darren with an expression like a well-trained, shackled guard dog waiting to be released into the melee.

Catching his own reflection in the window behind him, Will pushed his hair to one side, trying to interrupt the dome effect and gave himself a harsh diagonal sweep to his fringe. As he pondered which was worse, pudding basin or something that seemed to give him a slight resemblance to Adolf Hitler, he felt the tennis ball hit the window above his head and drop behind them.

Even thirty years on Will would never know what possessed Carl to pick that ball up. He held it as though he had picked up a sweet, baby bird that had dropped out of a nest. He then threw it back as a toddler would, trying out the technique for the first time. Maybe it was. The ball flew gently vertically up where it hung for what seemed minutes, before a slight gust of wind blew it onto the roof behind them.

A picture of the four lads' faces then would have painted a picture of the future. Carl looked as though he had been told he would be singing a soprano solo on the stage at the next day's school assembly, naked. Will looked at Darren, instinctively looking at the dominant force for guidance and Aiden had a blank look on his face, if it had registered it hadn't triggered any response. Darren however faced forward, shoulders open, eyes wide, chin set, poised and ready for come what may.

The lost ball triggered an instant response in the players and within seconds Carl was being held by the collar and being lifted off the ground by a swarthy fat boy, twice Carl's size. A voice rang out shouting 'Go on Kostas, hit the twat'. Carl had gone all limp like a stick of celery that had been left out overnight; no fight whatsoever.

'That was my ball,' Kostas bellowed. He looked around, very aware of his audience. 'No-one does that. You bloody pathetic greasy goon.' Later Will pondered why he had got involved. He had seen Carl bullied before and paid no attention. Maybe it was the huge straight-armed swiping cuff from a large, open, chubby paw, that slapped Carl's glasses straight into Will's chest that caused him to react, or maybe it was just the incongruous nature of the fight. He would admit a long time later it was partly the acorn of friendship that was to blame.

Will jumped on to the outstretched arm that was still holding Carl and lifting his knees up, attempted to pull it down with both hands. It didn't work. He just hung there like a heavy wet shirt ineffectively trying to pull down a firm washing line. Darren however, was more effective.

He went around to the other side and in a swift practiced motion assumed a wide stance and proceeded to snap fast uppercuts into his target's ribs at the side and back. His shoulders, hips, legs and feet all pivoted in an almost smooth dance-like sequence. His weight shifting slightly from side to side as each sharp punch fired out.

Will was mesmerized. He was now sitting on the pavement, Carl forgotten. He didn't punch like a child, Will thought at the time. You would have thought his features would be constricted into a growling rictus grin. Instead it was a face of peace and focus, like how his dad's face looked when he was enjoying a complicated jigsaw puzzle, completely lost in the moment.

Kostas let out a roar and casually threw Carl on top of Will. He turned around, face ablaze with fury, teeth bared and swung a huge heavy right, seemingly in slow motion after Darren's blurring speed.

Will gasped, but then immediately thought that even he could have ducked that. Darren wasn't there to duck however. He stepped forwards and cracked two jabs straight at the mouth ahead, shoulder rising on his right and left as each shot snapped out. He had made no attempt to dodge the incoming blow, but instead let it glance off his shoulder and top of his head. As his opponent's body twisted off balance, he released another right uppercut to the stomach.

The silence pounding in his ears, as he got up, Will realised he was seeing something special and something natural. It was clear Darren was born to fight. This was not a bible story though and Goliath managed to grab an arm.

With sheer brute force he twisted Darren around and got his arm under his chin, squeezed and leant back. Darren's feet kicked out, but it was clear he was helpless, his face reddening quickly as he gasped for air.

Will felt powerless as he remembered the strength of the arm he had tugged on. He desperately looked around the sea of gormless wan faces for any kind of assistance. His spirits rose as he saw what must be a teacher in a tracksuit observing from some raised steps about fifty metres away. It took about three seconds before he realised with certainty that the man had seen the fracas and done nothing.

As his hopeless gaze returned to Darren's purple face he heard a pounding sound and a large body came out of the corner of his vision. He felt its momentum as it bore past him and from a low angle and powering up hit Kostas so hard in the hip that he lifted him and his choking victim a foot in the air. He then lay on top of him, elbows next to each ear and hands holding the head in place by firm grips in the hair, as Darren rolled away hauling air into his lungs.

This time there was no weight disparity and Kostas struggled and cursed up at Aiden's blank face, but he was stuck. A curtain of fear fell down his face all of a sudden as he saw Darren get up. Darren's jigsaw face had returned. He walked to the pair in the lover's embrace and looking straight down over their heads, gave the target a calculating stare and pulled his foot back.

'Enough,' commanded a loud mature voice. The watching teacher had finally come over and gently pushed Darren away. He didn't seem angry, or even inclined to do anything bar stopping the possible head football that was going to occur.

At that point the bell rang and he shouted for everyone to get back to their classes. He pulled Aiden off and helped Kostas to his feet. Kostas looked winded and unsteady on his feet. His lip was split in two places, trickles of blood going down his chin, staggering like a drunken vampire. As a last ditch attempt to save some dignity, he spat a final threat.

'You're a dead boy.'

Darren looked him in the eye and slowly replied, 'Careful what you say. I won't always be eleven.' Kostas blanched and slunk off as the rest filed back into the school.

Will had a look back when he got to the door. The teacher was still standing there staring at them, a half smile on his face. Darren walked through the other children who parted for him like Moses and the Red Sea. Carl followed behind, hoping to bask in the respect that was on the faces of all the boys and the shock that was on the girls.

Will felt surreal, as ten minutes later they were in the midst of a test with questions being fired at them with little thinking time. Near the end Will looked around at the others. He knew he was a bright lad, but even he had been missing answers. Aiden was faring worse than him, his big hand seemingly struggling with the small pen he had been given.

A now red throated Darren was doing about as well, but that was maybe because he was focusing on Carl. He wasn't cheating, just watching. As the next few questions came, Will saw why. Carl was writing the answers down immediately as though he did not even have to think, like copying them out of a book. Oddly enough Will noticed he had the same expression on his face as Darren had when he was fighting. Cursing he realised he had missed the last two questions and resolved to concentrate.

The papers were passed to a different table and the answers read out. The teacher stood at the front and joked, 'Now anyone got them all correct?'

Little giggles echoed around the room until a girl in the corner stood up and simply stated, 'Carl did.' A gasp went around the room, necks straining to see who had managed the impossible. Carl only had eyes for Darren though and Darren was returning the stare, gently nodding his head. In this way, Will concluded, deals were done.

6

3rd September 1985

Will rose out of his saddle, arms straining at the handlebars. He could still just about see his bastard brother and his pal up ahead, their purple blazers billowing in their slipstream. Nathan had promised his dad in front of Will that he would stay with his brother on his first ride to school, but as soon as his friend had met them they had sped off and his smaller bike couldn't keep up.

He was desperate too, as they were approaching Edwalton Avenue which was just before the bridge and the dreaded underpass. It was here Nathan had been telling him that the kids from the other nearby school waited in a line so they could shower you with spit as you went past.

As his brother went out of sight, he saw a familiar boy cycling up the close on a bike that was way too big for him. It was Darren and Will gasped in relief. He saw a slight look of annoyance cross his new friend's face as he waited for him. He wondered whether it was on seeing him, but decided it was more likely his unwieldy conveyance which was weaving down the road. Just as well it was mostly cycle path to get to school or his mum wouldn't have let him cycle and Darren's life expectancy would be measured in days not years.

'Have you got your games kit?' Will asked.

'Yep,' said Darren. 'It's before lunch isn't it?'

'Yes. Although I've never played rugby before, what's it like?

'Violent,' Darren answered with a big grin.

Will wasn't as pleased at that prospect. He had seen rugby on television, but had never held a rugby ball before.

'Is it like American football?' His mum let him watch that after scouts on a Friday night.

'Yes, you catch the ball and run to the end. Apart from those jessies wear protective padding.' As they got to the crest of the road, he shouted, 'Last one to school buys the sweets.'

They both steamed down the sloping path, Darren's whoop of 'Aaaa-gaaa-doooo,' echoing around and Will's relieved cheer bounced back as they went through the empty underpass. As they came out of the dark and up the other side Nathan and his friend jumped out from behind a bush and spat at them both as they streamed past.

★ ★ ★

At eleven o'clock in the morning Will found himself standing on the edge of the games field. His shoelace had broken and the head games teacher, who was the teacher observing the fight and was still wearing the same tracksuit, was trying to repair it.

As he waited he stared at the throng on the field. Misfits and loners stood near the centre circle, whilst the more boisterous and confident were already trying to kick the ball at the posts and throwing the ball to each other. Darren was amongst the latter, passing the ball with accuracy and speed.

Aiden and Carl were standing on the edge of the centre circle, laughing about something as they watched the ball play. From a distance Aiden's size was comically obvious. He was a good head taller than Carl and his thighs were the same thickness as the smaller boy's waist. Although Carl's sports kit was oversized it looked like it had been ironed with military precision. This seemed to make his legs look more twig like than they could possibly be. Will suspected Carl's rugby career would be a short one.

Aiden however stood next to him almost bursting out of his. He winced as he remembered the noise when Aiden had collided with the boy yesterday. As he watched, three lads had made their way over to the pair and had begun pointing. You didn't need the hearing of Superman to know abuse is being delivered. The three boys' bodies rocked as they found whatever insults they were throwing hilarious.

He could understand Carl not responding but Aiden could have mown these lads down like grass. He suspected Aiden was a gentle soul and as he wedged his newly laced shoe back on he raced towards them with trepidation. Darren then came into view. He stopped in between the two groups and even from a distance Will could see him talking earnestly to each individual, pointing and looking from face to face for understanding. He then peeled away and left them to it.

As Will reached them he heard all three lads apologise profusely to their feet and they too left quickly.

'What was that about?' Will panted as he arrived.

'Nothing much,' Carl beamed. 'I don't think they will be doing it again.'

The teacher called them together and introduced himself as Mr Wheeler. He was about fifty and despite his age seemed in good shape, heavy but strong. He had a full head of hair, greying at the sides and a slightly dodgy looking moustache.

'Welcome to The Prince's School. This,' he declared, 'is a rugby school. Ergo, we play rugby.'

'Can't we play football?' a young-looking, ginger haired lad piped up.

Wheeler strode up to him and bellowed at him, so close his hair moved. 'Football is a swear word, this is ball to hand. If I see anyone kick the ball, I will kick them. Now listen to the rules.'

Considering he was a teacher it was the most cursory of explanations. The swirling wind kept snatching words away and the majority had blank looks on their faces. He picked up something about forming a mule and forward passing resulting in pain.

'Now I shall show you how to tackle. A volunteer please.'

Someone pushed the ginger haired boy forward, who now had a face like someone was shoving him toward a cliff edge.

'Name, boy?'

'Ingram,' he replied.

'Ingram sir!' Wheeler thundered as he fired the ball into the boy's midriff. To his credit Ingram caught it with only a faint huff as it hit his stomach. However he was standing for only a few more seconds as the teacher shouted 'Watch' and ran over and drove his shoulder into Ingram's thigh. There was a collective 'ooh' as Ingram's face slid along the grass.

'Once you are on the floor you must let go of the ball. Now practice in pairs. If you tackle properly, neither you, nor your opponent will get hurt.'

Will suspected Ingram would beg to differ as he watched him struggle to his feet, modelling a bright green side to his face.

Will felt a big paw on his shoulder and turned to a smiling Aiden. Given no choice he told Aiden to run toward him with a ball after stepping away to give him space. As Aiden arrived he put his shoulder down and dove toward a meaty thigh. It was like hitting a phone box.

As he sprawled on the floor, he looked up and caught Darren wiping out Carl next to them. In the background the teacher followed proceedings with a hawkish stare. Luckily before the horror of Aiden tackling him materialised, the teacher got a game going.

He gave the ball to Aiden as the two sides lined up and simply said, 'Off you go.'

Aiden looked at the ball as though it was a ticking bomb, before setting off at a country ramble. Ingram's poor day continued as he was the first person Aiden walked through. It wasn't until Aiden was almost at the try line that he was thwarted, although it was the teacher who knocked and dragged him to the floor. Will caught the teacher wincing when he thought he wasn't being watched.

What followed was thirty minutes of slapstick action. The teacher's shouted unbidden instructions merged with squeals of bent fingers and bumped heads, as twenty-eight lads barged after the ball carrier, like so many ducklings chasing their mother. Will actually found he quite liked it.

He scored two tries and found that he was a natural tackler although he had dropped the ball more times than he had caught it. If you went in hard and tight in the right area, it didn't seem to matter what size the person you tackled was, they still came down. Admittedly he hadn't tackled Aiden, as their class had been pitted against another.

Darren was loving being on Aiden and Will's team. Naturally Aiden had been put in the front row of the scrum. He was almost too strong. When he pumped those thighs, he was prone to send the scrum into a crumpling spin with Aiden left confused on top of a pile of bodies. As boys cried out about being winded and crushed, Darren was nipping in on agile feet and darting away. Will sprinting and rapidly joining him as they made for the try line, taking turns to score.

Will got the ball near his own try line after a line-out that more resembled a monkey's tea party and looked for a pass. Seeing three players bearing down on him and Darren for once under a pile of players, he panicked, and forgetting the teacher's warning kicked the ball as hard as he could. Misjudging the shape, instead of firing it long, it raced up in the air and went sideways to the wing.

Will looked to the ball's probable trajectory and saw Carl, who was standing as though out for a light stroll, was at ground zero and for a moment time stood still. Carl had excelled in his own way, managing to stay at least ten metres away from any of the action. His shorts and shirt were still ghost white as was now his face as the ball tumbled down to him, as if pulled by a string. His hands went up as though to catch a beach ball five times the size of the incoming missile and Will flinched at the inevitable. The swirling ball smacked Carl directly on the forehead with a wet splat.

Carl hit the deck like a hanged man when the rope is cut. The ball bounced straight into Aiden's hands who had almost reached Carl, as Will had just stood there gawping. Aiden froze there for a few seconds as though he had just caught an expensive vase that had been knocked off a shelf, before Darren screamed in his ear, 'Run!'

Aiden had about thirty metres of clear ground in front of him and it was the first time he had got some impetus without having three or four kids hanging around his feet.

He knew it wasn't, but Will almost felt like the ground was shaking as Aiden pounded away at the wrong angle straight towards the bulk of the opposition. He suddenly realised that despite his size, and given enough time, Aiden could run. It was a sight to behold. If he had looked around he would have seen the teacher grinning like the proverbial cat, at odds with the bladder-loosened faces of those in the line of fire.

Will realised a second inevitable collision within the same minute was about to occur. As Aiden's momentum hit full ramming speed, the first two boys at point of impact simply stepped out of the way. The two behind, possibly unsighted, were not so lucky. They were bounced out of the way as though they were inflatable dolls battered by a runaway horse.

The next three boys were trampled like the victims of a buffalo stampede and Aiden was clear. Unfortunately he ran through the try line and possibly only stopped due to the rapidly approaching hedge. Wheeler slapped Will and Darren on the backs simultaneously and winked, Will's kicking indiscretion forgotten.

'You three are going to be the Clint Eastwood of my attack, the Good, the Bad and the Beefy.' He looked at his watch. 'Straight to the showers everyone,' he hollered. He frowned at one of the boys who was sobbing and holding his arm as if to keep it attached to his body. Ingram's face was now grass green on both sides and Carl was still prone. His forehead was sprouting a lump the size of a golf ball, sitting proudly above his right eye. Will heard

Wheeler mutter under his breath, 'I suspect I better make my way to casualty.'

7

Will, Aiden and Darren all cheered and waved as Carl and two others were driven past them in the teacher's car after they had showered and were walking back to school. Will and Darren had spent all their dinner money on sweets before school and Will was regretting that fact, so they jumped at Aiden's offer to come around his for lunch as he lived near the school.

'Are you sure your mum won't mind?' Will asked. His mum would have blown a gasket if he had rocked up at the house unannounced with two unexpected lunch guests.

'No, she loves it. My dad works on the rigs off Aberdeen, he does six weeks on and then he is back for six weeks.' Aiden's eyes lit up at the thought of food, almost like a mist had cleared. 'My mum as you may have guessed is a bit of a feeder,' he continued. 'She throws herself into her cooking, especially like now when he is away, as she likes to keep busy. She also bakes wedding cakes and such from home. My sister is paranoid about her weight, so there's always extra for yours truly.'

Will was expecting a huge house in part as a reflection of Aiden's large stature. The house however was an average three bed Victorian terrace. They walked through a narrow dark alley between the houses and came out into a back garden which was bursting with flowers and plants.

It reminded Will of the local florist, but with a pleasant sun bringing the best out of everything.

They entered the kitchen at the rear of the house which Will was expecting to be baking hot and chaotic, with the waft of home cooking tantalising their taste buds. Instead it was white, sparse and bright. Dust motes hung in the air, caught by the sunlight coming through the windows and gave his mother a saintly glow as she looked at them from the kitchen sink.

What was large and warm was the greeting. His mum kissed them all on the cheek which left Darren looking particularly bashful. She ushered them in to the next room, a thousand questions being fired off in a strange lilting accent that Will could not place.

She was blonde, buxom and her sunny infectious manner soon had the boys laughing and shouting across the table, calling her Ingrid as she insisted. The dining room was empty except for the huge oak table and the matching high backed chairs they were sitting on and a large comfy looking armchair in one corner next to the window. A radio cassette player was quietly playing on the window sill in the corner, as it always would be over the years ahead.

As Ingrid left to prepare a little lunch, Will asked about the armchair. Aiden laughed affectionately and said, 'It's for Grandpa, for when he comes over from Sweden. He has a bad back but likes to be involved, so he sits there. My mum leaves it there after he has gone back as she says she then feels he is with us all the time.'

As they chatted Will marvelled at the change in Aiden's demeanour. He had come alive, leading the jokes and pouring the orange squash which his mum had brought in. He even got them all to cheer at his toast to 'Moffa' which apparently meant Grandpa in Swedish. It was when his sister arrived that he became the most animated though.

As she arrived, Aiden leapt up and swung her around in a hug-type dance, before plonking her in the seat he had saved for her next to him. Will had never really noticed a girl like her before.

Her hair was white blonde but her skin was a healthy pale brown as though she spent all her time outside playing tennis and riding horses. She had curves in all the right places as his dad would say, but was slim and willowy. It was her eyes though, they were the crowning glory. Light blue with heavy lashes, that made him stare even though he tried not to, as though he was being hypnotised.

Will wasn't the only one captivated by her beauty. Will dragged his eyes away and first looked at Darren. He had an almost shocked look on his face, which was gradually being replaced by one of desire or possession, like a cat who had just seen a pretty bird land in the back garden. Will looked at Aiden to see if he had noticed, but he was chatting animatedly with her, a look of fondness and pride on his face.

As Aiden got up to his mum's call, the girl asked who they were.

'Darren and Will,' they both replied in unison and she wrinkled her nose and giggled out loud, healthy white teeth showing, which seemed to dispel the tension that Will inexplicably sensed. He just sat back and watched as she and Darren chatted, although it was more of an interrogation than a conversation.

'So, what's your name?'

'Freja, said with y, but spelt with a j.'

'How old are you?'

'Thirteen.'

'Do you like sport?'

'Yes, I do.'

'Do you have a boyfriend?'

At that one she laughed, although she had a small smile on her face as she answered the question. 'Interested are we?' she teased, as she reached over and squeezed Darren's cheek. Will wasn't sure if it was the patronising gesture to a cheeky child or just the touch of her hand to his face that caused Darren to redden visibly, but she was now the cat, toying with a piece of string.

'I heard about your fight.' She leant forward as she said this, eyes wide.

Darren's eyes narrowed. 'Oh yes, from Aiden?'

'It was all around the school,' she replied. She paused and then said, 'Bad boy, are we?' Although she said it in a way that it was not a negative thing.

This time it was Darren who leant back in his seat. 'That's for you to find out, Freja with a j.'

Will felt he didn't understand the dynamics before him and it would be many years before he understood that some girls were just drawn to danger. Much to his chagrin, it would often seem to be the attractive ones.

All of a sudden Will's attention was distracted by the plate of food which was presented in front of him, the like of which he had never seen before. His plate was crammed with eggs, bacon, beans and fried tomatoes. In the centre of the plate were three sausages. They were massive. They sat there like enormous spent artillery shells, smoke pouring off them in waves.

He looked up at Aiden's smiling mother wondering if she had made an error and mistaken him for a thirty year old farmer, just in from the fields. She patted his shoulder and smiling at Darren said, 'Would you like to say grace?' She let him stew and fluster for a few seconds, before laughing and saying, 'Just kidding' and left them to it. Aiden was already ploughing through his with some efficient conveyor belt technique, making choking sounds as his mother's comments amused him.

Aiden sniggered as he saw Darren's fork battling with one of the behemoth bangers, one escaping his jab and scampering across the table towards Freja. She burst into a fit of chuckles at his phallic offering, handing it back to him between two delicate fingers and raising an eyebrow, causing him to furiously blush again.

Will settled into the task at hand, ravenous after the morning exercise. Soon though he began to flag and his mother's words seeped into his mind, oozing slowly to his conscience as he quickly realised he would never eat all this. 'It's rude not to finish your plate when you are a guest' was one of her many odd mantras. He persisted, finding his breath becoming shallower as his stomach expanded.

Noticing that the others were all pre-occupied with their herculean tasks, he slipped two of his sausages into his trouser pocket and asked Aiden to use the toilet. He cursed out loud as he closed the door, feeling the warm grease leak through to his leg. He wondered briefly who he could blame for it; his mum for her crazy rules or Aiden's for torture by food.

He slipped them into the cistern, a trick for disposing of unwanted vegetables he had picked up from his brother and returned to his seat. Darren stared at him through suspicious eyes. He had put his cutlery down and looked bloated despite half his plate being full. Freja had left a larger amount. Aiden's plate however was clean as a whistle as though a starving dog had been given five seconds at the remains and he was eyeing up any possible seconds.

Before he could bring himself to look at his own plate, Ingrid returned and whisked their plates away. Will almost passed out when she said, 'Don't worry about eating everything, not everyone is quite the hungry little one, like our boy here. Now who's for ice cream?'

★ ★ ★

As they staggered back into the sunlight, Will realised why Aiden looked so sleepy at school, he was probably stuffed to the gills. They waved to Ingrid, who threatened them with a spatula if they didn't return soon. Darren and Freja grinned at each other as they left, knowing it wouldn't be long before they would be seeing each other again.

As they trundled back to school, Will couldn't help looking at every flat, sun-baked surface and wishing he could pass out on one, like some gigantic snake with a whole cow in its stomach. He could hear the other two chatting about going to see the film 'The Goonies' at the cinema that weekend, but was too full to offer any opinion.

Suddenly Darren stopped, and halting Aiden with a tug on his arm, he looked into his friend's face.

'I'm going to marry your sister,' he declared, as though it was as inconsequential as saying 'I'll have toast for breakfast'.

'Is that OK?' he added, almost as an afterthought but only to be polite as Will could see he believed it was now a mere formality.

Aiden cocked his head to one side and seemed to ponder the statement.

'Sure,' he replied. He then laughed and said, 'I will be able to have her bedroom then.'

8

29th August 1988

Will gave his brother the finger as he rode past him on the way to the school. He had grown over the last six months and his dad had finally relented and bought him a full size racer but Nathan refused to compete with him. He clearly did not want to give him the satisfaction of beating him.

To be fair to Nathan he had been right about the other school spitting on them as they went past. It had become a habit to cycle as fast as you could as you ran the gauntlet. There was possibly nothing more disgusting than having someone else's warm phlegm land on your forehead. Darren had put an end to that for the most part last year by getting off his bike and demanding to know who was the hardest. Despite there being about six of them, it appeared no-one was.

Nathan hadn't been quite right about the sodomizing in the toilets although it was rumoured that Ingram got his head flushed in one. Kostas as usual was the guilty party. Ingram denied it after saying he had been wetting his hair down from the tap but he never used that particular toilet again. Carl had also taken a sound beating from a bully called Rudd in the same toilets a couple of days before the end of the previous term and even though he hadn't said anything, Will knew that Darren had taken it as an affront to his own reputation.

As Edwalton Avenue came into sight, Will could see Darren was there as usual. Three years they had been cycling to school and come rain or shine Darren was always waiting for him. He had never actually been to Darren's house, in fact he didn't even know which one it was, only that it was at the bottom.

Darren hopped onto his bike and gave him a toothy grin. They had spent nearly all the holidays together. The four of them had been to the ABC cinema to see Tom Hanks in 'Big' and even managed somehow to get Carl in to 'Die Hard'. Darren had asked loads of questions to distract the teller and Aiden had stood up close to the window, his bulk blocking a clear view of a clearly not fifteen Carl. The teller had given them all a long look but the queue was huge and snaked around the block and in the end he had just waved them through.

The film struck a chord with Darren. He had been back twice on his own to see it and even took Freja the last week before term started as she finally relented to Darren's continuous requests for a date. They had all shot up in height that year and Darren was now level with her so maybe that was why she had agreed, but there had always been an inevitability about it. There was a strange connection between them that Will could always feel when the two of them were in the same room together.

Darren had never shown any interest in any other girls to his credit and that date was the first for all four of the friends with any girl. Will suspected he was missing something as he couldn't see the point of spending time with the female of the species when he was having so much fun with his mates, even though despite his obvious indifference he still seemed to receive valentine's cards and confusing love letters.

The four of them had settled into a rhythm of doing virtually the same things all of the time. They went to Aiden's after school, loving the atmosphere and refreshments. They had tried Will's house for a change but it just wasn't the same. Carl's lounge had been their location for about twenty minutes once, but as they watched television his dad came in and turned it off stating in no uncertain terms 'You don't want to watch that rubbish'.

Carl always had to leave early as his accountant dad generally got home at six and expected him to have been doing his homework for a good hour under the watchful eye of his teacher mother. They were friendly enough to the boys, but you could tell they were not over enamoured with their son's choice of friends. Carl however was as happy as Larry, revelling in the relative security and safety of being part of what he called 'the gang'.

The weekends were generally spent with the four of them tearing around on their bikes or going out in the countryside. Will suspected the oil rig job paid well as Aiden's dad had a large shiny new Range Rover. When he was back he had all the time in the world for the boys and would take them fishing and on long walks.

Will had expected a giant sized individual, but Aiden's dad was just really tall. Freja was the apple of his eye, but he surprisingly tolerated Darren's single-mindedness. Maybe he just recognised his own devotion in Darren's eyes.

As they approached the bike sheds at the back of the school where they always parked, Will's heart sank as he saw Daniel Rudd waiting for them. He had his mate Flanagan with him and they both wore an intent look.

Darren dropped his bike on the grass and went over to them and Will did likewise, feeling he had little choice.

In his mind he could hear his mother shouting at him at breakfast that morning over the din of the radio. 'You've had a good holiday, but it's the start of a new year now and you've got to work. Buckle down Will, it will be worth it.' His mum's face had been all keen. He still felt sad when he thought back to his mother's crumpled face after he had come home last Christmas and told her he had been put on report for letting a teacher's tyres down. He hadn't done it either, Darren had, but he wouldn't rat on a mate.

She had signed his report card each day sniffing as she handed it back. She hadn't told his dad though, saying that he had enough on his plate. The next time he was put on report, though, he forged her signature. She didn't need to know about the cigarettes which Darren had brought in and they had been caught smoking in the park. He hadn't enjoyed it, Aiden had refused and Carl had been sick but the seed had been sown.

As Will looked at Rudd's mean squinting eyes, he suspected his mother didn't have this in mind when she said get stuck in. Rudd was in the same year as Kostas and was a pea from the same pod. Both of the lads waiting were taller and wider than them but the years had narrowed the gap. Rudd and three of his mates had picked on Darren before after finding him alone in a classroom. Darren had told him about it immediately afterwards.

'No room to fight in there Will and there was four of them. I may like a fight but I'm not looking for a beating and that boy is twisted. I will be ready one day and he will hurt.'

Will had been in the toilet still battling with his side parting that day when Darren had come in to stop his nose and lip bleeding. Darren always seemed to be covered in cuts and bruises, yet Will had never seen him lose a fight bar the Kostas altercation on their first day. He remembered looking at his calm face as he expertly wiped the blood away as though it was an occupational hazard of being Darren Connor. He wondered not for the first time what he got up to when he wasn't with him.

Rudd had an owlish face, with permanently narrowed eyes. He had a scar running down from the centre of his nostrils to a thin top lip which was unable to cover the four top incisors, giving him the impression of a permanently angry rabbit. He had the beginnings of a wispy moustache which he would no doubt use to cover that lip as he grew older. It should have been a comical face, but instead it looked wrong and evil.

Flanagan didn't look like he wanted to be there. Will had heard of him through his brother who was in the same year as these two. He had a nickname; Flick Knife Flanny, as he had apparently bought one on a French trip once. A poor nickname, Will considered, which he didn't look like he would be living up to. He watched Flanny trying to look cool whilst casually eating a Milky Way but his furtive eyes betrayed his nervousness. Darren and Rudd didn't look nervous. Will hoped it would go without saying that he would be fighting Flanny. Rudd spat on the floor and said, 'Gonna run away again pussy?'

He had a slight swagger about him and stood rolling his shoulders. Clearly not his first fight and he looked used to winning. Darren looked up from one to the other and then before anyone else involved reacted, stepped sideways and slammed a shockingly fast fist directly into Flanny's face. To be fair to Flanny he didn't hit the deck, he just sank to his knees with a stunned look on his face.

As blood poured from his chocolate covered nose, he just perched there with a shocked look on his face. His contribution to proceedings was over.

By now there was quite a crowd gathered and Will heard a few shouts of 'Go on Darren'. Rudd had made few friends with his violence and intimidation over the years, but no-one had had the guts or strength to challenge him, until now. Rudd assumed a boxer's stance, seemingly not bothered by his companion's demise, his jab hand poised to strike out.

As the two combatants squared up to each other a female voice froze them with a high pitched 'Stop'.

It was Freja, who had joined the crowd which now numbered around forty. She walked forward on unsteady legs and stood between them with her back to Rudd.

'Don't do this Darren,' she loudly said. 'You have been involved in too much fighting. Don't give him what he wants.' She paused and searching Darren's eyes she quietly said, 'If you want to be my boyfriend Darren, it all stops here.'

Will suspected only he heard the last bit, but he imagined everyone could hear the gears crunching in Darren's brain; a 'Does not compute' sign flashing red and blaring alarms. Suddenly she was jolted forward, almost falling until Darren steadied her in his arms. He pulled her to one side and looked at Rudd's grinning face.

'Out of the way please. Let me sort this piece of shit out and then I'll sort you out, if you get my drift.' He laughed, winking at a stunned Freja.

Darren leaned into Freja, and whispered in her ear.

'Just this last one, please?'

Freja stared at the distance for a moment and simply nodded. Will expected her to leave but she came and stood next to him, chin held high.

They squared up again, Rudd edging forward until he came in range and shot off a rapid jab. He was so quick that Darren only half evaded it and he staggered back under the stinging blow. Encouraged by his success Rudd stepped it up a gear, punches peppering towards Darren's face. Darren ducked most with ease and blocked some with his forearms, until Rudd missed with one and followed through with his elbow.

Darren went down on one knee and looked up as gasps came from the circled spectators. Shaking his head slowly, his hand rubbing the side of his already flaming head, he got to his feet. This time he went forward, but as Rudd's strike came in, he shifted to the side and caught the extended hand at the wrist and yanked it towards him.

Twisting it away from himself, he pulled down and driving his elbow into Rudd's shoulder, bore him to his knees. Using the straight arm as a lever he pushed him down again so his forehead was touching the concrete. Rudd strained in frustration as he was held there, stuck, until he dropped to the floor from a winding punch to his unprotected ribs.

All gathered expected this to precede a brutal pounding, but instead Rudd was allowed to get to his feet. His eyes were now mere slits, teeth bared as he let out a slow growl, his face frozen in anger. Sore but unbroken, like a snarling bear, starving but wary of its dangerous prey.

They began to circle each other, causing Flanny to shuffle out of the way. He crawled toward the mass of watchers, who parted for him, then reformed as though swallowing a tasty morsel, eager for more action.

The two combatants began to trade blows, both blocking and dodging, but it soon became clear Darren had the edge as Rudd's face snapped back every few seconds, his face rapidly reddening. As it went on Will realised Darren could have finished it a long time ago. Instead, as a last hurrah, this lad was going to suffer and suffer he did.

No-one moved or uttered a sound as his nose split, blood pouring down and turning his white shirt into a dark red bib. His cheek split open and his right eye began to shut. Rudd's blocking arms now flailed around like a wobbling, loose windmill in a weak breeze. Darren finally stood back to admire his handiwork before punting Rudd straight in the groin. As Rudd's head shot down and forward, with expert timing, Darren crunched his knee up into the falling face.

This straightened Rudd up but his eyes had rolled back into his head, his hands lolling at his side. Will would remember the moment for a long time after. It was quiet and peaceful. The only sound except for Rudd's laboured shallow breathing was a car revving in the distance. Then he heard the solid impact as Darren slammed an open hand into Rudd's chest. Rudd cannoned backwards and clattered on and into a line of bikes hung in their racks.

Freja took Darren's hand and they walked off into school. Will watched the crowd quickly disperse in silence, many ashen faced after their first and probably last experience of extreme violence, until it was just him and Rudd, who dangled there like an exhausted desperate butterfly in an unyielding web.

As he stood there he felt things spiralling out of control. The wind whistled the withered autumn leaves around him. Now the only other sound was gentle sobbing from Rudd. Will grimaced as he realised that his new academic trouble free start to the year had not even lasted until the first bell.

He couldn't blame Darren though, he hadn't looked for trouble, he had just found it waiting for him. What Will didn't know was todays meet had been planned since Carl's beating. What Will also didn't know was how seriously Darren would take Freja's threat. Today's fight had been a foregone conclusion, but it would also be Darren's last scrap at school.

Shrugging he turned and followed the others, feeling a sense of doom as life happened to him and it seemed he was powerless to exert any influence over it. As he thought on this, the first bell rang for registration. He paused under the clock tower entrance, then walked back to Rudd.

Taking a deep breath and trying to avoid the blood, he hauled Rudd out of the bike shed. He half dragged and half carried him into school through the empty corridors. Encouraging him like you would a tired toddler he got him into the nurse's room and gently dropped him into a chair and propped him against an arm.

He shouted, 'You ok?' at him and received an imperceptible nod of the head in reply.

He heard footsteps coming so he whispered loudly in Rudd's ear.

'It's probably best for all concerned, you included, if you say you fell off your bike.' He gave him what he hoped was a reassuring squeeze of the shoulder and slipped out the door.

When he arrived at his home room everyone was in their seats. Their form tutor this year luckily was the games teacher Mr Wheeler. He slapped Will on the back as he walked in, saying, 'I think we can let the top try scorer turn up a few minutes late.'

They had won the rugby league every season but it was always tight. Teams had wised up to their threats very quickly. Darren was a gifted player but easy to provoke and they had spent many games a man down after he had been sent off. Aiden was still amazing, but like a herd of cavemen pulling down a magnificent woolly mammoth, they realised numbers mattered and he could be stopped.

The classroom was set up into rows of two seated table and chairs. Seated at the front and far side were Aiden and Carl. They both waved wildly at him, like a pair of happy meerkats. Darren was seated behind them, gesturing to the empty space next to him.

Will explained what he had done with Rudd, whilst examining Darren's multi coloured face and head. None of the teachers seemed to mention his bruises much, almost as if they couldn't see them. Darren was in good form and said he had some exciting news.

'We are going somewhere cool Friday night.' Will imagined a party, but was a little surprised to hear the destination.

'Army Cadets. It will be awesome. You get given a free uniform, all you have to buy are boots. You get to shoot stuff.'

'Like what?' Aiden asked.

'Terrorists,' Darren said laughing and tussled Aiden's still dome-like hairdo. As Will contemplated and then accepted that shooting stuff would be pretty awesome, he noticed that both Darren and Carl's hairstyles were basically identical now. Shaved at the sides, a parting and a quiff, like two smaller Morrisseys from the band 'The Smiths'. Following a pause of disquiet, he put his hand to his head and realised his was the same. Will couldn't remember whether it had been a rational choice or if they had just steadily morphed into copycats.

As they agreed to meet at Aiden's on Friday night at six-thirty, Will wondered whether they did everything

Darren wanted because he told them too, or they did it because Darren had the best ideas.

Will was last to leave the room as the next lesson bell rang. Wheeler stopped him and asked if he was up for the season ahead. Will nodded and they both shared a moment as they watched Aiden dip his head to get under the door.

'You know,' Wheeler said. 'If I could take half of Darren's aggression and give it to Aiden and half your sense and give it to Darren, we would be awesome.'

Will pondered this for a minute. 'Yes,' he replied. 'But then you wouldn't need me.'

9

2nd September 1988

Will pushed his bike down the alleyway to Aiden's back garden and rapped on the back door. Aiden's mum answered and chastised him as usual, but he doubted he would ever just let himself in. The house, as was the norm, was full of life. Aiden's parents had been slow dancing to The Hollies latest song which was emanating around the house. His dad pointed to the lounge rolling his eyes.

When he got there he found Aiden laughing in Moffa's chair, with Darren and Freja crooning 'He is heavy, he's my brother' as the chorus came along. It was weird seeing them hold hands, but he guessed he would get used to it.

'Come on you two spoon heads, we don't want to be late and doing press ups in the rain on our first night,' Will joked.

They wandered up the road to Carl's, whose house was around the corner from the cadet hall. Will thought he would be nervous but he didn't feel that way. He had his best friends with him and he was excited. His mum had been upset about him quitting scouts almost overnight, saying not to rush into things and he had even had to sit through an uncomfortable meeting after an impromptu drop-in from the scout master on Wednesday evening. Afterwards he had contemplated how casually he had thrown in the towel on something he had been doing for years, for something he had not even been to yet, but had shrugged and thought 'What the hell'.

When they got to Carl's house they were surprised to see him answer the doorbell without his coat and shoes on. Carl was usually itching to get going. He whispered, 'My mum and dad are discussing whether I can go.'

His dad came into view and loomed over him at the door and with a distinct lack of eye contact stated, 'His mother and I have discussed it and have decided Carl won't be going, he needs to concentrate on his school work.'

Carl looked shocked and confused, like a dog that had just felt the heat of his owner's newspaper for the first time. Without further ado, the door was closed.

A little stunned, the trio walked on.

'That was pretty weird,' Will said. 'Especially considering he is perhaps the only person in the school who doesn't need to concentrate on his school work.'

'My dad would never stop me trying something,' Aiden contributed.

'Hell,' Darren laughed. 'It was my dad's idea!'

The cadet hut was a single storey building at the bottom of a car park at the edge of Westwood Industrial Estate. It looked more like a warehouse than a meeting place. There were about twenty-five kids hanging around outside, aged between twelve and seventeen. All had army uniforms on, berets included and nearly all of them seemed to be smoking. Will would never give Scouts another thought.

As they waited outside they stood on the edge of the group, but before they felt uneasy a few of the older boys came over.

'First night lads?' a gangly lad of about sixteen asked. He had a crew cut, bad skin and the shiniest pair of boots Will had ever seen.

'Yes Corporal,' Darren barked back.

Will and Aiden stole a glance at each other a little taken aback, wondering how the hell he knew that. Will also noticed for the first time that Darren had a pair of what seemed to be army boots on under his jeans.

The other cadet took a glance at Darren and said, 'I know you, don't I?' He was of similar stock to the Corporal. Lean and wiry, beret tugged down tight over really short hair.

Darren at least had the grace to look sheepish as the boy continued.

'Yes, we went to the same junior school, All Saints. You had a scrap with my younger brother. Beat the shit out of him.' Will gulped as he continued. 'Well don't worry, he doesn't come here. He's a gobby little twat anyway, probably did him some good.' He smiled, 'I'm Smith, and this is Corporal Cockhead.' He roared with laughter and peeled away to the door shouting, 'Fall in,' at the top of his voice.

They were the last to get in the building and the cadets had all lined up on parade. Three rows of eight, all neatly spaced. They all stood with legs comfortably apart, hands joined behind each back. Corporal Cockhead turned out to be Corporal Cockburn. He told them to join the back of the others and just copy them. 'Don't worry,' he winked. 'You will soon pick it up.'

A thin immaculately uniformed man in his mid-forties with a bright ruddy face came out of an office and marched to the front of the group. His bearing was so crisp it was almost robotic. As he got towards the centre, Smith and Cockburn, who were now at the front, came to attention and saluted him. Smith shouting, 'Officer on parade, at-ten-shun!' With a stamping of feet the parade all stood tall.

'I'm Sergeant-Major Lander. Welcome detachment.' The man marched up and down, looking at uniforms and barking comments out.

'Is your iron broken private?'

'Bull those boots son.'

'Push those shoulders back.'

'New recruits, excellent. The army needs big strong men. You will do,' he blared in front of Aiden.

'Get some boots, you will be marching here, not running,' he ordered Will. Will looked at his trainers and then at the footwear of the man in front of him, realising Cockburn now had the second pair of shiniest footwear he had ever seen.

When the officer stopped in front of Darren he paused. Darren was staring straight ahead, no eye contact. When he talked to Darren he had dropped his voice several octaves and spoke rather than commanded.

'I knew your dad son. He was the best soldier I ever knew. I was with him when it happened, it was a terrible shame. He saved a lot of lives that day. A great man.'

Will looked over with a confused look on his face. Darren had never mentioned his parents in any detail before. He turned to his other side and looked at Aiden, who shrugged. Darren just stared forward. Rigid at attention, but Will could see his eyes watering.

★ ★ ★

The moment was forgotten quickly enough as they were engulfed in an evening of army life. They did map reading and learnt how to strip down weapons. The guns were ancient Lee Enfield 303 rifles with the firing mechanism removed but it was still brilliant fun. They drilled in the car park, the three friends all getting told off for laughing their heads off as they marched. Aiden was useless and Will kept getting out of sync with some of the other newer cadets, whilst Darren kept singing under his breath 'Heh heh, we're the Monkees'.

Darren, Will noted, was not out of step though. They had something called NAAFI at break which was like a tuck shop. The first night was free much to their delight so Will spent the fifty pence his dad had given him to pay dues on a Twix and some black jacks.

They were exhausted afterwards as they walked back to Aiden's, but buzzing. Everyone had been really friendly and they had learnt loads in one short night. As Will fondly remembered the feel of the gun he remembered the comment about Darren's father.

'Was your dad in the army then?' he asked.

'Yes, the Paras,' he quickly and proudly replied. 'He gave me his boots.' His eyes seemed to glaze over a bit and he ruefully added, 'He doesn't need them now.' He stopped and put a hand on each boy's shoulders and quietly said, 'It's complicated, I'll tell you all about it one day.' He never would.

10

23rd August 1990

Will nearly fell off his bike when he saw the empty wall. Five years of school and he had never beaten Darren to the meeting place at the top of the avenue and yet today oddly he was nowhere to be seen. His scalp felt all prickly and itchy and he felt the hairs stand up on his neck. Forcing himself to breathe deeper he shivered despite the morning sun. He hoped that wasn't a portent of doom for his GCSE results which he would be receiving in approximately one hour.

He searched his memory to see if he had made a balls-up on the timings. He smiled as he realised he had used Carl's favourite phrase, in reference to his incident at rugby in their first week. He still had a tiny dint in his head all these years later. Jesus, he thought, five years ago. It felt like he had been at school forever, yet if his results went badly, it would all be over today. Checking his watch he realised he was fifteen minutes early such was his haste to get away from his mother's doleful expression that morning.

She had kept saying in a misty eyed manner, 'They will be good, won't they?' His father had just shaken his head in the background. He had grown distant from his dad over the last few years. All the things they used to do together like football matches and the cinema he now did with his friends. Meanwhile his brother had been sniggering in the background. He had assessed the situation more pragmatically and come to the conclusion that seeing as Will was hardly ever seen doing any homework then Nathan would be having an enjoyable afternoon at his brother's expense.

He sat on the wall and let his mind trickle through the previous months. They had all joked that if they failed their exams and couldn't stay to do their 'A' Levels then they would sign up. Will shrugged at this again, in a way he wished he was going to fail and he would be going to join the army.

He had found school life increasingly tedious. He had struggled to drum up much enthusiasm for any of his subjects except history, but that was only because they had been studying World War Two. His interest had waned for that as well when they moved back five hundred years and studied the Tudors. Henry VIII's villainy being one of the few moments of interest. The lessons had seemingly become longer and longer, in particular Religious Education, where he swore his fingernails grew during some weird time loop. Like in the science fiction films where the astronaut goes away for a year and comes back to find everyone is forty years older.

He shivered again when he thought of Maths. It was the one subject he was nervous around as he knew his general brightness would get him through the rest of the exams. In Maths however he had more or less spent the last five years just copying Carl's work. It wasn't that he couldn't do it, it was just Carl was a master and it was miles quicker than doing it himself. Well that was what he had told himself anyway. Darren had been the one to copy at the start but him and Aiden had ended up in a different set than Carl for everything except English and it was Will who had taken advantage of Carl's brilliance.

It was distinctly possible Darren and Aiden could have failed some of their exams and he suspected Aiden in particular had endured a sleepless night.

Will had not picked the cheating baton up lightly and he had felt a bit guilty with the plagiarism at the start but he was way past that now. It had got to the point where he had to change some of Carl's answers to get them wrong as getting one hundred percent right each week wasn't feasible. Not for him anyway. Carl wouldn't be joining the army either, despite their best efforts to drag him down to their level, his brightness was off the scale.

Turns out Will couldn't do the math, as they say in the States. The advanced exam for his set had been a sweating, clammy, dry throated horror show. Some of it might as well have been written in Latin and his calculator seemed to have the artificial intelligence of a dandelion. It was the one time at school where time had been fleeting and he had walked out at the end cement-footed and wild-eyed.

His general laissez-faire attitude was one of the reasons he kept getting in trouble too, as idle hands made mischief. He actually laughed out loud getting an odd look from a passing granny when he recalled the English class where Aiden had sneaked Carl's exercise book away and Will had drawn an enormous dripping penis on the next empty page. They had slid it back and watched him as he opened it to write down the homework. Aiden said afterwards he had wet himself a little bit he was laughing so hard and that was before Carl had turned the page. Just the anticipation of it was enough.

The English teacher was ancient and old-school with a zero tolerance attitude to disruption. So they were desperately trying to be quiet but both making snuffling and snorting sounds like two happy pigs. When Carl turned to that page Darren, who had been sitting on the other side of him, saw and laughed loud and hard. On realising his error he tried to stem the sound but that caused him to eject an eight centimetre candle of snot from his nose, which made him laugh more, the offending article swinging like a huge epiglottis hanging from his chin.

A massive bellow came from the teacher at the front of the class.

'Silence. Silence. Silence' he had thundered as he came over to their table.

Aiden had buried his face in his book, head bobbing as he sniggered and Will pretended to do his shoe lace up, shoulders heaving as he unsuccessfully tried to think of something serious. Darren said after he was choking back his laughter so much that he was almost suffocating but the shock, then dawning look of realisation, followed quickly by fury on the teachers face when he saw the giant offering was too much and he tipped his head back and roared with glee.

He was frog-marched out of the class to the headmaster's office, wiping his slimy nasal discharge on Ingram's shoulder as he left the room. There, he informed them later, he was branded a foul pervert and placed on report for four weeks. He didn't deny having done it, accepting his punishment with stoicism.

In some respects they should have left him on report for the duration of his last year; it would have cut down on meetings. He once farted so loudly in assembly that Will felt the vibrations through the legs of his chair five metres away. The mass chuckling soon turned to anguish as the stench crept over the waiting ranks like mustard gas on a battlefield. Will was sure he even saw some teachers smile at that one. However, true to his word to Freja, there had been no more fighting.

He hadn't actually needed to. Nobody wanted to know, certainly not Rudd, who was comical in his avoidance techniques when he came into accidental proximity to Darren. Both he and Kostas returned to the relative safety of bullying new arrivals.

Thoughts of his mates made him check his watch, and it was now a minute past ten. Darren's time keeping was exemplary so there must be something up. Feeling a weird sense of trepidation that he could not explain he walked his bike down to the bottom of the avenue. Strange how he hadn't been down here before.

It was a wide, tree-lined road with three bungalows at the bottom. The middle one, which looked all the way down the street, had a slow, curving, shallow ramp leading to the front door and remembering Darren's comments about his dad's boots realised it had to be this one.

He lightly knocked on the door, fearing what may open it.

'Lad,' someone suddenly shouted. Will visibly jumped in the air, his nerves bow-tight. It was only the elderly neighbour whom Will had not seen as he was bent down gardening. He looked over and raised a quizzical brow.

'Be careful if you go in there, lad.' He seemed to consider saying something else, then looked at his watch and instead quietly said, 'You will probably be alright now?' Then nodded his head and disappeared out of sight.

Will considered this and decided knocking again would not be needed.

As he turned to go the door opened and swung open to reveal a dishevelled man in a wheelchair. He had a dirty, old, blue football shirt on, tired red shorts and a pair of ancient-looking sandals. Will dragged his eyes away from the withered legs and saw a face that looked like it had lived a thousand lives and one of those seemed to have cost him an eye and most of the fingers of his left hand. His skin had a yellow tinge and the few remaining teeth looked lonely and unloved.

'What?' the man asked, his gaze narrowing. In that moment Will could see Darren, and maybe a glimpse of the man this broken shell used to be.

'Is Darren here?' he replied, trying and failing to keep his voice steady.

'Are you a mate from school?' To Will's nod of confirmation, he said, 'Come in.'

Will really didn't want to go in but edged into the doorway. The house had a clean smell but there was an underlying hint of tobacco and something like marsh gas, however the hall and kitchen beyond were spotlessly clean.

'Darren is out,' he said slowly and gave him a weak smile. 'Seems he is out a lot nowadays.' Will got a sense of crushing loneliness from the tired eyes that looked back at him and felt sorry for the man. He imagined being an active decorated soldier and then being imprisoned in a wheelchair to live a life where your only child won't even bring his school friends around.

He pondered for a second if there was a Mrs Connor but sensed there wasn't. The house was tidied in a way a diligent man would. The few personal touches were distinctly male; a few photographs of soldiers, a ship in a bottle and a painting of what looked like a spitfire.

'But he is a good boy,' Darren's dad added, as if he could read his mind. 'He keeps this place spic and span, does the washing and cleaning now his mother's gone, all the shopping too, so I don't need to go out.' He very slightly flinched at that, as though he would very much like to go out. 'I can't complain. He got a call last night though. He put the phone down afterwards very slowly and then simply ran out of the house. He didn't even say goodbye.' He muttered under his breath afterwards, 'He does that a lot lately too.'

He backed up his wheelchair and seemingly forced himself to grin.

'Come and have a cold drink. I've got some biscuits. It would be great to hear what kind of a man Darren has grown into. I taught him everything I know.'

It was Will who involuntarily flinched then, but his dad just laughed.

'Yes, I bet there are some tales to tell.'

'I'm sorry Mr Connor but it's results day today and we are all meeting at Aiden's house so we can get them together. It's just he wasn't where he normally is. Tell him I've gone to Aiden's and I'll see him there.'

'Who is Aiden, another friend?' he asked, looking pleased that he had some because it looked like he hadn't met any.

Will smiled back and again felt sad that this man knew nothing of his son's life. He clearly didn't even know what an important day this was.

'Will you come back and chat? I need to know my son is ok?' he almost begged.

He held out his good hand and Will shook it, thinking that there would have to be an extremely unlikely run of events to make him returning here a possibility. He got on his bike and zoomed down the street to Aiden's without a backward glance.

11

When he got to Aiden's street it seemed eerily quiet. The sun was beating down now and Will was so thirsty he thought for the first time he would let himself in and get a glass of water. As he pulled up outside, he noticed an empty police car parked on the other side of the road. Thinking nothing of it he went around to the back door. He knew when he woke up this morning his world would be changing today. It would, but not how he expected it to.

He put his hand on the door handle and smiled, but before he entered it was opened from within and a very serious looking policeman came out of the house. Will stepped out of the way and let him by. Aiden's dad followed him out. Will at least thought it was Aiden's dad. When he saw his face it was as if all the goodness had been leached out of it like a dried peach. It looked like suddenly he had too much skin on his face. He had unshaven pasty jowls and heavy bags where before there had been none. He reminded him of pinhead in the Hellraiser films. Eyes so dark and distant that Will knew something terrible had happened.

'Come with me Will, sit down here.' Aiden's dad took him over to a bench and sat him down. 'There is no easy way to say this son, so I'm just going to say it. Freja has been killed in a car accident.'

For one of the few times in Will's life he was fully aware. All of a sudden he felt the rough edges of the bench under his hand, saw the cat walk along the fence, heard its claws drag on the wood. He could hear a bird singing and the clink of milk bottles. He had to force himself to breathe. His eyes felt too big for their sockets all of a sudden. He didn't know what to say, or do.

'How?' was all he said. Expecting it to come out dry and ragged, appropriate to the situation, but it came out normally, like he was checking a football result.

'She went out in her car last night to get Darren a good luck card. She was only going down the road, lazy little sod. Her car and another misjudged the lights. Freak accident the police said. Normally there would be no injuries, but Freja's car was blindsided and she broke her neck. Just like that. Here one minute and then gone.' He took a deep breath and continued, even though it was a terrible effort.

'She wasn't back for some time. I don't know why but I walked down there. Maybe I heard the sirens. I don't know, but I seemed to know. I ran the last bit, never ran so fast.' He stopped talking, screwed up his face. He took another huge breath through his nose and opened his eyes and continued. 'I ran straight down the middle of the street, through the backed up traffic, like a madman. There wasn't a mark on her car.' His speech slowed almost to a standstill. 'The car I bought her.'

He stopped. Will looked over expecting him to be crying, but he wasn't. His jaw was clenched and Will could see him swallowing that piece of information. To save it for another time, when he would be able to use it to punish himself.

He quietly continued.

'They were working on her when I arrived. They didn't see me arrive. The first thing I heard was one of them say 'She's gone'. I don't remember much after that. We went to the hospital. I saw her. I rang Darren. He saw her. We came home.'

They sat on the bench in silence for a few minutes. Will felt weird, almost wired. Was this shock, or was he missing some basic human feelings. He had to say something, but his mind was like an Antarctic landscape. He blurted out the one thing lurking at the back of his mind.

'We need to get our exam results.' Then he instantly felt dreadful for being so insensitive and began to apologise. 'Sorry, I..'

His dad stopped him by placing his hand on his arm. 'Life goes on Will, the world keeps spinning. Don't worry about not knowing what to say or do. No-one does. Go on in, get them out of the house. I'm just going to sit here for a minute. Good luck.'

Will stood up and walked to the door. He looked back into the garden. James Hill was sitting amongst the flowers in their busy garden, his head bent down as though in prayer. He could be in a cemetery now, Will thought and again wondered why he himself wasn't crying.

He walked into the kitchen treading quietly like a burglar. He could hear some quiet music from the dining room and something else in the background, an almost mewling keening sound. He crept in and found Darren and Aiden sitting in chairs next to each other. Both had a similar expression to Aiden's father on their face. Red, puffy eyes staring into a void.

Will still didn't know what to say. He sat down opposite them and tried to get his head around it. The radio was playing. 'Nothing Compares To You' by Sinead O'Connor echoed around the room. He thought of Freja. He realised what a big part of his life she had become. She had been like a pretty bird that he could admire from a distance. She used to hug him all the time, giggling as he pulled away all embarrassed. She was probably someone he never appreciated. He looked at his two friends and knew their lives had been broken. Will could now hear chants of 'No, no, no' and howls of rage coming from upstairs. Darren reached over and turned the radio up a notch, but Will could still hear it. All their lives would never be the same again.

They sat there in silence barely moving, like three expressionless, lights-out automatons. Will felt as if the room had been pumped full of air. Too much air. The pressure pushing in on him. Increasing with every second. He thought of Freja and for a moment couldn't remember her face or her laugh, yet there were pictures of her all over the room. These photos seemed to take on an almost otherworldly glow, almost as if her spirit was lifting itself out of them.

He rose out of his chair and walked to the big picture of Freja and Aiden sitting on the bonnet of the Range Rover taken that summer. Freja laughing at the camera, her arm playfully around his shoulder, Aiden gazing at her. The breeze tussled her hair whilst she displayed the thumbs-up sign at the camera. He felt the urge to touch the photo and consented to it, stroking her face. He could remember her now. Her hair had been so soft, light to the touch. He remembered how she would tap her manicured nails on the table when they played monopoly and she was winning. A happy look on her face, no poker player was she.

He realised he had loved her and that photo was how he would remember her.

The radio slipped onto Maria McKee and 'Show Me Heaven'. They endured a succession of sad songs on Hereward FM's 'Housewife's Hour' as they sat there mute and stunned. Songs he would in the future feel the urge to hide from whenever they came on. Wherever he was in the world he would feel the need to change channels, leave shops where they played, talk loudly in bars, or he was instantly back here in a world he didn't understand.

He couldn't take anymore. His brain couldn't cope. He flicked off the radio and went to the door.

'Come on guys. Freja would want us to go.' He didn't know if that was true, he didn't know why he hadn't shed any tears, not even a trickle, he just knew he had to get out of here. They finally looked up at him through red rimmed eyes. 'Carl will be waiting for us,' he added. They eventually shuffled after him, like liberated prisoners of war, through the croaky screams from above and passed Aiden's stunned father, still frozen on the bench.

12

As they paced to school Will felt as if the world was a three metre circle around him, the only sound the scuff of trainers as they walked. When they approached the gates, Carl came belting over, but stopped fifty metres from them, as if they were carrying a big sign declaring 'PLAGUE', written in dripping, red blood. He just kept looking from one face to another as they approached. Darren stopped in front of him and said through gritted teeth, 'Freja's dead. Car accident. Let's not talk about it.' Darren and Aiden walked past him into the school, leaving Will to put his arm around a bewildered Carl.

They were virtually the last to get their results, being over an hour late. They had to go to their home room, where their grades were waiting in sealed envelopes. Mr Wheeler was waiting, compassion oozing from every pore. He didn't say anything just handed them their results. They all looked at each other and opened them at the same time, as agreed, what seemed now a millennium ago.

Will's fingers felt like a big bunch of misshapen bananas as he fumbled his letter open and had to stare hard at the paper to get the information to go in. He had passed them all, even scraping a C in maths. It didn't seem to mean anything. Carl broke down next to him. Will suspected he would be the only person in the country to get ten straight As and sob like a baby receiving its first jabs.

Darren threw his letter on the floor, said, 'Let's get pissed,' and strode out of the room, some kind of decision made. Aiden stooped down and picked Darren's letter up and gently helped the weeping Carl to the door. Will followed but was stopped as he was about to leave the room by the teacher calling his name.

'Will. I'm so sorry for you all. There are going to be some tough times ahead. You are the one with the sense in the outfit. Try and hold them together. Grief affects everyone in different ways, there is no wrong or right way, but we are all here to help.'

Will nodded. The left side of his cheek edged up a few millimetres in an attempt at a smile, before following his friends out into the sunshine. He appreciated the gesture but in a way wished he hadn't said it. When he told them all later, it almost seemed like he had told them to do what they liked and blame it on bereavement.

As he joined Aiden, he noted Carl getting into a car and Darren running down the street.

'Where are they going?' he asked. As Aiden replied, Will realised it was the first thing he had heard him say that morning.

'His parents said they are taking him out for a posh dinner to celebrate. He tried to get out of it but they were not to be refused. I suspect they knew what the alternative was. Darren said he had something to do and would meet us at the pub shortly.'

The only pub they could get consistently served in without presenting fake IDs that would not stand close scrutiny, was in Eastfield, a fairly rough area on the edge of the town centre. As they walked together Will searched for the words to talk to Aiden.

'I'm sorry mate. I just don't know what to say, or think.'

Aiden put an arm around him and sniffed his reply. 'You have been a great mate Will. You are one of the good guys. Just hang around, that's all.'

★ ★ ★

Will looked up at the rusty sign for the Anne Boleyn Public House as they arrived. She too looked like she had received terrible news. As pubs went it was a dreadful one. It was big and roomy, but sparse and cold. It had little alcoves and booths for quiet chats and a room out the back with a wooden floor for dancing. You walked into a small entry hall and then could go left to the lounge, or right to the bar. Will had never seen anyone in the lounge. He had never seen anyone on the dance floor for that matter.

Trade was poor and the beer was flat. The landlord was a drunk and quite happy to serve them in their uniforms, never mind quiz them on their ages. The décor was foul, unloved and bathed in nicotine and tar. The carpet made a noise like Velcro as you walked across it and most went home for a shit, so basic were the toilets.

It had its good points though. No teacher would be found here. It had a great pool table and the landlord's daughter Angela was a short-skirted vision of something forbidden.

Angela was serving, batting her eyelids and bending provocatively as she served them three lifeless lagers. They moved to a booth and Will smiled as Aiden purposely left Darren the pint with no head on it.

They both supped the millimetre of froth off the top of their pints, Will wondering not for the first time if there were better things to spend his money on. They had all taken jobs at the Tesco superstore in town after term finished and were saving up some money. The plan was to have a have a huge blow-out after the results came out but Will and Darren had been sacked from the bakery department two weeks back for seeing who could make the biggest jam donut with the electric jam pump. Amazing how big they could get really, but a couple had exploded and the manager caught them creasing over with laughter, jam dripping off their faces, their uniforms, the walls and the ceiling.

As security walked them off, they passed Aiden who was crouching behind the deli-counter stuffing slices of ham into his mouth. When they told him they had got the boot, he just took his hat and apron off and walked out after them, giving a fond last look to the cheese section. Will suspected their profits would have improved dramatically after their eighteen stone mouse had left the premises.

'What grades did you get? Will asked.

'I got Cs in everything, except French, Religious Education and Pottery. All fails. I'm disappointed with pottery,' Aiden laughed. His various pottery projects were placed in his parents' garden amongst the flowers and bushes, like strange sentinels. Will had thought his huge gargoyle was amazing, until he was told it was supposed to be Dracula. It now had pride of place in their vegetable patch and like all ineffective scarecrows was covered in bird shit.

Aiden opened Darren's letter up. He beamed.

'Cool. He got enough to get in for A-Levels too. We will all be together.'

As he folded Darren's letter back into its envelope Darren slid into the booth next to them with a pleased look on his face.

'Now what?' Aiden groaned.

He paused, exaggeratedly lit a cigarette, and leaned back.

'I've been to the army recruiting office. I'm going to sign up. The Parachute Regiment. Just like my dad. Operation Desert Shield man, I'm going to do my bit.'

It seemed forced to Will. Like he had made a snap decision at a crazy time. Maybe it was just his way of trying to take some control of the nightmare they had found themselves immersed in. This was the time he would later realise was when he should have mentioned going around to see Darren's dad, but for some reason he didn't. Weird how he was thinking of that and not the departure of his friend to some far-off country or the tragic death of Freja, but it was like he couldn't grind the proper emotion out of himself.

Aiden however looked stunned. He simply asked, 'When?'

'I'm not sure. There's a load of tests, medical, intelligence and fitness. My dad has to give me permission too.' He looked away. 'I can't go back to school. What's the point? It's all bullshit.'

When he looked back, blazing anger shone out sharply from his face, like a sun flare and then was gone.

Will looked at Aiden and saw his big friend's face fall. For a brief few minutes they had forgotten what had happened. He knew Aiden was now thinking he was losing two people.

Darren drained his pint and stalked back to the bar, pulling hard on his cigarette. Will had a sense it was going to get messy, but if this wasn't the day for that, he would never know what was. He looked over as Darren was served. The barmaid was giving Darren a real eyeful of her cleavage as she poured the drinks and for the first time

Darren was responding. He took a five pound note out of his back pocket and slid it between her ample breasts. She smiled and went to the till. She got his change and walked back in front of him. Never taking her eyes off his, she wedged the change back where the note had been.

Slowly Will turned his head to the side, praying to the absent God that Aiden wasn't watching. Instead he timed it as Aiden dragged his eyes away from the loaded scene, and wide-eyed, looked straight at Will. And time stood still.

Will never did know how long they stared at each other, but only Darren returning with a flushed face broke the spell. Aiden drank the rest of his first pint and then emptied the second pint down his neck in three huge gulps. He then stood up, looking at Darren first, and then for much longer at Will.

'I'm going home. I should be with my family,' he declared.

Will felt his heart tell him to stand up and loudly declare 'I will come with you'. Instead his mouth froze, as though he had suffered a stroke. He didn't want to go back to Aiden's house. He didn't want to think any more. He wanted to be eleven again and cycling with his friends, death something that was seen on television.

He suddenly realised things had changed. He wanted to feel alive. He needed to get drunk. He would like to know if the barmaid had a friend. He joked to them both, 'I should stay and make sure Darren doesn't resume his fighting ways.' He almost winced as his weasel words hung in the smoky air, see-through and without value.

He watched Aiden leave; his shoulders drooped. He didn't go after him though and as he sipped his beer, he could almost feel a small piece of what was good in him

Ross Greenwood

dying, gone forever. He thought he would never feel so wretched again, but he would be wrong.

13

12ᵗʰ August 1992

The letter from Darren was propped against the teapot on the dining room table. He ran his hand along the shiny wood towards it and carried it into the lounge. He hated that table. It had in effect been his homework prison for the last seven years. He smiled to himself, well not anymore he thought. In two days they would pick up their A-Levels results and that would be it. No more study and no more being shackled to the same spot night after night.

Despite his habit of revising with a few beers and usually a James Herbert novel, wedged and therefore concealed, in his massive Biology textbook, he suspected he would pass at least two of his exams and that would be enough to go to South Bank Polytechnic to study Economics and Politics. He shrugged at that. He knew he wouldn't be going though. His parents did too. They had given up chastising him about his ambivalence to it all and one night a few weeks back his dad had taken him to his local and quietly and slowly had a word.

'I would say that it's probably best if you didn't go on to university. It's expensive and even though we are happy to support you, we would need you to tell us that you really want to go. That you will study hard when you get there. Make it worthwhile. We don't think you can.'

Will had looked him in the eye and found he couldn't really disagree. He didn't even reply, just sat opposite him with a resigned look on his face. He didn't even know where South Bank was apart from somewhere in London. He knew nothing about the course and absolutely nothing about any facet of college life there. He had only applied there because everyone else had been applying to places and it was one of the few colleges that would take his predicted grades.

Will and his dad spent a decent night together in the end, and he had even bought some of the 'A job will be the making of you' bullshit his dad was selling. It had been funny to start with; watching his old man get sloshed and tired. However it soon became depressing as even though he tried to hide it, as his dad got drunk and reading between the lines, he knew he had disappointed them. He could feel his relationship changing with his parents and knew he would be moving out soon whatever he did. One day he would go home a success he thought, but God knows at what.

As he slid Darren's letter open he paused and thought about the last year at school. He had known he was getting left behind but felt powerless to stop it. The other kids in his year, and by this he meant everyone, were constantly chatting about grades and courses, where they were going to study and what they were going to be. They were full of talk of great seats of learning such as St Andrews, Durham, Loughborough and of course Oxford and Cambridge. They came in to the form room bursting with enthusiasm after going to visit their prospective colleges, having met the tutors and seen the halls of residence.

Will had encountered none of this, hadn't even known it was possible. He didn't even know who to ask about it, or whether he even wanted to. The other three places he had applied for had rejected him and whilst it had been a bit depressing getting the rejections, on balance he had been more relieved than upset. South Bank had been the fly in the ointment but he hadn't even rung them to enquire as to things and knew now he never would.

The worst students to listen to were the ones who stated 'I'm going to be a doctor', or 'I'm going to go into law'. How the hell did they know this and why couldn't he think of anything to do. Any sense of direction would be fine, so he suspected he would cling to his dad's 'A job will be the making of him' charade and see what panned out.

Carl needed four A grades to get into Cambridge University, which was a foregone conclusion and the only option his parents had given him had been Mathematics, or Mathematics with Physics. His father had been the polar opposite of Will's parents. He had taken Carl to meet his old tutor at his house for afternoon tea, helped him fill his application form in and generally encouraged him all the way. Carl though didn't seem to be relishing the prospect, a little look of distress arriving upon his face whenever it was mentioned.

Poor old Carl he thought. A single child with the weight of expectation on his gifted narrow shoulders as much a heavy burden as an excessive load on an elderly donkey. His parents' ambition had deprived him of many joys. He had missed out on clubs, nights out, holidays and generally just being a child due to his parent-imposed crippling homework regime. Girls were a total enigma to him. Even though his parents had loosened the reins fractionally since the last exam, this afternoon's trip to the cinema being a good example, his potential was still continuously dangled in front of him like an enormous slippery carrot. Occasionally to touch, but never to hold.

Thinking of a donkey reminded him of one of Darren's previous letters entitled 'The Mule'. The total contents were one small paragraph which stemmed from one of the exasperated teachers calling Aiden a thick mule as he tried to navigate a fairly simple algebra query in front of the class and they had often kidded him with the nickname.

'Donkeys form very strong bonds with other donkeys and animals and even short term separation from a companion can be stressful. Donkeys show limited fear response to novel situations and this can be mistaken for stubbornness rather than fear. Teaching a donkey requires a different mind-set; they cannot be rushed into doing something they don't want to do!'

Will had laughed his head off. He hadn't mentioned the letter to Aiden, even though he doubted he would have minded, but it was good to see Darren's sense of humour was intact.

It had just been Will, Aiden and Carl at the cinema today. The three muskehounds as Carl liked to call them. They hadn't seen Darren for eighteen months now, the regular letters to Will the only contact they received. After the ubiquitous questioning of Carl's age at the new Showcase cinema they had sat at the back for 'Basic Instinct'. Aiden always sat at the side, one thick leg down the aisle, the other taking more than his fair share of the foot space. Carl sat next to him automatically as his slight frame and Aiden's gargantuan one almost made two normal sized people. Will still had Carl pushed over onto him and he had chuckled as he felt Carl tense at the beaver shot part of the film.

Aiden however had become very popular with the ladies. In one perverse way Freja's death had been the making of him. Aiden did not talk about Freja and any attempts by Will or Carl to do so were more liable to push him into a distant uncommunicative state. Aiden spent a lot of time now with that sleepy look on his face that Will remembered so well from their first day, but the sloppy grin was generally missing and most of the time Will had no idea what he was thinking.

Aiden's big adjustment had been when he had a rugby ball in his hand. The first game of the season had been as shocking as the news on that awful day. Will had caught the ball from the kick off and jogged toward the opposition, allowing Aiden to get up to speed on his shoulder. He had then, as usual, slipped the ball back to Aiden to hit them and break the line. His lumbering gentle giant friend though had vanished.

What hit those first players was angry. A powerful, pumping, driving, aggressive force of nature, like a tsunamic wall of water, clogged with huge logs and boulders, washing everything before it. Try after try was scored, the only celebration a long glance at the heavens and then a straight armed point at Will wherever he was on the field. The pent up emotion and unanswered feelings had found an outlet and it was nigh on unstoppable.

As the season had progressed Aiden had thrown himself into training and the large plump boy had turned into a granite battering ram. They had won the league and cup two years running at a canter despite the rest of the team being decidedly mediocre. Will had reached six foot in height and filled out, but had reached a plateau in skill and he knew his rugby career would end as the sixth form did. He missed the camaraderie with Darren, often passing the ball to the empty space where he would have been. Aiden never rebuked him but he was all business when he was on the pitch.

Other teams had turned up full of confidence, snapping the ball around in complex manoeuvres, beautiful tries and pleasing technique. However they were powerless to prevent Aiden's tide of wrath. By the second half they were broken, minds and bones and the scouts came calling. Aiden however didn't want to listen. He told them he wanted to focus on his exam results which oddly he did. Freja had been academically gifted and Aiden had tried to fill a gap for his parents for which he was never intended. He had been offered and accepted a course at Loughborough University. A place with a strong rugby tradition and also where his sister had been heading before fate intervened. Ostensibly he needed three Cs, but Will suspected they would take him if he turned up with his cycling proficiency test certificate in one hand and a rugby ball in the other. Will didn't even know what he was going to study and suspected that Aiden might not have known either.

As his mum used to say, time and tide wait for no man, and change was coming.

Apart from the donkey communication, Darren's letters always started the same and this one was no different. He slumped on the sofa and as always read it aloud, imagining Darren's face and voice as he did so.

'Dear Will.

You are a dick.

Obviously due to the top secret nature of manoeuvres I am unable to reveal everything, however I have drunk vast oceans of beer, and pleasured many women.

Finally we are being sent into full combat roles. I might as well have stayed at home if I had known I would have to wait until I was eighteen before I would actually be allowed to shoot at people! I think about you guys a lot.

I have been all over the shop, Germany and Ireland to name a few, but it will be cranked up a notch at a date in the near future.

Thanks for the letters, they follow us around, but eventually catch up with me.

Sorry I haven't been back yet, but I haven't been able to face it.

Tell Aiden I love his news, but I could still kick his ass, and tell Carl to buy some johnnies. I will be home soon. D.

Will smiled, stood up and stuffed the letter into the back pocket of his jeans. The house was quiet and he felt restless as he wandered around the rooms. His girlfriend Sara had asked him to come around but his probing hands had been halted by her at second base and listening to her gabble on about her desire to be a vet wasn't worth the lack of progress. Thank the Lord she was off to study at Liverpool soon and he could extricate himself from what was rapidly becoming an unsatisfying association. A shiver had gone through his spine last week when she had mentioned marriage admittedly in an incredibly roundabout way, but he had stared at her in shock, a bell in his head tolling the end of their brief union.

He checked his watch and saw it was five p.m. He decided to go and see Darren's dad anyway. When he had received Darren's first letter he had wondered whether Darren had written to his father and decided to go and see him. Of all the moments of that terrible day it was for some reason the last comments from Mr Connor about coming back that were imprinted clearly in his mind.

He had tried to put reason to going there, saying he was easing a tired man's loneliness, but deep down he knew he was betraying his friend. Every time on the way there he had convinced himself this was the last time, but his dad had been so grateful, it never was. He would listen with a focused but ecstatic look on his face and usually ask him to read it again. He never mentioned why Darren wasn't writing to him and Will didn't bring it up.

He had ended up staying longer and longer on each visit. The stories he told were amazing. Tough times in Ireland, missions abroad and even the tale of the Falklands War and the grenade that had robbed him of his raison d'etre were told vividly and humbly. He did say his wife had left him, but had not offered an explanation. The man had given everything for England, but now sadly, he just drank for England.

He would crack open a beer at midday, no earlier but rarely later and by late afternoon he would be steaming. It was then Will had learnt to leave. He would become aggressive, confused and belligerent. He would tail off mid-sentence and slip into a thousand-yard stare. Will had wondered where he got his booze from, but once his leaving had coincided with a taxi arriving and he saw the man walk to the front door with a clinking carrier bag.

★ ★ ★

Will left his bike in the back garden and let himself in the kitchen door at the rear of the house. He regretted it almost instantly. Mr Connor was slumped in the wheelchair next to the phone in the hall and stared at Will with bleary eyes.

'I got a letter,' Will said.

'Read it,' was the slurred response. So he did. When he had finished he looked into the man's eyes and saw fury. 'Come here,' he drawled and beckoned Will over.

When he was within arm's length the man burst into a foul-mouthed tirade.

'That ungrateful little shit. I gave him everything. All my experience, all my time and the littler fucker doesn't give a shit. I knew he was a bad egg, I tried to knock it out of him, but he's rotten. You fucking kids are all the same.'

Will was too stunned to move and looked at him slack-jawed. He then stared in amazement as Darren's dad took what looked like a rounder's bat from his lap and proceeded to swing it at Will's head. Maybe it was the fact he was slaughtered that gave Will the time to react, or maybe the years had slowed his arm, but Will managed to grab the bottom of the weapon and stop the blow in mid-air, inches from his face.

They stood locked together, both straining for heavy seconds, before Will yanked it away from him. The sudden movement caused the wheelchair to topple over and Darren's dad fell to the side and his head hit the tiled floor with a heavy smack. Will backed away from the groaning figure, an incredulous look on his face. Shaking his head he let himself out and quietly walked his bike down the empty street, vowing never to return.

14

13ᵗʰ August 1992

Will arrived outside the Anne Boleyn at seven p.m. It was a warm night and he just had a smart shirt and jeans on. He could see Aiden walking towards him in the distance, dwarfing those around him, so lighting a cigarette and leaning against the wall he waited for him. Funny he thought how they spent so much time here now. They were old enough to get into any pub, yet they chose to spend a lot of time here. Tonight they had planned to down a few and then go into town. They often said that, but rarely did they leave. Will still felt spooked about what had happened the day before and was looking forward to a few beers and forgetting about things for a while.

The pub had actually become quite popular with the sixth form at the school. Will used to ponder how it wasn't raided, but there was never any trouble. Maybe they knew and thought at least it keeps the kids out of town. The landlord now was in the final stages of his self-destruction and was virtually unseen. Falling objects, possibly himself being one, on the ceiling above were usually the only signs of his existence. Death by alcohol was the slowest suicide on the planet, but a popular one.

Angela ran the show now and actually ran a tight bar. A cousin had arrived from somewhere in Ireland to help. Between them they coped with the trade and if there was any over exuberance Aiden was happy to go and ask them why they were trying to ruin his night which usually cued much back-peddling. It just wasn't that sort of place.

They walked in together and found Carl at the bar. He had been there for a while judging by his pint. They had for some reason got into the habit of going out the night before big events, dragging two nights out of any birthday, Christmas and even once a driving test. Aiden's nervy failure the next day had curtailed that particular celebration. Carl was giving what he thought was full patter to the Irish girl, Mary Rose.

He was only good for about two pints, then he would start to wilt like a flower in the midday sun. He had a real thing for Mary Rose, much to the others amusement. She was an unusual looking girl with mad, curly black hair, as pasty as Carl and had small mouse-like features. Carl called her 'The adorable squirrel' and by pint three he would lose his composure and be begging her for a date until she laughingly told him to feck off.

They took their drinks to the pool table and Aiden and Will started a game. Carl used to watch like they were performing incredible magic tricks, his pool skills on a par with his ball catching efforts. As Will potted the black with his back to the door, he saw Aiden and Carl look wide eyed over his shoulder. Turning around, he saw two men at the door. One was a wiry and fit-looking black lad of about eighteen with a serious look on his face. The other was Darren.

They stared at each other for a few seconds before Darren's face broke into a cheesy grin and he walked over to Will and gave him a bear hug. Will could feel the hard muscle of Darren's back as he squeezed him in return. 'Welcome home,' he said.

As Darren hugged the others, Will shook the stranger's hand. He introduced himself as Dean. He seemed keen to go to the bar, so Will accepted his offer of a pint and went and joined the others at a table. Darren was explaining his absence, and his return.

'After what happened I felt so angry I didn't know what to do with my time except to stew on things. I just threw myself into getting fit as fuck and being exhausted was the only way I could sleep. Every time I saw you guys, I re-lived that moment when I found out. I stopped coming to the pub as the hangover the day after was so bad I thought life was meaningless and had dangerous thoughts.

When I got to the division training camp it was insane. The training was full on and no-one knew anything so I gradually got through it. I didn't come home at all and I went to Dean's house on leave. We joined up on the same day. He is the only one who knows. I planned to come back soon anyway but I got a call from the police this morning.' He paused and took a sip of his beer, seemingly enjoying their looks and raised eyebrows. He then stood up and grinned, 'Just nipping to the bog.'

Will felt the temperature go up in the room, feeling as though he was being pulled toward a giant sun. His back suddenly itched and he felt sweat beads begin to form on his forehead. His mouth dried and his extremities tingled.

'Nice to have Darren back.' Aiden said.

'You docile donkey. What about the police thing?' Carl looked at him and shook his head.

All three friends turned their heads to Dean, who raised his hands in mock surrender.

'It's not for me to tell you. It's shocking news though,' he said with a straight face.

As Darren returned, Will feigned a cough so he didn't have to look at him. He was sure his friend would clock his worried face. His left leg seemed to be twitching of its own accord as Darren sat next to him. He straightened it out under the table and even though he was dying to slam the table with his hand and scream 'Spit it out' at Darren he dare not say a word. He took a huge gulp of his drink but then found he couldn't swallow it.

Carl put him out of his misery by saying, 'Spill the beans then Darren.'

Darren looked around the table and then whispered, 'My dad is dead.'

Will choked and then sprayed the drink in his mouth in a great spume that covered Dean in frothy lager from head to waist. There was a terrible silence as Will looked at Dean's shocked face. He stood up and quietly uttered, 'Shit, man.'

The charged atmosphere was extinguished by Darren, Aiden, Carl and then finally Dean bursting into laughter. Will thought his heart may give in. He quickly fired off, 'Sorry. That is shocking news,' but still couldn't bring himself to join in with the chuckling. He was itching to ask how, but didn't want to appear desperately interested to see if his life was going to be blown apart.

'He had a care worker who came every morning to get him up and stuff,' Darren continued in a conspirator's tone. 'She found him in the kitchen this morning in his wheelchair still. His chair had toppled over and he had hit his head. The floor was a complete pool of blood apparently. He had probably been there for hours and eventually bled out. Nice way to go according to the Doctor who said he would have felt dizziness and a weird light-headedness before passing out. That's assuming of course that he didn't spend the last few desperate hours of his life hoarsely shouting for help that would never arrive, as that would be a really nasty way to go.'

'I'm sorry mate. How are you feeling?' Aiden reached over and touched Darren's hand.

'OK,' Darren simply said. 'He should have died years ago.' He stood up and left them all with shocked expressions on their faces and went to the bar. 'Five lagers please,' he said to Angela who had come down to the bar to do a stock take and was looking at him like she had just seen Kermit the Frog walk in. 'Alright darling,' Darren schmoozed to her.

Will said to Dean, who was drying his face with a bar towel that a laughing Mary Rose had thrown at him, 'Come on, I'll show you where the toilets are.' As he walked out of the bar he looked at the quiet interplay between Darren and Angela. Something was awry. She had been keen as mustard that GCSE results night. Will had left them snogging in the bar at the end of the night, the only ones left. They hadn't been back to the pub for a while after that as Darren had been AWOL, Aiden at home and Carl abroad with his family. When they did come back she never asked after him and he didn't want to bring the sensitive subject up with Aiden as his sister had still been warm and her boyfriend was copping off with a barmaid. Wheeler did say people would react in a strange way. Angela seemed wary now though, like someone letting a dog back in the house after it had bitten someone.

The toilets had improved moderately under the girls' efforts. They had been cleaned and there was actually soap but the acrid smell of urine still made your teeth itch the moment you opened the door. He held Dean's shirt under the hairdryer to dry it, shocked that it was actually working, as Dean washed his face and arms, grimacing at the cold water.

'Your mates didn't seem very shocked by his dad dying.'

'They had never met him,' Will replied without thinking.

Dean stopped what he was doing and looked at Will with a confused look on his face.

'Really?'

Will nodded, praying that he wouldn't ask if he had met the deceased. He tried to move things long.

'He keeps his cards close to his chest and his dad wasn't very well.'

'Aye, that's true enough. His dad though was a total legend in the Paras. A real hero. He got the Distinguished Conduct Medal after the Falklands. A very tough man apparently. The acorn hasn't fallen far from the tree either as Darren is a double hard bastard. We had an instructor for unarmed combat who used to be a martial arts expert. After six months Darren could easily beat him so they had to bring in some bloke from America to push him.'

As he put his shirt on, he paused and seemingly weighed the question up before finally asking it, 'This girl who died. Were they close?'

'Like atoms,' Will said.

Dean took a deep breath and then surprised Will.

'We need to look after him, he is close to the edge. He needs a war to focus on. Let's hope today's news doesn't push him over the edge. He has issues.'

Will waited for him to continue but he was just searching Will's face as if looking for confirmation.

'Do you know how his father got injured?' Will responded.

'Yes, the whole battalion knows. He was a brave man, brilliant under fire and was well respected. His team would have followed him anywhere. He stormed a machine gun nest at Goose Green in the Falklands War and saved some men who were outnumbered and pinned down. He killed all the ones who didn't abandon the post except one young soldier, a boy really. He only looked sixteen and was lying on the floor crying in the aftermath. He had a young son of his own at the time, Darren was nine I think and maybe that is why he took his eye off the ball for a second. As he picked him up off the floor the boy released a grenade which he had been holding. Blew the boy to pieces and took some important bits of Darren's dad too.'

Will took a deep breath and thought so Mr Connor had been telling the truth when he had been talking to Will, however he had not mentioned the age of the soldier.

As they walked back into the bar Darren came bounding over.

'You took your time boys, you bum each other or something? You should have taken Carl with you, I said I would get him laid.'

As the night went on the drink flowed and the usual madness ensued. At one point Kostas from school turned up. Will suspected it was a close call as to whether he instantly soiled himself, so surprised and nervous was he at unexpectedly finding Darren in there. Darren however was all full of bonhomie and forgiveness, so Kostas stayed until near the end when he was ejected by Mary-Rose for being sick on the juke box. Carl passed out and Aiden picked him up like he was a sleeping child and carried him home. Soon it was just Dean, Will and Darren at the bar.

'When is the funeral?' Will slurred.

Darren, who had been drinking like he had been bitten by a snake and beer was the antidote, still seemed relatively normal.

'God knows. I won't be going anyway. We are due to be leaving tomorrow. Fuck him anyway,' he replied aggressively.

Will was shocked by the statement, but he had seen the drunken violent nature of his father first hand. Still it seemed a bit harsh he thought, after all he had done for his country. Suddenly Angela appeared and dragged Darren to the dance floor, somehow getting the soiled jukebox to play Boys to Men's 'End of the Road'.

As they watched the smooch descend into a full on snog Will said to Dean, 'Surely he will go to the funeral won't he? I'd have thought he would be organising it.'

'God knows mate. Still after all those years of abuse, kicking the shit out of his mother until she had enough and left and then turning his attention to Darren you can't blame him. Apparently he had a bat which he used to hit him with. He told me all this the one time I saw him really drunk, but I guess you already know this.'

Will tried to get his fuzzed up mind to work and process everything but his brain couldn't hold the information. It was like trying to catch thick gravy in a colander.

'Sometimes he would wake him up by hitting him with it through the covers,' he continued. 'Darren never fought back until the night he left for basic training. He still feels guilty about it now.'

Will stood there stunned. All those years of Darren coming to school with bruises and marks and them all thinking he had been scrapping again. All he could utter was the same phrase as Dean earlier, 'Shit, man.'

Dean suddenly noticed his visage and panicking, roughly grabbed Will's arm.

'I thought you knew. Do not tell Darren any of this, I dread to think what he would do.' Will nodded, unable to talk as his brain grappled with this new troubling revelation. Mary-Rose appeared as the song finished and 'Save The Best For Last' by Vanessa Williams came on.

'Which one of you strapping young fellas wants to dance?' She looked at Will as she said it.

Will looked at her and thought of Carl's keen little face and forced a smile onto his face. He quickly replied, 'It would be rude not to give a dance to our guest.'

As they walked hand in hand to the dance floor Will slipped out of the front door into the cold. Sobering up fast he staggered off home, the foundations of his youth crumbling.

15

14th August 1992

W ill was woken up on the sofa by the birds tweeting outside the window to find his father disdainfully looking down on him. He lurched into the kitchen like a mariner who had just arrived on land after a year at sea drinking his own urine and downed a pint of water. It felt as though someone had filled his mouth full of sand whilst he slept. As he stood with his hands rested on the sink, he let the previous day's memories wash over him.

Basically he had killed someone. Left them to bleed to death alone on a cold kitchen floor. That fact was going to take some getting used to.

He felt jittery and even though he had seemingly got away with it, part of him was expecting the police to come and barge down his door. He thought he should feel worse though than he did. He certainly didn't feel the need to hand himself in. Maybe the truth coming out about him being a raging alcoholic, wife beater and child abuser had eased his conscience and he had been defending himself after all. The almost imminent revelation of his exam results that morning seemed utterly irrelevant.

After showering he looked in the mirror and the same Will looked back. Well a little bleary eyed he thought. He brushed his teeth with vigour and nicked some of his dad's mouthwash and aftershave thinking about the mauling he would get off Aiden's mum shortly. It was still an hour before he met at Aiden's house so he decided to walk. The long way, so he didn't have to go anywhere near Darren's place.

He concentrated on walking fast and the fresh morning air helped revive him. It was going to be hot again but it was lovely now. Stupid idea, he thought, getting drunk the night before, but he knew he would do it again. Eighteen years old and my life already revolves around booze.

When he arrived at Aiden's he put a mint in his mouth and knocked on the back door. Aiden opened it immediately and Will stepped into the kitchen. He looked remarkably grim, his face like chalk. Not like Aiden to suffer so bad with a hangover he thought. Eight sausages and he was usually right as rain. Aiden shouted to his mum, 'Will's here.'

His mum was at the sink staring off into space. She had tied her hair back into a bun, but it was spilling out and her clothes were grey and seemed ill fitting. Will walked over and said 'Hi' in her ear. She turned to him slowly, eyes all blurred and wiped a tear away with the back of her hand. She crushed him with a bone cracking hug and Will hugged her back. His family were completely non-demonstrative and he had always loved that about Aiden's family, but the hugs felt different now.

She hugged him as if she was trying to pull some strength from his body. Great heaving sobs wracking her frame. He looked over her shoulder. Someone had put a plaque on the wall with the poem that had been recited at Freja's funeral and Will was back there in the church almost immediately as he started to read it.

'Do not stand at my grave and weep,
I am not there, I do not sleep.

I am the thousand winds that blow,
I am the diamond glints in snow,
I am the sunlight on ripened grain,
I am the gentle autumn rain.
As you awake with morning's hush,
I am the swift-up-flinging rush
Of quiet birds in circling flight.
Do not stand at my grave and cry,
I am not there - I did not die.'

Darren had gone up the front to say the words, shambling in a baggy suit. He had frozen as he looked out from the lectern at the massed ranks of friends and family, tried to get the words out, but no sound came. It was Aiden who went up and hugged him. Gently taking the poem out of his hands he had spoken the words in a loud crystal voice that had echoed through the anguished howls of his mother. As Will had looked over at her, his own tears had distorted her so she looked like the person on the painting 'The Scream'. His father stood there like a melting statue, eyes closed, tears pouring down his cheeks. Even if Freja hadn't died that day Will thought, many other things had.

Will wondered then if Aiden knew the reason why he rarely went around his house any more was because of his mother. The atmosphere had become oppressive. The radio silent. His mum just sitting unmoving in Moffa's chair. Sometimes she didn't even register them arriving or leaving. If she did she always gave him a huge hug, but it felt like she was retreating somewhere. That and the myriad of pictures of Freja everywhere, more seemingly springing up every time he visited, dulled his mood and he knew he would rather forget than be constantly reminded.

Eventually Aiden had to prise his mum's frail body off him. As he helped her onto a stool he said, 'There now mum, we will have to go. I won't be long.'

As they walked toward the school Aiden explained.

'We both got a letter this morning, from my dad. He's not coming back. He has taken a job on the wells in Nigeria. He said he couldn't continue like this. Every time he saw us he felt his will to live disappear like melting snow. His words. For fuck's sake. Doesn't he know he had two children?'

Will didn't know what to say, it was more torrid information for him to take in. With a brain that felt like a sodden sponge, the news just flowed off him. He squeezed his friend's shoulder but just kept walking.

When they arrived at school they were marginally late and had to walk against the tide of excited students. Will felt like an invisible apparition as people flowed past him and wouldn't have been surprised if, like in the film 'Ghost', they had walked through him too. This time they had to go into the teachers' room to get their results. A secret place usually only seen from the doorway. Normally it would have been a daunting experience, especially today as the walls were lined with bespectacled earnest tutors enjoying human emotion at its rawest.

Will looked at his Biology teacher in the far corner. He was a slippery, greasy, perpetual student type who could never have functioned outside the safety of a strict school. For a nanosecond their eyes met and then the teacher broke the lock and gazed at his teacup. That didn't bode well for my Biology result he thought.

He got his envelope and followed Aiden to where Carl was waiting outside. He was standing as agreed under a giant conker tree at the front of the school. His slim childlike figure looking like the softest breeze would carry him away, at odds with the huge muscled trunk beside him. Behind him on the other side of the road standing next to his car was Carl's father. He stared at them with a determined look on his face.

'I got the grades,' Carl stated with an unhappy look on his face as they stood in a circle. 'Four As.' He looked back at his father who began to beckon him over like Ahab calling him to his doom. 'I have to go. I'm in the doghouse big time. I sneaked into bed without being rumbled, but the room kept spinning like mad every time I closed my eyes. I realised I was going to be sick, so I tried to get out of bed, but my foot was all tangled in the sheets. I hurled up a dinosaur's dump sized mound of vom and then fell asleep in it. I woke up having spent the night rolling in it, with both my parents staring down at me. Very disappointed they are. I'm guessing I won't be going out for a while. I have to go, I hope your results are what you need.'

With that he turned and ran to the car. He stopped and gave them a 'V' sign before his dad pushed his head down and him into the back like a policeman arresting a felon. Will opened his results, 'Economics B, History D and Biology E,' he declared. His dissimilar subjects were testament to him being clueless as to any future direction.

Aiden knew about Will's decision to get a job and work. They had looked through the local paper together laughing. Aiden's standard response to each job description was laughing and shouting 'No way, that sounds shit'. It hadn't been encouraging but the thought of earning some money and getting a place of his own was. The decision was made.

Aiden opened his and nodded, his face displaying no emotion.

'Good enough?' Will asked.

'Aye, good enough.'

They walked in silence to the pub, unspoken acceptance that a beer was needed. The Anne Boleyn was still shut when they got there but after some meaty banging from Aiden, Mary Rose cautiously opened the door.

'Is it just you?' she said.

They both nodded and she let them in. They caught Angela in her dressing gown sitting at one of the tables. She saw them as they walked in and quickly walked out the back, but not before Will saw the livid red marks on her neck. Mary Rose poured two pints with a dour face. As she plonked them on the bar, she spat out what was on her mind.

'Darren is barred. I don't want to see him here again.' She stared hard at them both, daring them to challenge her. Will daren't ask why, because deep down he knew.

They drank their pints in silence. Will smoked a cigarette and watched mesmerised as the smoke danced across the room, caught in the sunlight beaming through the windows. As he tried to focus on anything but the events at hand, he realised one thing. He had to leave this city. There would be nothing left here for him but bad memories. Aiden finished his drink and plonked his glass down on the table.'

'I have to go, be with my family,' he said.

'I'll come with you,' Will quickly replied. There was no-one to say goodbye to so they walked out of the front door and as they left Will looked up at the sign creaking in the light breeze. He knew he wouldn't be back at this pub for a long time. It would be fifteen years.

16

24th December 1995

Will felt like his lungs were rattling in his frozen chest as he slumped further into his seat struggling to keep warm. He thought he had prepared well for the journey with his old army cadet boots over thick socks, two jumpers - one thick, one thin, gloves, scarf, heavy leather jacket and thick, insulated thermal hat but he was still cold. Possibly his own fault he ruefully admitted.

He had been committed to a quiet weekend so as to feel good for the Christmas break, but a tough Friday at work and his resolve had vanished like newspaper on a fire. He had met a girl that night and they had woken up together and then spent the next two days drinking, in bed, or both. An almost out of body experience as he had been permanently drunk and was now struggling to remember what she looked like, or whether he even liked her. Even a trip to the cinema was now just a wobbly dream. Then he had woken up on Monday morning, alone, feeling poisoned and furtive with 'the fear' from too many days of excess. With all this baggage the journey back to Peterborough was swiftly turning into the 'Retreat from Stalingrad', brought to you by British Rail.

He had eaten his sandwiches waiting for the first cancelled train out of Hertford and was now starving. He had planned to take the fast train for the last leg even though it cost an extra ten pounds. However, when he had arrived at King's Cross the long snaking queue at the ticket office had reminded him of the footage of people queueing to get on the last chopper out of Saigon. Desperate faces trying to be civilised, but close to the edge.

He had heard the announcement of this slower train arriving and just got on without a ticket knowing they didn't always have a guard. It had already taken three hours and he should have been home long ago so he had thrown caution to the wind. He had then had to spend the journey uncomfortably straining his neck looking for the ticket conductor as they stopped at what felt like every lamp post on the way up the line. Each stop rewarded him with an icy blast of cold air when the doors opened. When they finally left Huntingdon station Will relaxed a little. The train was so full now that if the conductor existed he would need to be as slippery as a lavishly greased pig to get through the mass of humanity that would be wedged around him.

As they passed by the brickyard chimneys and entered into the outskirts of Peterborough, through the industrial district and past Asda, he felt an unexpected fondness fire up inside his cold body. He was looking forward to seeing his friends. He had not been back to the city for two years and rarely before that. Nearly everyone he knew had started new lives elsewhere and the strong bonds of his friendship with Carl, Darren and Aiden had withered. Missed phone calls and sporadic letters were not enough to maintain a good connection. Typical blokes he thought, useless at keeping in touch. Although it didn't help that if you went to a good school, chances were the majority would go away to university and the majority of those would not return.

Will smiled though. He could see Aiden and Carl waiting for him as he cleared the condensation from the cold window. Aiden incredibly with only a shirt on and Carl for once almost the same girth, padded out with an awful grey duffel coat. He knew instantly they would pick up where they left off.

Aiden shook his hand hard when they met and took the bag off Will's back as though it was full of helium. As Carl shook his hand they stood in a tight circle, smiling at each other before Aiden broke the spell. 'Come on,' he said, 'I've got the Range Rover.' As Will climbed into the front passenger seat of the roasting hot vehicle he almost cried out with relief, feeling like a suicidal chicken sliding into a welcoming oven.

'Is your dad back then?' Will asked without thinking, gesturing to the dashboard with an open palm.

'No, he's dead.' Aiden sighed.

'I'm so sorry mate, what happened, if you don't mind me asking?' Will gulped in shock.

'Well they don't know for sure, but he slipped off a rig by the looks of it and drowned. Strange though, twenty years on the job and not so much as a broken fingernail before that.' As they stopped at some lights, Aiden reached over and shook his leg. 'Don't feel bad. It was six months ago and I hadn't seen him for years. The insurance paid out too.'

Will did feel bad. He realised how distant they had become and vowed to make better efforts in the future.

'How did you know I would be on that train?' he said to Carl in the back, wanting to change the subject.

'That was the third one we waited for. We spent the time catching up in McDonald's and then having a beer. It's good to see you Will.'

Will beamed back at him. Typical, that they would wait for him like that. Sadly he suspected he wouldn't have done so if the roles had been reversed. That was the reason they had not been in touch, he considered. It was him that had moved to Letchworth, Stevenage, Hemel Hempstead and now finally Hertford. He could have written to their universities at any point. Although he guessed they could have sent a letter to his parents' house.

This was one of his worst character traits. He could see every side to every story, meaning he could never seem to make a meaningful decision or a positive judgement. He should have been a lawyer. He would have been able to argue both sides so successfully that no-one would know what was going on and the case would be thrown out.

They pulled up outside Aiden's house. Will had agreed to stay at Aiden's tonight, telling his parents that he was getting a lift from down south on Christmas Day morning so he wouldn't have to see them until the big day. They hadn't been very pleased about that, but it was an improvement on last year where he had spent two weeks in Australia and had forgotten to ring them until he was drunk. Ten in the morning for them, ten in the evening for him. He wasn't sure if his mum was crying with relief or sadness at her flaky son.

Bastard Nathan had also got engaged this year, no doubt just to try and make him look bad. He would be in the background tomorrow afternoon when his mum had slugged back too many snowballs. Him with a simpering, victorious grin and her peering at Will, all motherly concern, asking Will if he would like to get married one day.

★ ★ ★

As always, they made their way around the back of Aiden's place. The front of the house looked tired though; woodwork peeling, the small lawn overgrown and he hoped Aiden's mother was fine. The back was considerably different and he breathed a sigh of relief. He had expected a mass of weeds and dead nettles but it was pristine. Hedges and bushes trimmed, flower beds weeded and even Dracula had been given a wash.

His mum had clearly been waiting for them and swept him and Carl up in her too thin arms. She ushered them in to the welcoming kitchen, pouring them a glass of wine from the bottle on the table. Next to it was a colossal steaming turkey that Aiden patted lovingly as he walked past. A turkey for two Will realised sadly, but probably just enough, as Aiden's bulk negotiated the door to the dining room.

As they sipped their wine, Will nodded in the direction of the kitchen.

'How is she?' he simply inquired.

A flash of worry crossed Aiden's face.

'Not great I'm afraid, but better since I came back. My dad's death knocked her for six though. I think she thought at some point he would come home.' He shrugged adding, 'I suspect that may have not been her first glass of wine today either.'

'I'm so angry with him, even though he is dead. Family was all my mum lived for and as heart-breaking and meaningless as Freja's death was, he shouldn't have left her.' He tailed off with, 'I'm going to lose them all now, I can see it.'

Will didn't know what to say, repeating Mr Wheeler's mantra about it affecting people in different ways was not going to help. Will left his friend sitting in the big armchair looking out of the window and took his bag upstairs. He thought 'I will make this a good night for him tonight whatever'. He went into the smallest bedroom and put his stuff on Freja's bed.

He had slept in there once before and imagined that it would be unnerving as he had suspected it would bring back bad memories. He had also assumed it would upset Aiden's mum but apparently it had been her idea. She had said 'If we hide from her life then we will forget her'. He remembered her saying it at the funeral, that and 'We were so lucky to have her for as long as we did', but it always felt like she was trying to convince herself not others.

The pictures on the walls though were all of happy times, many of them of her and Aiden giggling and chuckling as they grew up. It was more a celebration of her life than a mausoleum that ambushed you with pain as soon as you stepped inside and he had slept fine.

17

They arrived at the Dunton Arms in the town centre at six o'clock and the place was overflowing. Two girls with garishly applied lipstick and dressed in scanty elf costumes came staggering out arm-in-arm as they approached.

'Fuck you prick,' one of them bellowed at the doorman.

'Merry Christmas Ladies,' he laughed.

The other one staggered over to Carl and gave him a wet kiss on the cheek and said, 'Merry Christmas cutie pie.' The pair burst into laughter and rolled off down the street.

'Bad Elves,' Aiden sniggered.

'Good elves,' Carl corrected, with a look on his face that he could go home now and not have been disappointed with the evening. The trio were grinning as they pushed through the double doors into the pub.

The Dunton was a new breed of Wetherspoon's pub. A huge open place with a twenty five metre long bar. There were chairs and low tables at the sides, stools and high tables closer to the bar and then a big expanse of floor space in front of the bar. Not that you could see the floor tonight as the place was jammed. It used to be a library and many features remained, including the high ceilings, giving it a cool vibe. That combined with the reasonably priced beverages meant it was the place to be and the phrase 'Drunken in the Dunton' was a popular one.

Will loved early Christmas Eve drinking. Everyone was in great spirits, work was finished, all had just been paid and there was the promise of good times ahead. Family and old friends came to stay and old mates were back from university, jobs elsewhere and travelling. Factories and offices had kicked out early and last minute Christmas shopping challenges had been completed. Now they were all uniting in the usual British celebration technique. Will was not disappointed with the view in front of him. He would not have been surprised had a troop of monkeys been swinging from the lamps, chased by a crash of rhinos, so manic was the scene.

It seemed like someone had walked into the street and shouted 'Free beer', so frenzied was the crowd. The noise was deafening. No music, just talk, shouting, laughing and cheering. Stinging smoke hung heavy in the air, condensation pouring down the steamed up windows. Perfect, Will concluded.

They barged their way through the crowd, past scores of red faces from cold and drink. This was usually Aiden's finest hour and he stepped up to the task. He ploughed through the throng like an icebreaker crunching through the arctic. His best Clint Eastwood 'Dirty Harry' sneer on his face.

Many who were jostled turned around to argue, but melted away when confronted by such a huge presence. His usual technique when faced with a bunch of lads was to growl 'Security' and steam forward grimly looking over their heads. Carl and Will following tucked up behind in his slipstream, like pilot fish hugging to their shark. A space opened up at the bar as they arrived and Aiden docked into it.

They ordered two pints each so they wouldn't have to return to the melee at the bar for a while and finally managed to settle next to a fireplace in the corner.

'Darren would have loved this,' Will shouted above the cacophony.

'He would have had a fight, a snog and be helping behind the bar by now,' said Aiden fondly.

'I had a letter from him waiting at home for me.' Carl said as he presented it with a flourish.

'Read it,' Will encouraged, only slightly put out that he always used to get Darren's post. 'I've not heard from Darren for ages.'

'Dear boys,

You are dicks.

Merry Christmas to everyone. Sorry I can't be there to see you all, you know I would love to be. Me pulling all the best girls and you lot fighting for the scraps as usual. I heard you were meeting up again after I rang Aiden's and spoke to his mum. She sounded pissed and it wasn't even lunchtime, ha ha.

Thanks for the shed-loads of mail you have sent me over the years, however I have read both of them now, so please feel free to put pen to paper once more.

Work is pretty boring at the moment. Typical. I'm all ready to go and it's a world love-in! I joined the departmental boxing team to burn some free time and kicked some ass, but sadly I was ejected. Apparently there are some rules around elbow use.

I'm getting a mobile phone soon. You know how I like to be on it, like a car bonnet. Then you can ring me, you bunch of lazy bastards. D.'

They all stood in silence for a while, clearly thinking of Darren. Will wondered if the others felt guilty for the lack of contact like he did. He could feel a dark weight of

glumness move over them like a big black cloud
threatening rain on a spring day so he quickly changed the
subject.

'So Carl, tell me about these posh rich sorts at
Cambridge. Have you got them eating out of your grubby
Peterborough paws?'

'I was going to come here and say it's fantastic, I've got
a girl on the go and a great social life et cetera but now
I've seen you, I can't.' Carl looked nothing short of
despondent. 'I'm lonely guys. I feel like an outsider. They
are nearly all rich, foreign, or both. They all seem to know
each other or if they don't their upbringings are all the
same. They don't bully as such, just leave me out. It's like
I am not even there in the room and in some ways that's
worse. I had a year out at an accountant's in London,
Andersens, who are keen for me to return and that was
better, but basically I've got five months to go and I can't
wait for it all to be over.'

'Can you do the work?' Aiden queried.

Carl looked at him and gave a downbeat smile. 'Well I
won't bore you with the details, but I don't find it
difficult. Some of it takes a while, but its maths, so there is
always an answer.' Will caught Aiden's despondent face
after that exchange and filed it for later.

'No birds then?' he asked.

'There was a girl, for a while. A Chinese girl.' Carl
looked momentarily happy as he remembered. 'I used to
call her Mileena like in Mortal Kombat. She loved that,
used to like me to say it when she gave me a BJ which was
a little odd, but a man in my position makes hay while the
sun shines and I made a lot of hay that way. I think her
real name was, Ming-Hao. It meant something like
tomorrow's flower. Apt really as every time I got ready for

big business with the big boss, so-to-speak, she said tomorrow.'

'What happened?' Aiden laughed.

'She got sectioned and went back to China.'

Will and Aiden cracked up and Aiden slapped Carl's back causing him to spill his pint. They carried on talking about sport and politics but mostly reminisced about school. Carl though was still a bit down. He kept taking his glasses off, cleaning them with his shirt, taking a big sniff and putting them back on again. Will found himself counting how many times he was doing it.

'Seriously though guys, I really miss everything. I feel adrift when I'm there but it's like I can't do anything about it. I couldn't wait to come back and see you lot tonight. I've got some good news too, my grandad is ill, so my parents have gone to see him and won't be back until tomorrow evening so we can go back to mine. I sneaked some beer and wine in too and I've got a boot leg copy of that Seven movie.'

'Cool,' Will smiled. 'Well not about your grandad, but about the other stuff.'

Twenty-one years old and sneaking drink in was a little amusing. He had already seen Seven that weekend with the girl whose name was currently evading him, but didn't want to steal Carl's thunder. Besides, maybe two drunken viewings equalled a normal one.

He decided to tell them his life wasn't going great either.

'My social life is ok, but work sucks. Insurance Administration. I did not see that coming. I keep thinking something good is going to happen, but how can it, short of winning the lottery? I need to do something about it but what? There has to be more to life.' To get off his own depressing mundane existence he turned to Aiden, but sensing something he stopped.

Aiden finished his second pint and handed his glass to Carl. 'Here you go Carlos, how about you get the Big Boss to the big bar?'

Carl looked over to the bar which could reasonably be described as a mosh pit, took a deep breath, squared his shoulders and uttering, 'Once more unto the breach, dear friends, once more', reluctantly set off.

'What is it mate?' Will said, searching Aiden's face for answers.

'I'm not happy either. Uni sucked. I knew my place here, but I couldn't seem to get any purchase there. My course was a mystery as well. They gave me a mentor as they knew I might struggle and they wanted me to play rugby with my free time. He more or less did my work for me in the end. He said it was quicker than trying to drive it into my thick skull. You can imagine the confidence boost that gave me. Obviously I fucked the exams up. Three years down the pan. I might as well have stayed on the deli counter at Tesco. At least I liked the cheese.'

Will suddenly realised that Aiden must have finished his course six months ago and felt guilty about his lack of contact all over again. He had drifted away and as his ex, Sara, used to say 'Not tended the garden'. Although he had thought she had been referring to shaving her lady parts, it seemed to apply in this case too.

'Surely the rugby was going well?' he suggested.

Aiden puffed his cheeks and exhaled deeply. 'I lost it, whatever I had, I lost it. The anger seeped out of me and all of a sudden I was just another twenty stone meathead. I was still good, in the team and stuff but I was not great anymore and my heart wasn't in it. So I came home and spent time with my mum. This dad thing has really hit her. You've still got your family Will, don't think you have nothing.'

Will hung his head, but all he could think of was what a tool his brother was.

'Here you are lads,' a clearly happy Carl shouted as he returned much quicker than they expected. 'Look who I bumped into.' Will looked behind him at the wistful face of his ex, Sara. She came up to him and pecked him on the cheek.

'Hello Will, remember me?'

He had a flashback to a tearful goodbye at the railway station. Her tears not his. A promise of letters and visits thrown at the shutting door as the guard blew his whistle. He had forgotten all about it by the time he had got back in the car to go home. Someone up there he thought, was really trying to ruin his night.

'You remember Alice don't you?' Sara said pointing at a tall, thin, boring-looking girl with a severe bob. She did look familiar, possibly in his French class, although he was pretty sure he had called her Lisa whilst she was at school. He gave her a big welcoming grin, as Sara pointed at a third girl. She was small with messy mousey hair and poorly applied make up. She was attired in a horrific tie dyed dress. There was a strong hint of the undergrowth about her too, like a vole or an otter and not a particularly clean one.

'I'm Deidre, and I'm from Liverpool,' she gushed in an irritating 'Come-on-down, The Price Is Right' manner, hugging him like he was Bruce Forsyth. He looked at Carl over her head ready to roll his eyes, but Carl was looking at her like Cleopatra had just been wheeled in on her finest chariot. Not for the first time did Will wonder where Carl got his penchant for woodland animals from. 'Come on you,' she screeched at Carl, 'Let's go and put some songs on.'

As she dragged him off to what Will was sure was a non-existent juke box, he overheard Alice telling Aiden she had loved watching him play rugby as she squeezed a beefy bicep. Aiden too seemed to have perked up, Will reflected. Sara was looking at him and he pondered apologising but realised he couldn't be arsed.

'How are you enjoying college?' he said.

'You cheeky twat,' she retorted. 'That's it? Why didn't you write?'

'Why didn't you?'

She seemed flummoxed for a few seconds. Someone else had clearly been in the pub a while too. Pressing his advantage to escape any heat he added, 'You were starting a new life, miles away. I know what university life is like. I wondered whether you would write, but you didn't.'

She mellowed quickly and as she droned on about how amazing it was and how great everyone there was, he reflected on how she had changed. She had lost weight, grown her hair long and even though it was pulled into a simple pony tail it accentuated her prominent cheek bones and caring green eyes. She only had a touch of lipstick on, but her lips were full and Will remembered the many enjoyable hours he had spent locked to them. He just managed to stop a grin hitting his face as he looked at her aquiline nose, recalling Darren asking if he had managed to bang Julius Caesar yet. She too had a tie dyed top and long flowing skirt on. Will had never appreciated the wacky student look but he saw Aiden snogging Alice out the corner of his eye and realised he may as well enter into the spirit of things as he would no doubt be taking one for the team regardless.

A couple of hours seemed to evaporate as they do when you are having a good time. Around nine o'clock a breathless Deidre and a doe eyed Carl returned from one of their many wanders and declared in ecstatic unison that it was time to go to Carl's, as though the carriages had arrived and they were going to the Ambassadors ball. As they shuffled through the now thinning crowd Will felt Sara squeeze his hand. He smiled at her and felt a familiar stirring down below and looking at her realised that base two could well be reached and breached tonight. Things were looking up.

He half focused on those they passed as they got to the door. Clearly anyone with half a brain had realised it was time to go unless they wanted to spend the big day hanging out of their arses. With a melancholy sigh he noticed the majority who were left looked to him as though tomorrow held no aces and this was as good as it was going to get.

18

As Carl opened the front door of his parents' house Will remembered he hadn't been inside since the time Carl's dad had freaked them out by turning the television off. He almost tiptoed into the house like a mouse expecting the cat to leap out on him at any moment. As Carl took drink orders Deidre declared it was party time and brought out what Will suspected was a big lump of cannabis resin. He looked at Carl for a response but he was away with the fairies and Will resigned himself to it.

He wasn't a big marijuana fan. He had endured a particularly unpleasant experience only a few weeks back where he had partaken of a few spliffs of infamous white widow bought to him by a now departed hippy colleague called Ronald Belling. Ron, as he preferred to be called, had been to Amsterdam. This in itself was very odd as he rarely spoke to the guy. He was a little bit strange, although many were in the I.T department. He also seemed intent on convincing Will that he wasn't a 'Corporate weasel'. In fact the only meaningful connection he could remember was after he had left the toilets in an extremely foul state at work one Monday morning after a boozy Sunday. Ron and he had crossed paths as he left the scene of the crime and he asked 'Which trap have you used?' Assuming he was talking about the fact there were six toilets, like in a greyhound race, he had said 'That's for you to find out my friend, roll the dice'. When the guy had come out they had both raised their hands in unison and nasty for poor old Ron, they both displayed the number three. For the following week as they had smoked outside the building together, Will had amused them by calling him 'Hot Pot Ron.' He had given him the present a few weeks later as a leaving gift even though it was Ron who was leaving.

He had sparked up ostensibly to remember Ron, but had ended up watching Goldeneye on an extremely good quality pirate video copy his house mate had acquired.

The film had been brilliant and as the munchies had taken hold he had realised he was ill prepared for such over powering urges. He had then savagely unwrapped the present he had bought for the departmental secretary for staying late to do some work for him a few days prior. So engrossed was he in considering how great he would be as 007, that he managed to destroy an entire four hundred gram box of wine gums. After passing out, the next morning he woke on the couch and began to fart so violently that he had begun to worry that his ring-piece would shatter.

He had to ring in sick the next day as he was too spaced out to contemplate going to the shop to replace the item, never mind to make an appearance at work. He had ended up getting her a nice box of chocolates, causing her to wink and flirt at him ever since, which was exactly what he had been hoping to avoid by getting her such a shit present in the first place. He had not seen teeth that dirty since he had last watched 'The Return of the Living Dead'.

However there was going to be no escaping the demon weed and Sara fired up the joint in the living room. This surprised Will and elevated her in his warped opinion. She had been such a brown-noser at school, it was quite exciting seeing her be the naughty little one and he felt that stirring again. She passed the joint to him and he took a long deep pull, forgetting his lightweight nature with the enclosed product due to the beers he had consumed. He passed it to Aiden who had a few mini puffs on it, prompting immediate shouts of 'You bender' from the others. Alice took it next and immediately accused Aiden of bum sucking it, which caused Will and Sara to collapse into giggles. Good times, Will concluded through already narrow eyes. Sara and Lisa declared they were going to the toilet and left the boys to it.

Aiden was slumped in the armchair, a big smile on his face.

'Great night eh? Just like old times. First time I've been out in ages too, although I'm kind of trading on past glories. What do you think of my new friend?'

'She seems…' Will searched for a word other than plain, as he didn't want to say that, although he wasn't sure exactly why at that point. His scrambled brain churned like a slush puppy machine. He eventually said, 'Keen.'

'Surely a good thing!' Aiden replied. 'She actually fancied you for ages at school but you called her Leslie for five years. Apparently she was waiting for you to realise and apologise and then she was going to ask you out, but you never did. Then you started seeing Sara her friend and that was it!'

Will tried to absorb that piece of information which he suspected cast his character in a rather poor light and took another toke. He then watched as a hot rock rolled out of the end of the joint and landed on his new white shirt. Despite it being expensive and brand new and him being in an uncomfortable position on the world's most unforgiving sofa, he didn't feel able to move.

Where had they found this couch he thought distractedly as he watched it sizzling. If his parents had just lined up a row of assorted cacti and they had thrust their derrieres straight on them it wouldn't have been much more disagreeable. Or maybe that was the point; to prevent anyone from having any pleasure in the vicinity of their television.

Carl and Deidre came back with another rolled joint and she began to give Carl a blow back of frightening intensity. Will laughed out loud, secretly hoping that Carl's ability to process dope was vastly superior to his prowess with alcohol. As they ran off upstairs again like a couple of four year olds at a kid's party, Will looked at Aiden to see if he looked hungrier than him. He did. He always did.

'Best you get in the kitchen and start bringing the food in,' he ordered in a jokey manner. He imagined trays of heaped nachos dripping with cheese and freshly cooked steaming garlic bread.

He realised a bit later that he had closed his eyes and was drooling, several minutes or several hours could have passed by. Opening his eyes he saw that Aiden still hadn't moved, so suspecting the former he nudged Aiden's foot with his trainer. Aiden suddenly said, as though he had been considering a particularly expensive watch purchase, 'I can't imagine Carl's parents having a house full of E numbers, or meat for that matter,' he said. 'Maybe we should just ring for a pizza?'

'Great idea genius,' Will deadpanned as he looked at his watch. 'I suspect even Mr Domino is hanging his stocking up at midnight on Christmas Eve.'

Aiden let out a bark of laughter or a grunt of annoyance as he dragged his weight up, like Frankenstein getting out of his chair. Groggy and stiff, he hobbled into the kitchen.

Through the smoky haze, Will saw the door to the stairs open and Carl scamper around the sofa in a Harry Potter cape and just his boxers, with a squealing Deidre chasing after him waving either a wand or possibly a ruler, shouting out 'You are a bad wizard' to which Carl squealed 'I'm a good wizard'. At least Will thought that was what was happening, he could have imagined the whole thing, but he didn't mind. He felt as though he was sinking into an enormous warm fluffy white cloud on its way to heaven. Hopefully there would be a McDonald's at the gates, Saint Peter encouraging him to supersize his meal and then winking at him whilst slipping some free chicken nuggets into his takeaway bag.

'What's hummus?' Aiden popped his head out the kitchen and shouted.

Will groaned and as Sara and Lisa came in took one last drag on the joint. He didn't notice the enormous boulder of magma roll out this time and it dropped onto his chest, seared through the cotton and landed throbbing on his nipple. Yelling 'Arghh' at the top of his voice he shot out of his chair rubbing his painful chest and knocked his can of lager over on to the carpet, which seemed to amuse the girls no end.

Will handed Alice the offending article and she stared at it with a curled lip and then looking around she ground it out on the nearest ashtray type item. This turned out to be a large, cream, porcelain Buddha resting on a table. Having left the butt sticking out the top of its head she left it looking like Caspar the friendly ghost, and over a decade of being friends caused Will and Aiden to catch each other's eye and to convulse into peals of laughter.

Seeing as he was standing up Will went into the kitchen, desperate for something other than hummus and no doubt its healthy unwelcome friends Mr Celery and Mr Carrot. He remembered wanting a kitchen towel for something, but the reason had temporarily escaped him. The fridge contents were indeed a salutary lesson on how to live to a hundred but never enjoy a meal.

Frustrated he began opening doors and found the first of two unnerving finds that night. At the back of the pantry was a battered old Roses tin, pushed in a corner with a newspaper placed on top of it. He slid it out, and like Indiana Jones peering into what he hoped was going to be treasure, but could well be plutonium, stole a quick glance inside. He was hoping for a chocolate cake maybe, or even some biscuits. Milk chocolate digestives would be really nice. As his mind wandered, he thought hopefully though not a dead animal, or worse a baby.

It was instead full to the brim with Cadbury's Crunchies. Very odd Will thought, but definitely better than vegetables and dip. He returned to the room with his prize cradled in his arms.

When he got there Aiden and Lisa had disappeared this time. It was too much to keep up with. 'Cotton Eye Joe' was just starting to blare out of an old but serviceable cassette player that had been placed on the coffee table and Deidre seemed to be constructing something involving about six tobacco papers. Just looking at it made Will feel like someone had tied one of his trainers on each eyelid and was ushering him to the land of nod. Blinking in slow motion he sat next to Sara and turned to look at her.

'Crunchie?' he offered.

'Don't mind if I do she said,' pleasing Will by also looking decidedly worse for wear.

'Carl,' Will asked. 'You didn't mention you had a secret sweetie stash. Or music for that matter.'

'The Crunchies are my mum's. She loves them, and I'm not allowed to go in that tin. She says it's the only thing that gets her through the day. The music is NOW 30 my friend, I bought it myself!' More odd revelations for a twenty-one year old that Will wondered if he would remember in the morning. All things considered Carl looked to be holding up fairly well under the onslaught of disabling substances. It was as if adrenalin and nervousness were cleansing his body of all impurities, readying him for the deadly task ahead. He suspected Deidre would not be a considerate lover.

Will started sniggering to himself again as he thought this is the moment Carl has been training his whole life for. This set off Sara to his right, who made some deep throated noise as she finished her chocolate bar and lobbed the packet over the back of the sofa.

He passed Sara another Crunchie and tried to flex his face. His cheeks ached from laughing or was it the speed he was powering through his friend's mum's treats? The tastiness having gone up a notch due to their new illicit properties. Just one more bar he thought as he too lobbed his second wrapper over the back of his seat, noticing but not caring that he had eaten that last one before the song had finished.

A clearly hammered Deidre stood up to present her dope filled creation. As she went to light it the contents dropped out of the middle and fell like snowflakes onto the carpet. Will, Carl and Sara all neighed with laughter, particularly at Deidre's face, who looked like her grandma's wedding ring had slipped off her finger and plopped straight between the bars of a drain cover. The next song came on, 'Stay Another Day' and recovering her poise, Deidre dragged Carl up and began to slow dance with him.

Will found through his confused state he was eating this final bar to a rhythmic banging which was coming through the ceiling as though someone was trying to break through with big heavy swings of a large blunt axe. Will found his head swirling as the banging speeded up. Carl and Deidre spinning faster and faster, Wills teeth grinding harder and harder and Sara's laughter getting higher and higher. Suddenly it stopped just as the tape finished leaving a wide eyed silence and a guffaw exploded from Will's throat firing a huge squirt of chocolate and honeycomb goo straight onto the television, where it slid down like a slick slimy slug.

'Upstairs with you my boy,' Will heard through the heavy silence which was only broken by the odd merry whimper from Sara. He strained to open his eyes and wiped the moisture out of them in time to see Carl's face after that instruction. It was the same face he had worn when bracing himself to go to the bar earlier that night. Gritting his teeth, head down and muttering under his breath, he followed Deidre out of the room and with heavy footsteps followed her upstairs.

'Little boy with big job to do,' Will said to Sara.

Sara got up and came and snuggled up to him.

'Will,' she smiled. 'I have honestly never laughed so much. I missed you.' She gave him a hot, soft, wet kiss on his cheek which felt so lovely he purred like a cat. She disappeared into the kitchen, and after a clinking of cups and a hissing kettle came back with two strong coffees.

She drank hers quickly and then laughing, with meaning in her eyes, whispered in his ear, 'Upstairs with you my boy.' She hauled him out of his seat and helped him up the stairs like a survivor from a place crash. She shimmied off her clothes with no inhibition, leaving what appeared to be matching underwear on. She then walked to the light in the corner as if to turn it off but stopped and turning around, gave him a big wink and slid under the sheets of a big double bed. He caught all this out of the corner of a puffy eye as he had been unsuccessfully trying to balance his coffee on a book on the bedside table.

He hopped on one leg as he removed his jeans, promptly falling off to one side and decided it would be best if he removed his clothes whilst lying on the floor. Leaving his boxers on, he got into bed next to her puffing like he had just done a hundred press-ups. He realised for the first time that night that the heating must have been on full blast as it felt like a mid-summer day, so warm and close it was. She rolled over to him, and uttered, 'Will,' and began to kiss his neck. He could feel something under his head and, reaching around, he found a sturdy grey thing, which might have been the world's heaviest nightie or more likely was someone's shroud. Maybe it was for Grandad, if he didn't make it.

He threw it to the side of the bed leaving an unusual musty smell in the air. It hit the wardrobe with a worrying clunk and as he turned his head to see what he'd broken, found himself staring into a grinning picture of Carl in his school uniform. There would be no need for any more press-ups he thought, if he couldn't get that image out of his mind.

He suddenly felt woozy and weak and a little bit freaked out that he was practically naked in Carl's parents' bed. He blew out a breath and tried to will his body into action. So stoned was he that he could imagine what it must be like for people with locked-in syndrome. Your brain is working and you can hear what's going on, but you can't respond. He suspected he may be able to move his forehead if a large angry hornet had alighted on it, trying to fend it off with a bushy eyebrow, but that was all.

As her kisses began to patter down his chest, he thought of lunchtimes on the school field, trying to get his hand inside her bra, where he would have given his left nut to be in the position he was in now. His priorities seemed to have become skewed over the years.

Dragging his mind back to the present, he realised her head was rapidly approaching what was only going to be a massive disappointment, or in this case a tiny disappointment. Worse for him maybe, would be listening to her platitudes afterwards. Something awful along the lines of 'It not mattering', 'It happens to lots of guys' and 'I only wanted to cuddle anyway'.

With a superhuman effort he dragged himself up and said, 'Let me just finish my coffee,' and reached over to it with a set of numb fingers that seemed to belong to someone else. He caught the handle with his thumb and sent the cup jolting into a wonky dance like a spinning top just before it comes to rest and then it fell on its side, coffee pouring all over the flat surface and down onto the carpet.

'Jesus,' Sarah chuckled. 'You can't get out of it you know.' She kissed him on the forehead and added, 'I'll get a cloth.'

Will looked over the side of the bed and as luck would have it most of it had drained onto his white shirt. That shirt was like a May Fly he sighed, destined to live only one day. Although he was pretty sure the insect had sex before it expired, to go out with a bang so-to-speak, which might be something he might not be able to manage. He noticed the cabinet drawer was slightly open and when the noisy sounds of drunken lovemaking stopped humming through the wall next to their room, he could hear the drip of liquid.

Wincing, he sat up, pulled the metal handle and slid the drawer open, worried about what he had ruined. What was nestled in there, like a hamster cosy in its nest, shocked him out of his stupor. He lifted it out with both hands and marvelled at its weight. It was the biggest vibrator he had ever seen in his life. Both on screen and off. Incredulous, he placed it back in the drawer as shocking visions appeared in his mind. He heard Sara come back in to the room so he slammed the drawer shut and leapt back into the bed.

He heard her chuckle as she wiped the floor but did not say anything. The sneaky cow must have noticed his shirt had saved the day. As she got back in beside him and said, 'Where were we?' one especially gruesome image formed in his mind; Carl's staid, fifty year old teacher mother, kneeling on all fours on the bed. Her long, thick, tartan skirt pulled over her hips, sensible knickers around her ankles, strong shoes on twitching feet as she drove that monstrosity inside her.

As Sara's hand reached into his boxers, he horrified himself by feeling himself respond to the images. He was indeed a sick man. Then realising this was his opportunity, he reached out for a firm breast and with a sneaky smile rolled on top of her.

19

24ᵗʰ December 1998

He walked through the arrival entrance of Peterborough station just in time to look through the open doors and see Sara's car edging past the taxi traffic at the front of the building. She saw him and gestured to the short stay car park and drove off in a puff of smoke. He despised that car. It was an old Citroen 2cv that Sara would not be parted from. She poured her money into it like a desperate person on a fruit machine, knowing you were going to lose but doing it regardless. It looked like a battered upside down pram and was slightly less reliable.

The amount of times it had let them down was legendary. The V98 music festival that year had been a prime example. He was ambushed into going with promises of great times and spent two long days in inclement weather feeling like he was missing the point. They had bought some ecstasy tablets on the first night and he had never really recovered. Obviously Dolly wouldn't start for the return journey, no doubt feeling as lively as he did after being slumped in cold mud for forty eight hours. They had to wait until everyone else was gone, so they could be dragged to the nearest main road by a tractor and then wait for the AA. Depressing doesn't even start to describe it.

It was only ten o'clock in the morning yet a ferocious tide of people already rushed in and out of the railway building. History had taught Will to get home early on Christmas Eve. He stepped around a young couple who were so stereotypically student that he would put money on them being embarrassed by their clothes and hair when they looked back, many years from now, on this year's family photographs. They looked overjoyed with each other though. Squealing and crying, hugging and kissing, as though he had just pulled her out of some particularly rough surf to stop her from drowning. He searched his memory for when he last looked that happy and wasn't drunk or under the influence of some other kind of chemical and found himself wanting.

He put his Bergen rucksack in the boot of the car looking at it fondly. He had bought that for Army Cadet Camp over ten years ago and it was still in good nick. It was one of the last links to that time he thought, that and his friends. He climbed in the passenger seat next to her and struggled to get the seatbelt on. The car seat was as comfy as sitting on an enormous piece of ravioli that had been left out in the sun.

She reached over to kiss him on the cheek, but missed and hit his ear as the car juddered as she fought for first gear. Will thought back to those two students and felt down. Finally with an angry oink the car went into gear and they pulled into the surprisingly light traffic. He looked over at Sara, still in her Vet's uniform and felt happy for her. She had exactly what she wanted, well workwise anyway. He suspected there would be a few things she would like to change about him.

He thought back over the last few years and it felt like he had just drifted to this point. After that spontaneous Christmas Eve party at Carl's house three years ago they had all woken up late and rushed their separate ways, no time for embarrassment or future plans. He had made more effort to keep in touch with the boys though. On the last Sunday of each month he would sit at the scuffed dining table in whichever shared house he was in and write them a letter. He had considered writing to Sara but Liverpool seemed so far away and that night quickly became a blurred furry spot in his mind, smothered by many more memories of the same ilk.

It was only when he had gone back to his parents' house six months later for Nathan's depressing wedding that he had given it much more thought. His mum had told him he had some post on his old bed and there he found a pink envelope resting amongst a few white circulars and bank statements from empty accounts. He knew straight away who it was from. His handwriting looked like a disabled spider limping home from a heavy weekend with Keith Richards. Whereas hers almost looked like it had been typed. He could remember the moment he opened the letter very clearly, like another signpost in his life to look back to. It was midday and he could hear his brother and the best man nervously laughing in the sunshine in the back garden. The sounds were softened by the double glazing though and he felt warm and peaceful as he sat on the bed and read it.

He could still remember it now, word for word.

Dear Will,

Thanks for a great night on Xmas Eve. I know I should wait for you to write, but this time I won't. I love you Will. I have done, for what seems like forever. I know you wanted to go faster than I did when we were at school, so I hope the other night caught us up!

Write back to me Will.

Years of love

Sara

He had then turned the envelope over with trepidation and looked at the franking date. It had been sent on the 3rd January, it was then the 27th June. He had lain back on the bed, crumpling his suit and felt like a total shit. Generally going to a wedding on your own is a singularly depressing experience anyway. That little titbit of information was not going to make it better. Then to really make it worse he got steaming drunk. He had been calling his brother 'Nathan the knob end' at the bar in a loud obnoxious manner and then slipped into a rant about what a waste of space he was and also a shit excuse for a human being.

He hadn't realised the father of the bride had been talking to Will and Nathan's father just behind them. He had wondered at the time why Nathan was just standing there lapping it up and grinning. His father had grabbed his arm like a naughty school child and dragged him outside and given him a humiliating dressing down. Nathan was the golden boy now. So he had left and gone to sit in the park nearby to consider where it had all gone wrong. When he returned to the party, he had missed the speeches and his mother's look should have incinerated him in an instant, like a magnifying glass over an ant.

He was brought back from that horrendous memory to the present by Sara's terrible driving. Looking at the gearstick instead of the road, she missed a cyclist by the moss on his tyres, leaving him with an expression that suggested ten years had been shaved from his life anyway. It was Darren who had said some women don't drive cars, they just steer them like they are possessed. A shiver went through him as he realised it was like being driven by his own mother.

He looked at her with affection though. She was telling him about Alice's new boyfriend. He sounded like some squeaky clean lawyer type, very different from Aiden. That took him back to the miserable night after his brother's wedding. He had gone out with Aiden to cheer himself up. He had wanted to see his old pal too, although he had wondered at the time if he had just wanted to spend time with someone who was doing worse than him in the old race of life and he had definitely wanted to get out of his parents' house.

He had been too hungover to face any more alcohol so they had decided on the movies to see the cinematic classic 'Waterworld', with Kevin Costner. As they left that bitterly disappointing choice Will had been pondering the quote by Mason Cooley, 'Regret for wasted time, is more wasted time', when he had actually walked into Alice. Standing next to her was Sara holding hands with a bloke that could have passed for a young Charlton Heston. Nasty to see. Especially in his present weakened state.

All three of them stopped and there was a pause whilst Sara looked at him like she had just recognised someone she had caught burgling her house previously but had run away before the police arrived. The void was broken by another man of equal leading-man stature coming up laden down with popcorn and drinks stating it was about to start on screen one. Sara and Alice said 'Hi ya' with a distinct lack of eye contact and were zoomed away by their Hollywood dates.

Aiden and Will looked at each other. Aiden simply muttered, 'O joy.' As they watched them trot into the same screen that they had been in, Will clung to the fact that they too, were about to have a torturous experience. Then he realised with a sickening churning in his stomach that they may not be there to watch the film.

Sara was dressed in ridiculously tight jeans, high boots and a tight fitted white shirt and she looked amazing. Will rolled his tongue back into his dry mouth.

As she got to the door she let the others go in first and then, with every fibre of Will's being willing her to do so, she stole a glance back at him. Will suspected after that if he'd missed that look, he may well have not pursued it. As it was, he did. He returned her imperceptible smile and raised a hand. As they walked back to Aiden's, Aiden told him with an incredulous face that Alice and he had been on a few dates afterwards, but she had eventually dumped him with a well written Dear John letter, telling him he was boring. Will had laughed at that disclosure, Aiden not so much.

When he had returned to his own home he had looked for the telephone number of the girl from the previous weekend hoping for some distraction in the old fashioned way but it was nowhere to be seen. To add to his gloom, he had then wasted an entire afternoon frantically ripping the place apart. Another person he had let down and would never see again.

He had then sat at his scratched table and thought about Sara. He knew there was an element of wanting what you can't have, especially with him not having anything at the moment but eventually he picked up a pen and wrote to her.

So here we are Will thought, three years on. It had turned out that she had really liked this Heston bloke and it was all a huge decision for her. Will had expected her to dump him and that would be it. Instead it had ended up as a big drama, agonisingly conducted through Royal Mail. Just as it got to the point where he felt like telling her to choose 'El Cid', so exhausted was he by all the palaver, she arrived at his house on the morning of his birthday in November and they had gone straight to bed. They had then seen each other sporadically until they had settled into a twice a month arrangement. He would return to Peterborough one weekend and a fortnight later she would go and visit him. It was hardly rock and roll.

Sara pulled up outside Aiden's and stalled the engine. Will recalled one of his dad's little phrases, 'Mark my words, you will end up with someone like your mother and will be thankful for it'. A deeply disheartening thought at twenty-five, Will concluded. He saw Darren and Dean parked outside the house on the other side of the road a few cars up with a wildly gesticulating Carl in the backseat clearly in the middle of some amusing tale where something unpleasant happened to him.

Laughing now, Sara kissed him properly, wet and keen and made a 'Mmmm' sound.

'I will see you at my house,' she said. 'Three o'clock no later,' she added with a stern look.

'We are only going for a pizza,' he laughed. 'Darren is only back for a flying visit, Carl is off to Liverpool, and Aiden has…' He tailed off and gave her his best winning smile.

'I'm sorry Will, but my parents said no to him coming. It's a full house and you know how they are about Christmas being just family.'

Will kissed her again and got out the car. It was his turn to go to hers this Christmas, something he was not overly enthused about. He had asked if Aiden could come for dinner as by all accounts his mother was in a weary way. He had asked for Aiden's benefit and for his own, so he could have an ally as he never really felt that welcome there. He strongly suspected that he had been bad-mouthed due to his elusive behaviour over the preceding years and her dad usually looked at him like he was an unwelcome cat that had sneaked into the house and needed shooing out. Her mum, too, looked at him in a slightly unusual manner. Maybe it was his paranoia but it always seemed as though she was pleasantly tolerating him and making the best out of a bad situation. It was like he was a phase to be endured, until her only child wised up and got a decent human being.

20

Will rapped his knuckles on what he assumed to be Dean's car, startling Carl so he banged his head on the window. It was a silver Vauxhall Cavalier SRI that looked like it had been a lovely car once, until it had been driven full pelt around the world twice - in first gear. Gesturing for Dean to turn off the noisy engine Will waited next to the car, waving smoke out of his face as Darren got out.

'Are you coming in?' Will asked. He studied Darren's face as Darren looked at the fading door and the piles of rubbish that were now accumulating in the front garden. He had lost a little more weight, or maybe just trained it off. He looked like the older, harder brother of the Darren he went to school with. He retained the same intense eyes as if life around him was a finely balanced game of chess and he was always considering his next move, or maybe, the next five moves. His hair was now in a crew cut showing off a few scars where the hair now refused to grow.

He surprised Will and nodded his head. 'Yes, this last time. The world is changing, so it's time I changed. I'll tell you more about that later.' He then purposely strode towards the alleyway between the houses. Will followed after him, stepping over faded sweet wrappers and mouldy leaves.

Will and Darren stared at each other, no words necessary as they got to the back door. The back garden too looked neglected and that had been Aiden's mum's pride and joy and they both shared a look. Darren took a deep breath and knocked lightly on the door. A minute passed, so Will knocked louder this time and when no response came Darren tried the door. He pushed it open and gestured for Will to go in. Will edged into the kitchen as though he was entering a mine field.

Suddenly Darren pushed him and Will staggered forward and slid on what appeared to be a blackened banana and tripped into a load of bottles. The bottles bounced all over the hard floor, making a loud tinkling sound, leaving Will feeling like he was playing whack-a-mole as he tried to still them all at once. 'You bell end,' he snarled at Darren who was looking very pleased with himself. Darren then frowned, at the same time as Will creased his nose.

There was a funny smell in the kitchen. It reminded Will of the disposal chute at the bakery. Sweet and rancid at the same time and it was then as he looked for the source that he noticed the work tops were cluttered with old takeaway boxes and dirty plates. The sink was piled high with mugs, nothing else, like a tower of skulls. Wanting to break the nervous pressure that was building inside him Will opened the door to the hall and bellowed, 'Aiden,' up the stairs. Darren came past him and went into the dining room and Will followed. It was empty of life but looked like squatters had been staying there. Pizza boxes covered the table but had been arranged in a pattern, almost like a modern day laminate. There was the same musty smell here. Will watched Darren's eyes jump from culprit to culprit, like Robocop looking for crime, as he scanned the array of half eaten tins of food, semi-drunk bottles of milk and rejected toast crusts that littered the floor. Darren then froze, eyes widening, as he caught sight of the photograph of Aiden and Freja sitting on the car looking at the camera.

A full minute passed and then a tear crawled down his cheek. Steadily the volume of water increased and he closed his eyes as they began to stream down his face. Will began to step out of the room, to give his friend this last goodbye. Unexpectedly, a dull solid thud echoed from above and both Will and Darren's heads snapped toward the ceiling. They both edged to the bottom of the stairs and looked up. Darren wiped his eyes with the back of his sleeve and then put his arm across Will's chest. He made the universal sign for quiet with his hand and then took the lead up the narrow staircase.

Will followed, trying to mimic Darren's crouching gait. He copied the technique of keeping one foot close to the bannister and the other close to the wall and together they ascended in near silence, the only sound the slight sucking of the filthy carpet, as though it was loathe to let them advance. All the doors were closed at the top and there was a heavy curtain pulled across the only window so it felt like it was dusk, despite the fact it was not even midday. The only sound Will felt he could hear was the roar of his own blood rushing around his body and he moistened his lips. He shifted the weight of his straining muscles.

He then put a foot on the top step and broke the peace as the floorboard let out a high pitched sound like the wailing of a mother shrew that had come home to find an owl sitting in her empty nest. He immediately took his foot off the offending step which then let out the same sound in reverse. He looked at Darren in disgrace, who just shook his head and mouthed the word 'Dick' to him.

Darren opened the nearest door to them. He did it swiftly and stepped back against the doorjamb as though a swarm of bats would escape. It was Freja's old room. The curtains were pulled back so a weak wintry sun highlighted a mass of swirling dust which they had disturbed. Will could almost feel the thick air and knew the room was empty.

The next room door was pushed open and the mystery was solved. Freja and Aiden's mother was lying on the floor next to the bed. One naked leg caught in the sheets, causing her nightie to ride up to her waist. A more emaciated human being Will had never seen. The air was dank with sickness and a myriad of other bodily smells that pharmaceutical companies prevent us from recognising and Will put a hand to his mouth.

Will took a step closer to the prone form. He found himself examining the body as though it was something he had just run over. It seemed to have a yellow hue, but that could have been because the only light was coming from a weak single bulb on a nightstand. If it wasn't dead he suddenly knew, it would be soon. He went to pull the blanket over the scrawny bottom, to save it some dignity, when he saw a slight bunching of the back muscles.

Then a long slow fart was pushed into the air. It was like the dying gasp of a wounded soldier. It lasted about ten seconds, a strange meandering sound as though the body barely had the strength to expel it. It tailed off with a gentle high pitched parp. Sickened and amused at the same time, Will raised his eyebrows at Darren who looked mortified. Suddenly a smell so nauseating, so fetid and heavy, that it felt like his brain was being pulled through his nostrils, assaulted him and he gasped in shock. Returning his shocked look to the body, he started when he realised the eyes were now open and then a skeletal hand shot out and grabbed his knee.

He involuntarily jumped back and hit a solid object, which was Aiden and he would have fallen back on the creature if Darren hadn't grabbed him by the upper arm and held him. How the hell had a twenty stone giant made it up the stairs without them hearing. Aiden was clutching a bottle of vodka and was gently sobbing. He stepped past Will and picked his mother up off the floor as though she was a rare, expensive, spilled parchment and gently placed her on the bed. Darren had gone white as a sheet and he mumbled, 'I'll wait in the car.' He slipped out of the room like a wraith.

Will tried to compose himself.

'Sorry man, we thought it was a burglar,' he whispered. Aiden didn't bother to clear his eyes and spoke in a strong loud voice as though it would clear the air.

'You don't need to whisper. She can't hear you. My mum left a long time ago. All this thing does now is ask for vodka when it wakes.' He paused and then shrugged as though he needed to tell someone. 'Her liver has failed. Her kidneys too I think. The doctor said it's a matter of days, weeks maybe. He said vodka is as good as morphine. I forgot you were coming.' He sat on the side of the bed and held his mother's hand. 'I'm sorry Will, you shouldn't have to see this.'

Will had never been more at a loss for words in his entire life. He returned his gape to the person who had once been one of the most powerful life forces he had ever encountered. The skin seemed to sag around her ears, leaving her nose protruding like an exposed cliff. His mouth moved but no sounds came out.

'Can I help?' he eventually managed to stutter.

Aiden put a heavy hand on his shoulder and said, 'Yes, it's bath night tonight.'

Will was too dumbfounded to disguise his features and a look passed his face as though he had done a massive fart and then followed through. Aiden laughed.

'You're a good friend Will. Go. This is my burden to bear and I'm happy to carry it.'

Will stood there stunned and Aiden got up and hugging him, turned him around and gently pushed him toward the door. Will stopped at the top of the stairs, but couldn't bring himself to turn around and on wooden legs staggered down the steps. He burst through the back door almost at a run and he knelt, head tilted back, hauling huge great gasps of clean winter air into his lungs.

21

Will drained his second beer and finally gathered his thoughts. The others had been talking but he hadn't heard a word. He took a deep breath and joined the land of the living. Darren seemed indifferent to their recent harrowing experience and was explaining the Balkan war zone to Carl, Dean nodding beside him and Will tuned in.

'It's carnage out there. Starving people shooting each other over bread. Snipers picking off desperate mothers as they search for food. Mass graves everywhere. It's genocide man. And these are normal people, in jeans and trainers.'

An unusual phrase, Will thought as the spotty waiter put their empty plates down and said, 'Help yourselves please.'

'The SAS are already there,' Darren continued. 'But now they want the best to keep the peace.'

'This is what we've been trained for,' Dean cut in. 'This is what we are ready for.' The pair of them looked at each other and grimly nodded.

Will considered whether having these two fervent-eyed individuals there was going to improve the state of affairs. He stood up and said, 'Let's eat.'

He stood staring down at the collection of congealing pizzas and sodden pasta dishes and felt like his mouth was full of cotton wool. He took two slices of pepperoni, returned to the table and ordered another beer. The others came back, plates laden with calories and Will looked at Carl properly for the first time. He seemed different. More poised and confident.

'Glasses?' he enquired.

'I had laser surgery,' Carl grinned. 'Gruesome and expensive, but I love it.'

Will smiled. It was good to see him looking so well. He was still painfully thin, but his clothes looked expensive and his watch loudly declared money. He took a bite of his greasy cardboard.

'So tell me Carlos, what's new?'

'The accountants took me on after my degree. Sixty grand a year to stare at spreadsheets. Can you believe it, just to stare at a company's VAT returns? Work is good and my love life is great.' Carl puffed himself up.

'Still donking Deidre?' Darren chuckled.

'Yes, I love her lads. I would see her all the time, but she's a slippery one. I asked her to move in but I can't seem to pin her down. She has all these amazing plans to save the world's most needy.'

'Is she still in Liverpool?' Will asked.

Momentarily Carl lost his candour. 'Yes, I only get to see her every couple of months, she works for a charity. One day lads, one day.'

Will decided to ignore that unusual comment and stated the plans he already knew. 'So Christmas at hers then?'

'Yep,' Carl gushed. 'Meeting the family, well her sisters anyway. She was adopted or something.' Carl seemed to collapse into his seat and then manfully tried to get his money's worth from the 'Eat as much as you can' fare. Alarm bells rang in Will's head. There was a lot of information there that didn't add up, but he wasn't in the mood to dissect it. So Will changed the subject.

'Tell Dean about that Christmas morning.'

Carl brightened up immediately and almost glowed. 'It was the best Christmas Eve ever,' he began. 'Well, we had a party, didn't we Will? Booze, drugs and girls. Anyway, after the others left in the morning, Deidre said she was still horny, so not wanting to disappoint a girl, I took her back to bed. We must have fallen asleep. I woke up to someone shaking my shoulder and looked straight into the eyes of my parents.

'My mother was almost catatonic with shock. My dad took me downstairs and made me look at the lounge. It looked like the field at the end of Glastonbury. They ended up having to replace the carpet and some knob head had put a joint out on my mum's prized Buddha.'

He leaned in to the table and said in a hushed voice, 'Well I thought my dad was going to rip me a new arsehole. Instead he held his hand up, I was waiting for him to belt me with it. Instead he high fived me! He said 'We won't mention this again on two conditions. One, you tell your mother I really told you off and two, it never happens again'.

'My mum came down after and asked who had been in her room. I said I couldn't remember. I was expecting her to go off pop too, but she just looked dead shifty and began cleaning. It wasn't until I told Will that he confessed to spilling coffee over my mum's giant dildo!'

Carl creased over with laughter, his forehead resting on the table. To give Dean his credit, he also laughed, although Will could tell he wasn't sure if he was amused or alarmed.

Will looked at the two squaddies who were now eating like it was their last meal on death row. The two boys from the pub all those years ago were long gone. They ate like soldiers and they looked like soldiers. Will smirked to himself as they devoured the food, synchronised as the food went from plate to mouth. Not a scrap of spare flesh could be seen on either of them. They even had similar shirts on; two different shades of blue, but both tight and very short sleeved, showing off tanned veiny forearms and muscled biceps.

Darren caught him looking at them.

'Good to see you Will. That was some fucked up shit earlier.' His mouth laughed, but his face didn't. 'This is a new start for me. I'm a corporal now. I'm going to finally put Freja behind me. I've dealt with it now and it is time to move on, and up. You should have joined up Will, we need guys with brains, not like this dip shit.'

He rolled his eyes in Dean's direction, who looked up and spluttered 'What?' spraying food on the table and laughing.

Will wondered whether shagging everything that moved had been an appropriate way of dealing with his girlfriend's demise but smiled at his friend who emanated good health and vitality.

'So where are you going lads?'

'Kosovo,' Darren and Dean barked and clinked beers.

'I can see the future,' Darren declared with jaw clenched affirmation.

If Darren had that vision, he would have stayed at home.

22

11th December 1999

The drive up from London had been uneventful, but it had been good to try and get his thoughts straight in his head. He couldn't believe Darren was getting married. It was quite a surprise. He can't have known her two minutes as he had never mentioned her before, although Darren did like to play his cards close to his chest. Will pondered the fact that people did get married and maybe his shock when Darren had rung him was more a reflection of his own inability to commit. His main concern was more likely that today's events were going to shine a spotlight on his own relationship with Sara.

It had been a quick call with Will barely saying ten words. The usual congratulations, even if you didn't really feel that way. So stunned was he that he hadn't enquired into how they had met, if there was a stag do, a best man or any of those things. He had just written the date down, said 'I'll be there' and then Darren had rung off, saying 'Carl next'.

As Will parked outside Aiden's house he found himself thinking about the millennium in less than three weeks. It felt as though everything was changing and changing faster than he could process the information in his brain. The millennium was like a huge iceberg lurking in the dark, destined to be hit at high speed. A lot had happened. He had lost his job for one.

Lost indicates carelessness and he had always been guilty of that, but this hadn't been his doing. Rumours of financial horrors lurking in the company accounts had been around his office for years. Overheard shifty comments from managers at the coffee machine had spread through the building like a flu virus. Worrying cost cutting had also been rife. His department had then been called to a hotel for a meeting yesterday.

Will smiled as he recalled the meeting. When they had arrived the Director was there. Ironic really, as Will had never even seen him before then except in the shiny annual financial results statement. There was a nervous buzz of excitement in the air as they shuffled into the room, as though a bolt of electricity was leaping from person to person.

He sat next to Donald. He was in his late fifties and possibly the most boring person on the planet. The only interesting fact about him was the overabundance of dandruff he seemed to produce. Huge flaking chunks of it would tumble out of his hair as you talked to him. Will gave him a reassuring pat on the shoulder and tried to knock some of the bigger bits off. In the not so distant past that sort of thing would have grossed him out, but seeing death knocking on the door of Aiden's house seemed to have hardened him. Also he would do anything to distract himself from hearing about how many more years Donald needed in the pension scheme before he could retire.

Donald mouthed 'Restructuring,' at him and gave him a thumbs up. Will felt like mouthing 'Redundancy' back, but figured he would find out soon enough. He could almost hear someone quoting John Donne in a doom laden voice, 'Ask not for whom the bell tolls, it tolls for thee'. Today's news was going to be a blow for many. Will had searched for his own feelings on the topic and was not surprised to find he didn't really have any.

He didn't care about his job, the people he worked with or his pension. He was bored with London. He had found it was a place where rich people had a good time. Everyone else was overcrowded, overworked and he was over it. Change was going to be forced on him and he was grateful for something to knock him out of his inertia.

As it was, he had quite enjoyed the meeting. As the main man stood at the front and cleared his throat, Will decided to face-watch as the news came out. Snippets came back to him now as he stared at the 'Sold' sign in Aiden's front garden.

'No easy way to say this, financial black hole, overextended, onerous commitments, unemployed with immediate effect, garden leave, redundancy terms.' Will had almost laughed out loud as he saw the faces around him change. Eyes widening as the news sank in, looking at each other as though waiting for someone to say it was a joke. Then tears from the girls, great sobs of despair, people hugging, and Donald, well Donald was angry. His retirement dreams escaped from him and fluttered out the window like an elusive moth.

Where had these idiots been these last six months? They had run out of pens last week. Donald however had argued the case as if it was still up for debate. It wasn't. The best bit was the redundancy terms and Will had to stop himself getting out his seat, punching the air and shouting 'Yeeeesaaahhhh'. Will quickly worked out he was going to get ten grand and wasn't going to have to go back to that depressing warehouse of an office again. Result.

He had left the meeting and gone back to his house - a shabby six bedroom house where a room cost you five hundred pounds a month and for that you got to live with a steady flow of other disillusioned transients who had fallen for the story of Dick Whittington. The last person he had liked had moved out a week ago; an insane Australian agency crash nurse, who earned five hundred pounds a shift in London's poorly organised and frequently desperate hospitals. He used to lie on the sofa, smoking bongs and laughing at daytime television and if he got a call to go in, he used to have a shower and leave, stating 'I'll be straight by the time I arrive'.

Very concerning. Nice guy though and he had given Will his car when he went back to Oz. Will had tried to give him some money but he had refused saying it wasn't worth much and he couldn't be arsed to sell it. So Will drove him to Heathrow, and at the departure terminal received a dead arm, a 'Good on yer, cock' and a shit Renault Clio.

Will had woken up this morning with a small celebratory hangover and without much thought, packed all his stuff into his new car and with no backward glance, drove home. He was two months behind on the rent too having been successfully playing dodge the landlord when they found out he lived in America. So, with that little bonus in his mind he had whistled his way around the M25 and up the A1 to 'Hit Me Baby One More Time', 'Tragedy' and 'Mambo No.5'. It was funny how he still called Peterborough home, seeing as he hadn't lived there for years. It wasn't until he got to the outskirts that the radio had played 'Nothing Compares To You' and thinking of Freja his mood had soured. Not helped by the fact the radio was broken and he couldn't change channel or turn it down or off.

Aiden let him in the back door when he arrived and showed off his gardening prowess. Brutal was how Will would have described it. There was nothing left, as though it had been napalmed. The house looked much the same. Grandpa's seat was gone, as were all the photographs and it looked like no one had lived in it for years. He could see why he was selling up. There were a lot of bad memories here.

'When does the sale go through Aiden?' he asked.

'Three weeks,' came the gruff reply. 'I thought I would get a head start.'

'Where are you going to live?'

I'm not sure yet,' said Aiden as though it wasn't important.

'Jesus, do you not think you should start considering it?' Suddenly Will had an idea. 'Why don't we get a place together?

He hadn't seen Aiden look so happy in a long time and he felt a warm affection for the big man. 'What about your job Will?'

Will held out his hand and as they shook, he smiled and said, 'I will give that up for my friend.'

23

Sara picked them up in her brand new car, a Honda CRV 4x4. A chuckling Will clambered over Carl who had been kissing Deidre in the backseat and sat between the two lovebirds. Aiden had to go in the front or they all would never fit in.

'That's enough of that rubbish you two, especially on such a serious day.'

'To the church, driver,' Aiden said. Sara flicked him her middle finger and drove in the direction of Peterborough's registry office.

Sara drove in her usual manner, oblivious to the rules of the road and he again wondered how she had passed her test. She pulled up in the last remaining space as though she was parking a cement truck and they all got out. Will mentally relaxed each muscle and saw the others do the same.

'Busy isn't it,' Deidre commented. 'I didn't realise Darren had so many friends.'

Will shook his head at Deidre's clothes. She had some awful multi-coloured baggy romper suit type thing on, with the customary Dr Martens and resembled the back end of a pantomime horse. She had no make-up on and was sporting a hairstyle Ken Dodd would have been satisfied with. She was about as appealing as a turkey sandwich on Boxing Day evening. Carl however was proudly clutching her hand as if he was about to announce the winner of a beauty pageant.

Sara was dressed in a tight-fitting, light blue trouser suit. Her hair was in a taut, long ponytail which she knew always did it for him. She was laughing at something Aiden was saying, or maybe she was just amused by his ill-fitting brown suit which looked as though it had a secret double life masquerading as his pyjamas, so creased was it. In comparison he thought he looked pretty good, catching a clear view of himself in a nearby window. One of the few bonuses of working in an office; you have a lot of suits. He kept himself trim by jogging and used the tightness of his trousers as motivation to keep the weight off.

They walked into the place and Will spoke to an old lady who seemed to be there to give guests directions. There were people everywhere, all in smart dress, laughing and joking and taking photographs. The lady directed them to a room and held the door open so they filed in. This room had just five people in it. Darren and Dean both dressed to the nines, two large foreign looking shaven headed men in their mid-twenties and a tall achingly beautiful girl in a white dress.

Will found it hard to pull his eyes away from the girl. She had an olive complexion, high cheek bones, hair swept up in a bun and everything about her screamed 'model'. Her dress was white and simple, but clearly accentuated her slim lines and the bump that sat high on her stomach. This dress indicated she was pregnant and wanted everyone to know. As Will processed that face, Darren came into his line of sight.

'I know, she is amazing,' he said.

Will shook his hand, until Darren dropped it and hugged him. It was good to see him. He looked well too.

His features seemed to have softened slightly. Whereas before his gaze sometimes felt like it could carve through you like being swept over by a diamond laser his smiling face had a happy twinkle to it. He hugged everyone in turn then beckoned the three foreigners over.

The girl glided over and stood proudly in front of them. No demurring bride was this one.

'This is Kristina, from Pristina,' Darren said with obvious affection, a laugh and even a little bit of awe. 'These are her brothers Agon and Alban. Pristina is the capital of Kosovo. This is Carl, Aiden, Sara, Deidre and Will. Everyone who is important to me is now here.'

'Who are that lot out there?' Deidre asked.

'God knows, previous wedding maybe.' Darren looked over her shoulder and shrugged. They all stood there for a few seconds, in two rows, two banks of five. Will noticed these three strangers had hard eyes. Maybe it was normal where they came from, but the extremely light blue eyes seemed out of kilter with their tanned skin and they all looked like they had lived tough lives. Just as Will started to think it was beginning to resemble a scene before a shooting a man came in.

'OK, the time is here, let's get you youngsters married,' he declared.

They naturally went to the seats on the side they knew. Darren and Kristina stood at the front. Dean stood to one side of Darren, the best man puzzle resolved. Will considered this briefly and wondered if he or one of the others should feel put out. They had known Darren for a long time and maybe that role was better suited for one of them. He then realised he hardly knew Darren at all now. He was hardly ever back in town and his letters and phone calls were perfunctory at best. As for being best man, Will concluded he didn't care about that either.

Will had never been to a registry office do before and found it unsettling. It was like getting married in a meeting room in a hotel. There was no music and it all seemed rather serious. Maybe that was the point. The registrar put in some personal touches about fresh starts but it was clear he had only met the pair of them very recently. They all applauded at the appropriate stages, with particularly noisy thunderclaps coming from the two henchmen types.

★ ★ ★

Soon it was all over and they found themselves walking through some French windows into an area with a kind of stone love seat. The happy couple sat on it and gazed into each other's eyes. One of the brothers, Will would never know which was which, whisked a disposable camera out and began taking photographs.

'Get your camera out Will,' Sara whispered in his ear.

'Why, I thought you didn't like cheese?' he joked.

She shot him a dirty look. Will suddenly could picture his camera perched proudly on Aiden's kitchen worktop and grimaced.

'Oh no, please tell me you didn't. You useless, selfish, twat. One thing he asks you to do and you can't be bothered to take responsibility for that,' Sara spat at him.

She gave him a last angry look, then got her own camera out and moved away. That was a little vitriolic he thought all things considered, but alarm bells began to ring. He had been concerned that this event would highlight his own relationship's status quo and it now looked like that was going to happen.

It was definitely for the best that he didn't tell her today about coming back home and moving in with Aiden. It would make as much sense as lighting the fuse on a stick of dynamite and placing it in his underpants. He then had a dawning thought. Sara had bought her first house a few months back; a three bed sensible place at the top of her budget. A family home he now realised. He also now remembered snatches of drunken conversations about the future and children and the dreaded 'M' word. As they took pictures of the bride and her brothers he found today's events hadn't helped to change his mind about this heavy commitment. He didn't want any part of it.

It seemed like a huge step to him. Just one girl for the rest of your life, everything joined in the middle, until you separated and she got it all. Someone having the right to tell you what to do. It didn't sound very appealing at all. Not for the first time in his life did he realise he might be missing something. Surely if you wanted to get married you would be dead keen and he certainly was not that. Maybe he was with the wrong girl he ruefully admitted. He did love her, in his own shallow way. She was bright, funny, good in bed, ambitious, sensible and faithful. Six adjectives he suspected would not be used to describe his good self very often. It all seemed so serious this marriage lark. He considered whether he would be more excited about doing it if they eloped and went to Paris, or a beach without all this guff, but that held no appeal either.

The issue was he could feel her wanting to move onto the next stage and someone else's wedding was going to bring that topic to the surface like a fart in a bath. As he was dragged over by a laughing Carl to take a group shot after the registrar offered to take some he decided all he needed now was for the bride to throw her bouquet and Sara to catch it before looking at him and bursting into tears. If he didn't take the next step he was going to lose her, and he was pretty sure he didn't want that either.

After another round of kissing, hugging and congratulating which Will struggled to join in with any enthusiasm, Darren cleared his throat.

'OK guys, we will meet you at The Swan Hotel. Dinner and drinks on me!'

'You can show me the way in my car,' Dean said over his shoulder. 'The others will be in Darren's car and he always tries to lose me when I follow him.'

'Sure,' Will nodded. He then caught a glance off Sara and could almost hear the 'Kerching' as his negative balance went up a notch to a new high.

⋆ ⋆ ⋆

Will was itching with questions and Dean was cool, so he could ask stuff without worrying about offending anyone. He climbed into Dean's jeep, pleased the SRI was nowhere to be seen and they followed in convoy with Sara behind.

Let's get to it Will thought as they were only ten minutes from the hotel.

'So Dean, how the hell did all this happen?'

'Well,' he paused. He had a distant look on his face. 'This goes no further. It's a nice story in a terrible war torn kind of way, but a tough one to tell. We were the peacekeeping force in Kosovo, us and a load of other EU nations. Man, you would not believe the shit we have seen.' As they stopped at some traffic lights Dean lit a cigarette, his hand shaking. 'It seems crazy that people would do that to each other. You kind of expect it in Asia or Africa, but it all seemed the more shocking as it was a fairly normal place you know, brick houses and apartment blocks. Dead bodies in suits freak me out.'

'We were the liberating force in Pristina. The Serbs retreated as we got there but they had been there a while and had time to commit some awful crimes. I hope I never see so many dead bodies again in all my life. Executed, like cattle. We broke into a house as we could hear a terrible bawling. Darren and I went in, it went eerily quiet except for this gentle sobbing. Chilling shit man. When we got in there, Kristina was crying on the sofa.' He stopped as if to wonder whether to continue, then taking a deep breath, he did so.

'I don't know what had been done to her, but there was a lot of blood and she was only half clothed. When she saw us, she ran into Darren's arms and clung to him like a limpet. She then looked in his eyes. She ordered him, 'They are still here. Upstairs. Kill them'.

We went upstairs, Darren took point. I've never been so scared. There it felt like every civilian was issued an AK47 on their first day at school so you knew you could be shot around any corner. House clearances are not for the timid.'

Will looked over at him. He had trickles of sweat running down the side of his head despite the car being freezing.

'I kicked the door in and Darren went in with his pistol raised. There were two men cowering in the corner. Boys really, eighteen or so. They had camo trousers and boots on, but T shirts. Fucking Man Utd T-shirts. If they had guns I never saw them.

'One tried to climb out the window, so Darren shot him in the back. He then pulled him into the middle of the room and whilst looking at the other one, pumped two rounds straight into this kid's groin. The other one, well, scared doesn't even begin to describe his features. Appalling thing, seeing a grown man piss themselves through fear.

'They deserved it Will, fucking rapists. My sister was raped, she's still fucked up now. Anyway, Darren put his gun away, and drew out a knife. Not a huge one, but it must have been razor sharp. The boy never moved.' Dean sniffed and blinked his eyes trying to clear the tears.

'Darren held his throat, pinned him to the wall, and ran the blade along his stomach, you know, horizontally.' Dean took a deep breath and then spat the rest out as though he had to get it out now or he would never be free of these memories. 'He punched him in the stomach and pulled his intestines out. They just hung over his belt like a red octopus bulging out of its hole.'

'Darren just left him standing there. He came up to me and gave me his pistol. I watched him walk back out; Kristina was at the door, nodding. She took his bloody hand and guided him down the stairs. I couldn't believe what I'd seen. This kid was alive and started to walk toward me, like the god damn living dead.' He shook his head. 'All I could think was this guy could talk, so I shot him in the head. When I got downstairs Kristina was washing Darren's hands in the sink.'

They pulled up in the car park at the back of the upmarket hotel. Dean rested his head on the steering wheel. Will let out a long gasp, he doubted he had taken any breaths since he had left the register office. Completely and utterly stunned he tried to open the door, but felt like he barely had the energy to pull the lever. Dean suddenly reached over and grabbed his hand.

'You cannot tell anyone Will, not a soul.' He looked Will in the eyes. 'I'm sorry, I had to tell someone. We did right Will, didn't we?' he whispered.

What do you say to that? Will patted him on the leg, and said the first thing that came into his reeling mind. 'It was war Dean.'

24

H e got out of the car and walked on what felt like stilts to the small side bar in the hotel and mumbling with a mouth full of glue, ordered a double whisky. He downed it in one and felt a hard slap on his back. He spun around and found Darren grinning at him.

'Wrong bar buddy, we got a private room. We just wanted a small intimate dinner. Then we all go out and do some damage! Come on.' He put his arm around Will and guided him out the room. Will had a last look back, expecting to find his soul suspended on the ceiling by its fingertips, refusing to be dragged into this madness.

He followed Darren into the room and found it was all set up for a small private wedding. There was one big table, with two larger chairs at the head of it and eight more seats around the sides. The others were all seated, so Will slumped into the one free space between Sara and Aiden. Dean was sitting opposite him and he could feel his eyes on him. To his great relief he found a full glass of chilled white wine in front of him. He still felt like he was going to go off pop, so he picked it up and stood up.

'The bride and groom,' he loudly declared.

Everyone stood up and followed suit, Will noting he wasn't the only one downing his glass in one. The two brothers appeared to have finished a bottle of wine between them already and they couldn't have been in the room more than five minutes. Will dropped into his seat with the finesse of a sack of potatoes falling off a lorry. Sara reached over and touched his cheek.

'Are you ok? You look like you have seen a ghost.'

Will considered this and thought more likely a monster. He smiled at her though as he replied.

'Ah, you know how weddings make me nervous.'

Darren saved anymore grilling by rising to his feet and chinked his glass with his spoon. They all quietened down.

'I love a good speech,' he began. 'But I'll do my best to keep it short.' They all laughed. 'Kristina here today, has made me the happiest man in the world. The moment we set eyes on each other, you took my breath away.' The girl's all 'ahh'd'. Will found his gaze locked to Dean's, both grim. He wasn't the only person to have had his breath taken away that day. He looked up to the happy couple and found Kristina staring at him, like a hawk eyeing up a mouse. He forced a grin onto his face and prayed for this nightmare to be over soon.

'And we are having a baby. I will protect this boy with all my strength and power.'

Will kept his grin on his face, knowing he probably looked like a stroke victim, but went along with the cheers. He was really thinking that was a fairly scary choice of words. He also had a nasty thought as to the father of the child. He didn't know the dates and maybe it was Darren's, but it was perfectly possible that Darren had disembowelled 'Dad'.

★ ★ ★

As it turned out, Will enjoyed the dinner. Two bottles of wine and that whisky had perked him up no end, as well as an excellent meal. Will surmised that he must be a bloody cold fish to be able to forgive and forget about something like that so quickly, which should have seen him galloping straight to the authorities. He considered that for a minute and had known it was never an option. Loyalty to Darren and Dean maybe, an element of they had it coming perhaps, or more likely he just didn't want to think about it again. As that sank in he tried to match the violence to the boy he knew at school. As the pieces slotted into place in his mind, he now wondered why he had been so astounded.

As the waitress cleared the desserts away, Darren announced that it was time for the boys to go to the cigar room. This brought a chorus of 'Hurrahs' from all the men present, whom Will noticed to a man were looking more and more dishevelled and rosy cheeked. Even Sara and Deidre were loud and energised. Only Kristina remained immaculate at the head of the table, if she had been drinking he hadn't noticed. He guessed not, in her state.

The men followed Darren into a small cosy room with six high backed comfy chairs surrounding a big blazing open fire. Large portraits, heavy curtains and thick carpet added to the sense of warmth and refinement. They all found a seat and lit up the cigars that a clearly worse for wear Dean had passed around. It was a nice touch from Darren, Will concluded and the earlier shocking news faded even further into the background.

'So who is next?' Darren queried with a raised eyebrow.

'Will,' Carl shouted and burst into a fit of giggles. Someone else had clearly been partaking of the liquid refreshments. The others all laughed at Will's expense as Carl continued.

'Actually, I have something to ask you lot. Some advice is needed here. I've been thinking about it for a while, ummm and well, I can't decide, Ow!' Darren had thrown a coaster at Carl and hit him on the knee.

'Spit it out you joey.'

Carl took a deep breath.

'I might ask Deidre to marry me.'

Will groaned out loud and had a coaster fly past his ear for his trouble, considerably faster than the one that had hit Carl.

'Go for it Carl mate,' Darren said. 'I feel complete.' Will groaned again, even louder after retreating behind his chair.

Darren ignored him and gave Carl a serious look.

'What's the worst that could happen?' he said.

Will could not resist replying, 'She might say yes?' He got hit on the side of a head with another coaster from an impossible angle immediately after and saw Aiden grinning at him on his left.

'Ignore him Carl,' Aiden laughed. 'Will doesn't care about anything enough to commit. He is detached from reality. I say go for it too.' Darren cheered.

'Wait, wait, wait,' Will said. 'We haven't asked our new friends here.' He pointed to the brothers, who had produced a bottle of brandy from somewhere and were pouring it into their coffees like they were about to go over the top at the Somme. Will could only remember one of their names and shouted it out.

'Heh Algan.' So distracted were they in their pursuit of drunkenness that he had to get out of his seat and tap one of them on the shoulder

'Algan, what do you think of Carl marrying Deidre?' The one he thought was Algan directed a sharp look at him. He stood up, causing a brief flutter in Will's bowels.

'It's Agon or Alban.' He peered closely at Will, and then roared with laughter. 'Ah very funny, you joke yes, excellent joke. Which is the one you call Deidre?'

'She is the one with the crazy hair,' Will explained.

'Ah,' Agon or Alban said. He looked over at Carl and then roared with mirth, 'Ah, the one like the ......' He then spoke to his brother in heavily accented dialect, before his brother said one word.

'Clown.'

'Yes, that's it, the one like the clown. This very bad idea, unless you run circus.'

He bellowed with amusement again, looking at Will who had a massive grin on his face. 'Ah,' he shouted. 'You make joke again.' Gesturing to Aiden he roared, 'Better you marry the fucking elephant.'

Will put his hand on Aiden's shoulder and whispered, 'I do.' To be fair to Carl he laughed along with the rest, but when they had finished wiping tears from their cheeks, he stuck his chin out.

'I love her, I don't even know why, just that I do.'

'Do it,' Aiden said. He and Darren started chanting the words. Will raised his palms and they quietened down. He tried to look serious as he stared directly at Carl.

'Ok fair enough, ask then. Even if it is a bit cliché, at someone else's wedding.' More jeers from Darren and Aiden.

'My point is,' as he scrabbled around in his brain for what that might have been. He blurted it out when it came back to him and realised that he was drunk as a lord.

'What if she does say no? Things won't go back to how they were. There will be a huge elephant in the room every time you meet.' This brought a big cheer from the raucous Kosovan contingent. 'You will both see you want different things and you have no future.'

The last comment tailed off and sounded very final. Carl and Aiden's faces dropped, but Darren suddenly leapt out of his seat and rugby tackled Will to the ground.

'Bah humbug, scrooge motherfucker,' he yelled. 'Enough of this, lets join the ladies, I want to dance with my wife.' Will got to his feet, wiping ash and what looked like a pat of butter off his sleeve. He looked at his watch; Five thirty p.m. It was going to be a long night.

25

They eventually settled in a big, popular, Irish bar nearby called O'Neill's. It was quiet when they arrived and they settled into a booth in the corner. It reminded him of the Anne Boleyn. Nothing like a wedding to make you nostalgic Will mused. It was one of those places that catered for food in the daytime and eventually transformed itself into a late bar with a decent band and a dance floor. Darren sneaked a word and what looked like a few quid to the warming up musicians.

The lead singer soon did a remarkably good rendition of Robbie William's 'She's The One', which was apparently their song. Darren and Kristina did a slow dance, both clearly infatuated with each other and he felt Sara's hand hold his under the table.

As the night went on he felt like he was the constant at the table as more drinks were bought and people came to chat with him. He wondered if that was how it felt to be in a wheelchair as he seemed to have lost control of his legs. Darren and his new wife came and sat with him and Will probed their future.

'So what's the plan, lovebirds?

'Kristina is going back to Kosovo,' Darren said. 'She can't stay here for long on her visa. I, my friend, am joining the SAS. Being in the midst of all that lunacy has made me really want to get involved, to test myself, push myself to the limits. The Paras seem to be more involved in peacekeeping nowadays, if it's not other nations, it's our own squaddies. I've got more to offer. I've passed the tests and I'm off to Sierra Leone in a few weeks. All hush hush you understand.' The information rolled and jarred around Will's addled mind like a roulette ball that wouldn't land.

Darren left to go to the bar, feigning mock horror at Will's insistence that he had drunk enough. Kristina took his hands in hers. Up close her beauty was more striking, but the strength in her eyes made Will uncomfortable and he was glad all of a sudden for a girlfriend who was so easy-going.

'Your friend, he is a good man. A great man. Did anyone tell you how we met?'

Will tried to hide the look of dismay that animated his face in an instant. There was no way he wanted to hear that fairy-tale again.

Her laugh softened her features and for a while she looked like the young girl she was, before the soldiers came and destroyed her life.

'Don't worry, I will keep it short.' She took a sip of the pint of lager that Darren had plonked down for Will with a winning smile, and grimaced. 'Your beer tastes unusual.'

She spoke softly in a low voice. Her English was much better than her brother's, softly accented and lovely to hear.

'They had been in our town for many months, the Serbians. I think they knew the English were coming. It was what we all prayed for. The English and Tony Blair will save us we whispered to each other. The other nations are without a spine. The Serbs must have known that and it was like the fall of Rome. They killed my parents. I found them at their house, sitting next to each other on the sofa. Full of holes. Nothing had been taken, they didn't have anything to be taken. My sister disappeared and we are still to find her. My brothers were away fighting, or they, along with every other man their age, would have been rounded up and executed.

'So many people, children too, just shot for nothing. The first moment we knew we were safe was when your Parachute regiment, in their maroon berets, walked up our streets. When I saw Darren's face, I knew he would help.

'He did help,' she said and squeezed his hand hard. 'He did what needed to be done. Now I will go back and re-build our country, with my son. I want to call him Tonibler, in honour, with the Albanian spelling. Did you know that many hundreds of children have been named after him? They said that if the English think you are in the right, they will not let you down.

'I think I will have to just call him Toni though. When I told Darren my favourite name, he told me to "Jog on". I still don't completely understand that saying, but it makes me laugh for some reason.'

Darren came back. 'One last dance,' he said and pulled Kristina up out of her seat. The band was now doing a bad cover of Sixpence None The Richer's "Kiss Me". Kristina stopped suddenly and leaned back into Will playfully ruffling his hair.

'You should give that girl what she wants, or maybe it's time for you to jog on.'

And then she was gone.

Will put a hand to the crown of his head and sobered up quickly. His head was sweaty and a bit greasy but he could definitely feel a thinner patch there where she had touched him. Excellent, he thought. I'm going bald, more brilliant news.

Carl slid into the seat where Kristina had been, looking as happy as Will felt.

'I asked her to marry me,' he exhaled. Will suspected someone else's night had taken a tragic turn for the worse too.

'You were right Will. Don't say I told you so. She said no. Just like that. She could have at least said she'll think about it, and then told me no later.'

'Maybe she'll change her mind.'

'Unlikely, she's decided to go to Australia for a year. Find herself, travel and have new experiences.'

'Ah, general euphemisms for shagging around. Quite possibly with some bronzed lifeguards in budgie smugglers. Very unpleasant to hear.'

'Thanks for that Will.'

'You should thank them. It will be their pleasure to do Deidre many times, probably in the ass.'

'Fuck off Will.'

'Pleasure.'

'Beer?'

'No thank you.'

Carl took a huge breath and stated, 'You are having one anyway, cos we're going to get wasted,' and he staggered and weaved his way through the crowd.

Will wondered how wasted it was possible to be and still be awake. To his great joy it seemed the night though was finally drawing to a close. Darren, Dean, Kristina, Aiden, Agon and Alban came over, all slick skinned from dancing on the heaving floor.

'Dean's offered to walk Kristina back to the hotel. She is going to freshen up, for a night of indescribable pleasure at the hands of yours truly.' He wiggled his fingers at Will, like Wallace, taunting Gromit. Will watched Kristina supporting Dean as they left the building. 'I'm going to stay with my best friend for one more beer, we are off first thing tomorrow and I won't be back for a while.'

Will considered the phrase 'best friend' and then it was too late as his shout to Darren's disappearing back of 'Carl's getting me one' barely made it to the end of his table.

'Deidre's going to the toilet and then home,' Sara said as she came to sit next to him. 'I said I would go with her unless you particularly want me to stay.'

Will considered the fact that even though Deidre had summarily dismissed Carl, she would probably still want to talk it to death.

'No worries, I'll see you tomorrow.'

Carl plonked another pint next to Will's virtually untouched one and forlornly wandered off after Deidre who was scuttling away to the toilet. Then Darren came back and put another one next to it. Sara looked at him in a disgusted manner.

'Is this what you want Will?'

Will looked at the table, missing the loaded question, and laughed, 'I don't mind this,' he shrugged. He noticed a disturbance behind Sara and saw Darren on the dance floor squaring up to a wide, almost neckless bouncer. Darren's back was to him but he could see from the set of his shoulders he was ready to go. The bouncer's face was purple and angry, his expression determined. He was shorter than Darren but almost comically muscled. Three more bouncers arrived behind him, big men, as the two Kosovan's came and took their place next to Darren. Even though they were not outnumbered, the other bouncers looked decidedly nervous, their eyes fixed on Darren, despite the hulking presences of his new brothers-in-law.

The space around them rapidly cleared with people shuffling backwards fast, but with interested eyes. Will recognised two of the bouncers from school; Rudd and Kostas. No wonder they looked like they didn't want to be there. Aiden suddenly materialised on the scene behind Darren and the thickset bouncer had to strain his head to look up at him, his neck not made for vertical movements. As the first look of doubt flashed over the stocky man's face Darren's fist flashed out and all hell broke loose.

Aiden was right, he did feel detached from life. His friends were fighting now and he couldn't be bothered to get involved. Stupid really, on your wedding day. Will got pulled back from his role of disinterested observer of the fracas by an angry request.

'Are you even listening to me? When are we getting married Will, when are you moving in?'

He was only half concentrating and smirked when Rudd's head ended up wedged into what must have been a poorly constructed chair. The fight would have been over quickly if the police hadn't arrived. Now it was anyone's guess what was going on. He was distracted by the pandemonium behind him as he casually replied.

'I don't know Sara, I would have thought I would have to be really excited to want to do one of those things.'

As soon as it came out of his mouth he realised he had said what was on his mind out loud and his head snapped back to look at Sara's face. She didn't say anything, simply stood. Her face was expressionless as she picked up one of his drinks.

Strange thing, to have a pint poured over you. Quite shocking. She took her time too, like pouring a pint of Guinness. She then did the same with the other two pints, each one progressively colder due to its later time out of the barrel. Blinking beer out of his vision, he gasped with surprise. She gave him one last filthy look, but now with tears in her eyes.

'Goodbye Will,' she sobbed. And that, as they say, was that.

26

25ᵗʰ May 2002

'North Acton, this is North Acton.' Aiden and Will stepped off the train into sunshine. It was a little past five in the evening and it had been and still was, a glorious day. The promise of an excellent summer hung in the air and they were both in great moods.

'Where is that numpty?' Aiden laughed.

Will looked up the empty platform as the tube rattled off. They were the only two to get off and the only other person there was a dishevelled man in his forties who looked like he had fallen asleep on a bench. The way he was perched at an angle seemed to defy the laws of gravity, although judging by the state of his clothing he may well have set in that position.

'London baby!' Aiden again laughed.

'West London,' Will corrected. As they walked past the snoring figure Will stopped.

'Now Aiden, what has this fine fellow been up to?'

'He's had early beers.'

'And now what wasteful incident has occurred?'

'He's peaked too soon.'

'Correct.' Aiden had been chomping at the bit all afternoon but Will had managed to restrict him to a couple of beers at Kings Cross so they weren't partied out by eight p.m. He suspected it was more for himself than for Aiden. He was nearly thirty years old now and wasn't quite the man he used to be. He remembered being in the Anne Boleyn when he was seventeen and some guy at the bar telling him he was thirty. He recalled thinking thirty was absolutely fucking ancient and why the hell wasn't this man home with his family? That man from all those years ago probably had as much interest in a family as he did now. Not that he himself felt ancient, he just didn't quite have the energy he used to and he suspected tonight would call upon all of his reserves.

The station was at the bottom of a sloping path and he followed Aiden's long stride up it. Living with Will had seen a resurgence in the old content Aiden. He seemed happier now than at any time since that terrible accident. With Will's encouragement he had got a job as a postman and he absolutely loved it. They had opted not to mention the police caution for affray that he received for the brawl after the wedding and there had been no comeback. Typically Darren had somehow escaped from the melee and got away scot-free. They loved him at the Post Office too. He was reliable, conscientious and diligent. Even the money was ok.

All the walking had trimmed Aiden's physique up so he looked quite frankly a magnificent sight in a tight shirt. He had girls throwing themselves at him, oddly enough nearly all small ones. To Will's mind Aiden never took up enough of the opportunities, but he said he was always worried about squashing them.

Will, sadly, was envious. Obviously a little bit about the girls but more Aiden's enjoyment of his new vocation. He had looked for work, for something different, but the money was always shit. So he now worked as a manager in a call centre for yet again, another insurance company. Each day he went in he could feel his spirit shrivel that little bit more. He felt like a conker, having come out shiny, new and beautiful, but then had been left on the side. Now he was wrinkling and drying out, getting harder and stiffer.

Still, call centres were good places for meeting young impressionable birds. He was no nearer thinking about settling down than he had been at any point. His mum kept saying you'll meet the right girl, a soul mate and then you will know. Well that was blatantly romantic bullshit. His arsehole brother had shelled out three kids now, each one presented to Uncle Will as a trophy to magnify his own empty existence.

He suspected settling down was a mind-set. You got to a point where you started to feel old and then any old soul mate would do. Then you climbed on the treadmill of life, had children which turned out to be ruinously expensive little things who sucked the essence out of your sex life. Before you realised it, you hadn't had any for a year and it was too late. Gone forever. You got divorced, lost the house you had been doing two jobs to pay for and ended up like matey boy on the bench, lashed at tea time and snoozing in public. He stole a look back. Gravity had won and the poor bloke had fallen off. He was now lying on his side, still asleep, legs still crossed.

When they got to the top of the path it felt like they had come out into an industrial area. There was a huge Carphone Warehouse building stretching as far as the eye could see, but there, waving as he walked out of a depressing-looking pub over the road, was Carl. They shook Carl's hand, easy smiles all round. He came back home regularly, claiming he was lonely in London, so they saw a lot of each other.

'I know, I know,' Carl started. 'It's not what you expected, but I live ten minutes' walk from here. Darren is waiting at the flat. You'll love it.'

Whilst Carl's social and love life were generally mediocre at best, his professional one was blooming. He had escaped Andersens before it went bust and was heading for partner at another huge accountancy firm. Will almost didn't want to hear, but felt he should give his friend his moment in the sun.

'So how's the job going?'

'Job is good, well, it's dull and a bit shit really, but I got the promotion. They gave it to me in the end. You are now looking at the UK VAT Manager for Delaine and Todd.'

'So what does that mean?' Aiden asked.

'One hundred and fifty thousand a year.' Carl tried not to look smug, but failed miserably.

'I feel sick,' Will muttered.

Aiden slapped Carl on the back and cheered, 'Cool, beers on you wee boy!'

★ ★ ★

As they got to Acton high street, Will found he had been trying to work out how much that would mean taking home a month and found himself at the horrifying figure of around nine grand a month. His own plan had been to save around that figure up, go travelling to Asia and have a year's working visa in Australia. He had reached the magic amount now but it had taken him four years to get there. Now he was getting on a bit and his mind was strangled with indecision and inertia whenever he thought about it. Spend it on what to all intents and purposes would be a beer crawl around Vietnam, or do the sensible thing and use it as a deposit for a house.

The infuriating thing was the fact he had blown his ten grand redundancy money more or less on beer crawls around Peterborough. A couple of insanely expensive holidays to Ibiza and Majorca had done for the rest, along with his 'free' Renault Clio which seemed to consume money like he was throwing it into a log burner. He reckoned it would have been cheaper if he had just got a taxi to work each day.

Carl opened a grimy looking door between two shops on a busy main road and they walked up some mucky looking steps to another dirty looking entrance. As Carl fumbled with his keys, Will imagined him opening the door on to a scene from 'Trainspotting'. Broken tables, rubbish everywhere, filthy furniture and filthier junkies slumped dying on the ripped lino.

'Wow,' Will gasped as he stepped in. He had walked into a bachelor's heaven. It was a massive open plan apartment stretching from one end of the shops to the other. The floor was a continuous sea of hardwood with an expensive looking modern kitchen at one end. The other end had three doors which he suspected would lead to bedrooms. In the middle of the room was a huge television that had been mounted on the wall. Everything quietly said elegant and expensive. A long classic looking sofa and two of the biggest armchairs Will had ever seen looked at the television.

On one of these armchairs the back of Darren's head could be seen as he watched the screen. He spun his chair slowly around like Blofeld in Dr No, but instead of the cat he was stroking a bottle of Jack Daniels. With a stony expression he looked from face to face.

'Well, well, well. Look what the Carl dragged in.'

'I bet you have been practising that shit since Carl left,' Will laughed.

Aiden looked as gobsmacked as Will. He went and sat on the other big armchair and put his feet on an amazing looking coffee table and he also simply uttered, 'Wow.'

'Get your fucking clodhoppers off that table you heathen, that's a Vitra Noguchi. Cost me fifteen hundred quid.' Carl rushed over and tried to lift Aiden's legs up.

It could have been Tutankhamen's sarcophagus for all that meant to Aiden, but he removed his feet regardless. Will walked into the immaculate kitchen and opened the fridge door. There was a lot of booze in there and not much else. He raised an eyebrow at Carl and opened the oven door. As he suspected the oven was unused.

'Carl, either you have the best cleaner in town or you must eat out a lot.'

'I do have a cleaner actually,' he replied.

'Is she not allowed to clean doors?' Aiden's voice echoed around the high ceilings as though they were in a church.

'I'm not sure what she does to be honest. She's here for two hours, I give her twenty quid and she leaves.'

'You would need to pay me more than twenty quid to peel your sticky Y fronts off the floor,' Darren said.

'Very funny,' Carl replied. 'I hide them before she arrives or I would never be able to look her in the eye.'

'What's for dinner?' Will asked. He sat down at the large glass dining table that had been set for eight and picked up a knife and fork. 'I could eat something the size of Aiden, lightly fried, with a few thick cut chips on the side and a selection of seasonal vegetables.'

Carl took a bottle of champagne from the fridge and poured some into the flute next to Will's hemp placemat.

'Apologies sir, but I'm afraid we are all out of sautéed elephant. Popular dish, but we struggle to get the stock. If sir would like to peruse the menu I'm sure he will find something equally satisfying but maybe not as stupid, although we are getting good reviews for our Mule Mariniere.'

Carl chuckled as he slipped what appeared to be Hungry Carlo's pizza menu in front of him. Will looked at Carl and grinned. He had seen so much of him lately, that he hadn't realised he had changed. His complexion was finally free of acne and despite what must be a terrible diet he looked healthy and fit. Still painfully thin, but there appeared to be some muscle there too. His clothes too, were as perfect and understated as the flat.

'Excellente, Monsieur, with this culinary treat you are really spoiling us.' Will was about to throw the menu down when he saw a picture of one of the pizzas. 'Actually they look alright. Meat feast for me mate.'

'Me too,' Aiden shouted.

'Me three,' Carl added. 'Well we are a classy bunch. Not tempted by the range of artichoke options I see. What about you Darren?'

'I'm alright mate, not hungry.'

Will wandered over to him sipping his champagne. It wasn't like Darren to refuse a pizza. He gingerly sat on the sofa which looked as comfy as a park roundabout, but was surprisingly accommodating. Darren was staring back at him. He had aged Will thought. Again they had not heard from Darren for years. They didn't even know where he was living, whether the baby was called Toni or not, or even have a telephone number for him. He had just got in touch mid-week via Carl and arranged to meet. Cloak and dagger as usual Will thought as he noticed Darren's eyes had returned to their calculating state and it reminded him of the stare of his wife Kristina.

'So how is married life treating you Darren?' Will asked Darren who paused before he replied.

'I don't want to talk about any of that shit. I'm here to forget about all that. I've got a pass for a week and I just want to get fucked and live life.'

Will and Aiden exchanged a glance.

'Fair enough mate. You sure you don't want to experience Hungry Carlo's Lebanese fayre. It says here his kitchen has virtually no rats and if you find more than three cockroaches on your pizza, your next pizza is half price. You can't say fairer than that.' Will laughed trying to lift the dark mood that was hanging around Darren.

'I said I'm not hungry,' Darren growled. He took a deep breath. 'Sorry. I'm tightly wound. I've just got a week and then I'm back to Afghanistan.' He looked up with a haunted expression that Will thought he would never see him display. 'Crazy shit out there. Sneaky fucking war. It's all roadside IEDs, amputations, snipers and suicide bombers. Goddamn towel-heads. I just want a straight fight, not die burning in a fucking armoured truck, or worse,' he looked at Will, 'And end up messed up like my old man.'

'So tonight, we forget, and we enjoy.' With that comment, he presented the biggest bag of cocaine Will had ever seen.

Will looked over at Aiden for support, ready to give it a miss. They had generally steered clear of any class As of late. It wasn't that Will didn't enjoy it, but it had started to take its toll and after doing some he didn't feel normal until about Wednesday of the following week. So combine that with its ruinous price and it was not to be done lightly. Waking up on Sunday with that broken feeling was bad enough but at least you could drink the blues away in the pub. Monday at work however was a different story entirely. He did not miss cowering in his seat, sweat dripping down his body under his shirt, praying that no-one would talk to him and completely paranoid that everyone could see him for the ne'er do well that he was.

Unfortunately for Will, Aiden looked like all his ships had come in at once and he had already pulled a credit card out ready for chopping. Darren rolled a couple of chunky rocks over to Aiden and taking a lock knife out of his pocket began to prepare his own. Watching the boys go about their business all of a sudden felt surreal for Will. He could hear Carl on his mobile in the kitchen ordering the pizza he now knew would never be eaten.

He thought back to those first days of school and wondered what twists of fate had led them to be sitting here snorting coke off the world's most expensive coffee table. Said table now had four long lines expertly prepared, sitting proudly in front of Darren like so many poodle legs.

'Bloody hell Darren, you trying to kill us,' Will said, shaking his head. 'Carl, I hope your luxury accommodation came with his and hers defibrillators.'

Carl came over and sat next to Will on the sofa and stared at the four innocuous looking humps.

'One each eh?'

That surprised Will and he turned to look at Carl. When it had come to drugs he had always drawn the line at marijuana. Darren had often got four of a variety of narcotics, but his friend had never weakened.

'Go for it Carl, everyone should try it once,' Darren encouraged. 'You could do with a bit of coke confidence when it comes to chatting to birds.'

If Carl had been teetering on the edge of making a choice, then that statement pushed him over.

'Ok,' he said. 'What do I do?'

Darren smiled, a kind of weird smile, which reminded Will of Nick O'Teen. That thought led him on to thinking of the Grange Hill song, 'Just Say No.'

'Right, grab yourself a note, any one will do, my personal preference is a twenty. On your salary, you will probably have a big stack of them in your toilet for wiping your Aris with.' Darren looked around as he said that, pleased with his little joke. 'Besides you may find the smaller notes fold in on themselves, leading you to a less than perfect yeyo experience.

Roll your twenty up, not too tight, and place in your favoured nostrillo, whilst blocking the other with your finger.'

'Then bend your heed to your product, on your overpriced Kendo Nagasaki,' Aiden said. 'And snort. Wham, bam, thank you Afghan.'

'Right,' Carl said, drawing a thick wad of notes out of his back pocket. Passing them each a crisp twenty with a smile, he suggested, 'Let's all do it at the same time.'

'What, are we twelve?' Will commented, thinking as he said it that it wouldn't be too far from the truth.

Needless to say they all perched on the end of their seats, rolled up notes raised in preparation. Will looked down at his chubby line, guessing that there must have been at least ten quid's worth in that one bit. He felt a familiar grumbling in his stomach. For some reason whenever he was about to do coke he felt like having a shit.

'Um Carl, if you haven't done any before I don't suggest you do all of that in one go, do a quarter or something.'

'Bullshit,' Darren laughed, 'It's all in…'

'Registers a win,' Aiden finished. Carl cocked his head at Will as if to say 'C'est la vie'. Will put his free hand on his forehead for a second, looked around the table at them all, and took a deep breath.

'Fuck it,' he said and the four of them hoovered it up in one go.

'Jesus fucking H Christ,' Will roared as he shot out of his seat. His nose was burning like someone had stuck a lit cigar in it. Aiden and Carl were milliseconds behind him. Darren however was just sitting there with a smug look on his face.

'That shit is ninety percent pure my friends, also known as rocket fuel.'

Will felt a huge surge of energy rush through his body. Suddenly he was covered in goose bumps and it felt like his skin had shrunk by twenty percent. He felt a reassuring tickle run down his throat, confirmation that this indeed was what all the fuss was about. His bowel clenched and he scuttled to what he hoped was the toilet door and opened it to something perfect. He sat on the comfy toilet seat, admiring the wall to wall tiling and funky heated towel rail and expelled the contents of his guts like cement pouring out of a lorry. He found himself laughing, loudly.

He practically skipped back into the lounge and found Darren and Aiden giggling like school children. The source of their amusement was Carl who was pacing back and forth like a demented scientist, uttering 'Oh my God, oh my God.' He then flumped down on the sofa, sweat pouring down his face.

'I don't think I can uncross my eyes,' he whispered. Will went to the kitchen, found the glasses and poured a big one full of water. Handing it to Carl he rubbed him on the back.

'Drink that you will be fine in a few minutes. You should know better than to trust Tweedledum and Tweedledarren.'

'Nice shit?' Darren enquired.

'Very enjoyable thank you,' Will replied. He felt so good it was crazy. Why had they stopped doing this stuff?

The doorbell went so he trotted down the steps. He opened the bottom door to a slippery looking fellow clutching three large flat boxes.

'Yes,' he enquired, his smile splitting his face from ear to ear, making him feel like a Smash alien.

The guy looked at him like he had opened the door naked.

'Your pizzas sir.'

'Oh yes, sorry, wonderful. That was quick.' He took them off him and stood smiling. Stopping himself talking was almost impossible.

'We are only downstairs, sir,' the guy laughed, no doubt realising he was talking to a half-witted clown whose meds were out of synch. As Will went to close the door, the man shouted after him.

'That's nineteen pounds eighty please.'

'Oh sorry, I thought that cheeky fucker Carl had paid.' Will sniggered as he pulled out his coke twenty and unfurled it like a sacred flag. This action seemed to take an extraordinary long time and all of his attention. He handed it over to the bemused courier.

'Keep the change my friend. Three cockroaches max eh?' and, chuckling to himself, closed the door on the bemused man who was now shaking his head.

He could hear the talking before he even opened the flat door, it was as though he was about to walk into a bus full of chickens. The joys of chong. Everything was interesting. Money, women, politics, star wars, stamps, ironing, you name it.

Darren had gone from not wanting to talk of his domestic situation to practically shouting about it. He tuned in to the acidic diatribe.

'She's changed, man.' Weird Will thought, how people say man a lot when they are high. 'She's all involved in the local politics. Fervent is what she is man. Anyway, I feel like a stranger in my own house. Well, her house. Anyway, they feel like strangers. Her and little Tony. I can't seem to bond with him either. He doesn't even look like me. Her booze hounds brothers are around all the time too, chatting shit. In the end it's a relief to go back to war and if that doesn't say it all, I don't know what does.' He came up for air, and necked an industrial measure of JD. 'Relationships eh, what the fuck?'

'Yeah man, confusing,' Carl slurred, as though he was the sage of all sages. Will slid the pizza boxes onto the kitchen table.

'Pizza anyone?' he proffered. No-one even looked at him. Aiden seemed to be nodding his head to an unheard tune, whilst the other two continued their concluding.

Will opened one of the boxes and shook his head at what looked like a fantastic creation, before closing it and wandered off in the direction of the fridge. No Hungry Carlo's here.

'Put some tunes on man,' Aiden demanded. Carl selected a remote from the bewildering array on a stand that seemed to have been constructed just for the purpose of holding them and 'The Ketchup Song' came on.

Will sat at the table, frowning at Carl's dodgy taste in music and pulled his packet of Benson and Hedges Gold cigarettes out of his pocket. Taking his time, he selected one and slowly lit it, the end seemingly flaring over brightly in front of him. The beat of the track seemed to make his spine vibrate as it filled the room.

'Oy!' Carl jolted him from his reverie. 'This is a non-smoking establishment.'

'Smoke this,' Will said as he gave him the finger. This caused them all to burst into laughter. As the mad wave of euphoria slackened slightly, Will joined the others on the sofa and picked up the zip lock bag of the magic dust.

'Why have you got so much of it?'

'I called in a favour,' Darren said knowingly.

Will wondered what the hell kind of favour that could have been, before he realised he didn't care. He felt supercharged. The night was young, they had a bag full of happiness and a whole city of women were waiting for his charms. He always felt cocaine accentuated your natural charms and considering he thought he was an amusing decent type of guy, this made him superman. He looked at Darren and thought that seeing as he was a bit of a lunatic, he should probably steer clear of it. Darren still hadn't shut up.

'A lot of the world's Special Forces use stimulants to keep them going, especially at times of war. Obviously only for a short period. You make mistakes if you're tired you see.' Will suspected the quartermaster wouldn't be doling out eight balls with the ration packs anytime soon but held his tongue.

'Let's get in the mixer then lads,' Will said.

'Hang on,' Carl chuckled. 'I need a dump.'

When he left the room Darren went over to the boxes and slid a heavy looking pizza out. He then walked over to Carl's pride and joy, the table of wealth and placed it upside down on it. He then placed the pizza box on top of it and as Aiden wandered past with another beer he gave him a shove. He was about as stable as Bambi and heavily sat on top of the box.

Instantly he looked like he had sat on a sharpened stake and jumped off it. The three of them looked down and as Carl returned from the toilet declaring himself 'Fit and ready sir' they collapsed into peals of laughter.

He ushered Carl down the steps which seemed to have become an unnavigable obstacle course. He felt like ED-209 from Robocop as he gingerly descended, but he also felt like the lord of all creation.

★ ★ ★

The next four hours disappeared like a raindrop on Venus and they soon found themselves in a less than salubrious establishment called The Outback. An Australian hangout, calling itself a home from home, when it was little more than a dusty barn with a bar selling overpriced drinks. Maybe that was home from home. There were scantily clothed backpackers everywhere and Will could see Aiden and Darren grinning, gurning and grinding on the dance floor, surrounded by a horde of them.

Carl was next to him at the bar regaling two blonde haired beauties, who may well have been twins, with a tale seemingly so interesting it must have been the secret of life. Will stood there amazed. He had never seen Carl hold court in such a way before. One of them left to go in the direction of what was uninspiringly signposted as 'The Dunnies' and he watched still as the other one preened and fluttered her eyes. She grabbed Carl's arm at what he assumed was the punchline and moved in for a kiss. Carl's world had been ignited tonight, it was anyone's guess what would emerge out of the flames.

Will drained his beer and waited and noted the disappointed look on the other girl's face as she returned from the toilet. He placed his empty bottle on the bar and moved in for the kill. Life was good.

27

26ᵗʰ August 2006

Will pulled into Cherry Hinton Road with a smile. It was one of those days in England when you don't want to be anywhere else. The sky was blue with the occasional wispy cloud floating across it and there was a gentle breeze to take the edge off the warm sun. It made Will think of summers long gone in his parent's back garden and drinking ice cream floats. He pulled into number nine and let himself into his own back garden. The fuckers might have at least mown the lawn before they left he thought. It looked like the modern day pictures of Chernobyl. As though everyone had just put down what they'd been doing, or got off the swing they were on and then legged it, never to return, leaving this crazy wilderness to develop over the following twenty years.

If he sat in that with his ice cream he would be odds on to come out with Lyme disease, that's assuming one of the snakes didn't get him first. He shut the gate and went back to his car but walked past it and stood on the other side of the road, turning to see what he had bought. What he and Aiden had bought really and he laughed at the thought of his friend trying to get his head around all the legal terms, timescales, bullshit and expense. In the end he had just left it to Will, said he trusted him and to just point and show him where to sign.

So here they were. They were now the proud owners (Barclays may have something to say about that statement) of numbers seven and nine Cherry Hinton Road, Peterborough. Not housemates, but neighbours. 'Gaybours' as Darren had been calling them. Will had finally spent his life savings on a property in the new British Sugar housing estate. It was adios to travelling and he wasn't sure exactly how he felt about it all. His mortgage was pretty nasty all things considered, but as long as he didn't lose his job he would be fine. Great, he really was a slave to the wage. Aiden however had virtually bought his outright with the money from his dad's life insurance and the sale of the family home.

Still, everyone should buy their first home and move in with the sun shining Will decided. He walked back to his car, a maroon Vauxhall Vectra and shook his head. Thirty two years old and he was still doing stuff he didn't want to do. He had been pondering buying a black BMW as his Renault Clio finally entered its death throes. For some reason he had always fancied one. Nothing flash, or that new, just a three series. Instead his dad had bought a new car and the garage had offered him a derisory amount for his old Vectra. So his dad had arrived one Sunday morning and offered it to him for the admittedly low amount the garage had proposed.

Will had told him 'thanks, but no thanks', but it was as if the poor old Clio had been hanging on until reinforcements arrived, like the wounded hero waiting for the cavalry and had died the next day. This left Will to have to turn up in a taxi at his dad's house with his tail between his legs, late for work, before driving off in an old man's car. No swish BMW for him.

Still he was working in Cambridge now for what could only be described as a shonky loan company and he did not miss sitting in the daily traffic jam with the temperature gauge bouncing off red uneasily wondering if today would be another day to break down.

Yes, he had got to the age where he valued reliability over looks, how depressing. He had a massive loan over twenty five years which was equally disturbing. The most distressing part was to add to that, he had another job which he disliked but this time he had to drive for an hour to get to the damn thing. Whilst there he had to encourage people to take over priced loans that they neither needed nor could afford. As per usual life seemed to be getting away from him and he seemed to be under massive amounts of pressure and doing things he wasn't interested in. Love your job, you'll never work a day, hate your job and life sucks.

The parp of a van horn knocked him out of his reverie and he turned to see a grinning Aiden pulling up in the hired Sprinter. He realised it was the first time he had seen Aiden drive anything that didn't make him look like he was driving some kind of comedy clown vehicle. However, he still had to prise himself out of it as though he was climbing from a tight fairground ride.

He walked over to Will and as usual Will felt his mood lighten as he looked at his happy friend. Aiden put his arm around him in a matey manner and pointed at the house.

'One day Will, all that will be ours.'

Will thought of the twenty five years and didn't know whether to laugh or cry. They began to empty the van and as they did so it became evident very rapidly that Aiden had bought and therefore owned most of the things from their previous house. After Will had put his clothes on his bed in the main bedroom he paused to consider the two other rooms upstairs. He decided the smaller bedroom would be his computer room and slid the boxes for that in there and then he looked into the last one. A guest room perhaps, or maybe a baby room one day. Was that why he had bought a suburban semi when really he had wanted a funky apartment like Carl's? Still it would be lovely to have his own space and still know he could pop next door to see Aiden.

He heard the front door open and wandered down the stairs, surprised to find Darren there.

'Alright mate. I know you said you were coming to help move, but I thought that would mean you turned up tonight when it was all done?' Will said.

Darren laughed, and tapped a couple of big long boxes which had been poorly covered in cartoon wrapping paper and a smaller box.

'Aiden said you had bugger all anyway, so I bought you a couple of moving in presents.'

They carried them into Will's empty lounge, where he began to unwrap them. Noting the paper Darren had bought specifically.

'Barbie eh? Nice touch.' The first box was twenty four cans of Stella Artois. 'Very nice, and obviously vital.' The long boxes each contained a deckchair. 'Hang on a minute,' Will said and went to the car for his last possessions. He came back in and took out his old portable television that he used to have in his bedroom and rested it on the crate of beers in the corner. Darren smiling, set up the chairs in front of the set and sat in one. Will couldn't seem to find an aerial cable, so he shrugged and broke two cans from the 'table', gave one to Darren and sat next to him facing the small blank screen. They opened the cans in unison with a satisfying tssk and beaming at each other, clunked drinks together and took a sip.

'Hmmm, really warm, just how I imagined it, thank you,' Will chuckled.

'Piss off you ungrateful git.' Darren mocked looking hurt, but then Will noticed a scowl come over his friend's face and wondered what he was thinking.

'You're back early,' he said, giving Darren the opportunity to talk if he so wished. He did.

'I've been suspended Will. A few of us have. Dean's already gone. Medical discharge. There was a rumour there had been some unlawful killings.' Darren turned sideways and gave Will a piercing stare. 'Its war, killing is winning.' He let out a long breath.

'There is a price to pay Will. We did some bad things.' He shook his head as though that would make him forget. 'So I'm back for a good while and I hear through the grapevine that you have a spare room.' He stood up, gave Will a resounding smack on the back and a big smirk. 'I'll get my bag.'

Will took another warm sip and grimaced. He also let out a long breath and slumped further in his chair, blinking heavily. 'Excellent,' he muttered.

★ ★ ★

They had one more journey to make in the van so they all got in. Darren insisted on driving despite Will saying he wasn't insured for it. Darren said that his own insurance covered him for all vehicles and buckled himself in as though the dispute was over. Sighing heavily, Will clambered in next to Aiden. Darren drove confidently, swinging the van through the traffic at a speed which caused Aiden and Will to frantically work out how the seatbelts worked.

'See,' Darren chortled, lighting a cigarette whilst holding the steering wheel with his thighs. 'Who needs insurance? It's a waste of money. I don't even have it for my own car.' Will felt Aiden brace next to him.

'What time is Carl arriving?' Aiden asked, no doubt hoping to distract himself from the unpleasant experience he was having.

'Eight,' Darren replied. 'He is bringing his new woman with him.'

'Interesting,' Will commented with a smirk. Two things had increased dramatically in Carl's life. The speed he went through a gram of coke and the amount of girlfriends he bought back on his trips home. Will loved seeing these girls, even if he was very concerned that his friend seemed to be hurtling down the slippery slope of addiction like a fat kid down a steep hill on a well-oiled toboggan.

His dates however were invariably hilarious. The girls all seemed to be really messed up and customarily coke heads too. Carl didn't seem to care; it was as if he had missed out on interaction with the opposite sex all these years and now he was playing catch-up. Quantity, not quality was his new mantra. None of them so far had been even remotely attractive. Will chuckled to himself.

'What you laughing at Will?' Aiden queried.

'I was just amusing myself thinking about the crazy critters Carl's been dating.'

'I know, it's brilliant,' Aiden laughed out loud. 'God only knows where he finds them. He must live next door to a lunatic asylum for beasts from the forest and pick them up on release day.' Darren began laughing too.

'Do you remember that last one, the porky one? The one who disappeared halfway through the night. I thought I was going to shit myself I was laughing so hard.'

'Paula!' Aiden shouted.

Will remembered her in an instant. She had a really turned up nose, small eyes and looked almost exactly like a pig.

'It was Pauline, remember. Darren kept calling her 'Porcine' all night and she was so mashed she didn't even notice.'

They arrived at the flat Aiden and he had rented and got the last of their things into the van. Will could hear 'I Wish I Was A Punk Rocker' by Sandi Thom coming out of the van and thought about the memories that he was leaving behind here as he closed the door. Lately there had just been a messy collection of drunken experiences he would probably never give another thought to. He slid the keys through the letter box and whistling the song's tune, got back in the van and went to his new home.

28

That night, after Aiden said all the lifting and carrying had made him thirsty, they arrived at the pub early. It was actually more of a bar than a pub and the prices were appropriately priced. Darren was on good form.

'Who had the bright idea to meet in here?'

'Carl,' Will and Aiden replied in unison.

Will and Aiden sat down quickly on seats at the front looking out on the town square through big glass windows. They both said 'Lager' to Darren in unison too, and rolling his eyes he went off to get served.

'I've just been mugged,' Darren declared when he returned from the bar after paying for his round. 'In broad fucking daylight and he didn't even wear a mask. No change from ten fucking quid for three bottles of Japanese beer. I told him surely it should be cheaper if we are helping out poorer nations. I gave him a tenner and waited for my change, the greasy git told me 'That's it my friend'. I said 'How can it be? What are they, three pound thirty three and a third of a penny each the cheeky twat. I was gonna jump over the bar, tell him to have one for himself and stick it up his arse.' Darren paused to swig his overpriced beverage, nodding at its refreshing tang, before continuing.

'Then he told me it was happy hour, three for a tenner.'

Will and Aiden laughed at the punch line. It felt like Darren's suspension had lifted a cloud from him. He started regaling them with amusing tales of life in the forces, no doubt steering clear of whatever madness had led to his current situation, and seemed more relaxed than usual. Still a madman obviously, but a more chilled one.

Carl turned up at eight o'clock on the dot, looking gaunt but wealthy and his new squeeze didn't disappoint. As Carl introduced 'Syndi, with an S' to them all Will had to grit his teeth to stop himself bursting into laughter. He daren't look at the other two, but he could feel Darren tapping his shoe against his leg. She was the hairiest girl he had ever seen, not that she had a moustache or beard, just that her hair was a huge mass of black curls and her hairline seemed to be only an inch above her eyebrows. Her unruly styling across the shoulder made it look like she had long side burns too and no one could have missed the downy arms. He could also detect a hint of what no doubt was cocaine suspended in her nostril hair.

'I'm just going to powder my nose,' she said with a grin and kissed Carl on the cheek. She sauntered off through the now busy bar, swaying her hips with coke confidence and Carl gave them all death stares as they burst into gales of mirth.

'What is it, you tools? I really like her,' Carl stated.

'You always say that. We are just pleased to see you. Would you like a drink Carlos?' Darren put his hand around the back of Carl's neck and playfully squeezed it.

'Yes please mate, just get me a beer,' Carl replied.

'Anything for your Ewok?' Darren deadpanned.

Will almost wet himself at Darren's brilliant and amazingly obvious observation.

'Get her a Mojito you knob, I hope it bankrupts you.' Carl glared, but he smiled after, enjoying the craic.

Darren and Syndi returned at the same time, Darren with a 'Don't ask' when Will queried the financial implications of the cocktail purchase. Carl sat down leaving a space for his date, but she was like an ill-sitting hen, fluttering around the table, chatting to the people next to her and generally being a bit of an annoying nightmare. Will had to smile though as she drank her drink with a straw through her small mouth, her big eyes wide open as she concentrated. To be honest, as Ewoks went, she was a pretty one.

She knocked her drink over putting it back on the table and staggered off. Will assumed she was getting a cloth but she walked straight past the bar in the direction of the toilets again. Will leaned into the table with a smile; he did love a good piss-take.

'She seems nice, very friendly. Outgoing too,' Aiden began.

'A real winner, all in all,' Darren added.

'Yes Carl, she sure is one to cuddle up to on a winter's night,' Will commented.

As usual Carl took it in good grace.

'Very amusing you comic geniuses. She is actually a nice girl. Admittedly I have never seen such a hairy beaver. It was massively weird having sex with her, like sticking your winkie in some still warm road kill.'

Will tried unsuccessfully to push that image to the back of his mind.

'Who is next Carl? Jabba the Hut?' Darren asked.

'Boba Fett?' Will proffered. 'I was always suspicious of him.'

'Chewbacca! Carl you are a sick one,' Aiden creased at that.

'That is a nasty vision for his mum to open the door to, seeing her son crying into his pillow whilst a sweating

Chewy reclines next to him with a sedated expression on his face. Him grinning at your mum with a happy 'Grrrrrrrrrrr'.' Darren spat the last bit out as he was chuckling so much.

'Excuse me,' Carl said. 'I am the giver, not the receiver. I admit though, that you may be a bit disgusted with yourself if you had let the mighty Chewbacca have his wicked way with you. More than a bit sore too, especially if he didn't ring afterwards.'

'Anyway,' he continued. 'Don't mess it up for me like you did with Pauline.'

'It's not our fault she was so off her face and got lost,' Darren said, holding his hands up.

Carl handed Darren a piece of paper from his jacket pocket, who read it out.

'Dear Carl, you are a horrible excuse for a human being. How could you treat me so badly? As for your scum bag mates, calling me Porcine all night, did they think I wouldn't know it meant pig-like? I have never been so humiliated and to cap it all off you left me stranded alone in a town where I didn't know anyone. You are a complete asshole.'

'Asshole or arsehole?' Aiden asked.

'Asshole, it says. That's a little rude, but a fair reflection of that particular evening's events I would say. What's your point Carl?'

'My point Einstein, is that I am looking forward to round two with Chief Chirpa, so be nice. That Pauline was a nightmare anyway. That piggy little schnozzle couldn't half get through the powder, nearly ruined me. Talking of which, I'm off to the toilets, if anyone is interested.'

Aiden shook his head.

'Not for me either,' Will concurred. 'I have got tonnes to do tomorrow. I am sans everything. No sofa, fridge, cooker, washing machine, you name it, none of it. No food, nothing to eat it with and nothing to eat it off. No curtains, no lightbulbs, no idea.'

'No future,' Darren interjected.

'Correct,' Will agreed. 'So waking up with a chongover would not be the best way of resolving any of these issues.'

'I'm working tomorrow, overtime,' Aiden said. He drained his drink and stood up. 'So I will decline as I need to be tip top too. Same again anyone?'

'Yes please buddy and maybe later Carl,' Darren said and with that Carl wandered off.

'Don't you worry about being piss-tested in the army?' Will asked.

'Not really, most drugs only stay in the system for a couple of days. Dope stays in for longer but I've only ever been caught for a test once and then the guy doing the testing pissed in it for me.'

Any more probing on the subject was prevented by the return of Syndi. She fluttered around for half an hour, doing their heads in, like an 18-30 holiday rep, but eventually calmed down and proved surprisingly good company. As per usual they ended up in the same place, same seats in fact, all night. Will commented that they must be getting old, but Aiden pointed out they had been doing that for fifteen years. At midnight and chucking out time they all got in a taxi to Will and Aiden's. Aiden asked them in for a drink, but both Will and Darren declined. They hadn't discussed sleeping arrangements but Darren followed Will into his house and Carl and Syndi went into Aiden's.

Darren got on one of the deckchairs and seemed to fall asleep in an instant, so Will put his coat over him and went upstairs. As he tossed and turned in his own bed waiting for sleep to take him, he could hear sobbing coming from downstairs.

29

1ˢᵗ September 2008

'Can I borrow your car?'

'No.'

'Come on Will, pretty please.'

'No.'

'I'm only going to be twenty minutes. Promise. I've just got to drop something off for a mate and I'll be right back.'

'No.'

'I'll get a pizza on the way back.'

'Get a taxi.'

'It'll be twenty minutes before the taxi turns up mate.' Darren picked the keys up off the hook and jingled them in the air. 'I'll owe you.'

'Half an hour you've got. That's it.' Will looked at him with a resigned air. 'I've got to get those back tyres sorted this afternoon. If they get any balder they will be unscrewing themselves and be hammering on the door of the wig shop.'

'Are you sure anywhere will be open on a bank holiday Monday?'

Will gave him an exasperated look.

'Thirty minutes tops then mate. You're a good friend Will.'

'Just piss off Darren and mind those tyres. You are not Lewis Hamilton, so drive accordingly.'

Darren came over and kissed him on the top of his head. He grabbed a small rucksack which he had left next to the front door and bolted through it, slamming it behind him. Will gritted his teeth, he had really had enough.

It was a pleasant day and all the windows were open so he heard Darren fire the car up and turn the radio on full blast. Rihanna's 'Take A Bow' blared out for a few seconds, then silence, then Meat Loaf's 'Bat Out Of Hell' came on so loud it might as well have been coming out of the television in front of him. With a screech of tyres Darren roared off and the music faded into the distance.

Will put his face in his hands and let out a long sigh. A few more days and it would be over. Darren had been given an honourable discharge from the army for medical reasons last year but hadn't really been back to 'work' since Will and Aiden had bought their new houses. The army's equivalent of garden leave. Darren had in effect been living with him since then and whilst it had been a bit of a laugh to start with it had become a nightmare of swelling proportions since. Darren didn't seem to be able to get it into his pebble head that Will had to work during the week and therefore was not up for beers and joints whenever Darren was bored on some idle Wednesday.

A discussion at the start of the year had blown up into a full row which Will thought was going to end with him getting a good leathering. Instead Darren had put his foot through Will's forty inch plasma television. Darren had replaced it the next day and thought that everything was then hunky-dory. That was just one example of his increasingly erratic actions. You couldn't talk to him nowadays. His always short fuse was now almost non-existent and you found yourself treading on egg shells around him. He seemed to sleep for England as well, with

Will finding he was creeping into his own house after work so as not to wake him.

At night it felt like he had half of the town stampeding through his house and consequently it looked like it. It was like living with a drug dealer. To think he had been looking forward to his own space. To be fair to Darren he had helped him furnish it at the beginning and still paid a generous rent by direct debit into Will's account each month, but Will was more than happy to forego that now, before he lost his own mind.

All Darren had said about his discharge was that it was for post-traumatic stress disorder. Will didn't know what that meant exactly and Darren wouldn't be drawn on what caused it, but there was definitely something missing in their friend now. He had no empathy whatsoever and sympathy was in short supply too. He seemed to think he could do what he liked, when he liked and no-one was going to stop him doing it. Will had asked Aiden if he fancied a turn Darren-sitting. He had simply said 'No fucking way'. When Will tried to raise the subject again he had put his hands over his ears like a child and shouted 'La la la la la la la la, I can't hear you'.

And who could blame him Will thought? To start with Darren had taken security jobs in Iraq and would be gone for months on end, but he came back more and more wired each time. He would go on mad benders when he returned and when the cocaine made him chatty he would tell them about it. It sounded like the Wild West, Arab style, but instead of Colt peacemakers every man and his dog had a Kalashnikov under their bed. The money was amazing though, up to a grand a day guarding oil executives. However Darren said he earned his money and then some. Will wasn't sure what that meant either. Darren would joke that he had shot more people as a civilian than he had as a soldier. Will thought he had been joking anyway.

With all that money coming in you would have thought he would get his own place. Will had tiptoed around this fact, encouraged it and in the end ordered it. Darren on the other hand had done his best to avoid it. His standard response being 'Mate, my head's up my arse and you are my rock'. It had been left to go on for so long as Will had a lot of compassion for Darren's situation. The army trained him to be a cold hearted killer. Then after putting him in a steady succession of mind blowing situations that withered his very soul, sent him back home with a list of unneeded attributes. Darren had no support apart from his few close friends. Will, Aiden and Carl ostensibly. Everyone else had drifted away as Darren was just too much hard work and was often uncomfortable company. The guilt trips had eventually ceased to have an impact on Will too though and it had all come to a head a month back.

Darren had taken to just going out in Will's car whenever he felt like it. He had gone out one Saturday night in it and not come back until Monday morning. Will had missed a date with a girl from work because of it and he had been going spare as Darren's phone had been turned off and he had been wondering how the hell he was going to get to work.

Darren had finally walked through the door at seven a.m., looking like he hadn't slept for a month, thrown the keys on the kitchen table next to where an astonished and exasperated Will was sitting and simply said 'I'm going to bed'.

He went to the fridge and got a bottle of Will's mineral water out, walked out of the room and up the stairs. Will couldn't believe it. He had driven to work in a rage and returned ready for a showdown, but Darren didn't get out of bed for two days. Eventually Will cornered him and delivered an ultimatum. 'You have a month from today. I will be changing the locks.'

He had expected a scary meltdown but Darren had surprised him and made him feel like he was in the wrong. Unbelievable. He had acknowledged his unreasonable behaviour, saying he hadn't been taking his medication religiously and he knew it was time to go. He then thanked Will for putting up with him, saying he didn't know what he would have done without his support.

As Will recalled all this he gritted his teeth and resolved to put more effort in with Darren. Well, after he moved out anyway. He had promised to water Aiden's hanging baskets so went out the front to do that. Who would have thought Aiden would end up so house proud. His house was like a show home, with classy furnishings and luxurious carpets. It was clean and felt airy and relaxing. It was massively annoying, Will decided. He couldn't believe his house was the exact mirror of Will's. His own home could reasonably be called a shithole. It looked like the cast of Ben Hur had been around to continue the party after a particularly hot, dusty and thrilling chariot race.

As he pondered not watering the plants so they died, he was startled by a car roaring down their street with screaming brakes that juddered to a stop at the end of Aiden's garden. Waves of 'Two Out Of Three Ain't Bad' reached him. He couldn't believe it. It was Darren and after everything he had said about those bloody brakes. He looked at his watch, well at least he had only been twenty minutes.

Darren practically fell out of the car with an expression on his face like the hounds of hell were chasing him. He ran toward Will and threw the keys at his chest causing him to involuntarily catch them. Darren growled 'Fuck' and ran back to the driver's side of the car with the still open door and reached across and pulled his rucksack from the passenger seat. He then sprinted past Will shouting, 'You haven't seen me,' and disappeared up the path to the back of the house. Will cringed as he heard Darren kick the gate open which bashed hard against the side of the house and thumped shut again.

It was only then that he heard the sirens. If Darren's music hadn't been so loud, he would have heard them sooner, but it was only when the unmarked police car with the orange siren on top careered around the corner of the road that Will put two and two together. Oddly enough he didn't feel panic, not then, he was just totally dumbstruck. He stood there in his shorts and T-shirt, the light breeze billowing his clothes and watched the angriest looking policeman he had ever seen scramble out of the passenger seat and hurtle towards him. He was in jeans and a casual shirt and was holding what Will assumed was a police badge.

He wasn't a huge man, about the same size as Will. A similar age as well, with a shaven head trying to disguise advanced balding. He wasn't particularly muscly either but he must have been fit as he sprinted toward Will across the grass as though he had just come around the home bend in the Olympics. It was then that Will became scared.

'Stop, Police,' he bawled when he was about three metres away from the stationary Will.

His face was so contorted with such a combination of rage and hatred that it was like staring at a charging

Viking. As he got closer Will found himself putting his hands up in surrender. Will was actually surprised that when the policeman reached him he didn't pull out an axe, scream 'Argghh' and cut his head clean off. Instead he grabbed an arm and roughly twisted it behind Will's back just above his hips. Then the copper seized his other hand and wrenched that behind his back into the same position too, before yanking them both up towards his shoulders into arm locks. His head started to bow down and he was propelled forward.

Whilst he was being frogmarched back towards the waiting police car, he could hear the man muttering under his breath, 'You fucking piece of shit. Absolute scum, what is wrong with you people.'

He was thumped into the side of the car so hard that his head shot toward the bonnet of the car. With his hands behind his back he was unable to block his fall and as he stared at the rapidly approaching piece of metal he did the only thing he could think of and looked up. He later suspected that manoeuvre saved his nose, but he hit the surface with such a clunk he felt a wave of pain fly up his jawline and out the crown of his head. Higher level thought seemed to evaporate from his skillset. It was as if he went into survival mode and shut down the non-essential functions just to get through this terrifying situation.

He was then straightened up and as he swayed around like a wobbling weeble he was incredibly roughly cuffed by the other officer who had struggled out of the driver side door. Will let out a pathetic sounding 'Ow' as he was shaken like a rag doll. The second officer was well over six foot, his huge hands fumbling with the cuffing mechanism as he tried to release the big piece of skin he had pinched in them the first time he had shut them. This man was much younger but God knows how he had passed the fitness test as he was as fat as butter. Maybe he hadn't started out that way but judging by the unmistakeable stench of recently eaten Big Mac sauce wheezing in his face it was easy to see the reason.

Angry cop bellowed in his ear.

'I'm arresting you for dangerous driving. You do not have to say anything. But, it may harm your defence if you do not mention when questioned something which you later rely on in court. Anything you do say may be given in evidence.'

Will was so stunned it was as if someone had filled his mouth with golden syrup. His tongue felt as though his mouth was full of sludge and didn't seem to be able to make sounds. His brain felt like it had been over stimulated with the shock of what was happening and shut down. He would look back many times later and wonder why he didn't try harder to tell them it was Darren driving, not him. Every time he started to say something the angry officer bellowed in his face to 'Shut the fuck up'. Surely covering for a mate didn't stretch this far and this was completely beyond grassing on anyone. He assumed he would be able to explain what really happened later.

Even in his befuddled state he wondered whether they would have believed him anyway, such was the fury of the arresting officer. An enormous meaty paw thwacked his head down and he was manhandled into the back of the police car. Will looked out of the car waiting for someone to help, or maybe even to wake him up, but no one came, the horror was real. The driver reversed into Aiden's drive and they drove off at an improbably sedate pace in the direction of Thorpe Wood Police Station.

It was mercifully a short journey. As the car was unmarked it just felt like an uncomfortable taxi ride. Incredibly surreal, with the only interactions between the individuals present being a few evil looks from the front passenger. Deathly silent too, even the police radio only gave off the odd piece of static.

★ ★ ★

Soon enough he was standing at the custody desk. He was pushed into a seat as they waited for the custody officer to finish processing the girl in front of him. He tuned into the row they were having. She was so obviously a prostitute that even in Will's befuddled state he couldn't help but let out a small laugh. She had the shortest skirt on Will had ever seen, high heels and a halter neck top on. Definitely a hint of Pretty Woman about it all. Attractive in a thin way too. Her hair concealed her face but she was swaying on those heels like a reed of grass on a gusty day despite being held at the elbow by two officers.

'I was not selling my pussy,' she slurred.

'The plain clothes policeman, whose car you got into, whom you offered full sex to, for twenty pounds, begs to differ Mandy.'

'He's lying, I thought he was a taxi.'

'Is that how you pay for your taxis Mandy?'

'Sometimes.'

The officer shook his head and nodded to the officers next to the girl. They manoeuvred her around and escorted her past Will who did a triple take. So addled and haggard was she that she was the spitting image of Medusa. Body like Baywatch, face like Crime Watch sprang to mind. Her eyes had the look of someone who never slept, only passed out. There were some sick men out there if they were willing to pay for that. He would rather have put his dick through a cheese grater than in that honeypot of HIV. She focused her red rheumy eyes on Will as she was practically carried past.

'Don't believe them for a minute son, run if you can.' She disappeared cackling through some double doors leaving an acrid sweet smell in her wake.

The fat officer, fat cop, gave him a look that said just try it, which made Will incredulously smile again. He had the physique of someone who could only run when the canteen was running low on doughnuts. For that measure he got a pinched arm as he was dragged to his feet and pushed into the custody desk. He looked up into the face of a tired looking uniformed officer.

The arresting officer, angry cop, explained to the sergeant that he had been arrested for dangerous driving. He agreed to give blood for alcohol levels, praying last night's debauchery would have left his system by now. As though in a dream he confirmed his personal details, had his rights read to him again, handed over his personal belongings and was escorted to a cell. He was ordered to remove his belt from his shorts and his trousers, and quickly found himself alone, sitting on a thin blue mat like he remembered from the gym at school. He lay down and put his arm over his eyes to try and compose himself. It was cold and empty in the room, just him, the mat and an aluminium toilet with no seat. He found himself shaking slightly and wondered if it was the temperature or if he was going into shock.

★ ★ ★

Having handed over his watch he had no idea how long he had waited until they came for him, but it must have been well over an hour. As he sat up the mat came up with him, stuck to his head with some yellowy substance he hadn't noticed before. He had to remove it like peeling apart Velcro and felt another piece of his withering composure die.

He walked in his socks to an interview room and sat opposite the two arresting officers. There were no windows in there and it was even colder, as though they were in the bowels of the earth. Fat cop pushed a warm drink over to him and smiled. It was a humourless smile but it was the first positive piece of human contact he seemed to be able to remember. Angry cop glared at him though.

'You can have a solicitor if you want, but the duty one is busy and you will probably just want to get home. We just need to ascertain what happened and then you can be off and start putting this incident behind you.'

If Will had been on his game he would have seen through the angry smile a mile off, or held his tongue, but not knowing what he'd done, meant he had no idea how serious the trouble he was in. He looked at the two men, one by one and nodded. He didn't know what dangerous driving meant, it couldn't be too bad he thought, it was only driving after all. He just wanted to take a police caution or some points on his licence and get the hell out of there.

Fat cop reached over and pressed a button on a recorder in the corner of the room, and talked to the camera.

'Interview with William Reynolds, date of birth seven ten seventy-three, on Monday the twenty-fifth August at eighteen hundred hours exactly.' Three hours he had waited then, Will realised.

'So Mr Reynolds, tell me, what happened?'

'I wasn't driving. Someone else was.'

'We saw you get out of the car and run away,' angry cop said.

'You can't have, it wasn't me.'

'You were holding the car keys when we caught you,' angry cop added, waving Will's car keys in an evidence bag.

'Who was driving then, if it wasn't you?' Fat cop asked.

Will bowed his head as he thought. Incredibly he realised he wasn't going to be able to drop his friend in it even if he wanted to. They had their man and were not going to believe anything different. He suspected he wouldn't have if the roles had been reversed.

'Tell us exactly what happened?'

If only I knew, thought Will. He rummaged through his chaotic brain like a tired mother who was late for the school run looking for her car key in a bulging handbag.

'It all seems a bit of a blur now, I know I was wrong, but I just had a moment of ummm, lack of, ummm, I was ummm, hmmm, maybe you could tell me and I will tell you if that is a fair reflection.'

The two officers looked at each other, a little confused.

'OK,' said angry cop. 'We were parked up, observing a Bookmakers that had been the subject of an armed robbery the day before, when we heard a car being driven fast. I looked in the wing mirror and your maroon Vectra flew past us at a speed no less than sixty miles per hour. We pulled out, put the flashing lights on and activated the sirens. You drove through a red light, failed to stop for us and due to the speed you were going we lost sight of you for approximately thirty seconds. We then found you, running away from your car and trying to hide in your property. Would you agree this is an accurate reflection of this afternoon's events?'

Will looked in horror at the man. This sounded way more serious than he thought.

'Can you give me a minute to recollect?' he asked. He shifted on his unforgiving seat and looked at the ceiling, trying to remain calm. He had a pretty good idea that failing to stop for the police was frowned upon in a big way, but there wasn't much hiding away from the fact he had clearly been speeding and if two of them said he went through a red light his protestations were likely to come to zero. He stared at the single white bulb hanging above him, at least it wasn't so clichéd as to be missing a shade, but what was there was distinctly functional. The ceiling needed painting too he thought. A hand slammed on the table, jolting his attention back.

'Focus,' he was ordered.

There was a voice inside his head, saying 'Say nothing' but the two officers were now almost smiling at him, giving him encouraging looks.

'I may have been driving fast, but I'm pretty sure it wasn't sixty, maybe forty. I did go through a light, but it was amber not red. I didn't hear the sirens, or see the lights. I just went home. I wasn't running when you pulled up. I didn't realise you wanted to talk to me.'

Angry cop looked at Will like he had told him black was white. Fat cop cut in.

'Do you agree though that driving at that speed in a built up area with a school nearby was dangerous?'

'No-one was at school today.'

'No, but it was still dangerous at that speed.'

'I guess so,' Will mumbled. As he said that he noticed a spare chair in the corner and thought that's my solicitor's chair. 'I think I would like to wait for the solicitor.'

'Let's get you in to see the nurse first eh?'

He padded through to a bored-looking nurse, who gave him the most cursory of onceovers.

'Any issues?' she said.

'I'm cold.'

He found himself back on his mat, this time with an off-white blanket. He turned the mat over and checked for more sticky patches. Finding none, he lay down and pulled the cover over him. God only knows what it was made of, as it seemed to provide virtually no heat whatsoever, but made him sweat profusely. He tried to sleep but the increasing arguments and drunken shouts of the later residents of the holding cells prevented any of that.

He had no idea what the time was as he was led back into the interview room and came face to face with an attractive heavily made up girl in her late twenties. She flirted with angry cop as he left and gave Will a wet weak handshake that instilled zero confidence. She pushed her solicitor's business card over.

'Hi, I'm Jennifer,' she breezily introduced herself as though she was his waitress for the evening. 'I hear you have admitted to dangerous driving?'

'Well, not really, I just admitted to driving too fast.'

'Well that is dangerous.'

He let out a puff of breath.

'Do you have any previous convictions, or any kind of criminal record?'

'No, nothing at all, not even a speeding conviction, or a parking fine.'

'OK let me tell you what's going to happen tomorrow morning. You will be taken to Magistrates Court in the morning. The case may be transferred to Crown Court. If you have no previous you will be released on bail, and you will receive a court summons ordering you to go court for your plea.'

'So I have to stay here tonight?'

'I'm afraid so. Is there anything I can get you?'

'A cigarette please.'

She looked at him as if he had asked to rub his greasy face against hers, but she eventually nodded. Will rested his head on the table.

30

26ᵗʰ August 2008

H e woke up after a maximum of two hours sleep by a deep voice shouting 'Court in thirty minutes'. For a few seconds he thought he was at home. His protesting back soon shattered that thought and then it all came back to him. His stomach tensed, he felt sick and needed a dump at the same time. He looked over at the toilet and considered his options, concluding that any time spent near that shit-splattered tin pot would be horrendous and he definitely wouldn't be putting his face anywhere near it.

He was disturbed by a young uniformed officer bringing in a tray with some congealing microwave breakfast on it.

'Do I get a shower?' Will asked.

'Shower's broken, sorry.'

'Phone call?'

'You refused a call last night,' the man said checking a clipboard. 'You can make a call at the court.'

Will opened his mouth to complain, also suspecting the latter comment was a brush off, but who the hell was he going to ring anyway. The door closed on him and he peered down at the meal that looked like it was made of wax. He was starving. So he picked up the plastic fork, which was the only implement he had been given and ate it anyway.

★ ★ ★

Thirty minutes later, after a harrowing experience hovering over the pit of repulsion with his ass tingling from the world's most abrasive and non-absorbent toilet paper, his shoes and belt were returned to him along with his personal belongings. He was escorted on to a long kind of white van with five blacked out windows along the side. He could see other people behind the metal gridded doors as he got on the bus and walked down the middle to the back. He was wedged into a tiny compartment and his door was shut, enclosing him inside. He must have been the last one on, as the van gingerly pulled away shortly afterwards. Judging by the sky and the light traffic it was still fairly early although it was difficult to tell through the tinted windows. The barrier was raised as they left the police station and five minutes later they were driving down a slope taking them under a building boldly declaring itself to be Peterborough Magistrates Court.

It was a long four hours waiting in the holding cell. The duty solicitor had been to see him and had confirmed to him what the girl from last night had said about proceedings. She informed him in no uncertain terms he must get an excellent solicitor appropriate to these types of cases. One of his hands was then cuffed to a man from court security and exhausted, dirty and gritty eyed, he was led up some steps and through a wooden door into a bright, well lit room.

He looked out into the court room through the Perspex glass. There were three suited figures on a raised desk on his left who all seemed to be reading something in front of them. In front of them was a man on a slightly lower desk who was whispering something to them. The duty solicitor was facing them on a row of tables in front of Will and at the far side of the room was another desk facing him. The woman seated over there was the only one observing him, but when he caught her eye, she looked away disinterestedly.

The central figure at the top, a grey haired general practitioner type, looked over his glasses at Will.

'You may be seated,' he said. 'Are you William Reynolds?'

'Yes,' Will replied, but it only came out in a whisper.

'Louder please.'

'Yes, yes I am.'

'Confirm your date of birth.'

'Seven, ten, seventy three.'

'Mr Reynolds you have been charged with dangerous driving and failing to stop for a police officer. These are very serious offences. As this is the case we will be transferring these proceedings to Crown Court as our sentencing powers are insufficient in this case. You will be released on unconditional bail, and will be summoned by letter in the near future. Needless to say, failure to attend is also a serious offence. You are in a lot of trouble Mr Reynolds, however due to your previous good record, you are free to go. Release him please.'

The cuffs were taken off and the dock was opened so he could walk out. He was given some paperwork, guided through a door and suddenly he was on his own in the waiting room. He saw an exit sign on his right and walked towards it. He passed a metal detector door frame with people shuffling through and being scanned by a bored-looking security guard. No-one seemed interested in him, so he stepped outside and into the blessed open air. He took two deep breaths, and then quickly walked down the steps, desperate to be away from this place.

He put his hands in his pockets as he walked, remembering he had no cards, phone or money. Home was a thirty minute walk away. Embarrassed by his dishevelled state, he put his head down, swallowed and walked through the smart business people and happy shoppers whilst staring at his feet.

As he walked he made the decision not to think about things now. He knew what he wanted to do. When he got home the front door was unlocked. He picked up his mobile phone and rang work informing them he had been ill all night and only just woken up. He checked to see if his so called mate was upstairs. Not only was he not, but all of his stuff had gone.

There was a note on the kitchen table. He sat down to read it.

'Dear Will. I am a dick. I am so sorry. Do not worry I will make it up to you. I have plenty of money so don't fret about anything. I'll be in touch.'

Incredulous Will turned on the radio which was on the table, desperate to interrupt the humming silence of the house. Maria McKee's 'Show Me Heaven' was mid song. Will jumped up out of his seat and picking up the radio smashed it into pieces on the tiled floor. He went to where he kept his alcohol and yet again cursed Darren as he stared at his empty bottle of Jim Beam. All he had left were two bottles of a case of red wine that he had brought back years ago on a booze cruise to France.

The wine had tasted like a cross between vinegar and washing up liquid with a heady bouquet of pub toilet, hence their longevity. He couldn't face going out again though and unscrewed the first bottle. He sat at the kitchen table, poured the contents into a cleanish looking pint glass and drank.

Innocent lives can be ruined as quickly as that.

Ross Greenwood

31

14ᵗʰ October 2008

Will knew this day was coming. He had even had a month from the court summons to get his head and story straight, yet as he ascended the steps it felt like he was using his legs for the first time. It wasn't a hot day in the slightest yet he could feel the sweat building in his hairline. Aiden had insisted on coming and even though he had told him it was OK and he would be alright, he was now so glad he had agreed.

He looked over at Aiden who was carrying his bag. Jesus, he thought. His prison bag. His bag contained a couple of pairs of jeans, some trainers, some sports stuff, underwear, writing material, books, stamps, his toiletries and a towel. Apparently you weren't allowed the towel oddly enough, but Darren assured him the officers were likely to be so overworked and stressed that they either wouldn't give a shit, or would miss it.

Darren, who had made him pack the bag even though his solicitor had said it was extremely unlikely he would be sent to prison. Darren, whose fault all this was. Darren, who had disappeared for a week afterwards. Darren, whom he swore even found this all a little bit amusing. That was a long fucking week Will thought as they stood at the back of a considerable queue at the scanner. Great Will thought, a big queue means a busy day, no doubt means a lot of waiting. It felt like his life had been on hold since that sunny afternoon.

He hadn't told anyone apart from Aiden and Carl. Not work and certainly none of his family. However he knew it was likely to be in the local paper. He would have to hope that as he worked in a different city that no-one would see it. A suspended sentence would hardly be front page news. He had checked his employment contract and whilst there was nothing in there about dismissal for criminal convictions, it was all worded so that they more or less could do what they liked in the event of one.

Will had missed a lot of work lately because of this and his boss had clearly had enough. He didn't even want to start thinking that Darren's selfish actions could cost him his job. He could even lose his house. Will found himself gritting his teeth as he remembered and forced himself to unclench his jaw. As his grandma used to say, what's done is done, although that's easier said than done. Will shook his head; it felt as though all he had racing around his head in ever dizzying circles was a steady succession of clichés.

To give Darren his credit, he had arranged for a solicitor and paid for it all without being asked, but that hardly balanced it out. Darren had advised Will on what to expect at court as though he had been through it all personally. Although to Will's knowledge he was pretty sure Darren hadn't been before a judge before. How much did he really know about his friend now though? He had missed huge chunks of Darren's life and had no idea what he had been up to. Darren withheld things, he always had and he could have been remiss about anything.

Even though the barrister had been expensive and an expert in road traffic cases he didn't really have much to work with. Will would be going guilty at the first opportunity; today. The case was damning. Dangerous driving was a hell of a lot more serious than it sounded. You are as likely to go to prison for dangerous driving as you are for drunk driving. Dangerous driving meant the way you had driven fell far below the minimum acceptable standard expected of a competent and careful driver; and it would be obvious to a competent and careful driver that driving in that way would be dangerous.

Darren's driving had been dreadful. The punishment hinged on the presence of aggravating factors but as his barrister had told him the one time he had met him, once you went before a Crown Court judge, anything could happen. That hour's work had apparently cost Darren a thousand pounds. He would be focusing on Will's previous good character, putting it down to a one off event. Darren had been all apologetic afterwards, but how could you apologise for what had happened. Darren kept saying he would make it up to Will, whatever happened. Will told him to go to the police station and admit to it but the solicitor had been present and said at this stage they would just not have believed it. Darren now treated it as though it had all been a bit of bad luck and had even starting joking about Will getting bummed in prison.

His barrister was another who didn't seem to be taking it seriously. Heaven knows where Darren found him but they seemed to have history and had been cracking jokes together. Will hoped this was just due to his brief's confidence in his own ability, but it was a worrying feeling none the less. He could see his barrister sitting at the far end of the waiting room. He was head down in paperwork with the same cheap suit, but at least he was already here. He had been an hour late for their first meeting, totally disorganised, but with a gung ho 'It'll be alright on the night attitude'.

Will found himself worrying about his own suit, never mind why his public schoolboy lawyer couldn't afford a decent one. He had looked at himself in the mirror this morning and thought 'Would you jail this man?' He looked like what he was; a relatively wealthy single man with no children who didn't like to be told what to do. Even though this would not normally entail breaking the law, the judge was not going to know that. Will forced himself to exhale. He had been doing a lot of that lately, compelling himself to breathe.

Aiden caught his eye as they finally got to their turn to be scanned and he gave him a grin.

'Chin up man, it will all be over soon.'

'Yes,' Will thought, by tonight I will hopefully be in the pub and my body will start breathing on its own again. Darren had demanded they meet after but said he was 'Busy with business' so wouldn't be able to attend court. Will suspected he was worried Will was going to break and shout out 'It was him' whilst dramatically pointing at Darren. Sadly the time for that was long gone.

The security guard's metal detector was insanely sensitive. No wonder it had been slow going. It picked up his belt, his watch, his chewing gum and even his bloody Rennie. As they approached their man he looked up and they caught his unguarded expression and Will's nervousness went up to DEFCON one. He tried to recover, greeting them profusely with his posh blustering manner, but something had rocked him.

'What is it Henry?' Will demanded.

'It's the prosecution. They have added in a report about the condition of your car. God knows who wrote it, but it's so damning the only way it could have been a more dangerous conveyance would have been if you had mounted a lance on the front of it.'

'Oh,' was all Will could come up with.

'Oh indeed. All is not lost though. Let's face it, no one was hurt and it was only a single occurrence.'

Will shook his head as the man's demeanour indicated his lack of poise on this latest revelation.

'Why have you brought your bag Will? Your faith in me must be astounding.'

'I didn't want to arrive in prison without my pyjamas. I've had a special pair made with a back flap, so I don't catch a chill whilst I'm being passed around the bigger boys.'

'Well done Will, that's the spirit. You won't be going to prison today. If he is going to consider a custodial sentence, which is doubtful in your case, he will ask for a pre-sentence report to be done, so probation will produce one and you will come back in a couple of weeks.'

Bloody Darren, Will thought, but he still let out a steady stream of air in relief.

'You're first up, so that's good news anyway.'

Will sat down next to him and stared blankly at the television on the wall.

★ ★ ★

It was only twenty minutes later when his name was called but as Will made his way into the court he realised he could not have told you one single piece of information about what he had been watching.

He made his way into the room and was guided into the dock. The layout was very similar to his previous visit but he couldn't help feeling small, insignificant and lonely as the door was gently closed behind him. He looked over at Aiden who was the only person in the public gallery at the back of the court. At least someone was having a good time he thought as he watched Aiden take it all in with the look of a child at the fairground for the first time.

'All rise.' Will shot up like he had sat on a whoopee cushion.

The judge walked in like he was walking to his own funeral. His wig perched on his head looked like a dead lamb had dropped out of the air, but it was plain for all to see this man took himself and his role very seriously. He arranged his paperwork on his desk and peered intently at Will. Will wasn't sure whether to stare back and meet his eye or look down, ending up doing both, feeling like Churchill the nodding dog.

'Are you William Reynolds?'

'I am,' Will said clearly.

'Confirm your date of birth.' Will did.

'How do you plead to the charge of dangerous driving?'

'Guilty.'

'You may take your seat.'

'I have examined the details of your case intently Mr Reynolds and although it is not rare for me to hear of such a flagrant abuse of our laws, I still find it astounding. Before I pass judgement is there anything else I should be aware of?'

Will's barrister stood.

'My client is full of remorse for that day's actions m'lud. I hate to use cliché, but it was very much a moment of madness which will never be repeated. He is of excellent character as the testimonials confirm. He should be given credit for his early guilty plea and be able to continue his law-abiding life. Prison would have a damaging effect on Mr Reynolds as he has had no contact with that part of society. He is able and willing to pay a substantial fine and is aware his driving will be curtailed.'

It was a bizarre feeling, watching others discuss your future. It was a continuing theme in his life, but he had never felt more powerless than he did just now. As his brief sat down, Will felt short changed for Darren's money. That was it, that was his defence.

'Mr Reynolds. I can understand a moment's lack of concentration but that day's events shows a wild and wilful disregard for the rules. Not only did you drive in a manner which could easily have resulted in death or injury to an innocent party, you ignored our constabulary and tried to get away with it. You have not got away with it.

I would consider a suspended sentence due to your previous good character but the report on your vehicle tempers my hand. Your tyres were in such poor condition that at normal speeds you would have had trouble doing an emergency stop. I shudder to think what would have happened with you going at over twice the speed limit.

You will return here in a fortnight and I will pass sentence. Let me assure you Mr Reynolds, all options are open to me.'

32

28ᵗʰ October 2008

Will looked around at the other people in the court waiting room. There was very little joy to be seen, in fact he had seen more interaction and emotion on English public transport than here. Maximum effort to avoid eye contact and hushed furtive talking made Will think it was lucky the trials weren't out here or everyone would be getting years.

He wasn't as nervous as before though. It's funny what you get used to. The fear of the unknown at least here was gone. Whether he would feel the same after the verdict was a different matter. He caught Carl's eye and got a thumbs up from him. It was good of him to come up from London but Will suspected he would rather have been here on his own in the end. God knows what he would do if he was sentenced to prison. He hoped weeping in the dock like a bereaved mother was not a possibility.

Carl looked rough though, white and drawn with bags under his eyes that you could haul rubble in. Not so different to himself Will shrugged, whose insomnia had reached fever pitch. He had drunk the most of a bottle of night nurse late yesterday lunchtime knowing he would never sleep otherwise and had finally slept. Well, he had been unconscious for twelve hours. Now he felt like a zombie, heavy lidded and slightly gormless. His intellect had slumped to below Rocky Balboa levels but it didn't matter as the questioning was over. The decision had already been made and he was only here to hear it.

The barrister had finally explained what all options meant when they arrived today. It was a maximum of two years in prison, a massive fine and five years disqualification from driving. Will had needed to go to the toilet ever since he had heard that news and he had only just been when they arrived. He also informed them their case would be the second to be decided and unconvincingly joked that Will would be banging on the pub door by five to twelve.

As Will stared along the length of the waiting room over the heads of Darren and Aiden he saw a familiar figure and his heart slumped. Just brilliant. The last person on earth he would want here. Which fucker had told him? Bloody Nathan. He decided he would do without pleasantries.

'What are you doing here? Have they finally found your porn stash?'

'Very amusing William. I came to offer my support.'

'Who told you?'

He saw an almost imperceptible move of his head towards Darren but he recovered quickly. 'A bloke I knew well was here for non-payment of council tax a few weeks back and saw you.'

'Yeah, who?'

'Does it matter? Look, here is some money.' He gave Will fifty quid in five ten pound notes. Will was stunned; Will had never received anything off his brother except Chinese wrist burns and dead arms.

'What's this for?'

'If you get jailed today you go straight away. No popping out to get some cash to pay for concrete pants to safely shower in.' He looked well chuffed with his little joke, but Will didn't have a penny on him.

'Won't they just take my money off me when I arrive and give it back when I get out?'

'If you turned up with a grand they might do, but if it's just a hundred they put it in your private jail account and put some in your spending account straight away. It means you can buy tobacco and sweets on the canteen straight away otherwise you have the ball-ache of having to get money sent in, or worse earning it. That can take weeks and you are going to have some long nights of chain smoking in the beginning. Here, put this in your bag too.'

He handed him a plastic Sainsbury's bag which Will opened to find contained four packs of Haribo's and five packs of Benson and Hedges Gold.

'You always did like your chewy gooeys.'

'I'll be able to keep these too?' He looked for confirmation from the others. His barrister gave him a guilty nod and Darren shrugged.

'You get given a tobacco pack when you arrive if you smoke,' he said.

'Jesus, that's hardly likely to last me two weeks, didn't you dinkers think to mention any of this before?' He included his barrister on his sweep of dirty looks and looked up at his brother in a new light.

'Thanks.' He stood up and offered his hand.

'No problem, it's what any brother would do. It's the easiest thing to get into debt over tobacco when you arrive. You can get it on tick, but its double bubble and it soon adds up.'

'What's tick and what's double bubble. How do you know all this?' Aiden said suspiciously.

'I did some time a few years back. Just a few weeks for drink driving ironically. We didn't tell anyone. You've always been the golden boy Will.'

Some of the old Nathan shone through as he condescendingly replied to Aiden, speaking more slowly than was necessary.

'Tick is where one packet of tobacco is lent to you. Double bubble means you have to give two packets back on your next canteen, or it doubles again.'

It was all a lot to take in. His friends reached into their pockets and gave him all the notes they had. Darren even gave him his three remaining Mayfair cigarettes. Nathan handed him a condom.

'You may find it beneficial for your sexual health to use this when your new gentlemen friends come calling.'

'I think I'll give that a pass actually. All I need is for that to drop out my bag in a busy shower and they will think my ass is open for business.' Will looked at Nathan and unexpectedly found he wished his parents were there all of a sudden.

'All I need now is Sara to show up, maybe my parents, couple of my teachers from school and my current boss,' he said to distract himself.

They all laughed. Darren tapped him on the leg.

'I saw Sara.'

'Brilliant. I don't want to know thanks.'

'She was walking through the shopping centre here.'

'Don't tell me.'

'She was pushing a double buggy thing, with some tall prosperous looking handsome dude, probably called Rich Rupert. She looked really good too, really happy.' Darren roared with laughter.

'Cheers you git. What a brilliant thought to take with me to prison. It's a shame you didn't take a photo, I could have pinned it on my cell wall.'

'Heh, they probably haven't had sex since the kids were born, not with each other anyway,' Carl said when he had stopped laughing. 'He will be snorting coke in the train toilets on the daily commute to London just to get going and she will be downing a bottle of red wine just so she can face the school run. He'll have spent every posh holiday glued to his lap top trying and failing to maintain his finances, which have become a house of cards the current economic malaise will bring crashing down.'

'Yes Will,' Aiden added. 'You will be safe and sound with three square meals and the local armed robber doing your laundry for you.'

'That's better,' Will laughed. 'Just throw in a particularly nasty gardening accident involving a strimmer and Rupert's genitalia and I'll sleep like a baby. Maybe Darren could have been helping him at the time and been de-nutted as well.'

Their laughter was interrupted by Will's name being called. He took a deep breath, picked up his bag and nodded to his mates. Darren got up and shook his hand.

'If you do go down, don't worry, I know a lot of people in there, you will be fine.' Not particularly reassured Will strode through the doors to an echo of 'Good lucks' from everyone.

As he walked into the court he was directed into the dock. This time there was already a heavy set security officer standing in there who sized him up like a tailor would a client. As Will turned around to face the room, he heard the dock door being locked. His bag slipped out of his hands, both of which were now sweating freely. He didn't want to look over at his friends, so he faced the front where the judge was already sitting. He confirmed his details in a croaky voice and was told to remain standing for sentencing. The judge seemed to be in a poor mood and spoke in a rapid clipped fashion with flowery language that was hard to follow.

'Mr Reynolds. The report has come back indicating you are a law abiding citizen who has lived a crime-free life. You are a professional businessman and have no end of character references confirming your noble endeavours. I have taken this all into account.

'However, I cannot get away from the seriousness of that day's behaviour. The flagrant disregard for the law and lack of mitigating factors exacerbates your predicament. Untold damage could have been done to any number of innocent bystanders. It is a wonder no-one was incapacitated or killed. The aggravating aspects of the poor condition of your vehicle and your outrageous attempt to escape justice have led me to only one conclusion.

A short, sharp, shock is needed in this case. We cannot have people thinking it is acceptable to run away from the law. I am therefore sentencing you to six months in jail. You will receive credit for your full admission and early guilty plea, so this is reduced to four months. Of this you will serve two. If you commit further crimes in the following two months you will be returned to jail to serve the remainder.

'I hope I do not need to state that if I ever see you again for something similar, I shall not be so lenient. Send him down.'

Will had tried to prepare himself for this, but he was still shell shocked. He wasn't really sure what all that meant. The security guard handcuffing him immediately though left him in no doubt. He looked over at his shit barrister who was intently focusing on his nails. He scanned to his friends, who looked shocked and visibly upset. The last face he saw as the door opened behind the dock and he was dragged into the darkness beyond, was that of his brother Nathan. He was grinning like a Cheshire cat.

33

29ᵗʰ October 2008

It was the cell door being unlocked and pushed slightly ajar that finally woke Will. He just about caught the word breakfast being barked into the cell and opened his eyes. His first sensation was of feeling refreshed. Yesterday had been an insanely long day. His belongings had been taken off him and he had spent the next nine hours in a waiting cell under the court with a guy who looked and smelt like if he pissed himself it would be the first wash he had experienced this year. This tramp had woken up once when the sandwiches came around stating, "Gotta eat, who knows when the next meal is coming", before going back to sleep. At least that was all he said, although no-one else had talked to Will either.

Time had dragged like waiting for a delayed flight in an airport. Weird slow time in a strange environment. No communication of what was happening, or when. The transfer had been a blur. The thing he remembered clearly was holding his breath as he entered his cell, wondering what horror may be lurking in there, but it was a single and relatively clean. The officer called Duke had been pretty reasonable throughout the whole searching, stripping, and questioning routine since he arrived and gave him a smile.

'Don't get used to being on your own. We have no PNCs for you so we can't risk assess you for cell sharing.' Will had given him a blank stare so he explained.

'PNC, Police National Computer. Before we put you in with someone we need to make sure you didn't strangle your last cell-mate with your shoelaces whilst he was watching TV. You have probably got two days at most.'

So Will had climbed fully clothed under his ancient looking duvet, pulled his thick towel from home on top for warmth and slept. Maybe it was the fear of going to prison had gone as he was already here. Maybe it was the fact that the horrific foreign psychopathic cell-mate who liked to watch you sleep hadn't materialised. Probably a combo of those two things and the sleep deprivation he had been experiencing these last few months, but he slept like a baby.

When he woke though, his imagination ran riot. His mind began to process where he was and he could feel the wretched thing start to create unpleasant scenario's waiting for him as soon as he stepped out of his cell.

Before he could force himself to get up and face whatever reality was out there, which was never going to be worse than the things his mind was creating, his door was gingerly pushed open and Will had his first encounter with a greasy smack head.

'Just got here have you Bruv? Don't worry, it's not too bad here. You haven't got any burn have you?'

Will followed his longing gaze which had focused on Will's two remaining Mayfair on the cell floor. He then looked at Will's towel, his pupils expanding and contracting as though they were electronic. Will knew well enough to say 'No' but didn't want to make any enemies at the same time. Shame they had not let him keep his sweets. Not that this guy looked like he had the dental capabilities to tackle a cola bottle. He doubted he would be much of an enemy either. He looked so sickly and yellow that a slight cold would be enough to carry him across the River Styx.

Before he had to deny him a smoke they were joined by another prisoner. He shoved the junkie into the corner and he collapsed cowering onto another seatless toilet. Surely there is a hole in the market there, he strangely thought.

'Get the fuck out. If I find you anywhere near him again, the next cigarette you smoke will be in the infirmary.'

He slung him out as though he was a flatulent dog needing its morning constitutional and turned to regard Will with a cold but vaguely familiar look.

It wasn't until the man's face creased into a grin and he spoke that he recognised him.

'Fancy us sharing the same hotel,' said Dean, from all those years ago. Will couldn't have been happier than if his suitcase had been the first one out of the conveyor belt at the arrivals terminal. He jumped to shake hands, but Dean hugged him as if he was a long lost brother.

'Shit man, it's good to see you. I got a letter from Darren saying that you might be coming.'

Will stared again at Dean and felt another rush of relief to see a friendly face.

'It's good to see you. Did you just arrive here as well?'

'I've been here long enough to be a wing worker on this wing which is one of the better jobs here. This is the induction wing where everyone comes through, so I knew I would see you if you arrived. The screws are pretty sound on here, they are always looking for normal people to be wing workers, you know, the ones who aren't going to sell the toilet paper and make spears out of the mop heads. I'll get you a job on here. How long did you get?'

'Six months. But as I went guilty I think I got it lowered to four months, but I think I might have to serve two. Maybe, it was all a bit confusing.'

'I know, it's a head fuck, you are whisked away and no-one explains anything. I thought I had a whole bloody year to do, no-one said anything about doing half. Thank the lord I won't have to be here at Christmas. You will get a sheet of paper slid under your door in a few days telling you what day you will be released.'

As he said, that his demeanour changed and he gave Will a serious look.

'My wife got me sent here if you can believe it. We had a few drunken rows and she got a restraining order on me. I couldn't go within two hundred metres of my own house and my own son if you can believe that either. Anyway, she rings me up, drunk, come over, have a few drinks, see your boy, he misses you. So I do. I turn up and it's all good, same as before. I stay over. The crazy cow rings the police while I'm asleep, says I wouldn't leave and before I know it I'm in here. Absolute joke.'

Will nodded in agreement but suspected there was a whole lifetime of issues in play and his wife would have a very different version of events.

'I'm starving.'

'Come on then Will, I'll introduce you to the boys. Cornflakes today, do you like cornflakes?' Will shrugged.

'Good,' Dean laughed, 'Cos it's always bloody cornflakes, or rice crispies. I hate rice crispies.'

The wing was quieter than he was expecting; a more subdued vibe to it than an atmosphere of suppressed violence. They took their breakfast back to Dean's room and ate it companionably on the bed. Dean's room was spotless, the floor shining. One wall was covered with pictures of what he guessed was his wife and a little lad who was his spitting image.

Will noticed a picture of two squaddies in maroon berets. He got up and went over, bending down to see it on eye level in the gloomy light. As he suspected it was Darren and Dean. They looked so young and vibrant. He turned to look at Dean and smiled, but inside he was thinking 'Look at the state of him'. He could pass for fifty. Whereas before he had been whippet thin and sleek he was now chunky and jowly.

'I know, look at us.' Dean held his stare. 'What happened eh? I don't even know where I'll go when I get out. I can't believe I'm homeless.'

'Can't you go back to your parents?'

'No, my dad is long gone and my mum's old now. We had a few fallings out when I first got out too. It's not really fair on her at her age.'

Will wasn't sure he definitely wanted to know but in the end he asked.

'Why did you leave the army?'

Dean stopped eating his cornflakes and put his Tupperware bowl down on the floor next to his plastic stool and looked out the barred window.

'I lost it man. A lot of us did. We were exposed to enemy fire almost daily and even though I seemed to cope out there, I couldn't back here. I'd have flashbacks and night sweats, that's if I slept. I had huge mood swings and the only thing that seemed to make it better was drugs and alcohol. My missus took it for a long time, bless her.' Dean stopped talking and turned to look at Will. 'You can only take so much you know.'

'Have you thought about seeing if Darren can help you out?'

'Do you still see much of him? How is he?'

'He's fine, a little highly strung these days. Not seeing his kid hasn't helped.' Will found he was going through the usual platitudes but knew he was covering up for Darren. He wasn't sure why as he could see by the look on Dean's face that he knew what was going on.

'Don't tell him this please Will, but I don't want to see him. We did a lot of things you know. I know they were orders, but in the light of day I can't seem to live with the fact I did them. I don't think Darren can either and when we meet, well it's immediately brought straight to the surface.

'There are a lot of us here Will, ex-forces. We get burnt up and burnt out. You were scared to death sometimes but you felt alive, throbbing almost, a real buzz.

'Then you are out, discarded. Unwanted and useless. There aren't many job adverts for past-their-best assassins with an unpredictable temper and penchant for mind subduing substances. Not long after you're discharged you are sat on a cheap sofa staring at a shit television, day in day out. You were Special Forces, now you are a nobody, in a small dirty terrace in Huntingdon next to a virtual stranger, watching bloody Countdown.' He took a huge breath.

'Bet you glad you asked, eh?'

'Still,' he said recovering. 'We've got your back here.' He tried his best at the smile that used to animate his face but failed miserably. 'You'll be fine here mate.'

Worryingly, he was right.

34

24th December 2008

The holding cell was packed. Will doubted it was supposed to hold fifteen people but there was little prospect of trouble today. He looked at his watch and grinned. Six forty-five a.m. There had been no trouble waking everyone up and getting them out of bed this morning. Prison rules state that if your release date was on a Saturday or Sunday, you went on the Friday before as they didn't release at the weekend. They also stated you could not be released on a bank holiday, you went the day before. Will was due to be released on the 28th of December, a Sunday. So he would then normally have gone the Friday before, but that was Boxing Day. So here he was, with four times the usual releases, on Wednesday, Christmas Eve, like a child waiting for Santa.

He could hear varied bursts of conversation and laughter in many different languages, but you didn't need to be a linguist to know what was being said. For most, it was all they talked about whilst they were banged up and there seemed to be a clear division. For short termers and first timers it was all about where and what they were going to eat when they got out, how pissed they were going to get and what they were going to do to their missus. KFC was a popular choice, as was a blow job in the prison car park. As Darren was picking him up he would do without the latter. The thought of a proper chicken burger though had him drooling despite the early hour. The prison kitchens were still some way off cracking Colonel Sander's recipe.

For long termers and repeat offenders their joy was tempered. It was often drink or drugs that had got them in this predicament in the first place and by the look of some in here they would be making similar choices the moment they stepped outside. It was not quite so easy to celebrate when life had taught you that you would soon be back. Will suspected at least one would be back by this evening, if not here, then in the police custody suite which was the waiting room for here. One of the prison officers had told Will that he had released someone at four in the afternoon one Friday after they were given 'time served' from video court and as he was driving home that night after his shift finished at seven, he had seen him face down on the pavement being cuffed outside the nearest off licence to the prison. He had even put him back in his old cell on the following Monday.

Will joined in with the cheering as one of the youth offenders emptied a bowl of cornflakes down the back of another's jogging trousers. It was a carnival atmosphere. Will wondered when was the last time all those rich people rattling around in their enormous houses and driving their non-appreciated top of the range cars felt like this. This was gritty happiness. Will really understood the old adage that you don't appreciate what you have until it's gone. Take someone's freedom and a gentle walk in a peaceful park is a hopeful dream. Prison is an illogical place. You are locked up alone, but you can feel unhappy humanity all around you.

Will had been having a recurring dream of an unoccupied Olympic size swimming pool whilst he was inside. He would walk naked out of the changing rooms and slowly stride along the side of the water feeling the knobbly non-slip floor under his feet. The air would be crisp with chlorine and slightly chilled. Glorious silence would fill that empty space. He would go up to the five metre diving board and walk to the end. Then topple forward, ever so gently. He would slowly glide through the air and as he neared the surface he would hear the gentle lap of the water. He would burst into the icy clean coldness and race through and up, his ears bubbling and break through into the mist, gasping with shock, joy and freedom.

He would usually wake up then and think one day, soon.

Will had ended up staying on the induction wing. Good to his word before he left, Dean had got him a job as a wing cleaner and he had helped on the servery. He never had to relinquish his single cell - a perk of the job. He worked hard most of the time and got a simple pleasure from mopping floors and serving inmates. The prison kitchens cooked the food and it was then transferred to the wings in great big trolleys. Here the servery workers served it up in varying portions to the queueing masses. Due to that, he had eaten better than at any time in his life since he was a child. The servery workers short changed the new arrivals like it was a national sport. If you didn't know the rules, how did you know they were being broken? It was a steep learning curve in jail and Will had learnt quickly. Giving the massive gym nutters an extra bit of chicken to help quench their insatiable desire for protein gave obvious benefits. A 'He's alright' comment could be the difference between receiving a beating or not over the smallest perceived disagreement.

As one of the inmates was let out for processing, everyone cheered again. Despite the overused air in the congested cell Will took a deep breath. He felt good. Better than good. Two months without booze, drugs, takeaways and nightclubs and he felt like he had been scourged through with bleach, coming out bright, refreshed and energised. He could feel the muscles move under his shirt that gym three times a week and cell exercises had given him remarkably quickly. No rolling around in bed here with a hangover when it was your wing's turn for exercise.

An officer let the orderly in to clear the mess up off the floor.

'How long Eighteen?' a con called Jules asked the orderly. Will had worked with Jules on the wing servery. He had said he had been given a ten year stretch for manslaughter and had come back to this jail near his home for local release. Eighteen was a lifer but no-one seemed to know what he was in for. The room went quiet for the reply.

'Nine o'clock at the earliest,' Eighteen replied. 'They will let the courts out first, then you releases.' A big cheer went up in the room. Will thought he would google these two lifers when he got out to see exactly what they were in for.

Jules looked pensive. Jesus, ten years he had been in jail Will considered. Jules had described prison as a living death to him more than once. He had arrived all those years ago with a job, money, possessions, a house, a mistress, a wife and three children. Since then he had had to sit in a cage and watch them all slip away, in that order. He was not in any hurry to rush out to see what he had lost.

Finally they were walking out of reception to the main gates. They all stood in the vehicle lock as the huge electric door shut behind them and they were plunged into darkness. There was a mechanical grumbling and then the door in front began to let light in and soon they were staring at the hopeful and tearful waiting families. Loved ones, not quite believing they were going to be out until they saw them. Will weaved between the relieved and happy clinches and saw his friends sitting on the bonnet of a sleek Audi at the front of the visitors' car park. It was a good feeling.

He hugged them all in turn but found himself thinking how much older they looked. It had only been two months, but it was as if he remembered them from school. He got in the front seat, Darren of course was driving. He passed Will a can of lager.

'Where to Maestro?' he said.

'My body is a temple now fellas,' he said resting it unopened on the floor between his feet.

'McDonald's first.' He looked around at his mates and grinned. 'I was worried I was going to come out and find you had found a grubby hooker to bring along.'

'We did, but she had just finished such a busy night that she ran out of energy and we had to drop her back at her crack house,' Carl said.

'Shame.'

'All is not lost William, we kept her pants for you.' Darren turned to his side and grinned. 'Carl has got them on.'

Will looked to the back seat at Carl who gave him a comedy wink, then laughed a deep belly laugh. As he did he realised he hadn't laughed like that in jail and he had missed it.

They stopped at a cash machine on the way and Darren told him to check his balance. He gave Will his bank card which set alarms bells ringing in his head. Darren must have been in his house again to get it for him. He opened his mouth to complain, but Darren implored him to just look.

He entered his pin code incorrectly twice before he realised he had been entering the pin for the prison phone. He pressed the option for check balance and winced as the machine began to whir, expecting some nasty negative balance that was accelerating daily with onerous bank charges. The screen pinged to life and displayed eleven thousand four hundred and ninety-eight pounds and thirty-three pence in credit. He checked the recent transactions and saw two cash deposits of six thousand pounds. One on the day he had been sentenced and one yesterday. He turned back to the car and saw Darren tapping his chest with his fist as he looked at him.

Darren didn't say anything as he got back in the car, although by the way the two in the back were smiling he suspected they knew.

★ ★ ★

As he walked into McDonald's he found himself taking a big snort of air through his nose, savouring the smell of greasy food. He couldn't help smiling at the people behind the counter, normal young people and he found himself running his hand along the backs of the seats as he walked to their table as though he had never been anywhere like this before. Soon though he was tearing his way through his second sausage McMuffin and chuckling at Carl's story of his latest crazy female acquaintance.

'No current pyscho then?' Will asked.

'No, I'm conserving my energy for our holiday.'

'Holiday?' Will replied with a mounting sense of horror and excitement combined in equal measures.

'You tell him Darren, you paid for it.' Aiden said.

'With some help,' Darren nodded at Carl before continuing with a flourish. 'Will, with that day's heroic and gallant actions, you have been rewarded with a holiday for four to Thailand. Obviously you can't choose who you take on it. We go in a month my friend. The holiday of a lifetime. Fine food, great views, scuba diving and more lady boys than a frustrated ex-con like yourself can handle.'

He handed Will an itinerary and Will sat back in his seat with a small smile on his face. Prison had given him time if nothing else. Time to sleep and time to think. He felt like he was now thinking straight for the first spell since he left school. He had lain on his prison bed and wondered what the hell he had been doing all these years. He was off the hamster wheel now and he was not getting back on it.

Will had decided in jail he was now going to do something with his life. Nothing exceptional maybe, but break out of the rut he had found himself in. He was going to travel the world for a start. All those years he had wanted to go to Asia and never had. He didn't care if he was a bit old for backpacking, or if he might be lonely on his own. That, he surmised, had been his big fear. Well you were never more alone than being inside and he had coped just fine. He knew that might have just been because he only had a few months to do and that the awful waste of doing years would be very different, but he wouldn't be going back. He shouldn't even have been there in the first place.

Admittedly these plans had needed money, but for the first time he decided he would make it work whatever. He hadn't wanted to sell his house, but if that was what it took, so be it. He had decided if he had to work in B and Q until he was seventy-five because his pension was so poor then bring it on. Typical that now he had decided he didn't care about that, he wouldn't have to. He'd almost been looking forward to it.

All of a sudden he could see a whole world of opportunity and new experiences opening up to him. Maybe, just maybe, it had all been worth it. He felt fully alive for the first time and he could hardly contain his delight.

As they pulled out of the restaurant car park Will felt a little peaky. He wasn't sure if he just had eaten too much or he now wasn't used to food with flavour. Damn, it had tasted good though.

'What do you want to do Will?' Carl asked. 'It's your day. Do what you want and we will do it with you.'

Will looked at his watch and was about to say its canteen day and stopped himself. He realised at the back of his mind he had been thinking about getting the servery ready for the food trolleys. Forgetting about prison routine would take a while and he was pleased with that. Every time he realised he could now do what he liked, when he liked, it sent a bolt of joy through his body. He began to have some understanding for how Darren felt when he left the army.

Improbably though he wanted to go to his house and spend some time on his own. Sit on his sofa and watch television for as long and as loud as he liked. Draw himself a bath maybe. Even though he didn't like baths much as he felt like he was washing himself in a tight coffin it was the fact the option had been taken away from him for so long that now made it appealing.

'Do you need to do any Christmas shopping?' Carl asked.

'No, it's OK, I made you all bird boxes in the woodwork workshop.'

'Brilliant,' Aiden said. 'I've been looking for one for my garden.'

'I'm joking you moron, how much bloody time do you think I've done.'

'Yes Carl, I would like to get a few things for my nephews and nieces. I figured everyone else would understand that they would be getting fook all. Surely the pleasure of my company will be the only gift they want this year. My brother in particular can whistle, unless I can somehow buy a parcel bomb. That fucker wrote to me and told me he hadn't really been to prison, he had just read someone's biography of their time in jail. He just wanted the pleasure of watching me get sent down.'

'Very sneaky from Nathan, he is indeed a massive weasel.' Darren laughed out loud.

Carl though picked up on the vibe coming off Will. He was a good friend Will thought.

'Will, how about we drop you at your house, you can chill for a bit, then walk into town and pop in John Lewis. We will meet you for a nice pizza in Prezzo's or something, then we can have a few beers and see if we can find someone desperate enough to sleep with an old crook like you. We can pitch it like some Christmas thing, you know like they will be doing their bit for charity.'

'That's a great idea Carl, take me home and I'll see if I can find a long shirt to cover up my new hepatitis C infecting prison tattoos. Shall we say five p.m. in town?'

Will could see by the look that flashed across Darren's face that five wasn't acceptable. He had clearly been expecting them to be together all day and on some kind of crazy pub crawl around town. Will for the first time in his adult life didn't want to be pissed. He wanted to feel the way he felt today for the rest of his life.

However he knew that his friends wanted to go out and he wanted them to be happy too, so he agreed on three p.m. as they all got out of the car at Will and Aiden's address.

'Do you want us to come in with you? Aiden offered.

'Were you not listening cloth ears?' Carl said with raised eyebrows added. 'He has been locked up with a thousand men and wants some me time, if you get what I mean.'

Will looked at Aiden's dopey face as he got out of the car and saw that he didn't.

★ ★ ★

He opened his front door, stepped in and closed it behind him. He thought it would be like stepping on to the Mary Celeste with half-eaten food and unfinished drinks on the table but instead it was cleaner than at any time since he had moved in. There were a few dust motes hanging in the air but as he walked through the lounge he could see nothing out of place. The kitchen worktops actually sparkled in the weak sunlight like in a movie and the floor shone in a way that he had never been able to achieve when he had mopped it himself. In fact he recalled throwing the mop away last summer when a horrid odour had him convinced a squirrel or cat must have crept in and died somewhere, only to find the offending article was his cleaning equipment resting behind the door.

He looked at the fridge and realised it had never occurred to him to empty it before he went to court the last time and he wracked his brain thinking of what he had left in there. It would have grown powerful by now and would be lurking inside, ready to leap out and bite him when he opened the door. He popped the door open and laughed. It was spotless. There was a pint of unopened milk with a best before date of New Year's Eve, some new Lurpak butter, six free range eggs and a new pack of bacon claiming to be from acorn fed pigs. There was even some Tropicana orange juice and a four pack of Singha beer. He must have had the world's poshest squatters move in or Carl had been shopping for him.

He climbed the stairs, half expecting to find Mark Zuckerberg asleep on his bed but it was as clean and empty up there as it was downstairs. On his pillow was a pristine packet of Benson and Hedges cigarettes and a new zippo lighter with an SAS badge on it. He had never smoked in his bedroom before but prison necessity had overruled that particular standard and he took one out of the packet and laughed out loud when the flame caught and he saw that Darren had taken the effort to put gas in the lighter.

He blew the smoke back out and it hung in the middle of the room like a dirty ghost and he felt as though he had just lit up in a chapel. He went to the spare room which he used as an office. The door was closed which was odd as he never closed it. Inside it was an absolute shit tip. Just how he had left it. Clearly this was a step too far for the cleaning crew. He turned his PC on and cracked open the window to blow the smoke and tap the ash out of whilst it loaded up. He felt odd as he sat in his old office chair, like he was sitting in someone else's seat and would need to leap out when they came home.

He signed onto his Hotmail account and stared in dismay at the two thousand odd new messages waiting for his perusal. He considered looking at them and decided he wasn't really interested. He hadn't missed all this technology inside or the wasted hours constantly looking at updates on the BBC news website and pointless Facebook posts. He turned the computer off at the mains without even bothering to shut it down and grimaced at the taste of the cigarette. He was used to roll-ups now. Anything else was too expensive in jail when you earned two pound twenty for a day's work. He flicked the half-smoked fag out the window and gave a little cheer as it went plop in Aiden's fish pond.

He quickly trotted down the stairs, feeling like a stranger in his own home. He found himself touching and noticing things as if for the first time. He saw that he had missed that someone had arranged his post in a neat pile behind the door and decided he couldn't be doing with looking at that today either.

He opened the fridge again, almost missing the strange smell of various decomposing dairy products which used to greet him in the past, to get the milk out for a cup of tea but found his hand drawn to the beer. He pulled a bottle out of the pack and held it up for inspection. There was a golden lion under a bold SINGHA label and the bold declaration of it being 'The Original Thai Beer'. He opened the drawer for his cutlery knowing he was going to have to hunt for a bottle opener but even this space had been tidied so everything was in its correct place. Aiden really needed to get out more.

He reclined on his sofa which gave a reassuring sink in exactly the right spot and thought back over the last two months. How many times had he dreamed of this moment? Right now, back at home, on his own, total quiet. He slid his thumb through the cold condensation on the bottle and for the first time realised his friends had even put the heating on for him. He breathed in the aroma of the beer and it reminded him of being about eight years old and sneaking into a bar when he was on holiday.

A small voice in the back of his head reminded him of his promises not to go back to this old life, but this temple wanted some beer. He slowly bought the bottle to his lips so as not to spill any and took a small sip. He washed it around his mouth a little and took his time swallowing it. He let out a little sigh. It was that perfect.

He probably drank it quicker than he should have, but he knew that when he was lying on his death bed, hopefully many years from now, he would remember these few minutes of heaven.

He was disturbed from his trance by the sound of laughter from next door, so he jumped off the sofa and feeling light headed ran back upstairs. He found a T-shirt he had only purchased just before he went into jail and pulled it on in front of the mirror. It was much tighter than before. He tensed his new prison muscles and even though he didn't quite recognise the eyes staring back at him, he nodded at his reflection. He looked good.

He grabbed the remaining beer downstairs and putting his favourite coat on, stepped outside and rapped loudly on Aiden's door. It was party time.

35

10ᵗʰ February 2009

19.00 hrs

W ill heard the door being delicately pushed open and then the not so dainty stomp of a medium-sized brontosaurus come and stand next to his bed.

'Go away, I'm dying.'

'You can die tomorrow Will. Its full moon night, you are in Kho Phan Ngan with your best friends and tonight it's the pinnacle of all partays.'

'I feel like death warmed up. I'm not young enough for this madness. I can't even pass out even though it feels like I haven't slept for a year. I'm hungry but I can't face anything and I've more or less spent the last twelve hours rolling around in my own sweat. God only knows when I did anything that even closely resembled a log shaped turd. I'm spent mate. Go and have fun.'

'Come on Will, you'll feel better after a few beers. Think of all those scantily clad backpackers gyrating on the beach, waiting for your entrance.'

'Strong am I with the force, but not that strong.'

'Your thoughts betray you, I feel the good in you, the conflict.' Aiden laughed as he continued the Star Wars theme.

'There is no conflict,' but Will got up anyway. Last night he hadn't even begun to feel remotely up for it until he had forced down his fourth beer. That had been about eleven p.m. and he hadn't got home until six. No wonder he felt like a dying duck in a thunderstorm, but they were going home in two days and this would be the last chance to go out for a big one.

'Give us ten minutes for a shower then.'

'Sure, I'll wait on the porch and enjoy the sunset.'

Will laughed at that. The hut opposite was inhabited by two east European girls who felt it necessary to sit on their balcony naked for most of the day. Anywhere else Will guessed this might be unacceptable but here it just added to the surreal feeling that nothing was out of the ordinary. This combined with the fact they were easy on the eye and super friendly made waving to them a pleasure.

Will gasped as the cold water hit him. They had booked on the far side of the island so as not to be too close to the non-stop partying, but all it had really meant is they had a longer walk to the centre and then a longer walk back. They had also each paid for a hut on their own with air con and hot water so they could get up to mischief without someone else ruining it for them. Both the air con and water had been erratic at best but they had been too hungover to get out of bed early enough to do anything about it. The island was now overrun with thousands of people for full moon night, many of whom would not have booked accommodation, so the chance of moving was currently zero.

Will had kissed a few of those thousands of backpackers so far, but had not felt the urge to bring any back to his abode. The girl last night had been particularly keen but around five a.m. the energy had drained out of Will like escaping air from a li-lo due to a poorly positioned cigarette. It felt like even his face had begun to collapse. Only Darren was near him at the time, the others elsewhere in the mosh of humanity that was still stampeding up and down the beach-edge bars.

He had contemplated telling Darren he was off but knew he would just end up persuading him to stay. So as he was distracted giving a leathered-looking girl his full attention at the time Will had just slunk off when the girl whose name he now couldn't remember had gone to the toilet. The others wouldn't care as they had all been arriving home separately or in twos anyway, with hazy recollections and sore heads the next day. Darren had even woken up next to a girl who he swore he hadn't been with when he went to bed and said she had cried when he had asked her what she was doing there. Afterward, when Darren was elsewhere, Carl said he had seen him pushing a sobbing girl out of his door and telling her to 'Just fuck off'.

The walk home had at least given Will a chance to think. The first week of the holiday had been brilliant. It was like old times but in a really cool place. They had gone sightseeing in Bangkok and then taken a bus to Kho Phi Phi where the film 'The Beach' was filmed. They had just chilled, sunbathed and swum. There was some night life but it had a chilled ambience and even though they had shifted plenty of beers it had not been excessive. They had eaten fresh fruit and vegetables and picked 'today's catch' off the display to be cooked on a barbecue next to their table. It was all Will had dreamed about whilst he had been locked up and more. The people, both the Thai and the tourists, had been pleasant, friendly and relaxed. Will felt like he had entered a different world after the hatred, frustration and pent up vehemence of jail. He could almost feel the pressure being released from him as though he was a hot air balloon steadily going down after a long flight. Even Darren had relaxed a little and had not managed to find anyone to have a fight with since they had left the UK. Will and Carl had learnt to Scuba dive and now Will wanted more of this lifestyle.

That had been until they had come here to Haad Rin on Thailand's party island. The only word to describe it was insane. A line of bars along a sandy shore with a huge throng of the world's youth looking for and finding fun. Constant offers of drugs from every corner made you feel as though you were rude for refusing them. Before their arrival here Carl had even begun to put some weight on due to their healthy diet and lack of class As, but here he had discovered diet pills could be bought from the chemist containing industrial levels of ephedra. They gave you a buzz similar to cocaine when mixed with alcohol and they had all ended up taking them to enable them to continue to party when their bodies would normally have waved the white flag.

This was not what Will had wanted. Prison had been a waste of time and here felt the same. There was the same edginess as on a busy wing. Prison taught you to sense an atmosphere and this one cried out crime. Will seemed to see pickpockets, burglars, drug dealers and rapists everywhere he looked. He didn't want to go out tonight and he would be looking forward to leaving. Last night's solo walk home had left him with a plan though and he now accepted that he would do one more night, just for his friends, as in a way, that would be a fitting goodbye.

20.00 hrs

Will and Aiden arrived at their favourite restaurant and found Carl and Darren in a veranda seat. They didn't look too lively either.

'The big one eh lads? Full Moon night huh? Are we ready?' Darren said as they sat down.

No-one else replied.

'How about some shots to get us going?'

No-one replied to that either.

The tiny Thai lady came over to take their order. She was a terrible waitress. Will was pretty sure she had not successfully got any order one hundred percent right since they had arrived and it had become part of the night's ritual to laugh at her mistakes. Brits abroad loved a bit of routine.

'Four Changs please,' Aiden sheepishly said.

The other amusing part was her fascination and blatant desire when it came to Aiden.

'These beers all for you strong man. You drink many beer. You come back later when I finish?' She squeezed him as she spoke, as though she was checking a horse for musculature.

'One each will be fine thank you.'

They ordered food and as per usual the chef brought it out instead of her and practically threw it on the table. It was probably her husband and he may well have spat in it for all they knew, although as he shouted at them in Thai every time Will could always see a glint of humour in his eye and this time he winked at Will as he left. The food was always amazing but tonight Will had to really force his down, hoping some nutrients would be absorbed before it was jettisoned out of his derriere. It would need to be some pak choi to magically eradicate four days of excess.

'I am going to shag everything on the beach tonight, I can feel it,' Darren declared. 'Disco dancer, pole dancer, fire dancer, you name it. No-one will be safe from my charms. I want to go out with a bang!'

'Very romantic Darren. More like Northern Dancer. Whilst you are concentrating on that, could you please not antagonise the locals. I could do without any more drama,' Will said.

'If that little shit wants me to teach him a lesson, then I am happy to.'

Darren gave him an evil look. A small but incredibly muscled Thai and him had been jostling each other for the last few days. The barman at the Drop In Bar had told them he was 'The Man' on the island and an ex-Muay Thai boxing champion. Darren had just said 'SAS, game over'.

'I read on Google today that it is not unusual for someone to die on full moon night here,' Aiden said. 'Maybe it can be you this year. Stabbed up by Liu Kang and his gang.'

'I'm just off to the chemist, would sirs like their usual order?' Carl said as he got up from the table and pushed his mostly uneaten food away.

The thought of pumping more drugs into himself didn't seem to be an appealing prospect for Will, but the chance of him lasting the night otherwise were infinitesimal.

'The usual please,' Will and Aiden replied.

Darren got up, whispered something in Carl's ear and they both laughed out loud and wandered off down the dusty street.

21.00 hrs

They arrived at the Cactus Bar and sat on a bench in the sand outside in the dusk. It was busy but not heaving yet. Full Moon Night was a marathon not a sprint and Will told Darren so.

'Was it really necessary to get here so early?'

'I like to do a recce first,' Darren replied, 'Check out the scene. I don't want to miss anything.'

Darren had a loose vest top which showed off his wiry muscles but even in the dark Will could see he was sweating profusely. There was actually a nice breeze off the sea tonight so he was clearly already on something. Carl looked flushed too but he was so groomed he didn't look so manic. A sun tan had given Carl the final piece of the jigsaw and there was almost a film star quality to him. Who would have known being so thin would become so desirable. Carlbuncle was well and truly consigned to history.

They finished their beers and wandered further up the beach. There were already many people the worse for wear but they mostly appeared to be in the 'I'm so happy, I love everyone and everything stage' as oppose to the 'Kill me, or kill you phase'. They stopped outside a trance bar which already had people whirling and twirling to a hideous beat. Random laser beams of light lit up the black dance floor into fractions, making the dancers appear as though they were being electrocuted from different angles.

'If we get split up, let's meet here,' Aiden declared. 'We'll stick out like sore thumbs.'

22.00 hrs

As the four of them sat around a low table on the sand outside another bar Will felt the drugs he had taken pick him up out of the doldrums and felt the energy course through him. He wasn't sure where Darren had got the ecstasy tablets from but they had all taken one anyway. All of a sudden the music from the bar seemed to become clearer and his body picked up the rhythm of 'Poker Face' by Lady Gaga. They all stood up in unison, grinning at each other.

Will could feel his heart pounding as he danced with his friends. He knew it was partly the chemicals flowing through his bloodstream but he swore he had never felt this good. He had experienced some dark nights in prison where he had felt he would never have good times again. It was such a relief to know it was still possible. Aiden was bopping next to him, a huge grin on his face, arms in the air. Carl was sandwiched between the two eastern European nudists who had taken the effort to put some flimsy clothes on with a look of heavenly surprise on his face. 'Bastard' Will thought and tipped his head back and laughed out loud.

'Your round.' He felt a tap on his shoulder and turned to see a stationary Darren behind him. He seemed at odds to the swirling mass of people around him.

'I'll give you a hand,' he said.

Will let him be guided around a corner thinking Darren was just wanting to get served quicker and taking him to a less manic bar.

When he got down the path, it was quieter as a big tall wooden building cut out the music and all he could hear was the beat in the background. There was no bar though, just two local men with serious expressions on their faces, clearly waiting for them. One was the Thai fighter Darren had spent the last few days posturing to.

'Fuck this Darren. I just got out of jail. Let's go,' Will hissed at Darren.

'No, I'm here to fight, you are here to watch.' As Will wondered what the hell that meant the boxer and Darren walked further down the alley. Will followed feeling he had no choice in the matter, taking a sharp left turn until they were in a clear flat area of dried mud behind some shacks. The other Thai came and stood next to Will which elevated the discomfort his body was feeling at the sudden change in atmosphere. As the other two men squared up to each other, the man turned to him.

'Your friend lose. Slowly,' he whispered to Will. Will looked at the combatants. Both appeared supremely confident. The weak orange light from the single street light emphasized the greasy forehead and face of Darren but he looked relaxed and fluid as he rolled his shoulders. His opponent took his T-shirt off, bowed to him but never took his eyes off Darren's face and then it was on.

No wonder the bloke was self-assured. He was chiselled like no man Will had seen before. He suspected he would be able to find more spare flesh on Carl than on this rapidly moving individual. Suddenly Will's belief in Darren evaporated. He looked like what he was. A thirty-five year old washed up ex-soldier high on drugs. It seemed it was all Darren could do to dodge the myriad of kicks and punches that were coming his way. The poor light made it difficult to see what was landing and what was being deflected but it was evident to both men watching it was one way traffic.

Darren suddenly slipped a punch and no doubt realising he could not beat this guy in a boxing match got in close and got off a succession of punches to the man's midriff. His victim, though, twisted his body left and right and rained blows to Darren's head and face. Darren dodged them all bar the last one, an upper cut to his chin. He blocked it but the force of the hit knocked him backwards giving the other man space to direct an extended kick straight into Darren's solar plexus knocking him a metre back and he dropped to his knees. The other man held both hands up, nodding his head; a slow smile enlivening what had been a stony visage. He knew he had the best of his opponent.

Will looked at the man next to him and began to wonder how he was going to get out of this intact. His heart was going like a trip hammer and the blood coursing through his veins felt hotter than lava, causing sweat to ooze out of him like a cheap burger on a barbecue. He decided when the deadly blow came, he was going to turn around and sprint for the safety of the crowds as if his life depended on it - and it probably did. He looked at the man next to him who had adoration glowing in his eyes at his invincible friend and Will suspected he might not even notice if he slipped away now. Something though made him stay. Darren deserved what he was about to receive and Will was done getting involved, but this could end horribly and Will wanted to be able to help if he could and it didn't affect his own health. It did end horribly.

To be fair to Darren he pulled himself upright and engaged his enemy once more. Breathing hard he circled him, blocking the kicks that came his way. Fast and without warning Darren flung his watch, whose catch he must have loosened when he was kneeling, with an underarm throw at his foe's face. The man dodged it and threw an inevitable punch, but no doubt due to the surprise of the watch trick it seemed to lack its usual crispness and Darren slipped underneath his fist. It was then that Will's mind cleared. Darren wasn't a fighter, or a sportsman. He was a trained killer. He hadn't been boxing with this man; he had been working out how to disable him. He had been looking to destroy his opponent in the safest way possible with the minimal amount of damage to himself. Always a professional.

Darren got in close and clawed his thumbs into his rival eyes, as he raked and gouged he used his forward momentum to slam his forehead into the exposed nose. Will could hear the wet crunch of bloody bone from where he stood. As the man lost consciousness and began to drop to the floor Darren immediately threw a thumping uppercut under his chin, knocking the falling head back up and then he grabbed the man by the back of the neck. As the man fell forward with a slack face Darren propelled his face down, straight onto his own rising knee.

Will turned to look at the unconscious man's friend but he had disappeared, no doubt like Will should have done. He walked over to Darren who had turned the man over and was eyeing up the pulpy mess that had once been a face. As the man started to make a gurgling sound, no doubt choking on the blood which was pouring out of his nose Darren turned to face him. He gave him a blank look and walked past him, down the alley and disappeared into the crowd. Will went to follow him before whispering, 'Fuck.'

He bent down next to the prone form and proceeded to arrange his arms and legs in the right way and pulled his head towards him. He noticed the two front teeth were missing. With a grimace he propped the man's jaw open, wincing at the scrape of bone on bone, and put his finger into the mouth and fished them both out in a pool of blood and phlegm. He then rolled the man over into the recovery position. He stood up and spun around as he felt eyes upon him. It was just a small child watching from the shadows. Fearing the return of the other man with a mob and feeling very exposed Will trotted back down the lane and made his way towards the nearest bar toilet to wash his hands.

23.00 hrs

Will eventually found him watching a fire display on the beach talking to a young couple.

'Here he is.' Darren clapped him on the back as though he hadn't seen him for months. 'This is Jenny and John from Wisbech, small world eh?'

Wisbech is a small market town near Peterborough in the Cambridgeshire fens famous for jokes about farmers with webbed feet. John looked very much like he belonged in these tales. He was built like an ox, powerful shoulders and heavy dark bearded face, sporting a pair of biceps that looked as though he spent his working day throwing hay bales around. Jenny on the other hand was as different as it is possible for two humans to be. She was lithe like a dancer with an open doe-like expression on her face. She was sporting a bikini, some artful body paint and a pair of flip flops. That was more or less it, except she was wearing a look of intense animal attraction that had alarm bells jarring in Will's head. She stared at Darren as he spoke. It was the same meeting of souls as Darren and Freja all those years ago.

Darren had his hand cupping her neck as he leant forward and whispered something in her ear. The same hands that not thirty minutes ago had almost beaten someone to death. She was dancing on the spot, clearly under the influence of a modern chemist and grinned widely. Will could hardly believe it. This bloke looked like he could pick Aiden up and twirl him around his head like a pizza chef. He caught Will's eye and grunted, 'She's my sister.'

Before he let out a sigh of relief it appeared to Will that that fact might actually be more dangerous. Trying to distract John from the mating display that was going on under his nose Will tried to engage him in conversation.

'So what brings you to Thailand?'

John involuntarily sneezed before he could answer. 'Sorry, I feel like shit.' It was a heavy, booming sneeze that had sprayed Will's feet with snot. 'I picked up this cold on the plane and all this drinking and whatnot has made it worse. Fucking typical, although we have only been here a few days.'

'Just a holiday then?' Will asked as he worked his feet into the sand.

'No, we are travelling for a few months. I worked on the land but all those bloody immigrants arriving have ruined it. Sadly they work hard, undercut everyone and are more reliable to boot. I lost my job after having a load of time off for a car accident. I was struggling to get a new one, got some compo for whiplash and we decided to come and have a laugh and then look for new work when I get back.'

'Get on well with your sister?'

'Yeah, she's great. She just came out of a shitty relationship with some prick and needed a pick up. So here we are.'

It looked more like a prick up was on the cards. Will tried to carry the conversation but it was like cycling into a headwind. A lot of effort for minimal reward. He came to the conclusion fairly quickly that he didn't need to be here. He had done more than his fair share of wing man duties for Darren tonight. He was about to make his excuses when John sneezed again. It was a huge affair that wracked his body. Through sore, grainy eyes he looked at Will.

'Look, I've got to go back to the bungalow. She will want to stay out, so fucking look after her, or I'll be mad.'

Even in his weakened state, Will could see that an angry John would be a terrible thing to behold.

As John interrupted the kissing couple and informed her of his departure Will suddenly thought wait a minute. Why the hell was he looking after her? He hadn't even spoken to her yet.

As John clumped off barging his way through the crowds like a wrecking ball through an old warehouse Darren and his new friend came over to speak to him. Will watched Jenny's ever faster spot dancing as Darren whispered in his ear.

'Jackpot William, I'm going to fucking ruin her.' The girl gave Will two peace signs and stuck her tongue out at him. She was smoking hot and mad as a March hare. Right up Darren's street. As Darren stood back and gave him a wild eyed look Will could see flecks of blood on his head and a bruise beginning to form in his jawline. The pair of them staggered off in the direction of a nearby bar leaving Will shaking his head in bemusement.

24.00 hrs

Bollocks, Will thought, where are those other two pecker-heads? Although it was not surprising he couldn't find them as there must have been over ten thousand people wedged onto a small fire-lit beach. It dawned on him then that he could just sneak off. He had looked for them so wouldn't feel too guilty. Nice, he could get a tasty chicken burger from chicken corner and have an early night. He began to thread his way through the throng, looking forward to some peace and quiet when he felt someone tap him on the head.

'Where have you been you numpty, we've looked all over for you.'

Will turned around and looked at his two shiny faced friends. Carl seemed to be having trouble focusing and Aiden's hair was matted with sweat.

'That doesn't look like all you've been doing,' he replied, but he was pleased to see them.

'Aiden's in love.'

'Shut up Carl. In fact Will, I have found the perfect girl for you. Tonight you will meet the girl of your dreams.'

'Aiden's in love too.'

'Is that true?'

'Well I have found something rather lovely as well and luckily she is here with your ideal woman. Come on before some other skunks snaffle them up.'

For once, on matters of the heart, Aiden was correct. They were seated at a table surrounded by locals when they turned up which made Will's flesh goose bump, but they left as they arrived. It didn't take any guessing which one was Will's. The girl on the left was average build with a pleasant face but even sitting down Will could see she had the most perfect pert pair of boobs he had ever seen. After a minute of conversation with Elaine he was smitten. She was quick to laugh and easy going but there was a keen intelligence in the background that Will found almost as attractive as her cleavage. Game on.

36

11ᵗʰ February 2009

01.00 hrs

A full hour went by before Will even looked at the other girl. When he did he wondered how the hell he hadn't noticed. She was enormous. Not fat, just big boned. Her head came up to Aiden's nose giving her many inches in height on Will. She caught his astonished look and offered her hand.

'Hi, I'm Penny. Your friend's telling me good things about you.'

He shook her hand marvelling at how small his looked in comparison. She was pretty in a way that Shrek's wife was and emanated the same sweet temperament and demeanour with a strong persona. The four of them chatted for a while. The girls lived in North London which Aiden declared with a lack of cool 'Was only an hour away by train'.

Will noticed that Aiden and Penny were holding hands and even in the dark he could see they fit together. It was only then that he remembered Carl.

'Um, where's Carl?' he asked, suspecting Aiden would be as clueless as him.

'Those two crazy Latvians came back, don't you remember. Apparently he was going back to theirs as one of them had promised him it was his lucky night.'

'What! No way,' Will involuntarily slipped out.

'Don't let us keep you Will,' Elaine said.

'I'm sorry, I was just worried for my innocent friend.'

He gave her his best smile whilst desperately straining to keep his eyes away from her bosom. It felt like he was caught in their tractor beam.

02.00 hrs

The four of them found a bar to dance in. It was the only kind of dancing Will liked. A floor so packed that everyone's technique was restricted to unremarkable shuffles. Will and Elaine naturally danced opposite each other, being constantly jostled and manoeuvred into one another's personal space as the crowd ebbed and flowed. When they came apart after touching she would give him an impish smile and he thought he had never been more turned on. Their thighs slipped between each other's as they were next compressed together and this time they didn't separate.

He went to kiss her but she moved her head next to his so his lips grazed her ear, but she immediately hugged him tight and ran her hand over his bum and it was possible to be more aroused. He pulled her in tight, feeling her curves and knowing she would be able to feel his hard edges and breathed her fragrance in deeply. He closed his eyes as they swayed together and contentment flowed through him.

03.00 hrs

When they finally separated Will felt like a bleary eyed Rip Van Winkle awoken after a hundred years. She conga'd after him as they both agreed a drink would be a good idea. They still hadn't kissed yet, but it was in the post and that was an amazing feeling. Will ordered a beer for Elaine and a water for him. He was acutely aware of not wanting to mess this up by being all over the shop.

They joined Aiden and Penny who were both enjoying a chocolate pancake they had bought from a street vendor. As they ate in silent contented unison Will thought they already looked like they had been together for years.

'Having a nice time are we?' Will said.

They both just grinned.

'Do you want one?' Elaine asked.

Will guessed some food would be a good idea.

'Sure I'll get it.'

'No, it's my treat. Penny can give me a hand.'

The two girls walked to the cart giggling to each other.

'Penny says she's had enough of this madness,' Aiden said to him when they were out of earshot. At Will's horrified face at the thought of his night ending abruptly, he continued quickly. 'She thought that all of us should go. Get a few drinks to take with us and play cards on their deck. She's asking Elaine now to see if she wants to bring you. That's if your Vor Sprung Durch poor dancing Technique hasn't put her off.'

'I'll have you know my silky moves have had her trembling in my hands.'

'I suspect that's your breath, as it often has the same effect on me.'

No more discussion was needed as they returned, handed Will his pancake and began to walk away from the beach. They bumped into Darren and Jenny in the street, both looking decidedly worse for wear. Jenny in particular looked remarkably unsteady and had the rolling gait of a lifelong mariner who was experiencing a brief walk on land.

'Where are you guys off to?' Darren asked.

Will really didn't want to tell him. Experience had taught him adding Darren to an experience like this was like pouring petrol on a barbecue. He fought an internal battle for a few seconds, also feeling bad for considering lying to a friend. His loins won out.

'We are just going for a wander, you know, clearing our heads. Where are you two going?'

'She wants to do some more dancing, then we are going to find a quiet spot to get properly acquainted.' He spoke as if Jenny wasn't standing next to him. Will looked at her face and noted in some sense she wasn't. Her pupils were hugely dilated and her face wore the wasted, tired expression of someone who had given their all at the end of a particularly arduous marathon.

'OK mate, that's cool.' Remembering her brother's warning he added, 'Look after her eh, she looks like she is on her last legs.'

'I'll look after her alright.' He gave Will a cold wink and then put his arm around her shoulders and escorted her back towards the sea front. Will shivered and not for the first time since his thinking time in prison came to the conclusion that Darren was damaged goods. He looked up the mud path and saw the others had continued but in a slow amble, waiting for him to catch up. All other concerns were forgotten as he jogged after those breasts.

Will would never have guessed it would be eighteen months before he clapped eyes on Darren again.

04.00 hrs

The two girls were staying in a line of chalets in the opposite direction of the nightlife from theirs. When they arrived Aiden and Penny went into one without saying a word. Will and Elaine took a seat each on their porch. There was a flimsy table outside with four chairs ideal for cards. They both smoked a cigarette in easy silence. However after a couple of minutes they looked at each other and smiled. It was plainly clear from the creaking bed and chuckling that was emanating from inside that the others weren't coming back out.

'Come on, let's sit outside mine.'

She got up and went to the hut next door and disappeared inside. Will sat on a chair in the identical layout at hers and she soon joined him bringing two glasses and her mobile phone with some small speakers attached to it. She put the music on fairly quietly, just enough so they wouldn't have to hear the rutting beasts next door.

'Nice that you two have separate chalets. Looks like two weasels came on holiday hoping to get lucky.'

'Pot and kettle springs to mind. I hear that you boys have a similar set up.'

'That's purely because we all snore and sleep is very important for your mental health.'

'Judging by the state of you lot I suspect your mental health is way down your list of priorities. Beer?'

'Sure, I'll try one. People rave about this stuff, but I'm more a camomile tea man myself.'

She laughed and passed him a glass, touching his hand unnecessarily after he accepted it. He noticed as he took a sip that there were plenty of mosquitoes in the air around them and slapped a particularly juicy one resting on his knee.

'I know, there are tonnes around here for some reason. They didn't put anything about that on their website.'

'Sometimes it puts people off. Air con, hot water, double room, nice view, bring your blood type as any transfusions necessary are all inclusive.'

'Free Wi-Fi, linen and quinine.'

He quietly laughed. It felt good to banter again.

'We allegedly have hot water but I've yet to see any.'

'Our water is fine, but our air con doesn't work properly. It's about as strong and refreshing as someone breathing on you after sucking on a mint imperial.'

'You're lucky. Ours is totally boom or bust. It only has two settings. One is off or possibly broken and the other is nuclear winter. If you have it on for more than twenty minutes the temperature drops so fast that drinks freeze, your breath steams in the air and frost appears in your hair. But I've paid for it right, so I'm having it on.

Admittedly, I have to wear all of my clothes at once, but at least the mozzies can't stand it. And I've always felt sexy wearing both pairs of my holiday pants.'

'Silver linings, eh?' She giggled a sexy laugh.

'Yes. In the morning I get a certain satisfied pleasure from it. It's like walking on broken glass as I crunch their frozen bodies under foot.'

They sat in companionable silence for a minute, giving each other the odd little look whilst they savoured their cold beers. He slapped another mosquito on his neck and looked around him in the air for more, like a crazy man hearing voices.

She got up out of her seat and took him by the hand pulling him up.

'Looks like we will have to go inside. So I can bite you.'

05.00 hrs

As they lay there breathing heavily afterwards Will estimated he had lasted around seven minutes. That would usually have been a problem but she had lasted for only about four minutes and if he wasn't wrong had orgasmed again when he did. Her breasts were all they had threatened to be and they had fit together like precision engineered equipment.

Will thought what a way to break his post prison duck. She kissed him on the shoulder and snuggled into him as their laboured breathing subsided. He knew he was on holiday, he knew he was half cut and he knew he had only just met her, but he had the most incredible warm feeling. He really liked this girl. His mum always said when you meet her you will know. He felt a bit bad now for giving her grief all these years about her ridiculous Mills and Boon ideas about love.

He felt like he was in paradise. It was crazy but he already could see himself being with this sexy, clever girl for the rest of his life and raising a family. They would grow old together, still having a joke with a glint in their eyes all those years later. As they chatted in the afterglow, that brilliant heavenly feeling also lasted about seven minutes.

'So what job do you do?'

'I'm between jobs at the moment. I worked in insurance and, well, it's a treadmill. I got the opportunity to take some time out, get my head together. I want to do something different, something I enjoy. You know, find a job you love and you never have to work.' As he spoke he felt increasingly lame. He sounded like a dreamy naïve eighteen year old who hadn't comprehended dreams don't pay the bills.

'Good luck with that,' she whispered. 'All that work nastiness seems a long way from here right now and to be honest completely irrelevant.'

He loved her saying that and felt another rush of warmth. She was smart enough to know he sounded flaky but had chosen not to joke about it. Definitely a keeper.

'How about you, what do you do?'

'Well, it's all change for me.' She exhaled deeply. 'I've been working for a solicitors ever since I left Uni. It's a good job but it's full on. Long hours and I'm tired of London. Anyway, it's a global company, offices all over the world. So I have taken a secondment to the Australian branch, in Melbourne. I start in two weeks. I fly straight from Bangkok a week today. All my stuff has gone ahead of me and I can stay as long as I like. If I love it and they love me, they will sponsor me and I can stay.'

And just like that Will's vision of nirvana faded like the smoke from a snuffed out candle. She felt him stiffen and rolled on top of him.

'You can come visit, I'd love to see you again.'

Will knew deep down that wasn't going to happen. Australia had strict entry rules and suspected his custodial stay wasn't going to help his cause. Fate shits in his lap once more. He returned her kisses and this time when they made love it was somehow better. He knew now what people with terminal illnesses meant when they said life was improved in some ways. He felt every touch, every caress as though it was the last they would have. He had always had a bad habit of not appreciating something until it was gone. Well she was still here in his arms and this time he was going to savour every last intense moment.

15.00 hrs

A persistent gentle knock at the door roused them from their dozing state and Will slid out of the damp, sweaty sheets and opened the door.

'I'm going back to get my things. Penny wants me to stay at hers for our last night. I want to as well.' Aiden looked almost guilty, but he had clearly made his mind up.

He turned around to look at Elaine who had raised herself up on one elbow with the sheet only just covering her modesty.

'Go and get yours as well.'

Will grinned big time, went over and kissed her hard on the lips. 'See you in a bit.'

It took thirty minutes to walk back to their huts but in this time Aiden had declared he was hook line and sinker in love and was more animated and alive than at any time Will had seen, even including the time before Freja's untimely death. Apparently Penny felt the same. They were going to meet up when they got back, it was only an hour on the train after all and neither of them could wait.

Will had a strange combination of emotions running through his mind. A weird happy buzz, tinged with jealousy and sadness. He was happy for his friend though.

He was also happy for Carl. He greeted them from the East European's balcony, beer in hand. The railing blocked the view of below his belly button but Will suspected he was also naked.

'Happy days eh?' he said. 'Where have you two been?'

'We've been looking for you,' Will smiled. 'We thought you had been abducted.'

'I had, in the best possible way.'

Will explained, from a distance, what they were going to do and why and Carl beamed at them.

'No worries, I'll meet you at the dock tomorrow morning for the ferry back to Samui. Ours is at ten, then the flight back to Bangkok leaves there at four, so we have plenty of time.'

'Have you seen Darren?' Aiden asked.

'No, I checked his place and all his stuff has gone. He must have done the same as you. Looks like we all had a pleasant evening.'

37

12th February 2009

09:45 hrs

Will kissed a teary Elaine for the last time and walked up the gangplank. Aiden had found a spot at the side of the boat so they could wave as they left. To say Will felt blue was a gross understatement. He looked at Aiden who was waving like a schoolchild leaving his parents to go to camp. He had no misgivings that things weren't going to work out for him. He had even said he was looking forward to going home so it would be sooner when he could meet up with her again.

'Chin up Will, there will be other girls,' Carl commiserated.

Not like her he thought.

'It's probably for the best, otherwise I would have worn my penis down to a small useless stub,' Will joked, but he didn't laugh.

'I feel you, buddy, I'm going to have to put my John Thomas in a cryogenic chamber for a month when I get home, see if I can breathe some life back into it.'

There was still no sign of Darren, but that wasn't unusual for him to do whatever the hell he liked. Their thoughts were on other things and they waved until they were out of sight.

15.00 hrs

They stood outside the airport sweating in the afternoon sun. Carl broke the silence.

'Come on, let's go in, it's his fault if he doesn't show up.'

Will took a deep breath, but all of a sudden he knew it was the right thing.

'I'm not going either.'

'What?' they both chimed.

'I'm staying.'

'But Elaine goes in a few days anyway?' Aiden said with a puzzled look on his face.

'No, I'm not going back to her, I'm going to go to Kho Tao. I checked it out. I'm going to do my advanced PADI and if I like it, my Divemaster and be an instructor. I'm not ready to go back. I want to chill in the sun for a while longer. I've finally got the money and I'm already here.'

'Why don't you come home and leave in a bit, arrange things at home? What are you going to do with your house?' Carl said with a concerned look.

'To be honest I'm scared that if I go back I'll never get the inertia to come back and the chance will be gone. As for the house Aiden, I was hoping that you would rent it out for me while I'm gone. You should be able to get enough to cover the mortgage and then I'm in no rush to come back.'

'Sure, I'll do that for you. I'll miss you Will.'

'I know Aiden, but this is something I should have done a long time ago.'

'I'll rent your house,' Carl stated. At Will's frown he continued.

'I've been thinking for a long time that I want to move home. I'm tired of working for someone else and the bonkers hours. I'm going to set up my own accountancy firm. This is a sign.'

'Cool. Make sure you keep the house in the pristine condition you find it in.'

He watched the others walk into the airport and waved down a Tuk Tuk.

'I want to go to Kho Tao please.'

'No problem my friend, I take you to dock, my brother have boat. Very good price for nice guy like you.'

They sped off into the traffic and Will pondered his decision. He crossed his arms and a small smile tugged at the corners of his mouth. Nodding his head, he broke into a full grin, it was the right one.

38

24th September 2011

Will looked out of the window as the train trundled through the outskirts of Peterborough. The familiar sites were still there but he could also see new housing estates and roads. He thought back to that Christmas when he had come back, freezing in his seat and worried about getting caught without a ticket. Incredibly it was nearly fifteen years ago. The city had changed, but he wondered had he?

Well he had at least bought a ticket this time and he was relaxed and content. The train carried on surrounded by autumn trees shrouded in amazing colour. He thought of all the times he had been on this train and was sure that this was the first time he had ever really seen them. England was a beautiful place. He felt he had ticked a big box by seeing some of the world but he was ready to come home now. After he alighted he fought his way through the commuters all going the other way to London and felt like an alien seeing a crazy new civilization for the first time. He would not be going back to the nine to five, he knew that much.

However, at the back of his mind he could feel a small black spot of worry which whilst minuscule at the moment, he could feel strengthening. He was worried about what he would do for a job and money and for the first time in his life no longer felt young. He was so glad he had his house back here, because otherwise all he would be returning with was a killer of a sun tan and a pickled liver. He lugged his backpack around to the short stay car park and saw Carl flashing his lights at him, sitting in an elegant, sleek, silver Mercedes. The passenger seat was taken by a perfectly groomed creature who looked young enough to be his daughter, but judging by the kiss they shared as he went to the side of the car, she wasn't.

He opened the back door, threw his rucksack onto the far side, and slid onto the leather seat.

'I see business must be tough Carlos.' He smiled as he said it, noticing Carl looking dapper as usual. The interior of the car was a battlefield between expensive his and her scents which made Will very much aware of his long journey home. He hoped Eau de Thai Airways and hint of dive bum didn't invade the war and triumph.

'It's tough spending it all William. This is Adele, she's my secretary.'

He reached through to the front and shook her perfectly manicured hand. It was hard to tell what she looked like, so thick was the make-up, but her smile did at least reach her eyes behind the trendy glasses.

'So how was it?' Carl asked.

'If you read or replied to my emails you would not need to ask that question, but seeing as you are enquiring now, it was awesome, thank you.'

'I've been so busy setting up the business that I've barely had time to trump,' Carl laughed. 'I saw all your pictures on your Facebook. Trip of a lifetime eh?'

Will smiled thinking back, it had been. Indonesia, Laos, Thailand, Cambodia, Vietnam and Malaysia. He had travelled and worked as a diving instructor through them all. The pay was often accommodation and food but his money had stretched easily. He still had a bit left so he wouldn't need to work immediately, although he had almost fainted when he had been charged two quid for a water at King's Cross station. He could have eaten out for that in most places he'd been to and had a cocktail whilst he waited.

'Aiden is well pleased you came back. He wanted us all to be here. To be honest I hardly see him. I hate to quote Forrest Gump, but they are literally like peas and carrots. They told nobody about the wedding, just returned last Sunday and changed their status on Facebook to married. Gretna Green apparently, maybe homage to his Scottish roots. I guess they didn't want a fuss.' Carl drove as he talked, handling the car well. It was smooth and quiet and very different from the shambolic transport Will was used to.

'Instead they booked a table tonight to celebrate and invited their closest friends. She hasn't really got any family either bar an absent father. Just her younger sister who is coming I think.'

'Who else is coming?'

'No idea, I think he is expecting about fifteen but he said they were invited from all over the place and he wasn't sure who was going to make it.'

Will immediately thought of Elaine. He had pushed the thought away whenever he thought about the possibility of her coming. It would obviously be great to see her again but if she rocked up with some handsome boyfriend it would be a considerable downer on his return. They had emailed regularly to start with but as the months went by the time between each one lengthened. About six months ago she had hinted at a boyfriend and he had not heard from her since.

'How is Darren, I heard he managed to make the plane back then?'

'Yes, he reckoned he was getting some heat from the locals after a fight but was his usual vague self. He went back to the Middle East for a while but he said he's done with all that now and wants to buy a pub of all things. He is living with some lunatic he has been dating so I don't see much of him either.'

They pulled up outside Will's house around nine thirty. Carl laughed, 'I made up the spare room for you, but Aiden said you can stay at his if you want. It's good timing you being back Will. I've just completed on one of those new riverside flats in town so you can have your house back. I'll see you tonight at The Peking at seven. I've got something to do at the office.'

Will caught the little look between Carl and Adele and shook his head.

'Aiden is home as he is off work with a dicky knee. He said for you to knock around as soon as you get back.'

Will got out of the car and watched and waved as Carl smoothly drove off. He looked up at his house warmly. He found his key in his pocket but before he could let himself in Aiden opened his door, hobbled over and embraced him in a bear hug.

'Welcome home mate. Come in, I've got the kettle on.'

Will sat on the comfy sofa and looked about the lounge. It was still pristine and striking but there was now a homely woman's touch about the place. Flowers adorned the window sill and a big photograph of the happy couple sat above the fireplace.

'Eloped eh?' Will said, gesturing to the picture.

'Yes, Penny's idea really but I was happy to make her happy,' he said smiling. 'She couldn't be doing with the fuss and thought it would be romantic.'

'Cool. Was it?'

'Yes, it was brilliant,' Aiden gushed. His feelings for his wife were written all over his face.

'So things are great for you then, I'm pleased for you pal.'

'Not that great actually. I keep having gyp from my knee. No doubt lugging all those heavy post bags on top of all that rugby has left its mark. I've got an appointment with the specialist at eleven today but it doesn't look good. Work have offered me a job in the offices but you know me and paperwork.'

They chatted until Aiden left for his assessment and then Will let himself into his own house. He smiled as he walked around the place as it looked exactly the same as when he had left it eighteen months ago. He felt like a shower but the journey had caught up with him. He had never been able to sleep on planes, so he climbed into the spare bed and was asleep in seconds.

* * *

He woke at about five feeling refreshed and full of beans. He could hear voices downstairs but decided to have a shower. Afterwards he wandered into his old bedroom and checked the built in wardrobes to see if any of his old clothes were still there. It seemed to be the only place Carl had made a mark. The bed was new and freshly made and the hangers all had clothes with expensive labels hanging on them. Never mind he thought, he had brought a new shirt and jeans at the airport. He noticed Carl's feet were the same size as his and he chuckled to himself as he picked a smart looking pair up and took them with him.

Darren was downstairs and greeted him with the same firm handshake and calculating look he had given him when they had first met at school. However he then slapped Will on the back and picked up a big carrier bag.

'I got you a present.' He handed him a heavy parcel which Will opened to reveal a cool looking jacket. He pulled it on and was pleased to find it fit reasonably well. It was a damn sight better than his other options which probably had sand on them. All of a sudden his travelling days seemed a long time ago. No more sandals and shorts and beers in wooden shacks.

Carl gave him a bottle of lager and disappeared for a shower.

'How are things then Darren?'

'Great.'

Will deliberately didn't say anything, wondering if Darren would bring up Thailand. He didn't.

'Nice to be back?'

'Time will tell I guess, but yes it's good to see everyone. I even missed my family, well, obviously not Nathan.'

Darren laughed and chinked his bottle against Wills.

'What's your plan Stan?'

Will took a sip of his beer. He looked at the brand, which was Stella. It was very different to the local stuff he had been glugging, but was refreshing none the less.

'I'm not sure. Get a job obviously, but God knows doing what. I can't see me wearing a suit again, but I'm an ex-convict, pushing forty, no qualifications to speak of and a gap on my CV the size of the Grand Canyon.'

'Come work for me.'

'It's a long time since I worked behind a bar and if you forgive my lack of enthusiasm you don't know anything about running a pub.'

'You don't know anything about satisfying a woman yet you still give it a go.'

Will choked on his beer as he laughed. Just like old times.

'So that little skunk Carl told you did he?'

Will didn't even want to think what working in Darren's pub would be like so he changed the subject.

'I hear you live with a delightful creature?' It was Darren's turn to choke on his drink.

'She is frothing mad. And if that's me saying it you know it's bad. I'm going to move out as soon as this pub deal goes through. You haven't asked where the pub is.'

'Go on.'

'It's the Anne Boleyn.'

Will was dumbfounded. It was possibly the worst pub he had ever been in. He didn't want to piss on Darren's parade so he trod softly.

'Not the most popular establishment in town, hasn't it been boarded up for years?'

'Yep, that's why I got it so cheap. I'll do it up and I'm a man about town nowadays so I'll bring in the business. Think about it, I'll make you a manager, it can't be rocket science. You would be good at it. I'll need people I can trust.'

That last comment hung in the air.

'I'll think about it mate. Although it's nice to be offered anything.'

'So tell me about all the birds then?'

The mood lightened as Will explained how teaching diving and pulling the students was like shooting fish in a barrel and soon it was time to go to the restaurant.

Lazy Blood

39

The three of them stepped out of the house at six p.m. and Will noticed a variety of cars clogging up the street. Will knocked on Aiden's door and when it opened he found himself looking at Elaine. His voice caught in his throat as he huskily said hello.

'William. Good to see you again.'

She looked different somehow, but before he had chance to ask the myriad of questions that suddenly clamoured to be answered a tide of people swarmed out of the house. Aiden rapidly introduced the people who Will hadn't met which comprised Penny's sister and three of her old school friends and their partners. Either he assumed everyone else had met at some point or Aiden was chomping to get going so he just left it at that. The restaurant was an old grain barge situated on the river and was within walking distance so they all set off.

He tried to manoeuvre himself next to Elaine as the group walked along but instead found himself interrogated by Penny's sister Dawn. Dawn liked to talk.

'So anyway, when I'm finished Uni, I'm going to go travelling, like you did. Cool uh? Then I want to work in purchasing for a fashion label. I love fashion and fashion loves me. I want to work in the States too. I heard you've been in prison, cool eh?'

Will made a mental note to thank Aiden for keeping his little secret but it made him wonder if Elaine knew.

Try as he might though he couldn't escape the conversation. She seemed a nice girl but reminded him of why he had decided to come home. He had met many girls like this taking a year out and whilst they were invariably good fun they were also exhausting. Luckily for Dawn she hadn't inherited the gigantic proportions her sister had but she still had really long legs on ridiculous heels and long ginger hair. She trotted next to him like a hyperactive adolescent red setter.

However she could have been Angelina Jolie, naked and riding a St Bernard and she wouldn't have distracted Will. His gaze was up ahead, focused on Elaine's derriere. He realised what was different about her apart from the fact she had lost the sun tan and a few pounds. She was wearing high heels, really tight blue jeans and a white billowy shirt and looked smart. He had known her when they were all sweating on a beach and that was no place for heels or expensive clothing. She looked fantastic. They were only a few minutes from their destination now so he tuned back into the discourse next to him.

'I don't know how I would cope with prison. I mean, I'm sure I would be fine, but I couldn't cope without my lippy and straighteners. Was the food nice? I have to get my five a day, well seven a day really. Was it violent?'

She actually waited for an answer to that one. He had rarely told people about his spell at Her Majesty's Pleasure. Women responded generally in two ways, they either made a sharp exit, or they were intrigued and interested. Dawn clearly belonged in the latter camp.

'Yes, it was violent.'

'Wow, so exciting. I mean, scary too.' She droned on, and Will mused there would be violence here too if he had to sit next to her at dinner.

They had a big table on the top floor of the converted barge. It was a lovely restaurant with great views across the river and a pleasant atmosphere. They all sat down and much to Will's displeasure he found himself at the other end of the table to Elaine. He was sitting in between Aiden and Darren's girlfriend Yvette, who had been waiting for them to arrive. He gave her a warm smile and she returned it in a nervous manner. A couple of waiters poured them all a glass of bubbly and Aiden called for silence.

'Hi guys, thanks for coming, especially those who have come a long way to celebrate our union.'

He got some heckling for that phrase but he continued undaunted.

'Clearly I'm not one for speeches, so I would just like to say dinner is on us and the drinks are free.' That cued a good natured cheer especially from Will as the food was brilliant here but it was a lot more expensive than sweet and sour soup in Sapa.

'I would of course like to thank my wife for making me the happiest man alive.'

Once the 'Ah's' had settled down the group broke into a variety of conversations. Aiden was gurgling something to Penny so Will turned to his other side. After a few minutes, Will, who considered himself a good judge of character, came to the conclusion that Yvette wasn't any madder than anyone else at the table. Sure she was a bit timid and appeared beaten down and she also drank a tad too quickly, but Will guessed that living with Darren would probably cause most people to act in that way.

As the night progressed and alcohol oiled the wheels of conversation Will realised he felt part of something decent. There was no-one on drugs or absolutely shit faced, although Yvette was trying her hardest to remedy that last fact. There was good natured joshing and genuinely nice people having a pleasant time. Not at all what he was used to. Elaine was too far away for him to even shout to but he looked at her often and as the night wore on he found they caught each other's gaze on a regular basis. Penny was the type of drinker who got louder and more animated the more she consumed and as they waited for their desserts he heard her 'whisper' to Aiden in a voice that would have carried back to his house.

'Go on, you big lunk.'

Aiden stood up and the room went quiet. He walked around to Elaine's seat and then realised it had gone quiet.

'What? My lovely wife has declared she has had enough of me for a while and would like to talk to her oldest friend instead. As I am such a superb hubby I have offered to swop seats with Elaine.'

Elaine got up out of her seat and curtsied to him and as the volume of chatter resumed she made her way to the other side of the table.

Penny stood when Elaine arrived next to her and kissed her on the cheek.

'I'm just off to the little girl's room,' and disappeared. Elaine sat gently down and looked at Will.

'That wasn't very subtle.'

'No,' Will laughed. 'But necessary.'

He felt tongue-tied for a minute and lost for conversation. The things he wanted to say seemed a bit desperate. He had no idea what her situation was. She broke the ice.

'How was Asia?'

'Very good. All I had hoped it would be. I feel I've done it now and I'm ready to join society again.'

'Do you think you will go back?'

'Well never say never but my pension contributions have dipped dramatically just lately and if I don't get started on a new career soon I will be one of those fifty year olds over there with a grey pony tail.'

'You would have to buy a glue on one,' she giggled and it was the same sweet characteristic that he had found so endearing when they first met.

'Are you enjoying your new life in Australia?'

She was about to respond immediately then paused and took a sip of her drink.

'It's been an eye opener. It turns out working for a big professional solicitors in London is very similar to working for one in Melbourne. There are great beaches everywhere but if you're stuck in an office they might as well be miles away. Christmas was weird in your bikini too. I saw a really nice guy for a while which helped me integrate a bit better but I missed the British sense of humour.'

She pushed his shoulder when he made a disgusted retching sound.

'I expect you never kissed a soul?'

'No, not I,' he said feigning horror. 'It was more a spiritual experience for me. A journey, meditation, Tai Chi under the palm trees, a lot of vegetables. That sort of thing.'

He threw caution to the wind.

'I thought about you a lot.'

'I missed you too.' She looked at him intently. 'I feel a bit daft saying it. We only knew each other for a few days. I wanted to tell you how I felt by email but whenever I started an email saying it, I just sounded loopy. Even when I was dating you were there, skulking in the back of my mind.'

'It's what I do best. Are you going to stay out there?'

'No, tonight has confirmed it for me. I miss my friends and family too much. I'm going to resign when I go back.'

'Brad not on the scene anymore?'

'His name was Mitchell actually and no. He was a great bloke but my heart wasn't in it. I need to be crazy about someone for it to work.'

The waitress placed the smallest piece of ice cream Will had ever seen served in front of him and he grinned at her as they both shared the silent joke. He felt all tingly as he watched the waitress serve Elaine her morsel.

She put her hand on his arm after the waitress left and smiled at him.

'Do you think we could make it work? Do you think you are ready to settle down?'

He didn't need to think about it for a second.

'Yes, yes I do and yes I am.'

It was as simple as that.

40

6ᵗʰ April 2012

Will felt like trampling the Kelly Clarkson CD into the drive as he got out of his old car. All very well for her to sing about what doesn't kill you makes you stronger. He bet she hadn't just been sacked from her job in a pea processing factory. They had called it 'laid off' due to losing a contract, but he had stuck his head above the parapet about the piss taking with work conditions and breaks once too often and had known it was only a matter of time.

He wasted the time once more trying to lock his car, but no, definitely broken. He frowned and then thought what the hell it wasn't worth nicking anyway. He was sure there must be a hole in the petrol tank too, the speed it was getting through fuel and the insurance was ruinously expensive due to his driving conviction. That was another unpleasant little side effect he hadn't been expecting after his custodial stay.

That was the fourth job he had taken since he came back and they had all been dire. All soul destroying experiences where time stood still. He was usually the minority or even the only English person there as well to emphasize the isolation and depression. Even his stint as a temp sorting for Royal Mail had him stood next to a guy from India called Dilip who kept asking him in heavily accented English 'North or South?' They had been sorting the mail for those letters which the machine had failed to read due to them not having a postcode or poor writing. His geography was pretty good and he had worked hard in the hope of being kept on after the busy work period. He completed about four times the sorting of his confused colleague yet after the busy Christmas period he still got his marching orders. Incredibly he saw Dilip driving a Royal Mail van a few weeks back with a big smile on his face.

He let himself in the front door and flopped on the sofa. It all smelt very differently now Elaine had moved in but she hadn't been anal about cleanliness and they rarely disagreed about anything. She had a younger brother and understood it wasn't necessarily laziness when he stepped over dirty plates or washing; it just didn't register. He took a deep breath and thought 'Thank god for Elaine'. They had been getting on so well that Will couldn't think of a serious argument. Their sex life was perfect and she seemed happy too. She had taken a job for a reasonable sized solicitors on reasonable money with a reasonable amount of pressure. She cycled to work and lived next door to her best friend Penny. Life was good for her, it was just a shame he was so boracic.

He tried to have a nap but it was only eleven in the morning so he knocked round for Aiden. As he waited for the door to be opened he heard the window open above him.

'Jesus Christ Will, can't a man get some sleep?'

'Get up you lazy sod, it's nearly dinner time.'

Aiden came down and opened the door looking very groggy.

'Uggggggggghhhhhhhh,' he said, before wandering off into the kitchen. Penny was out working at the hospital as a radiographer or a radiologist, or something like that. She had explained to Will twice but it wouldn't stick and he daren't ask her again. Will followed Aiden who was now filling the kettle.

'Rough night? Surely not on a Thursday?'

'It was absolutely heaving mate and obviously a lock in. I don't know how Darren's done it but he must be making a packet.'

'Any trouble?'

'No, there never is. It's a bit of a mad vibe too, lot of druggies, but I don't think anyone wants to get barred, or more likely get Darren's back up. Not after that incident with that little gobby scouser.'

'Yes, I guess there is nothing like kicking the living daylights out of someone on a packed dance floor to keep everyone in line.'

'You not at work?'

'I got the tic tac this morning.'

'Again, oh dear.'

'Yes oh dear indeed. Typical isn't it. My home life is perfect now apart from I have to eat Asda smart price frozen cheese and tomato pizza because I can't afford Domino's.'

'It's not that bad is it?'

'Well no, not really. I just feel like a bit of a loser. She's at work all day paying the bills and comes home to find me passed out on the sofa and the house smelling of farts.'

'Some people like that sort of thing,' Aiden laughed.

'What sort of thing?'

'You know, dirty sex with tramps.'

'That's a nice thought, thank you.'

'Careful though, if she starts putting change in your cup of tea or peeing on you whilst you are asleep you have probably let things go too far.' Will did laugh at that.

'Don't drag Elaine into your own sick world. Talking of dragging things into this sick world, I'm now officially in the same boat as you. Elaine wants to stop taking contraception. So that cranks up the pressure a notch on me finding decent work.'

'Unfortunately we aren't in that boat anymore.' Aiden's face dropped. 'Penny found out this week she has polycystic ovaries and possibly endometriosis as well. We have been trying for a year now and nothing and it's unlikely she will get pregnant, even with IVF.'

'Shit sorry mate and here's me banging on about my petty problems.'

'Don't tell Darren please, he will only take the piss. Talking of he who must be obeyed, he keeps asking why don't you go and work for him.'

'I don't know, it all seems dead shonky and there is blatantly some illegal activities going on there.'

'He pays me ten pound an hour to sit on a stool and look out for non-existent trouble. That's got to be better than pulling dead rabbits off a vegetable conveyor belt.'

'Ten pound after tax?'

Aiden rolled his eyes.

'Hmmm, as I suspected. What does he want me to do exactly? I thought he made Kostas the bar manager.'

'Look, I'm going back to help with the delivery at two. Come back with me and have a word with him. Let yourself out quietly, I'm going back to bed.'

Will's mind began to whir.

41

The Anne Boleyn was open and already doing brisk trade when they arrived just after two. He had somehow got the post office crowd coming here after their early shifts finished and it also seemed to be full of trades people quoting prices, arranging deals and spending money. Darren reckoned it was the barmaid's legs that brought in the crowd. She was standing behind the bar as they walked in. Aiden cheerfully shouted 'Morning boss' and she gave him her usual piercing look.

Dawn was only about twenty but she was as hard as nails. In all Will's years he had never met anyone with such a perfect body, like a curvy gymnast, but she had a huge port wine stain birth mark down the left side of her face. He suspected childhood had not been easy and she was probably as effective a bouncer as Aiden.

Darren was in the 'lounge' as he liked to call it, nursing what looked like a Bloody Mary, clearly showing the effects of a late night. He looked up and did a pretend double take.

'Will, if I'd known royalty was coming I would have rolled the red carpet out. Aiden the delivery is out the back.'

Will rarely came in as neither Penny nor Elaine liked the murky underworld vibe about the place. They said it felt like at any moment the doors would be kicked in and they would all be sprayed with bullets.

'If I could afford your crazy prices Darren I would buy myself a tankard and keep it behind your bar.' Darren's prices were actually very reasonable, erring on the side of cheap and that too was a reason for the busy establishment.

'To what do I owe this heavenly pleasure then?'

As Aiden walked past he answered the question for him.

'Will got sacked.'

'Ah I see. Desperation has sent you to my doors, how lovely.'

Will had a feeling this was going to be made hard work for him and was tempted just to walk out, so he was pleasantly surprised when Darren changed his tune.

'That is great news Will. That thick, tubby bastard Kostas is fucking it right up. We ran out of gas for the pumps last week and bloody tea bags this week. Do you know what the mark up is on tea bags?'

Will wasn't really listening, he was looking around the place. He hadn't been in since it was finished, but it looked awesome. Darren had made it look like a traditional boozer. Big wooden bars, comfy seating, oak floor and he had even got a big painting of the lady herself hanging on the wall. He could see past a new pool table through to a shiny dance floor and found he was nodding.

'It looks good doesn't it?'

'It does Darren, really good.' Will looked Darren in the eyes. 'Must have cost a bomb.'

'Not too bad, as I called in a few debts. A lot of people owed me money, so I took it in labour. The rest, I stole.'

As per usual of late Will wasn't sure whether he was joking or not. He used to be able to tell but there had developed a distance between them since Will had taken the rap for Darren's misdemeanour.

'Talking of money, what do you want from me, and what will I be getting in return?'

'Twelve pound an hour clear and special bonuses.' As he said the last phrase Darren raised his eyebrows.

'Aiden said he only gets ten.'

'That's because he is the hired muscle, you my friend will be my business partner.'

'Anything illegal I should know about.'

'Plenty, but nothing too dodgy.'

'What about the old tax man?'

'I knew that would worry you Will, you are such a bender. However just this morning I have employed the best accountant in Peterborough to do our books. So it will be all above board. Tax, national insurance and free parking. What more could you want.'

'I take it that would be our friendly chef Carl?'

'Correctamundo. Cooking the books to perfection.'

Will pondered his options for a minute and decided he didn't have many. Twelve quid an hour was double what he was making grading veg, he was currently unemployed and he was church-mouse skint.

'What exactly will I be doing? I don't want you ordering me around like some skivvy.' Like he just did to Aiden, Will thought.

'Run the bar. Get another barmaid to help gravy face if you can't be arsed to serve. Cash the tills, stock take, generally run the show. I want us to focus on other lucrative ventures. I might need someone sensible to come with me every now and again, to pick up and drop off. You know, someone smart, who can spot an opportunity.'

'OK, let's do it and if I'm the manager you can start by not calling her that again.'

Will stared hard at Darren who held his hands up in mock surrender. At the back of his mind he had the nagging feeling he was offering his soul in exchange for diabolical favours.

42

Every now and again turned out to be eight p.m. that
same night.

'Where are we going?'

'Just drive towards Marholm.'

'Are you taking me for a nice meal at that lovely
restaurant with the striking topiary display?'

'Just a little drop off.'

Darren had insisted that Will drive his car, saying his
insurance covered any driver, although Will noticed he
smelled strongly of drink. When they arrived at the small
village on the outskirts of Peterborough Darren directed
them away from the centre.

'Carry on up here.'

'Left here.' As they drove down a small country lane
Darren checked his watch.

'Stop here.' The only light was from the moon and
Will felt strangely isolated.

'Twelve pound an hour is not going to get me dogging
you know.'

Darren didn't respond as he had all of a sudden
become very alert and serious. They waited for no more
than thirty seconds and then Will saw a smart looking
Audi saloon car turn into the lane and pull up directly
behind them. Darren still didn't say anything but pressed
a button on the dashboard and Will felt the boot catch
open up behind him.

Using the wing mirror he watched a man in a suit and despite the hour sunglasses, climb out of the car and approach the rear of their vehicle. He opened the boot, there was a pause of a few seconds, then he closed it with a firm shove. He then returned to his car holding a chunky brown manila envelope. He got in, put his seat belt on, reversed and slowly drove away.

'OK Will, we just need to pop to see an associate of mine.'

'Jesus Darren, how dodgy was that. I thought you said nothing too illegal.'

Darren paused for a good while as though he was weighing up what to tell him. His shoulders sagged slightly.

'It's only weed. It's a little side business. Marijuana is the new cocaine. All the growers are inside at the moment so it's all about supply and demand. I can shift the decent stuff for twenty-five pound an eighth. That's good money.'

'Excellent, maybe I can get Elaine to send me some of it when we are inside. Get some nice things for my cell.'

'We won't be going to jail for a little bit of possession.'

'I'm not spending my time sweating in your loft and watering your illicit shrubberies.'

'Don't be so melodramatic. I don't produce the stuff. There aren't any scales here or at the pub. I've got some growing rooms around the city, nothing large scale. If they get caught, they go to court, they know better than to mention names and they also know they only have a small amount of plants so all they will get is a smack on the wrist. It's only a class C drug now. It's easy money Will and remember, you haven't got any.'

That took the wind out of Will's sails and he let out a heavy breath. His mind was spinning as they pulled into an industrial estate in one of the rougher areas of the city. As they stopped outside a used car yard proudly calling itself 'Polish Porsche' Darren got out and beckoned for Will to follow.

They both walked into the reception to be greeting by a blonde Slavic looking lady bending over a coffee machine with a pair of jeans so tight you could see the pattern of her underwear. She was also wearing a tiny cropped T-shirt asking you to visit Poland.

'Is he in?' was all Darren said.

'Office,' she deeply strangled in heavily accented English sounding like Ivan Drago from Rocky.

Will dragged his eyes from the incredible sight and followed Darren as he left the reception area and walked around the side of the building. They went through a garage with a variety of vehicles that looked like their best days were behind them. There were a couple of heavy-set blokes in boiler suits idly standing around smoking. They gave them hard looks, but then seemed to recognise Darren and turned away. They looked as though the only time they would use spanners was if they needed to beat something, or someone.

Darren knocked on a flimsy brown door and it was opened by a thick set man with a shaven head and a light blue tracksuit top and bottoms. He had a thick gold necklace and piercing blue eyes on an emotionless face. This odd ensemble was made more unusual by the fat cigar he was smoking. He shifted the cigar to his left hand and then his face broke into a wide grin.

'Darren, always good to see you. Come in.'

He shook Will's hand in turn with a meaty shake and then followed them in.

'Who is your friend, Darren?' His accent was evidently eastern European but was moderate compared to the bombshell at the reception desk.

'This is Will. I told you about him. He is my business partner. I've known him since we were eleven. We are like brothers. Will, this is Radic.' He pronounced it raddish and a look of annoyance swept over Radic's face. He looked straight at Will.

'It end's with an itch, Radditch. I swear he does it to annoy me.' His easy smile returned to his face. 'Family eh? In our line of business it is best to keep it in the family.' He spoke slowly as though he was enjoying the words. He gestured out to the garage area. 'Ben has the money. You can get it now, everything is good. Let me get to know Will for a minute.'

Darren looked for a minute like he was going to say something but reluctantly left.

'Drink?'

'Please.'

He was expecting some kind of industrial measure of vodka as the man opened a small fridge behind him but he instead passed him a chilled bottle of Evian.

'So William, you like cars?'

'Yes, although I've had some bad experiences with them,' Will replied.

'Yes, I heard.' Radic beamed at him. 'Darren told me about your loyalty.'

'I don't see many Porsche out there.'

'No, not many Porsche.' Radic let out a big booming laugh. 'I'm not Polish either.'

Will found he was laughing too. He was a little imposing this character but he was quick to laugh and obviously enjoyed a joke.

'You like working with Darren?'

The question blindsided Will for a moment and he wasn't immediately sure what to say. He stuck with the facts.

'I've known him a long time. I trust him.'

'Good, good. A little wild your friend I think. You, however, I believe I can trust. I like you William. You seem, umm, what's the phrase, a decent bloke.' He laughed to himself again. 'You have a crazy language, very easy to up fuck.' He gave Will a serious expression.

'A man needs to be wary of men like your friend. Very dangerous.' That dark look passed over his face again but he removed it as Darren returned.

'But Darren is good for business no?'

'Come on Will, see you again soon Raddish.' Darren left.

Will took a final swig of his drink and placed it on the table. He shook the man's hand firmly.

'Nice to meet you Radic.' He made sure to pronounce it correctly.

★ ★ ★

Darren was in a foul mood when he got back in the car.

'Goddamn Polacks. Ordering me to get the money, he should give it to me.'

'He says he isn't from Poland.'

Darren shot Will a dirty look.

'What were you two talking about?'

'Cars,' Will said after giving it a few moments thought.

By the time they had pulled up at the pub Darren had cheered up considerably as they chatted about old times. As Darren got out he gave him an envelope.

'Your first bonus.'

He left Will in the car and went inside. Will took a deep breath and tried to absorb and process what had happened that evening. As he did so he idly opened the envelope. There was a small solid wodge of notes. His eyes opened as he counted it. Five hundred pounds in twenties. He let out that breath and knew this moment was a pivotal one. He thought about his options. He could carry on doing rubbish jobs for terrible money or he could sell his soul to the devil, but probably have a good time doing so. He didn't want to go back to prison but he trusted Darren when he said they wouldn't get into trouble. He was pretty sure though that the government had re-categorized marijuana as a class B drug and therefore had stiffer penalties.

He gave it a few more seconds consideration, then put the money in his pocket with a small smile. He walked into the Anne Boleyn to continue his new job.

43

11ᵗʰ April 2013

A gentle thudding brought Will to his senses. He opened his eyes which seemed to take an extreme effort and immediately put his hand up to cover them from the bright light coming through the window directly onto his face. His mouth was bone dry and he must have passed out without closing the curtains.

All of a sudden he remembered the importance of the morning and jerked himself upright. He was an idiot. He knew he shouldn't have gone to the Anne Boleyn last night. He searched his brain for someone to blame and came up with Aiden. Why had he listened to him saying it would be days before anything happened? What the hell would that bell-end know about it?

He reached to the table next to his bed where he always kept his mobile phone and found a congealing portion of takeaway chips in its place. He sobered up quickly as he searched for his phone thinking he may have missed the all-important call. He found his jeans on the landing and upended them. His phone and a strangely large amount of change dropped out and he found himself holding his breath as he turned the display on. 'Please no missed call' he whispered to himself. He stared hard as the light came on but the screen was illegibly smudged by some kind of dried brown liquid. Frowning he wiped it with his thumb but just proceeded to make what looked like dried curry sauce spread more. Panicking now, he began to lick the phone like a dog with a juicy bone, gagging at something that didn't taste of curry sauce, then wiped it on the carpet. He looked and noted the lack of missed calls and breathed again. There was a God after all.

He went into the bathroom to get some Rennie, Paracetamol and anything else that might help his fragile state and heard the banging noise again. It was coming from downstairs. He checked his watch to see it was only seven fifteen. That was way too early for the post nowadays, but it was becoming louder and more insistent. His muddled brain instantly put two and two together and came up with the police. In some ways he had been expecting it for months. Fighting back his paranoia he quickly surmised that if it was the police they would not be knocking. More likely they would have broken his door down at four a.m. and dragged him naked into the street.

Gingerly stepping down the stairs to avoid tripping on his shoes and socks which lay strewn down them he realised the sound was coming from the kitchen door. With relief he remembered the dog and he would want to be let out. That was usually Elaine's job first thing so no wonder he had forgotten. She had wanted to get the filthy brute, so she could look after it. It had been pure madness on her part to get the thing. He could hear her continuously saying 'I've always wanted one, go on Will'. He saw the door throb as it was hit again and felt he was to blame too. He should have done some research into what a Newfoundland was.

He eased open the door and was immediately accosted by the large furry head of an enormous Newfie. It was only a year old yet it was about the same size as a

Rottweiler already. He had looked in shock when she had bought home a puppy that had bigger feet than your average bear but obviously it was too late by then. Still it was a sweet natured docile thing and he felt some sympathy for it being locked in for so long.

That sympathy evaporated instantly as he entered the room and was assailed by a horrendous stench. The dog jumped up and put his massive wet paws on Will's chest and tried to lick his face.

'Down Pluto, down.'

Pushing the dog down he was greeted with a scene from hell. The kitchen floor was covered in huge pools of dark brown mucous liquid. In these pools were large paw prints. He stepped into the room and he felt himself gag as the smell hit his nostrils. Forcing himself to breathe through his mouth he unsuccessfully tried to dodge through the carnage as he went and opened the back door and felt the cold clammy goo squeeze between his toes. The dog disappeared into the back garden and Will noted the detritus of a kebab on the floor. With a brief glimpse of the past he remembered putting said item on the work surface when he came in last night. Obviously a tad too close to the edge for Pluto and obviously a tad too spicy for his delicate constitution as well.

As he wondered if they had a mop, and if they did where would it be kept, he heard his phone ringing. Realising he had left it at the top of the stairs he closed the kitchen door and quickly ran up them trying to remain calm.

'Hello?'

'Mr Reynolds?'

'Yes, speaking.'

'It's Nurse Thomas here. Things have moved faster than we expected and we think you should come in now.'

He found he was pacing the room all of a flutter but he could still smell the terrible aroma from downstairs. He looked at his shoulders and saw the liquid shit which had seeped into his shirt from Pluto's feet.

'Right now?'

'Yes please.'

'Erm, OK, see you soon.'

She ended the call as Will looked down at his brown footprints on the cream carpet. Yes, there was a God, and he had a sick sense of humour.

Paralysed with indecision he thought back to the conversation with the nurse. She had said right away but her voice hadn't carried any urgency. Did she mean amble in or did she mean drive like the wind. He suspected she wouldn't say the latter anyway as he might have driven like a lunatic and wiped out the school run.

All things considered he decided a shower was a necessity and went and got straight in. One speed clean later, taking great time and care with the soles of his feet he continued with his routine at high speed. With teeth brushed, twice, face shaved, mouthwash used, aftershave applied and fresh clothes adorned, he scuttled downstairs spraying deodorant over his body length and selected some shoes. He picked up his car keys and put his coat on noting the bright yellow stain on the sleeve and made a mental note to sort that in the toilets when he got there. He then heard Pluto snuffling behind the kitchen door.

His mind hummed with indecision. 'Feed the dog? Feed the dog? Feed the dog?' he murmured to himself. He recalled the scene of horror behind the door and decided 'Fuck the dog'. Abstinence is always best when you have a poorly bottom.

He jumped in his new car and then remembered he had left the back door open. 'Fuck that too' he thought.

They didn't have anything worth nicking anyway bar a fifty inch plasma TV and that was so big you would need to be King Kong to carry it away. So if someone wanted to fight their way through the kitchen of death, negotiate their way past a ten stone shitting machine and was strong enough to remove the daddy of the TV world, then they deserved it and a locked door would not have stopped them anyway.

44

He fired the Vauxhall Insignia up and got on his way. Suspecting he may well be drink driving he drove on the speed limit, resisting the urge to floor the accelerator. He pulled onto the parkway and followed the signs for the hospital. As he got nearer an ambulance, sirens blaring, steamed past and he prevented himself from racing after it. He pulled back into the traffic and resumed his journey. He tried not to think of the importance of what was about to happen. It would have repercussions for the rest of his life, he knew that much. Think of something else he reprimanded himself.

He focused on the smoothness of the drive. He had wanted a huge 4x4 but she had said they were too big for her. In the end they had got this. It was a good car at a great price, from her Uncle. Would he ever get the car he wanted? Annoying it was too, as with all the money he was making he could have had what he liked. Like that git Darren. He had rocked up a few weeks back in a brand new amazing looking black BMW X5. Worrying about their 'business' he had argued with him about it and recalled himself shouting 'You should have just got a number plate with 'DRUGS HERE' in the unlikely event that it isn't completely obvious'.

For the umpteenth time since he had worked for him he had been surprised that an ever more volatile Darren hadn't hit him and he wondered now if he wasn't just jealous as that was the motor he wanted. The pub was still doing a roaring trade but the control was beginning to fray at the edges. The special bonuses were getting bigger but Aiden was finding he was splitting up more and more fights and throwing more and more people out and some of them were very resistant. Darren, though, rarely barred people and by kicking out time the atmosphere was like that of a bath of petrol, waiting for someone to flick their fag end into it.

Radic had somehow got Will's phone number and was constantly trying to get him to work for him. It was getting so bad in the pub and with Darren's increasingly bizarre behaviour he was considering it, but he knew he really would be in with the big boys then. In light of current events he did not want to risk going down for a huge stretch but he felt stuck, as he couldn't face the minimum wage again.

He had hoped Carl moving in upstairs would have helped Darren's moods but the pair of them seemed to be off their faces most of the time. Carl had gone downhill since his girlfriend had left him for some bloke at her gym and the pair of them had got back on the class A's big time. They were both racing so fast down the slippery slope of addiction that surely even they could see the wall coming to greet them. Although maybe that was the dichotomy of drug abuse and enjoying yourself, as he had to admit they did seem to be having a good time except when they were complaining about how ropey they felt the next day.

It all seemed to be falling apart but today wasn't the day for such thoughts and he pushed them away. He pulled up in a residential street behind the hospital. It was a five minute walk from here but he was buggered if he was going to pay ten pounds to park there for the day. He strode off and put his hands in his pockets finding his cigarettes. He debated smoking one, knowing he would feel like shit afterwards but lit one regardless. He arrived feeling nauseous and dry mouthed, cursing his stupidity for about the third time that morning.

He found a vending machine on the way to the ward and gasping for a drink of any kind he reached into his back pocket for his change. Two pounds fifty for a water; un-bloody-believable. He didn't have any change. Obviously it was still all over the floor in his house. Cursing, he then spent the next minute desperately trying to slide a five pound note into the feeder which kept spitting it out. Just as he was about to smash his head through the plastic Perspex in a rage and remove the item with his teeth it was accepted and he pressed the button and a bottle of water dropped down. He waited for his change but nothing happened. He then noticed the 'exact change only' button was lit. Resisting the urge to growl out loud like an ogre as his fury reached new levels he purchased another water and then staggered off up the corridor.

★ ★ ★

They seemed to have put the maternity ward at the furthest recess of the hospital and he was freely sweating when he arrived. Why the hell were these places so hot, surely it just encouraged the germs? He stopped outside the entrance door, pressed the buzzer and glugged the entirety of one of the bottles of water, gasping at its coldness, whilst he waited for a response.

As he entered the receptionist smiled at him, 'Room fourteen Mr Reynolds, hurry along now. You can get your car park refund stamp when you leave.'

He looked at her stunned for a few seconds and then noticed the 'Free parking for partners' sign on the wall behind her. He pushed the information out of his mind and raced along the corridor. He checked his watch, seven fifty-five. Not too bad, all things considered.

Arriving at room fourteen he pushed the door open and strode in. As he went around the partition, the first sight he saw was the baby being passed to his girlfriend.

Jesus, he had missed it. He went over to the bedside and stared down at his new-born daughter. He looked at Elaine's sweaty, tired face and squeezed her shoulder.

'Is everything OK?'

'She is doing great, she was amazing,' the midwife answered. 'Your girl came so fast she almost arrived in the toilet. She got ten out of ten on the APGAR test though and she is absolutely beautiful.'

Thinking back to the NCT classes he had been forced to endure he recalled that was a good thing and couldn't stop a huge grin splitting his face from ear to ear.

'I'm sorry honey, they should have called you earlier.'

Will kissed her on the lips and then reached over and kissed his new baby on her soft head. His baby. What an incredible feeling.

He didn't feel any anger about missing the birth. He saw the stain on his coat sleeve out of the corner of his eye and concluded nothing else mattered anymore. His daughter was here safe and sound and she and Elaine were both healthy. He just felt relieved and enormously happy.

'Do you want to hold her? I'm gasping for a drink.'

Will smiled at her and eagerly nodded as he passed the extra bottle of water to her.

'I thought you might be. I got this especially for you.'

45

22ⁿᵈ August 2014

Will checked the text message again. Just three words.

'Get here now.'

'Yes, mine said the same thing.'

'I've had enough of this shit Aiden. I'm too old for this bollocks for a start.'

'I know, I didn't get to bed until four a.m. Then I get woken up by this demand at ten.'

Will must have been dead to the world as he hadn't even stirred. In fact, the only reason he was here now was because Aiden had let himself into his house and shaken him awake. Sam Smith's gentle tones were playing on the radio but even that was jarring on his nerves so he turned it off. He turned to Aiden who was driving with tired bloodshot eyes.

'What are we going to do, it's massively getting out of hand?'

Yesterday had been unusual for a variety of reasons. Darren and Carl had been off their faces before the pub had even opened and had not come down to the bar all day. They had become paranoid and anxious like the drug addicts they were. Both the bar maids had been given the day off to go shopping in London meaning the four of them were supposed to run the place. Therefore Will and

Aiden had to work like Trojans to keep on top of things even though it had been a slow day.

The first unusual thing was the visit by the local constabulary. Will always thought Darren must have them in his back pocket as they were conspicuous by their absence. The two guys who came in at three and then again at seven and asked for Darren, were so obviously plain clothes police they might as well have been wearing comedy helmets with flashing lights on them. Will had to give them some pony about not knowing where he was. This didn't seemed to be too much of an issue at three, but when they both came back at seven and Will told them what Darren wanted them to hear, which was he was away for a few days on business, they were clearly furious.

'We will be back at Saturday lunchtime,' one of them had snarled. 'He will be here if he has any concerns for his wellbeing.'

The other strange thing was how quiet it was. The bar had become a really busy east European hub. They were a rowdy drunken bunch but they were generally respectful and accepting if they got a whack for stepping out of line. Radic and his crew came in frequently, although it was noticeable every time they did that they rarely drank much. The rest were all manner of labourers, workmen, new arrivals and the wilfully unemployed. This attracted all types of bottom feeders and they were constantly moving along prostitutes who had come to ply their trade outside. Will suspected that when Darren was here he let them stay as he seemed to think it was all part of the experience.

This afternoon and evening, though, the 'east' was absent. Almost all of them, as though they knew something was happening and were deliberately staying away. The only one of any note who turned up was Radic, with two of his most threatening 'mechanics'. Will and Aiden told him the same story about Darren being away on business. He too had been unhappy.

'Tell your friend Darren I have given him many chances. This one is too much. I will need to meet him face to face on Saturday morning. I'm sure you will let him know'. He had then cryptically added 'I fear he may be going down. Do you want to go down with him? It's time to choose Will'. This last comment had made Will's blood run cold. The English regulars had still been in but they weren't a late bunch and they had everyone out, the tills cashed up and had done a general tidy up by midnight. What had made them late was the arguing with Darren. This state of affairs couldn't continue.

By this time Carl and he looked like a pair of wasted ghouls. They were grey faced and sunken eyed. Carl had looked comatose throughout the heated discussion, only volunteering 'Let's not fall out' before sinking back into his seat with only his eyes moving to indicate he was still with them. God only knows how he was keeping his business afloat. Darren had been fidgety as hell, pacing up and down and slamming his hands on the table but not actually volunteering any information. Will had noticed the yellow nicotine stains on his hands as he did so. The old Darren would never have let something so disgusting occur and it made Will even surer that he had lost it.

As they pulled up outside the pub they noticed that the front door was shut and both barmaids and a few of the post office crew were waiting outside. Will got out and opened the door.

'Why isn't it open?'

'You go and ask Tony Montana. I know he is in there cos I could see the bloody curtains move.'

'Ok Dawn, look you're in now, I'll have a word with him.'

'I've just about had enough Will. I'm thinking of going to London. I had a job interview yesterday and I think I'm going to take it.'

Will shook his head. They would be sunk without her organisation. As the patrons came in he noted that yet again there were none of the usual foreigners. Maybe they were like the titanic, a critical breach had occurred and it was only a matter of time before they too sank to the bottom.

Will and Aiden climbed the stairs to the living quarters and found Darren in the kitchen, pacing again.

'What's so urgent then?' Will asked in a quiet voice as he could see Darren was close to the edge.

As he walked up and down Will could hear him whispering, 'Think, think.' All of a sudden he seemed to realise they were there.

'We have two immediate minor problems and an imminent major one,' he said, recovering his poise quickly.

Will and Aiden looked at each other. It was Aiden who asked.

'What are the immediate ones?'

'The young lovers through there.' He pointed towards one of the bedrooms.

Will dreaded what he was going to see as he gingerly turned the door handle and pushed the door open. The room was dark but there was an unpleasant combination of familiar smells in the room. One distinct element reminded him of the smell of his old money box, which used to put his teeth on edge when he used to count and recount his savings when he was a child. The other brought back memories of opening a wheelie bin in the summer. He could hear rattling breathing as he flicked on the light.

What he wasn't expecting was to find Carl and Kostas lying on Carl's king-sized bed together. It took Will a while to get his head around the sight but as he stepped closer, he realised they were both either asleep or unconscious. It was also clear by the amount of blood on Kostas that he had received the mother of all beatings. It was his breathing that was causing the rattling. By the way he was curled into the foetal position he suspected he had at least one broken rib to go with a clearly broken face.

Will turned to Darren sharply.

'What the fuck did you do that for? It looks like you've nearly killed him.'

'You prick, I didn't do it. I got a call this morning but I didn't answer. They left a voicemail saying go and check your back garden. He was lying across the barbecue. I managed to get him up here but then he passed out.'

'You didn't think to ring an ambulance?'

'I can't think straight at the moment. That's why I employ you. I don't want the police turning up.' Funny that, Will thought.

'Did he say who it was?' Aiden chipped in.

'He just said 'Russians', that was it.'

Carl was further away against the wall behind Kostas's big back and as Will peered over the prone form he queried Darren.

'Why did you put him in bed next to Carl?'

'I didn't know what to do with him. He was all bloody and I've only just changed my sheets.'

Disbelieving his own ears at Darren's warped thought process, Will suddenly recoiled at the smell as he got closer to Carl.

'As you can see Carl's sheets are already a goner.'

Carl had gone to bed in just boxer shorts and a T-shirt but he had clearly soiled himself. A horrid, foul looking substance that reminded him of Pluto's transgression was pooled between his legs. He was also in the foetal position behind Kostas and Darren was right, they did look like two lovers spooning. Carl also had some black liquid dribbling out of his mouth, though, and Will was immediately concerned.

'Look, we have to take them to hospital. Aiden go and run the shower.'

'What are you going to tell them Will?'

Will wracked his brain for twenty seconds, eyes flickering as he thought of any kind of plausible explanation that wasn't going to raise too many questions.

'OK, we tell them Carl has been ill all night and we are worried he has ulcers. We say Kostas fell off a ladder when he was clearing leaves from the guttering.'

'OK, that makes sense. Give me a hand carrying Kostas to the shower,' Aiden replied.

'We aren't showering him as well you cretin. They might be a little suspicious if he turns up with internal injuries and a face like a squashed watermelon but clean as a fucking whistle. Just clean the shit off Carl and put him in some new clothes and me and you will take him to A and E.'

'What about Kostas?' Darren queried.

'You take him.'

'Why don't you take both?'

'Am I surrounded by imbeciles? They would think we must be having a really bad day if I pulled up outside casualty and dragged two near dead specimens in. You take him Darren.'

Darren didn't look happy but didn't say anything else.

Will grabbed Kostas' legs and Darren grabbed the shoulders of his jacket and they manoeuvred him as gently as they could towards the stairs. Kostas groaned in pain. Half way down Darren said, 'Shit.' Will looked up and could see Kostas's head slipping through the neck of his jacket.

'Put him down,' he shouted, but it was too late and he just shut his eyes when the thunk of his heavy head hit the next step. Kostas then began to sob.

When they got outside Darren dropped Kostas on the floor, shouted, 'Wait,' and ran back in the pub. He returned with a pleased look on his face and a newspaper in each hand. He strategically spread it out in the boot of his X5 and turned to Will with a big grin.

'Who's the genius now, eh?'

Will put his incredulous head in his hands. This couldn't be real.

As Darren pulled out of the parking space he wound down his window.

'Pick me up at ten a.m. tomorrow. We have a meet with Radic. We all better go.'

'I don't think Kostas will be up to much tomorrow, or Carl for that matter.'

'Well, maybe not. Carl will be fine. All of you. Here at ten. Don't worry about coming back today, the girls can handle it.'

'Is this the imminent major problem?'

'Yep.'

'What is it Darren, tell me?'

'We had a couple of failed deliveries and some missing stock. A lot of people are out of pocket. Don't worry, I will sort it all tomorrow.'

Darren then roared off, leaving Will open mouthed and mid question in the street.

He went back into the pub and found Aiden pulling some clothes out of Carl's wardrobe. He looked in the shower and saw Carl standing in the bath under the stream. From behind he looked like a small child, he was so thin and emaciated. Aiden carried him down the stairs like you would a new-born baby, with his hand supporting his neck. As they got in the car Carl seemed to show more signs of functioning but had still not said anything, so Will got in the back with him.

'You alright Carl? It's probably best if you go to hospital, or the doctors, get checked out.'

Carl mumbled something indecipherable.

'What was that mate?'

'Just take me home,' he managed to gasp out.

'You are home?'

'My parents.'

They pulled up outside Carl's parents' house and he shuffled to the door. Aiden and Will sat in the car and watched as it was opened and his mother came out, looked at him for a few seconds, and then pulled him into an embrace. As they reversed off the drive his father came out and stared at them. It was the look you would give someone if you caught them throwing rubbish in your front garden. He felt Aiden jump next to him as the front door was slammed shut.

'That's it, I'm done Will. No more.'

'I know, me too.'

'I didn't know whether to say anything but me and Penny have been talking about it for a while and we have decided to move to Cambridge. Her sister is there and she can see how toxic the situation is here.' He paused and then added, 'I feel a bit like I'm deserting you.'

'God, don't worry about that,' Will laughed. 'It's finally dawned on me that I have a family, one that I'm responsible for. I can't go to jail, even if it is only for a few months. No more pub and no more Darren, before he drags us all down.'

'Cool, let me know what he says when you tell him.'

Will laughed again, 'We'll tell him tomorrow, together.'

'Deal.'

As they drove back home Will thought of them dropping Carl off at his house like an errant teenager. Not so funny and more than a little depressing when they were all forty years old.

Will walked into his lounge when he got back and found Elaine tickling his giggling daughter on the carpet. What the fuck was he doing with his life?

46

23rd August 2014

Will put his spoon down next to the uneaten bowl of cereal. His stomach was doing somersaults. He gave Elaine a smile he didn't feel and went to get his car keys. That cheeky twat Darren had sent him a text with just the words 'Pick me up'. I'm just a glorified taxi driver, Will thought. Then he changed his mind. No. A taxi driver wouldn't feel like this. He felt like he did when he was walking into his A-Level Biology exam, woefully unprepared and nervous as hell. There was also the same determination and relief there too. The wanting to see it through and come what may, after today, it would all be over.

The door shuddered with Aiden's customary pounding so he kissed the girls goodbye.

'It's the right decision Will. Don't worry, we will be fine.'

He was going to ask her to marry him soon. He knew that now, as soon as he extricated himself from Darren's descent into hell. Talk about something bad to happen to make you focus on what was important. They had discussed his decision to quit last night and she had just said 'It's about time'. It must be the right choice as she didn't even know the half of it. As he lay in bed last night he had wondered what he had been waiting for. He had the right girl and they were blessed with a wonderful daughter. He had so much to be thankful for, so why was he risking everything? He thought of a quote by Fernando Pessoa that Carl used to have in a picture frame in his toilet. 'In order to understand, I destroyed myself'. He hoped that he had not made the same mistake. He stepped out of the house to a grim-faced Aiden who held out his hand.

'Let's do this,' Will said as they shook.

They stopped at Carl's parents' house and did rock paper scissors for who had to go and knock when no-one responded to the car horn. Will lost. He was relieved when it was Carl who answered the door.

'Are you coming?'

'No Will I'm not. It's over. I'm spent. I told my parents everything last night. They have got me into rehab, starting tomorrow. I'm looking forward to it actually.'

Will looked over Carl's shoulder and could see both parents giving him death stares. He was about to make his excuses and leave but instead put his hand on Carl's shoulder.

'I'm sorry Carl, you know, getting you involved in all this. I should have looked out for you more.'

Carl gave him a strange, almost contented look.

'Jesus, Will, are you my mother? Don't be sorry for anything. I've had a blast, an amazing time. Experiences, and women.' He looked sheepishly over his shoulder at his parents. 'So many women.' Grinning at Will he continued.

'Don't you remember what I was? I was the geeky one, Carlbunkle. My life was a road map of boredom and drudgery. If I die tomorrow at least I could say I have lived. But it's over Will. Or I will die soon. I'll be in touch, when I'm in a better place. Say goodbye to the guys for me.' He gave Will a surprisingly strong hug and nodding, closed the door on him.

'Carl not coming?'

'No. Rehab'

'Good for him.'

'Lucky him.'

★ ★ ★

When they arrived Darren jumped into the back of the car all full of joir de vivre as though they were off on a trip to the seaside and threw a heavy-looking holdall onto the other seat.

'No Carlos?'

'Nope, he wished us luck, but he had to go somewhere with his parents.'

Will felt he was better letting Darren find out about Carl later, he was going to get enough bad news for one day.

'Where to?'

'Out to Maxey.'

'What the hell are we going to the old quarries for? So they don't have far to dispose of our bodies?' As the words left his mouth, he began to consider that they might be true and he felt a shiver go down his spine.

'Chill out Will, it will be fine.'

He heard the bleep of his phone receiving a message but as he was driving he left it in his pocket. When they arrived in the general vicinity Darren directed them along a succession of ever deteriorating roads until the concrete completely disappeared and they were bumping along a muddy path. Will frowned as he felt his axle scrape the surface.

'Why aren't we in your fucking 4x4?'

'What, that car cost a bomb, I'm not ruining it out here.'

Will scowled but felt a flood of strength come over him. The git was at least making it easy for them to tell him it was all over.

They pulled up behind a huge slag pile, next to a dark, threatening gravel pit and Will turned off the engine. They sat in silence for a few seconds. Will had his window down but it was as though they were on the moon. Total silence. It was a pleasant day, but a pleasant day for what Will thought.

Aiden clearly couldn't stand the tension any longer. He blurted the news out.

'I'm leaving Darren. Quitting and going to Cambridge. Sorry mate.'

'Cheers friend, leave me in the lurch why don't you.'

Will looked at Aiden's crestfallen face.

'We are both quitting Darren. We have families now, responsibilities.' He looked into the back seat at Darren whose face was black as thunder.

'I take it we are meeting Radic?'

'Correct.'

'What for exactly?'

'I owe him and some of his friends some money.'

'How much money?'

'Half a million, more or less.'

'What the fuck? You lose a marijuana farm or something.?

Darren's face took on a smug look.

'You fucking idiot. You didn't really think it was that all this time. It was cocaine my friend, yeyo, Columbian marching powder. Well, mostly Afghan marching powder in our case.'

The realisation hit Will like a blow from a baseball bat. How could he have not known? All the fucking money, there had been tonnes of it. He remembered overhearing Carl once saying 'I can't hide this amount Darren, there's too much'. He had known that everyone in the pub was off their faces on it but why hadn't he done the math. Maybe he hadn't wanted to and had been happy just to take the cash. Suddenly he thought of the seriousness of getting caught.

'Fuck's sake Darren. You should have told us. If we get caught we are looking at nine to eighteen years, maybe even life. You utter wanker.'

'Oh shut up will you. Don't come the high and mighty with me. Don't think I don't know you used to go around my dad's house. We all have our little secrets don't we? You were quite happy to take the dosh.' He gave Will a condescending look. 'It's always been coke. Remember when you took the dive for me after the police chase and I went back for my bag.'

Will was too shocked to reply, so just bobbed his head in response.

'One kilogram of it was in that bag. All those trips back weren't about security work, they were arranging deals, transport routes. I've been doing it for years.'

'Darren, why didn't you let us know?' Aiden said with tears in his eyes. 'The police were at the pub this week.'

'You are too stupid to know,' he snapped. 'I owe some of them money too actually.'

'Why don't you just pay them?' Aiden said.

'I don't have that sort of money. We lost a shipment to the coastguard. To be honest quite a lot of it went up me and Carl's nostrillos. Pretty mad really, how much you can get through if you really want to. Kostas was carrying a hundred grand when he got turned over yesterday. I was going to use that to buy some time.'

Darren's eyes suddenly narrowed. He pointed with his head out the front window. Will followed his look and could see a transit van and a huge pick-up truck driving towards them across the bumpy flat waste.

'It looks like time's up Darren,' Will stated.

Darren avoided Will's icy stare and rummaged in the holdall he had brought with him. 'You might need this Will.' He handed Will a pistol. A really old pistol.

'What the hell is this for?'

'What do you think? If things get nasty, use it.'

'Jesus Christ.' Will turned it over in his hand. It looked ancient. 'Are you sure Davy Crockett isn't going to want this back?'

'I know,' Darren laughed, more of a bark than a chuckle. 'Don't worry, it will work and it's loaded. Just make some noise with it if necessary. You were a good shot at Cadets. Sorry Aiden, I could only get my hands on two. It's surprisingly tough to get your hands on firearms in this country. You should put these on too, just in case.'

He handed Will a pair of dark leather gloves and put a pair on himself. He then took out a black, shiny, new-looking pistol. Will could see the oil glistening on it as Darren expertly checked the magazine and flicked the safety catch off. He looked at them and smiled.

'Glock.'

Will gave Aiden a shocked look. His heart was going like a trip hammer. This couldn't be happening. The approaching vehicles were crawling towards them now, as though expecting an ambush. Will thought about his options. He remembered the text message he had received as he was driving and got his phone out, clumsy with the buttons due to his gloved hands. One text, from Radic. 'Decision time'.

'No signal here Will, you might as well be on Mars,' Darren laughed.

The massive pick-up truck stopped directly to the side of them about fifty metres away so they had to look to the left to face them. The transit parked directly behind the massive pick up so they couldn't clearly see who was in the cab. Then nothing happened.

After a minute Darren interrupted the still.

'I don't get it.'

'Get what?'

'Remember when we were out on full moon night, I said I was going to shag everyone, disco dancer, pole dancer?'

'Yes.'

'You said more like Northern Dancer.'

'Yes,' Will was exasperated. 'Surely you have other things to worry about?'

'I don't get it, why Northern Dancer?'

'It's a famous horse you numbskull.' Will looked at Darren in the rear view mirror and saw him quietly smile to himself.

'Ahh, I get it now.'

With that he opened the door and got out. He leaned back in.

'If any shooting starts, get out and shoot back. Distract them. I'll handle the rest.'

He then proceeded to walk towards the other vehicles and stopped half way. He held his hands out to both sides in a conciliatory gesture but as he did so his jacket rode up at the back and they could both see the gun tucked in the belt of his jeans.

Will could hear Aiden's heavy, fast breathing next to him and knew he was doing the same.

'Aiden, we could just drive off?'

Aiden didn't look at him but shook his head.

'Look, nothing will probably happen, we can't leave him here on his own.'

Will thought that's exactly what they should do. He felt his hand move to the keys and was just about to turn the engine back on when he saw some movement past Aiden. Three men had got out of the back of the transit and were walking slowly toward Darren. Will recognised two of Radic's more silent types who had a strong air of ex-military about them. They stopped a metre away from Darren.

Even though they had the windows down neither Will nor Aiden could hear anything due to the wind blowing all the sound away from them but it was clear they were having an argument of some kind. Apart from their breathing they did appear to be on Mars. There were no birds here, and seemingly no plant life. Just gravel and mud.

'Come on Aiden, let's go. He is going to get us all killed here. There are three in the front of that pick up and three more in the front of the van, who knows how many more in the back. If this gets nasty we will be MIA. They'll drop us in one of these deep pits and we will never be seen again. They won't even know what happened to us. We've got families Aiden, I've got a child. This is insane. We've been sucked into Darren's world without our permission, we don't owe him anything.'

Will looked at Aiden's face. He could see a tear rolling down his cheek and he saw his friend's resolve begin to waiver. He felt a surge of emotion for this big man, so loyal and kind. Aiden didn't deserve this. He turned the ignition on and fired up the car, looking at the four men in the middle as he did so. He would wonder later if that sound was the catalyst, or if things would have worked out the same anyway, as suddenly it was far from quiet.

Darren whipped out the Glock in a move so quick and practiced it was all a blur. He shot the first man in the throat, the second in the face. The third man began to move into a crouch, but he was slow and clumsy in comparison and Will saw the bullet, some brains and a spray of blood fly out of the back of his head. Darren was then running back towards them, zigzagging as he did so. Will and Aiden were still sitting in stunned silence as two men got out of the pick-up brandishing machine guns and sprayed bullets in their direction. AK47 by the looks of it, Will thought, having shot one in Thailand, surprisingly light.

Multiple bullets slammed into the car and Will's brain fired into life.

'Fuck,' he roared. He slammed the car into gear but another spray of bullets hit the bonnet causing it to shoot up and release a huge cloud of smoke and then the shooting stopped. Will felt the car die underneath him and then it was quiet except for a sound similar to a mangled helicopter blade slowing down. Darren picked himself up off the floor and ran around to Will's side of the car and pulled the door open.

'Out,' he ordered. Will was out of the car before he got to the 't'. Aiden tried to follow but he wasn't built for speed in an enclosed space. Will popped his head over the roof and saw the men had re-loaded.

Will put his head back in the car and desperately pulled at one of Aiden's arms, but it was like trying to pull a sleepy elephant along by his trunk. Soon the air was alive with the sound of gunshots. He could hear Darren returning fire next to him crouched over the bonnet and then he heard the inevitable 'Argh' as a bullet went into his big friend. Aiden bellowed 'Argh' again, louder this time and then screamed it, frantically hauling himself out of the car in absolute panic. He finally got himself out and dropped out on top of Will like a dead weight and crushed the breath out of him.

'Get up you fucking idiot and start shooting,' Darren hissed at him.

He managed to slide out from under Aiden and found his gun on the seat. All of a sudden it weighed a ton and felt poorly balanced. They were all going to die. The shooting stopped and again it was quiet, except for the sounds of Aiden snivelling and groaning next to him. Will looked at Aiden's prone form and could clearly see three entry holes in the back of his chinos. One was in his bottom and he had one in the back of each thigh. The bum cheek one was bleeding profusely. Aiden looked up at him, ashen faced.

'Help me, Will,' he gasped.

Will knew he had to stop the blood flow but all he could come up with was, 'Sit on your arse, it will seal the wound.' Aiden shifted up and leant his head back against the rear car door.

'Put your guns down. You can't win.' Radic's voice boomed through the air to them.

'Shit Darren, let's just fucking surrender. If we don't get some help for Aiden soon he will bleed out.'

'Fuck that, the Russians will just shoot us.'

'What do you suggest? A tactical retreat carrying Aiden on your shoulders? And he's from the Ukraine actually.'

'Still joking Will, even at the bitter end? I'm going to kill them all, or die trying.'

'Time's up, goodbye my friends.' Radic's voiced echoed out again.

Darren was looking over the bonnet and whispered, 'Oh dear.'

Will looked over the top of the car to see the pick-up was moving sideways on. He noticed there were now five dead bodies on the ground between them. He looked at the rear of the vehicle as it moved and saw there was a man on the back pulling off the last of a tarpaulin from an evil looking mounted heavy duty machine gun.

'Belt fed, fifty cal, five hundred rounds a minute, incredible stopping power,' Darren whispered. 'Checkmate to you Radic. Boys, we are dead meat.'

The first round screeched past Will's head like a missile. The second one hit the car and physically shifted it a few inches, knocking Aiden's head forward. The third went straight through the passenger side door, clipped Aiden's shoulder and whistled off into the distance. Aiden didn't make any noise this time, he just slumped to the side.

All of a sudden Will thought of a way out. His brain screamed but he knew it was the right decision, the only decision he could make. He lifted the gun up and pointed it at Darren.

'He's jammed it,' Darren laughed as he turned to Will and saw what was levelled at his stomach. His eyes narrowed. 'I told you I'm not going to surr…'

Will wasn't sure if he pulled the trigger or if the gun just went off, but the effect was the same. There was an almighty bang and the force of the blast in such close proximity blew Darren backwards. He staggered away, his shocked eyes never leaving Will's face and then he stood still. He seemed to give a small nod of his head, fell face forward and hit the ground with a thump.

Will didn't ponder his decision, he threw the gun away over Darren's prone form and ripped his T-shirt off. He tucked it around Aiden's shoulder and applied pressure, turning his face away from Aiden's horrified look.

He heard the sounds of many boots running towards him, and Radic appeared around the side of the car. He picked up Darren's gun and waved it in Will's general direction.

'Decision time eh? Not quite what I expected, but it will do.' He shook his head, but with a smile.

'What a mess eh? Although I did always like you Will.' He put the gun in his pocket and walked toward Will.

'Take off your gloves Will.' He grabbed them off him and picked up Will's ancient firearm and looked him in the eye.

Time froze as Will returned the look. His daughter's face appeared in his mind. He would never know her, or she him. Radic cocked the weapon and squeezed the trigger. The bullet roared above his head and Will opened his eyes.

'Say nothing to anyone, about anything. I'll see what I can do. I will ring for an ambulance when we get back to a signal.' He stepped away from Aiden's ever expanding pool of blood. 'He'll be fine. Big man, lot of blood.'

He then walked toward Darren and using his foot pushed him onto his back. From Will's side view he could see the small judders of Darren's chest as he breathed. A trickle of blood ran out of his mouth and down his cheek. Radic picked Darren's feet up and grinned at him.

'Look at you. Shot by a friend. Just like Jesse James.'

Chuckling, Radic dragged Darren's body away. Just before they went out of view Darren's head lolled to

Will's direction and his eyes opened and held Will's gaze for a split second, before they glazed and closed.

Will focused on the task in hand and re-applied the compression on the shoulder wound of his friend. As he did so Aiden's hand found Will's. His eyes were closed but he spoke clearly.

'Will, you did the right thing. You did the right thing.'

He heard engines start up and move off and then it was silent once more. Any thought that came in to Will's head he pushed away. He did not want to think about anything until he had the time and space to deal with it properly. About five minutes later Aiden's body slipped away from the car and hit the ground with a gasp. It was then though, that he heard the sounds of distant sirens. Relief flooded through him. Please let there be time. Suddenly an image of Darren filled his mind. Eleven years old, laughing as he cycled no handed down that underpass all those years ago and he began to sob. He had shot and killed his friend.

47

27th August 2014

The sounds of the prison waking up roused Will from his fretful sleep. He had been in bed for about twelve hours but he still felt shattered. As he had the previous morning, he woke up and thought of the horror of what he had done. He sent another small prayer up in the hope that Aiden would pull through and what he had done had not been totally selfish. He could hear them shouting 'kitchen workers' and unlocking the odd cell door so he suspected it must be around six thirty in the morning. His cell at least was on the right side of the prison so the morning sun gently shone through the gap between his curtains.

For some reason it made him think of waking up on holiday. The last time his cell was on the other side and the strong afternoon glare would turn your cell into a boiling hell hole, baking your brains and making you feel like you were going insane. He had wasted many hours dreaming of taking a frozen beer from a steaming cold fridge.

Will reclined back on his bed and let himself think of sipping a nice glass of tropical fruit juice from that same fridge, but was disturbed by his own cell door opening and the light from the wing landing flooded into the room. His mind searched for a reason as to why he would be unlocked. Maybe he had court or something, but before he could do anything he felt a heavy booted presence enter the room and the light was blocked out. A man with a big angry face stood over him as he lay there and a huge, strong paw grabbed his collar and pushed him into his mattress.

'You don't remember me do you?' the officer growled through gritted teeth.

Despite the grimacing visage Will did recognise him.

'You were the senior officer from reception the night I was brought in,' he replied in what he hoped was a placating way.

The man laughed but with no humour or change in facial expression. He leaned closer so their faces were only inches apart and talked in a quiet but hostile staccato fashion. Phlegm periodically hit Will in the face as each small sentence was spat out.

'It was Kho Phan Ngan, the party beach, five years ago. We met on full moon night. You, your big mate and him. I was ill and went home. My sister stayed with your friend. I woke up late the next day. She wasn't back. I didn't find her until much later. Do you know where she was?'

The memory crawled into Will's mind like a centipede entering his ear. The slim, tiny girl with the doe-eyed face. The one Darren had been with. He was the big man with the sickly sweat. Jenny and John from Wisbech.

Before he could think of a reply, or of the consequences of saying anything at all John continued. By now he was shouting, his eyes red, glaring and watered.

'They found her in the hills. Half-strangled and abused by your rapist mate.'

The man bunched his fist further causing the fabric of Will's T-shirt to draw tight around his throat. The elbow of a hugely muscled arm which had been resting on his sternum was suddenly dug in and he felt the weight increase on his chest causing his breathing to shallow.

'We had to come home,' he snarled as he tried to control his anger. 'My travels finished before they had begun. Her mind was gone. She wouldn't talk to anyone. She barely left the house for a year. Then a year to the day, she went up to the multi-storey car park next to the station and threw herself off it. Eight floors up. Strawberry fucking jam. My parents divorced. I haven't seen my dad in years. Nobody knows where he is and my mother had a breakdown from which they doubt she will ever recover.'

'I knew you pricks were responsible but I couldn't remember your names. I managed to find where you were staying later that night. I thought I had you, but you had gone. No doubt guiltily fleeing the scene of your crime. I swore on her grave I would avenge her. And now here you are, dropped in my lap, like lucky shit from a seagull.'

Will began to redden and choke as he ran out of air. Suddenly he was lifted out of the bed by his neck and was standing face to face with the crazy-eyed madman. Will knew then that his sister wasn't the only one to lose their mind that day. John looked to the door and nodded. Will followed his gaze and saw another officer retreat out of the room and close the door behind him. He then heard the key gently clicking the lock shut, leaving them alone.

John pulled him in so close he could feel his breath, warm and fetid on his face.

'This,' he snarled. 'Is payback.'

Ross Greenwood

The End

Epilogue

I was a prison officer at HMP Peterborough for four years before resigning to complete this novel. It was a tough job, not for the faint hearted. However not all prison officers are the same. This letter was given to me on my last day by an inmate serving seven years.

Dear Ross,
Thank you for your kindness, support and laughs over the last couple of years.
A place like prison needs men like you. Through the darkest points in our lives comes light and you, for me, have been one of those lights.
I hope and am sure you will achieve all you desire. Enjoy your new found freedom.
All the best,
Max

Acknowledgements

I'd like to thank, in no particular order, Kev Duke, Nicola Holmes, Lynsey Pooley, Alex Knell, Barry Butler, Sam Bernardis, Ann Bellamy, Yvette Smart, Jos Marriner, Alex Williams and, of course, Amanda Rayner.

Without your encouragement at various points along the way this book would never have been completed.

About the Author

I was born in 1973 in Peterborough and lived there until I was 20. I then began a rather nomadic existence, living and working all over the country and various parts of the world.

I found myself returning to Peterborough many times over the years, usually when things had gone wrong. It was on one of these occasions that I met my partner about 100 metres from my back door whilst walking a dog. Two children swiftly followed. I'm still a little stunned by the pace of it now.

This book was started a long time ago but parenthood and then four years as a prison officer got in the way. Ironically it was the four a.m. feed which gave me the opportunity to finish the book as unable to get back to sleep I completed it in the early morning hours.

My aim was to write an entertaining story set in my home town. I hope you enjoyed it.

If you would like to get in touch, read some interesting facts about Peterborough, or see some pictures of notable places in the city that may or may not have influenced the book, please contact me below.

https://www.facebook.com/RossGreenwoodAuthor/

http://www.rossgreenwoodauthor.com/

I've also written a book called Abel's Revenge. More or less it's a story about a couple struggling to raise children in London against the backdrop of an escalating serial killer.

I've written it in a slightly tongue-in-cheek style. My aim was to write a book that would make you laugh out loud, while still having dark themes. There's also the question of who is Abel. See if you can guess before the end of the book.

Please leave a review if you enjoyed this series.

Printed in Great Britain
by Amazon